Dancing through Fire

JoAnn Hague

ISBN-10: 1475114303
ISBN-13: 978-1475114300

Published by Tuesday House

Cover design copyright © 2012 by Kim West
www.kwestcommunications.com

Published in the United States of America

DEDICATION

To my writing friends – Lee Huntington, Sandra Love, and M. Ruth Myers –
who kept me afloat through the years.

I give special thanks to M. Ruth Myers, who helped me begin this writing
journey and who never wavered in her support.

And to my beloved family:
John – who is my first and finest fan ...
and Beth, Chuck, Cora, and Mike – who make all things worthwhile..

CONTENTS

INTRODUCTION

Dancing through Fire is a carefully researched account of the events from 1775 to 1782 which culminated in the massacre of more than 90 Christian Indians at Gnadenhutten in eastern Ohio.

This novel is a recipient of the OHIO ARTS COUNCIL FELLOWSHIP GRANT FOR CREATIVE WRITING.

All historic events are actual, and all secondary characters are real.

Although fictional, the novel's main characters are accurate depictions of Indians and Moravian missionaries during the American Revolutionary War.

1
APRIL 24, 1775 – JULY 1, 1775

The redness came today. Wind Maiden continued to hoe. Star-at-Dawning, her mother, worked beside her, breaking up the clods of earth. Wind Maiden glanced sideways at her: a wide, slow figure, laboriously picking over the ground. The heavy, black stroud of Star-at-Dawning was wrapped tightly about her massive hips and thighs; her white shirt was stained with perspiration though it was the Planting Time and still cool. The few silver buckles hanging from her shirt shimmered, clicked, and danced lightly in the breeze. She was warm and soft. She had sounds that tinkled and smells that were both sweet and bitter. Wind Maiden did not want to lose that yet so she waited and did not tell her.

When they had worked to the edge of their plot, her mother straightened her low frame. She turned her fleshy face to her daughter: "Enough. Home now."

The girl looked up. She knew she must speak. But when she spoke, today and yesterday would be gone forever. And she feared tomorrow.

"Mother, today the redness begins."

The older woman's face did not change its expression although the dark brown eyes, encased in rolls of fat, seemed to sink further into the face.

"Fourteen times I have taken in the maize since I first put you down upon the earth. The time is fitting. It is good."

In silence, they returned to Goschachgunk, Black Bear's Town, principal village of the Tribe of the Great Tortoise of the nation of the True Men, the Lenni Lenape. The village sat below the fork of the Elk's Eye, the Muskingum River. They walked along the wide path of the village, across the line of the second path that slashed through it.

From openings in the arched roofs of the huts, smoke puffed. Within, crouching women hovered beside the fire pits, tending the flames, shifting bread cooking in the ashes, stirring the broth in brass kettles placed over the fires. Other women squatted outside their dwellings, pounding maize in mortars held between their legs. Boys in breech clouts wrestled in the dirt. Wolf-like dogs roamed, tails between their legs, about the village. Not many, just a few bony dogs. Most had been eaten during the meatless, breadless days of cold winds and snow.

A circle of girls huddled together and passed around a small, dark object. They whispered and laughed. One glanced up. "Come listen," she called to Wind Maiden, shaking a small love beson in the air and giggling. "We cast a spell for lovers. I shall make one for you."

Wind Maiden paused to call back.

"No!" The snapped warning of Star-at-Dawning gulped back the words in the mouth of Wind Maiden. "You would cast the spell! Look down!"

The girl looked down upon the dirt before her. She had not wanted the blood. She did not want the power it gave her. Her body was her own. Then why had the redness decided to flow?

"I cast no spell, mother," she moaned.

Star-at-Dawning did not turn to look. "Yes, yes, it is good."

With slowness, with sad and dead solemnity, they walked past.

Their hut stood in the midst of the village. Star-at-Dawning stopped at the door opening.

"Bow your head. Do not speak. Hold back your eye from all flesh ... because of the power."

She turned, bowed, and squeezed into the darkness of the hut.

Wind Maiden waited outside. What evil would attack her family if she followed her mother inside? She inhaled, sunk her head to her chest, and closed her eyes. What was she now? The redness – could it do so much? She did not feel new strength. She was bruised and sore inside. Did the power work against her, too? She could not hide from herself. "I look at blackness," she thought.

How many nights must she sit inside the blackness? Twelve. Other friends had disappeared inside their own small, dark huts when first their redness had appeared. Twelve nights had passed and they had appeared, never again to giggle with the children and to run in their games.

"I do not like it," she decided. "If I do not choose to become a woman, can I stop the redness? I shall say, 'No! I will not go to the hut of separation!' Then I shall not become a woman."

And what was it to become a woman? She would find a husband, and she would cook and grind and scrape. Then, some day, she would look like Star-at-Dawning.

2

What husband would she take? The most fierce and the most powerful. Yes.

But not yet.Play now. Her teeth were white; she did not want them to rot to black stubs like the teeth of her mother.

Soon, Star-at-Dawning emerged, carrying an old, woolen blanket and a piece of glowing fungus, ignited from the smoldering fire and cradled in a clay bowl.

"Follow close against my heel."

Wind Maiden stared at the feet of her mother.

"Mother, I do not want them to know." She could play with the children if no one knew.

"They will know." The reply heaved with the knowledge of years. "Take the blanket for covering."

Wind Maiden hesitated. "I do not wish to become a woman yet, so I shall not go to the place of separation."

Star-at-Dawning shoved the blanket into the arms of her daughter. "The flow – it comes; it goes. You cannot stop it."

"Yes! Yes! My body belongs to me. I shall tell my manito."

"No! Is your manito more powerful that the Great Spirit? He has told these things to our Grandfathers. You live apart twelve nights when first the redness flows. It is the path from girl to woman. Later, you must live apart only when the redness comes." Star-at-Dawning frowned. "We do not question this."

They returned through the village, the mother walking a pace ahead, carrying the glowing bowl. Wind Maiden stumbled behind, draped in the worn blanket.

What power did she now hold? Could she bring bad hunting or could she poison food? Could she swell stomachs of babies and make them cry? Could she bruise the shin of Little Moon and make her limp? Little Moon had laughed when Wind Maiden had said that a dream told her that Grandfather Fire was her manito. She would look for Little Moon. A small limp through one night, maybe two, she would make – nothing more.

The girls in the circle, the women at their chores watched. The women gazed at Star-at-Dawning. They shared the secret. Shame pressed against the chest of Wind Maiden. She did not look up but followed the heel of her mother. Another time she would use her power on Little Moon.

The skin over the opening to the small hut at the edge of the village, the one to which her mother retreated for three days each moon, flopped half off. Star-at-Dawning pushed it aside. She glanced back toward her daughter.

Wind Maiden crouched and looked in. "Dirt – smell. Cold and damp. I do not like it."

Her mother did not reply. Wind Maiden crept in.

Dust from the ground of the hut puffed up. Wind Maiden coughed. She shuddered. She breathed quickly and lightly. She heard a rustling behind her and turned to see her mother crouching before the cold fire pit, stacking the partly burnt logs about a glowing heap of burning fungus and kindling. Wind Maiden observed the ponderous movements of Star-at-Dawning. She breathed more slowly. She watched the stubby fingers flit among the logs, retracing the movements that would not allow a fire in their family hut to die. Wind Maiden crouched, holding the blanket about her. She stared at the full, warm, soft hands, now moving in and out of shadow.

Star-at-Dawning turned to her daughter. She crawled toward her. The warm, fat hands clasped the edge of the blanket. Old, slow eyes met young, quick eyes. Then, Star-at-Dawning pulled the blanket over the head of her child, and the eyes of Wind Maiden gazed into darkness.

"Drink," said her mother.

"Not another," Wind Maiden whimpered. The raw smell of the time before and the time before and the time before clung to her stroud, her flesh, her blanket. It soaked into the dirt.

"You must spit out all evil so you can become pure."

"If I do not drink, then I will not spit out. If I do not spit out, my stroud will be purer."

"Drink," urged her mother.

"I hurt here and here," she complained, pressing near her protruding ribs where the clenchings of the heavings had bruised her.

"Drink," said her mother.

Mud and salt and bitterness oozed down into her. She heaved forward and gagged and gagged.

"Eat," said her mother.

"Why do I eat? It will be wrenched out of me again soon." But she was hungry. And the bread would soak up the bitterness of the other slime. "Bring water," she begged.

She sat, the blanket pulled over her. Her nose would rot and fall off. Already it could not easily sniff. "Wait," she comforted. "I shall take you from here." She cupped her hands over her nose.

She crawled to the corner where she crouched over a hole. But after the first night, not much came out. It escaped the other way.

She drank the water. It dribbled down her chin. She drank and drank.

"Drink," said her mother.

"Not again," she whimpered.

She drank and belched out the water. It gushed across the hut and sizzled in the fire. It seeped into the dirt.

4

She rolled into a ball, hiding inside the rough blanket. The fire crackled; her mother rustled. Then, quiet.

Footsteps retreated through the village. Voices laughed and shouted. Babies wailed. Feet pattered, pursued by more. A bark and a growl. More feet, more voices. Retreating, retreating. Silence.

In the darkness, she huddled. She shivered. She rubbed her nose. Loose strands of hair lapped against her face. She did not try to push them back.

"Mother ... Mother," she whimpered. "I ache. Sit beside me, Mother."

No one answered.

A scream puffed up and up. She pounded it down against the dirt with clenched fists.

A shivering puppy, nose wet and cold, she wound up herself and tumbled into screeching blackness.

~ ~ ~

"It is completed," said Star-at-Dawning, crawling into the hut. "Twelve nights and, now, morning." She pulled the blanket from off her daughter. "You are clean. Now we can wash away the filth that clings to you. You are being born a woman."

A woman. Wind Maiden wrapped the blanket around her. She crept out into the light. "Oh!" She squeezed closed her eyes and slapped her hand over them. She stumbled back and plopped onto the ground.

Her hand slid from her eyes, but, still, they could not open. She blinked and blinked until she could squint into the burning light.

She saw her wet and splotched and wrinkled shirt and stroud, her dirt-smeared hands and arms and feet and legs. She felt her tangled hair and dirt-stained face.

"No one should see," she murmured.

"All know," replied her mother.

Back through Goschachgunk, head bowed and blanket wrapped around, no longer to restrain the power but to hide the shame, she stumbled near the heels of her mother.

At a cold and gurgling stream, within the covering of the forest shadow, she tore off the foul shirt and stroud and bathed. Cold and clear, the water rolled across her skin. She touched her breasts, small but round. She washed away the evil and rubbed in woman. She pulled her black hair across her shoulder and watched it float upon the water. Her hands caressed it and smoothed it back.

Star-at-Dawning waited and watched.

Wind Maiden draped upon her slender waist a blue stroud. Red leggings fell to her ankles. Upon her feet, she wore deerskin moccasins, inlaid with the design she had copied from the moccasins of her mother. A blue linen shirt, covered with many-colored ribbons and silver buckles, hung over her stroud.

She smoothed her long, coarse hair then smeared the grease of the bear upon it, rubbing downward until it shone. She gathered back her hair and bound it in a red cloth wound several times about the hair and secured.

She stood, back straight, and turned her dark eyes upon her mother. Star-at-Dawning was a mushroom, low and flat. But Wind Maiden was a sapling, taller than many saplings among the Lenni Lenape. Her legs and arms were long and muscular. A soft, round jaw sloped down from high cheek bones. Small eyes and full lips of Star-at-Dawning were copied onto the face of Wind Maiden.

The mother lifted from her own neck two strings of wampum, reached up, and draped them upon the neck of her daughter.

She dropped her arms and murmured, "It is good."

Wind Maiden turned and gazed down to the ground where the head covering lay.

"The covering," said her mother.

With groaning slowness, Wind Maiden raised the head covering from the ground. She did not want to wear it.

"This is what we do …" Star-at-Dawning would say. The fathers and the grandfathers and the great-grandfathers …

Wind Maiden wiggled it onto her head. It was wide and grey and musty in smell. The shield fell from the top and cast her face into shadow. She raised her head up and backward, cocking it sideways until she could see her mother.

"Two moons …" she began.

"Yes. Until the deer put on red," interrupted her mother.

Wind Maiden humphed. "Why should I care if I offend the spirits by showing my face? My manito is stronger … "

"Close your mouth and dig a pit for your words," warned Star-at-Dawning. "Why beckon evil to yourself? It will find you soon enough."

Wind Maiden, the waddling duck, walked beside her mother to Goschachgunk.

When the deer put on red, the sun would be large and bright and dirt would be hot against the foot. Men would hunt, chasing deer whose red pelts would force good trade with the White Man.

But today, the men lounged in groups of three or four, recounting with wide gestures tales of prowess from the winter hunt. Some braggers wandered from group to group. Children crouched near the men, staring with wide eyes at the contorted faces of the tale tellers. Women scraped skins.

Wind Maiden cocked her head back to see her father standing outside their hut. Black hair was plucked out to the crown where a circular band fell in a braid down his back. The ears, slashed and distended, glittered with heavy silver ornaments. His face was stone, carved in frowning lines. He wore leggings above which hung a breech clout. Over his shoulder draped a small blanket of red and black and blue.

Wind Maiden crouched beside the door, leaning into its shadow.

She liked to hear her father talk in low and rumbling words. In the evenings, she would sit beside the fire pit and listen while he told her two older brothers about animal tracks and rifle shots and ferocious techniques of battle. And, then, her father would whisper stories of the hunt and of battle. His face would reflect the light of the fire and his hands would cast dancing shadows and Wind Maiden would smell vengeance and taste power.

An ancient one was grumbling to her father: "Look! We wear the clothing made by White Men. Leggings, breech clout, blanket. We forget the old ways! I weep. We offend the Great Spirit who gave us the skin of the deer and bear to wear. Now we become the dog of the White Man and lick up his morsels.

The father of Wind Maiden sighed. "Yes, old man. And they kick us from the land which the Great Spirit gave to us. We whimper and run away."

"The Great Spirit takes back the land from us because we do not obey," croaked the old man. "My words are coated with years. Once, the True Man would have heard my words. He can hear no longer. Destroy the ways of the White Man and cleanse the flesh of the True Man."

"Old man! I hear," said her father. He was Fish-of-the-Deep-Water and he was a hunter and he was a warrior.

He raised his hand, palm downward, and motioned left. "All this land ... " He stopped. His eyes fell upon Wind Maiden. "The little bird flies from the nest." He laughed. "A covering will not hide you from the prowling cat for long. Flee, big-eared maiden listening to the wind."

Wind Maiden crawled into the hut.

~ ~ ~

Wind Maiden worked in the field. She tended maize, potatoes, squash, beans. She stabbed at the fire and cooked above it and in its hot ashes. She did not play; she was no longer a child. She sat with the other women, weaving wild hemp into straps for carrying, listening to the jabberings that kept heavy eyes from closing. Always, she wore the covering that shielded her from everyone. Tear it off — it was the enemy who cloaked her in loneliness. Caress it — it was the friend who covered her in darkness and demanded nothing. Her eyes ached from straining to see around the visor. So more and more, she did not try. But all was as it should be because that was what her mother said.

Then the deer put on red. And, one morning, her mother said, "Throw off the veil today. The spirits smile because you are a woman."

Wind Maiden rolled over on her bench. Her brothers teased and jabbed at her until their father called them outside to pack for the hunt.

"Now. Find a strong hunter to marry." Star-at-Dawning spoke as she packed the dry maize called tassmanane for the men. "A hunter like your father. Then hunger will not grind the stomachs of your little ones until they wail."

Wind Maiden wrapped dried flesh in wide leaves. "I do not know men, Mother. Only boys. Hunters are mighty. They will not see me."

Star-at-Dawning smiled. "They will see you now. You are a woman." She patted the hip of her daughter and laughed.

Wind Maiden laughed, too, but she did not know why she laughed. Had the nights of vomit and the moons of her covering shaped her into some new thing, like a fuzzy worm in its woven tent that flies out one day?

Her mother laid aside the deerskin pouch she was filling. "You must go to the dance every night and dance beside the men. You will paint your face like this ... " She rubbed her soft finger under the eyes and upon the chin of Wind Maiden. She was crouching now, her round puff of a face near the face of her daughter. "Do not look at them, but cast your eye down." She lowered her own eyes. She laughed, her breath breaking with warmth against the eyes of her daughter. She looked up. She raised her hand: "You look up, sometimes, just to one — so he will know. Never look at more than one. Just the hunter like your father."

"I do not know a hunter to look at," Wind Maiden whispered. "I shall look at all of them."

"Never!" Star-at-Dawning shook her head. "You gaze at all and men will speak tales about you and jest with you. Then a good hunter will never marry you."

"Then I shall keep my head down all the time."

"No, no ..." Star-at-Dawning shook her head again. "Then no man will look at you. No, no, listen to my words."

Wind Maiden smiled. "I shall watch them dance. They will shout and jump. I shall choose a man who has many pelts." She bounced upon her knees. "I shall choose a man who jumps high and tells stories of the hunt."

She stood, stooped shouldered in the low hut, and walked about, shuffling her feet and glancing sideways at her mother. "I shall dance like this and I shall look at the hunter." She stopped. "But if he does not look at me ..."

"You look away and do not look again unless you feel his gaze on you," her mother interjected.

Wind Maiden resumed her shuffling. Star-at-Dawning smiled and turned to leave the hut. At the door, she looked back.

"Do not hear the council of your friends." She frowned now. "If they speak what I do not say, then they say what is bad. Young ones do not know; still they speak." Her voice saddened and she shook her head. "It was never so before. No. We honored the ways of our mothers." She spoke these last words as she turned back to the door and left the hut.

Wind Maiden followed Star-at-Dawning outside. She shuffled her feet, rocked her head from side to side, laughed, then rocked her head again.

8

"I am the white-headed eagle, soaring in the upper sky," she thought, "and I shall always fly free."

She bowed to grind maize for the morning meal, still rocking her head, now softly chanting a song of freedom. She would find the hunter who would sell his skins for wampum and ribbons and silver and fine linen. He would give her many gifts.

Wind Maiden glanced about the village, cocking her head sideways and back. "No!" She snapped her head down. "I do not wear a covering. I am clean; and I am free; and I am a woman now. "

She paused, gazing around the village, watching the women preparing meals and men lounging near their huts. She looked beyond them to the clearing near the council house.

"When the men return from the hunt, then! I shall dance there around the fire. And the hunter who jumps high and shouts, he will be my husband."

2
JULY 3, 1775

Sarah sat in the large, empty meeting house, her white apron spread over her full, grey skirt. She fingered her headband and felt the contours of the pink ribbon tied under her chin. She touched her cheek, then, noticing the dampness of her palm, rubbed her hands on the underside of her apron.

It was the third hour of the morning. The business of the Unity of the Brethren Community of Bethlehem, Pennsylvania, had begun two hours earlier. Sarah heard the cracking rumble of carts as workmen traveled to and from the plantations on the edge of town. The craftsmen clipped along the wooden walk, greeting one another with blessings. Yet, inside the meeting house, the somber emptiness of the room and the coolness of the bench Sarah sat upon separated her from the world without.

She studied the room, the benches lining the wall, the oak planks laid with precision upon the floor. Her wide, brown eyes, set against her pale, thin face, would, she knew, betray her bewilderment and fear. Today, for the first time in her life, Sarah would be alone with a man, a man other than her father. This man, whose face she could not even now envision, would be her husband. That she was to marry startled her. The already thin line of her lips grew narrower as she thought back to the events of the two days before.

~ ~ ~

Sister Marie had awakened her with other than the usual briskness Saturday morning, singing in German, "May the Lord be praised this day!"

Standing at the door of the room which Sarah shared with twelve other single sisters, Sister Marie turned toward Sarah: "Sister Glaser asks you to dress and come to her room presently."

Formality dispensed with, she hurried to Sarah's bedside and, leaning over the figure sitting on the edge of the bed, whispered, "God will surely bless you this day."

Such jumbled mystery! It confused Sarah. She dressed in her grey linen gown, pressed her hands along the folds of her skirt and apron, and hurried out of the room, smiling and nodding to her roommates as she left, but saying not a word.

Stepping with care to avoid the creaks in the floor of the upstairs corridor of the building which housed the forty-two single sisters, she passed the open doors of rooms similar to her own. She slowed her step as she approached the room of Deaconess Glaser. Her hand rapped on the door — a light, faint tap. Behind the heavy door, the familiar, low-pitched, almost masculine voice bade her enter.

Sarah pushed forward the door. "God's blessing, Sister, I ..."

"Please be seated, Sister Sarah." She indicated the chair near the window of the small, tidy room.

Sarah clutched her skirts, slid sideways around the bed, and sat down. The early morning July light pressed itself against Sarah's cheek, a warm comfort to her question-plagued mind.

The Deaconess came to the side of her bed and sat down not three feet from Sarah. The aging face with its scrupulously laid creases on cheek and chin studied Sarah's downturned features.

"Child," she began, "I have long watched with parental concern your growth in both the Young Girls' Group, and, for the past eight years, in the Single Women's Group. We have communed often. Our Saviour has been gracious unto you, and you have not denied Him. You are twenty-four, a weaver and knitter of yarn. Much alone in the world ... Am I not correct?"

Sarah opened her mouth to reply but, with relief, realized Sister Glaser did not require an answer; for, immediately, she spoke again: "Brother Christoph Zundel — do you know of whom I speak? — returned two months ago from the mission among the savages in the Ohio Country. He was weak, my dear, and tired, and ill-cared for. The missionary board has proposed that he take a wife to care for corporeal needs and to fellowship in his ministry ..."

Sarah's heart quickened. "What does Sister mean, Lord? I cannot understand what she means!"

"... Brother Zundel acquiesced, reluctantly. He is thirty-four, Sister, and conformed to bachelor ways. The board communed with the deaconesses of our Single Sisters' Group and, with us, chose six sisters whom we prayerfully determined would serve our God and our brother. Your name was among them. I myself submitted it."

The light which first caressed now chilled Sarah. She bit her lip and hardened her will against what she feared the Deaconess was about to say.

Sister Glaser smiled, nodded her head, and continued as before: "Brother Zundel chose your name, Sarah. He selected you as the woman he would choose to marry. He said he had often seen you yet never spoken to you. He admired your quiet industry, Sarah, your precision in your weaving, your ..." Deaconess Glaser hesitated.

Sarah sat motionless, her eyes and brows twisted into a mute protest: "He is mistaken! He could not mean me. I do not even know who this man could be."

The Deaconess leaned forward and tapped her ancient hand upon Sarah's tensely intertwined hands. "You are twenty-four, my dear; Brother Zundel wishes to marry you. You will not receive another proposal — you are twenty-four. His is an honor he pays you. Indeed. An honor." She paused, patted Sarah's hands, then withdrew her own.

"I have not been trained for work among the Indians! I cannot speak their language. And a husband ... Oh, I ..." Sarah formed these objections in her mind, but before she could summon the courage to speak them, Sister Glaser arose and said, "You may leave now. Retire to pray this day, petitioning our Saviour for His revealed will. Let us talk more later."

Sarah had avoided her other sisters that Saturday morning, passing quickly down the stairway and out-of-doors. Behind her, she heard the familiar clicking of tableware and the bumping of chairs as the single sisters prepared their morning meal. Few words would be spoken, only, short, courteous comments in an atmosphere of purposeful diligence. That reverential hum had, for twelve years, leant its order to Sarah's heart. But this Saturday morning, her heart pounded discordantly with it.

Sarah sought the secret places of her world. A favorite path led her behind the communal dwellings of the fellowship, down to the Lehigh River. From there, she walked upstream along the river until she could no longer see the buildings of Bethlehem. Before her lay the water ... a solemn, dutiful servant; behind her, the fields, yellow-green with small and tender and virgin plants. A massive oak stood near the water's edge. Against that tree, Sarah sat, folding her legs close to her body and spreading her skirts before her. Although the day was-warm, she huddled against the oak. In the stillness of those moments, she prayed.

She was alone and lonely, she whispered. Her parents were far away at mission stations in New York. God was her only Father, Jesus her only Brother ... now. Marriage? A river like that was too deep to cross alone. At the end of what course did her Lord await her? Christoph Zundel, Lord — she did not know this brother. A man of God?

Yes, a man of God.

Enduring privations among the Indians would be difficult, Lord — maybe too difficult.

No, not too difficult.

Could she become a good wife ... she, already a spinster, a woman who had conversed only reluctantly with men?

By the Spirit of God, yes — by His Spirit.

The peace of her Saviour began to settle upon Sarah's heart that moment. She arose and walked along the river's edge as her Lord shared with her the mystery of the tender plants, naked but faithful, open and fertile, barren but hopeful; for the promise of fruitfulness was upon them. Could she do less than to accept the same commission from God? Behold — she was a tender plant. But God's handiwork would make her fruitful through privation, abundant in love.

One hour before midday, Sarah approached Sister Glaser in the kitchen of the sisters' dwelling and, amidst the clanging of utensils in preparation for the noon meal, announced, "I have determined to marry Christoph Zundel."

She blushed, turned, and hurried from the room. As she slipped through the door, she glanced back to see Sister Glaser shake her head, pause to smile ... at what? A recollection, a half-formed thought? ... then return to the steady, rhythmic kneading of the bread dough laid before her.

That Saturday evening, Sarah knelt beside her bed to pray and to read scripture, as was her habit. She pressed her long, coarse sleeping gown close about her. The sounds of the other sisters in the dormitory as they prepared for the night hummed in the background. From the book of Psalms she recited, "Behold, the eye of the Lord is upon them that fear Him, upon them that hope in His mercy; To deliver their soul from death and to keep them alive in famine."

Sarah climbed into her bed. She nestled into the hum of the whispered prayers of her sisters.

"... To deliver their soul from death and to keep them alive in famine." She rolled that promise around in her mind. Through all the years with the brethren in Bethlehem, she suffered neither physical nor spiritual lack. But outside her community, all was ominous. Stories of slaughters, privations, starvations came from the west to Bethlehem, carried by Christian Indian messengers. Moreover, tales from the east now warned of rebellion in the colonies against the English king. Would starvation and death come from both the east and the west? She shuddered. Still, the promise of deliverance repeated itself in her mind.

She turned toward the wall and thought of Indians she had known in Bethlehem — Christian friends with solemn, smiling faces. As she dozed, those faces became alien and suspicious, angry and vengeful. A tall, vague figure approached her from the distance. She thought, "Christoph Zundel, Lord ... who is Christoph Zundel?" Then, she slept.

The next morning, Sunday, the betrothal of Sister Sarah Hannah Himmel to Brother Christoph Friedrich Zundel was announced from the pulpit during the public service. The banns were officially posted. With proper decorum,

Deaconenss Glaser introduced Sarah to her betrothed. They nodded at each other, both mute. He was tall, broad shouldered. His hair was blond, his brows bushy. The face of Sarah burned. She could not gaze more.

Stepping past them while leaving the worship service, brethren bowed. Sisters exited from the other side of the chapel. They spared a look at Sarah and left. Sarah glanced at the wood-planked floor and looked up. She would live the rest of her life with this man. They met too publicly! It happened too quickly! Brother Zundel muttered an invitiation to meet him the next morning in the meeting house during the third hour of the day. Deaconess Glaser consented to the arrangement. Sarah nodded.

So it happened that Sarah found herself sitting in the empty meeting house that next morning, awaiting her betrothed. How could she impress Brother Zundel? she wondered. She was hardly a comely woman. Neatness in appearance was her attribute, she felt ... hardly more than that. She patted her cap and felt her knotted hair beneath it and rubbed her cheeks for color. She examined her hands, long and narrow, calloused on their tips and sides from accustomed use of coarse yarn. Rubbing her fingers, she regretted their appearance. It seemed as if she had never before seen such awkward hands.

The heavy oaken meeting house door moved ponderously open. Sarah thrust her hands under her apron and sat rigid and still.

Brother Zundel stood in the doorway. He bowed but remained outside the meeting house. Although tall, he was not thin but solidly built. His blond hair was pulled back and tied. He motioned to Sarah with awkward gestures.

"Good day, Sister. I ... oh ... hardly think it appropriate for me to enter an empty room ... um ... uh ... empty but for you, that is ... um ... without a chaperone."

Sarah sat motionless, watching his square, firm jaw open and close.

"I should not enter, you see." He paused. "Oh ... I would much more appreciate not having to enter ... If I should come in to assist you out ... why ... I do not ... I ..."

His jaw clamped shut. He looked at Sarah. She bit her lip.

He coughed, straightened himself, adjusted his black coat, glanced from side to side, then said with a grave, deep, pulpit voice, "Might you kindly join me for a stroll out-of-doors, Sister Himmel? I would approach you to assist you, Sister Himmel, but ..." He coughed and cleared his throat.

"Oh, Brother Zundel!" Sarah rose from the bench. "I do, indeed, beg your pardon! I do honor your sense of propriety." With that, she placed her hand to her throat and nodded her head in a sideways fashion she hoped appeared gracious. She clutched at her skirt, stepped to the door, walked past him, and waited while he closed the door behind her.

Two brethren passed them with greetings and smiles. Brother Zundel returned the greeting and frowned. He turned to Sarah who was now standing erect, facing him: "We shall walk in God's Acre."

He strode past Sarah who turned, stumbled, and hurried behind with small, quick steps. She, too, was anxious to leave the main street and the scrutiny of all who passed by.

As they approached God's Acre, Brother Zundel paused to wait for Sarah. They walked together in silence. Brother Zundel attempted to shorten his strides while Sarah exerted herself in lengthening hers. Once she tripped on her skirt and twice he stepped on it. She was small, too small and frail; he was tall, so tall and strong. She hurried along with a slightly downturned head while he looked purposefully before him.

They entered God's Acre and walked in silence along the path. Two children played among the gravestones on their right while the mother rested against a nearby tree. Otherwise, the cemetery was empty. It was a sunny July morning, yet the crisp dampness of evening lingered. Brother Zundel did not alter his gait until he reached the rear of the cemetery. He then turned, glanced back at the woman and the children, and stopped. He faced Sarah who dutifully imitated him. They stood four feet apart, an uncomfortable distance for intimate conversation.

"Sister Himmel," began Brother Zundel. His voice was loud. He lowered it: "I am grateful you consented to the invitation to become my ... wife." Surely it was an embarrassment to speak that word, a confession to be hidden. He coughed on it.

"Why, Brother Zundel, I assure you, I am sincerely flattered at your generosity." Sarah flushed. Words of intimacy had never before been spoken by her. She felt altogether daring, as if she were exploring a new land previously sacred and forbidden.

Her mind swelled with wordless thoughts but not with words so she waited, looking up toward her betrothed. The large-featured face of Brother Zundel contorted. He jerked his blue eyes from her face to the trees behind her. No words emerged. They stood. Sarah, like brother Zundel, attempted to admire the trees. Both avoided the gaze of the other.

The minutes passed. Sarah felt a swelling urge to run beyond the village, into the forest, to a place where she could hide from this frightening man. The swelling throbbed until she contained it no longer and began to sob, first slowly, then quickly and uncontrollably. The tears formed, and she cried. She turned to run for shame.

But a hand, heavy and strong, clutched her shoulder and held her in place.

She looked back. He smiled. He did not release her.

Sarah's unformed fears fled, and she felt protected.

They sat together that day, leaning against an ancient maple, looking out over the hillside. They did not speak; they did not need to. Words would come later. Previously, Sarah had been in solitude and loneliness. Now she found company in solitude. Sarah's hand lay on the grass between them; over it rested the large, calloused hand of Christoph Zundel.

3
JULY 25, 1775 – AUGUST 13, 1775

Black Wolf stomped his foot and turned. He bowed his head and thumped his feet alternately upon the ground, muttering in time to the beat of the drum. Suddenly, he raised his head and arms, leaped, and whooped a shrill cry. The rest of the men followed him about the fire, leaping higher and higher and shouting louder and louder. The women followed, their bodies erect, their faces frozen in somberness. Wind Maiden moved with the women, shuffling her feet forward, then back; forward, then back. All the while, she watched Black Wolf.

He was tall and slender. Naked to the waist, his muscular body shone as the light of the fire reflected from his perspiring chest and arms. His face and forehead were painted red with black figures on cheek and chin. In the tuft of hair upon his crown, three black eagle's feathers protruded; two stood erect and one turned down.

Black Wolf faced the fire; the other dancers turned with him. They bowed their heads and dropped their hands to their sides. The traditional chants were on their lips, sung to the repetitious beat of the drum. The women swayed from side to side, shifting first one shoulder forward, then the other. Black Wolf, then the other dancers, straightened, looked up, and began, again, to stomp about the circle faster ... faster. The men whooped, leaped, and stomped; the women swayed and shuffled behind. The drum beat two long thumps, and the dance ended.

Wind Maiden looked across the fire at Black Wolf who stood, hunched over, with his hands on his knees, breathing deeply. The drummer sang and beat out a tale of the hunt; the fire crackled. Most of the dancers retreated from the light of the fire and waited for the next dance. Wind Maiden followed South-Wind-Blowing to a cluster of other young women. Laughing One leaned toward her.

"Black Wolf plays his flute at night outside my hut!" Her brow furrowed, yet no other sign of warning appeared upon her round, softly-carved face.

Wind Maiden frowned and said nothing. She faced the fire, standing rigid and still. Why did Black Wolf play his flute for Laughing One? Laughing One's arms were wide and strong. Did he want a woman who could carry heavy loads and hoe large fields? Her hips were full. Would babies fall like ripe fruit from beneath those hips?

South-Wind-Blowing whispered in her ear: "Laughing One is a slithering snake. Cover your ears against the hiss of her words, and set your eye upon the one you choose."

"Yes," thought Wind Maiden. "A man can play his flute where he wishes," she decided. "The nights are dark, and he can lie, unnoticed. He can play his invitation outside any hut; no woman can deny him freedom of night. Let Black Wolf play to Laughing One, or let him play to me. I do nothing." The corners of her mouth eased upward.

The smooth, brown skin of Wind Maiden glowed red in the light of the fire. She felt the vermillion on her cheeks set aflame. Her ribbons and silver buckles reflected the gleam. "The spirit of fire shares with me his power," she thought. "Grandfather Fire, make me burn as you burn."

Another dance was forming; Wind Maiden stepped forward to join the line of women. The drummer began the hollow call on his drum. Wind Maiden swayed and shuffled her feet. The silver in her earrings jingled slowly and rhythmically.

~ ~ ~

Wind Maiden arose late the next morning. She sat on her bench and recalled the night: the heat of the fire, the movements of the women, the dancing of Black Wolf. She stood and tightened her stroud about her waist. "Black Wolf is a strong hunter," she thought, "a member of the Wolf Tribe, known among the True Men for his fearlessness in battle. Someday, he will be a captain like White Eyes or like my father. I shall marry him." She set her mouth tightly shut and stepped into the sunlight.

She walked to a kettle suspended from three heavy, overlapping sticks. Using a half-gourd ladle, she scooped boiled deer meat and beans from the kettle into her wooden bowl. She picked up a wooden spoon from the ground, rubbed it against her stroud, and began to eat. She held the bowl close to her chin and chewed while she surveyed the village.

"But I must snatch him from Laughing One. He must see me, not her."

Her brothers, Red Face and Eagle-with-White-Head, knelt nearby, throwing dice. One-Who-Runs squatted with them. Wind Maiden watched the game. Eagle-with-White-Head placed the dice into a small bowl and cast them onto the ground. The dice were made of plum pits, painted black and yellow. Red Face grabbed them and laughed.

He smiled at One-Who-Runs. "My brother does not have a manito so he cannot win against me."

Eagle-With-White-Head grunted.

Wind Maiden lowered her spoon to her bowl: "My manito," she whispered to herself, "he will give me Black Wolf."

Red Face lifted the bowl over his head and proclaimed, "I am a fierce hunter and a brave warrior!" He cast the dice before him.

Fierce hunter? His arms were twigs. Where were the muscles? His mouth was thick and wide. The muscle was in his mouth.

"My brother prattles and creates tales like a woman." Eagle-with-White-Head said, nodding toward Wind Maiden. He was tall; his arms were trees. He was the son of his father.

Wind Maiden smiled and moved closer to the group. She liked being near her brothers, especially Eagle-with-White-Head, the younger. Red Face used words which pierced so Wind Maiden sometimes avoided him.

One-Who-Runs stretched and turned to observe Wind Maiden.

Red Face spoke to her: "Only your fleas awoke this morning while you slept on."

Wind Maiden sighed and stared at her brother. "I will not show him my anger. He kicks me because he cannot kick our brother."

Eagle-with-White-Head slapped the shoulder of Red Face: "Can the prattler throw dice, or can he only cast tales?"

"Ah — so now the toothless one snarls," jeered Red Face. The two returned to their game.

One-Who-Runs rose and walked to Wind Maiden. "I saw you at the dance last night."

Wind Maiden chewed a piece of meat from her bowl and watched his big, wide nose. Her eyes leaped from his nose to his smiling mouth.

"Black Wolf is tall and strong; his mouth is tight and fierce," she thought. "One-Who-Runs is a boy."

One-Who-Runs continued, "Did you see me?"

Wind Maiden thought of Black Wolf kneeling in the firelight. She sipped a spoonful of broth then answered, "No."

Red Face yelled. One-Who-Runs scratched his arm and looked back to the game. Wind Maiden ate the rest of her meat. "If I burn gifts to my spirit, he will give me Black Wolf.

Grandfather Fire is stronger than the manito of Laughing One, stronger than any manito. He will give me Black Wolf."

She re-entered the hut, emerged again with her carrying bag, and hurried toward the forest. "He will not take green sticks that little children gather or twigs that lie broken on the ground. I must walk deep into the forest where deer sleep by day. Then I can find strong, crisp sticks that will please my manito."

The woods were humid; insects were swarming. Women and children had come early to collect their firewood to avoid the stings of flies and mosquitoes. Wind Maiden frowned. "Good. I am alone." She walked beside the fork of the Elk's Eye and heard the smooth flow of the river on her left. The flies buzzed near her. She scurried from them.

Finally, she began to find fallen branches and dead saplings. A long, narrow, evenly-formed branch hung cradled between two, heavy, low-hanging limbs of a walnut tree. "That one — strong ... and hard," Wind Maiden decided.

She extricated the branch from its perch and rolled it in her hands, rubbing her fingertips down its smooth side. Turning, she walked back upon her steps with slowness, gathering kindling with her right hand and dropping it into her carrying bag which now rested against her back, suspended from a strap of woven hemp which hung from her forehead. In her left hand, she clutched the branch of walnut.

"He does not go to many places in the forest. He does not like the damp earth. I shall go to where he meets the hunters at night."

Wind Maiden turned right of the path, still gathering kindling while stepping through low brush. She stopped at a small clearing where she knelt, placed the branch on the earth, and slid the carrying strap from her forehead. The bag of firewood slid onto the ground.

"When my fire ignites as in the days of my grandfathers, my guardian spirit will be pleased."

She removed kindling from the bag until she found a small, flat piece of wood and, then, a round stick. She gathered a handful of kindling and moved to the center of the clearing where she knelt and placed the flat wood on the ground. She hunched over, swatted the flies from her face, and rotated the stick between her hands upon the flat wood. Flies buzzed in her ears and eyes. They must have been sent by her enemy, but they would not stop her from spinning the stick. At last, a small stream of smoke rose, then, a hesitant flame. Wind Maiden fed the delicate fire with twigs and bark and moss — just a small meal for a young flame. The fire crackled and brightened.

Wind Maiden retrieved the thin walnut branch. She broke it with her foot into three segments and laid the pieces in a triangle upon the fire. She stepped back two paces and knelt.

"I wait. My manito arrives soon."

Presently, smoke rose and sparks sputtered from the segmented branch. It flamed.

Wind Maiden slid a pouch from the waist of her stroud and rocked forward upon her knees.

She spoke aloud, her voice vibrating against her ears: "Grandfather Fire, forever wise, consume into smoke my offering." Opening the pouch, she took a handful of shredded tobacco and cast it into the flames. The fire cracked and surged briefly. Wind Maiden nodded, "He approves."

"Grandfather Fire ... Guardian Spirit ..." She imitated the chant of the singers at the sacrifices. "He who shares secrets ... He who gives power ... Warmth of all councils ... Light of all villages ..." She spoke low and bent near the flames: "Give me Black Wolf."

She arose and circled the fire, scattering into the flames a second, then a third, handful of tobacco, repeating her incantation each time. She knelt where she had arisen, settling upon the ground, to await the death of the flames.

"Now, when I dance before the fire, I shall move as smoothly as the red-tailed hawk glides. Black Wolf will see me. He will play his flute for me, and I shall be his wife." She rocked and watched the dying flames. "I snatch Black Wolf from Laughing One."

When the fire died, the flies returned. Wind Maiden fidgeted and stood. She selected a charred fragment of wood — "A reminder so Grandfather Fire does not forget his promise." — and dropped it into her pouch. She scattered the unburned wood and covered the site with dirt and leaves. Wind Maiden repacked her carrying bag with the remaining firewood and adjusted the hemp strap upon her forehead. She tucked the pouch into the waist of her stroud and turned toward Goschachgunk.

Star-at-Dawning awaited Wind Maiden outside their hut. "You become toad that hides in ditches," she scolded.

Wind Maiden slid the carrying strap from her forehead. She looked down at the bag. "I shall marry soon, Mother — a warrior and a hunter ..." She looked at Star-at-Dawning "... like my father."

The eyes of Star-at-Dawning widened in their fleshy recesses. She smiled, revealing brown stubs of teeth. "Which hunter is he?"

"Wait, Mother; you will see."

Star-at-Dawning tapped the shoulder of her daughter with two chubby fingers: "He must first send friends to ask for you. And he must distribute gifts to the friends and flesh and skins to us. Remember."- She raised her hand. "Move like the turtle. You must wait and watch."

The eyes of Wind Maiden floated past those of her mother and slid between earth and sky. "Sometimes the turtle is caught because he is slow," she pondered. "Yes," she said aloud and walked past Star-at-Dawning.

"Mother is wise in the old ways, but the old ways are gone. The Big Knife walks upon our heels. We no longer live in the land where our fathers faced the big sea. We must always run to a new fire. And when we run, we must go quickly or be smashed like a slow turtle. No — I must run or die."

~ ~ ~

The night was black; low clouds concealed the flicker of the stars. The fire shone orange and yellow, seeming to ignite the clouds themselves. Wind Maiden stood early before the fire, her mouth arched into a quivering scowl to hide her fear. She knelt and thrust a small, charred log into the flames. "For remembrance, Grandfather," she muttered. She arose and withdrew to an edge of the clearing.

A stout man strolled near, regarding her as he approached. He paused, gesturing to her to come from the shadows.

"Does he mistake me for a trading woman?" Wind Maiden cringed. It was not yet time for a woman to be at the place of dance unless she was a trading woman, trading herself with the men. "Go away," she hissed.

He stood another moment then laughed a low, guttural chuckle and walked on.

Three men,- wearing only breech clouts, fed the fire. The drummer approached, carrying a White Man's barrel with a deerskin stretched over the opening. He settled in his accustomed location and beat slow, rhythmic thuds with the heels of his hands. Then, he thrust the full palms upon the drum, increasing the beat.

Wind Maiden shook. She crossed her arms to hold in the shaking. She closed her eyes and saw the throbbing orange of the fire surrounded by impenetrable blackness. She yearned to yank the sound of the drum from the air and hide it in the blackness before her eyes so no ears could find the sound and follow it to the dance.

"No dance tonight," she pleaded within herself. She breathed in spasmodic jerks and opened her eyes. Several men and women had responded to the call of the drum and were gathering in the warm light. Wind Maiden sighed and scolded herself: "I am a little turtle who creeps away. Turtles do not kill bears. I reject the turtle. I am the hunter who kills the bear." She hooked her hands on her hips and chased away the shaking.

South-Wind-Blowing was approaching the clearing; Wind Maiden joined her friend. South-Wind-Blowing was older than Wind Maiden. She had married a man from the Tribe of the Turkey and had lived with him three years. No children. He had taken his rifle, skins, and dog and left because her belly was empty. She had sneered at him ... he could not fill a belly. She said she had left him. Now, she stood at the dance, waiting for another man.

"Those men," South-Wind-Blowing cast her eyes across the fire, "look on whom you please. Take the gifts one offers and share his hut." She glanced sideways at Wind Maiden. "If he does not please you, move to a new fire." She smiled. "And take new gifts from another man."

"I choose Black Wolf." The voice of Wind Maiden quivered.

"Yes," said South-Wind-Blowing. "Run, then, for soon he will take the snake to his hut."

Wind Maiden did not respond; her own thoughts burned her mind: "He is my hunter. Tonight he will see me. The fire is before my eyes. The promise burns in the flames." She watched the sputtering flames ... and Black Wolf.

He circled the fire in slow, confident strides. Wind Maiden saw two dark wolves carved upon his chest, one crouching, the other springing at an unknown prey. She looked into his face, half black, half red, fearful in its coloration. As he passed, he dropped an unseeing look upon her.

"Now," her heart pounded, "Now!" She looked and did not turn away. She saw his face relax in recognition, his frown disappear. Then, he walked on.

"He knows," she muttered, "and I have a hunter and a warrior." She shivered and wished the dance would begin.

Wind Maiden swayed like grain in the wind, erect and leisurely. Black Wolf leaped and plunged like a warrior in battle, circling and looking at Wind Maiden who returned his gaze. Their faces froze in grimness. During the intervals, Laughing One snarled warnings in coarse undertones at Wind Maiden who stood immobile and silent.

"Black Wolf chooses," she thought. "Laughing One cannot speak for him. Black Wolf chooses."

After the dance, Eagle-with-White-Head followed Wind Maiden to the hut. "Take care, little fawn," he whispered, "Black Wolf is a sly hunter. And he takes many pelts."

Wind Maiden turned. "You know nothing! The ..." She stopped. Grandfather Fire would be angered if she revealed his pact with her. "I know what I do," she concluded.

"No!" returned her brother. "Did you see One-Who-Runs at the dance? Did you see him dance for you?"

"One-Who-Runs is a boy. He is not a warrior. He cannot give me much deer meat and pelts."

Eagle-with-White-Head sneered, "And Black Wolf takes much deer flesh, little fawn. You forget you are speckled. You run freely in the clearing when you should be hiding in the forest." He hurried past her.

The next morning, Wind Maiden moved from chore to chore and finished nothing. Finally, Star-at-Dawning tossed her carrying bag to her: "I am weary from watching you pace in circles. Hurry into the woods where you can chase firewood. The mosquitoes will suck the running from you." She chuckled, shaking her head.

"Black Wolf, the hunter," whispered Wind Maiden. She meandered along the path. A fire filled her mind; next, swaying, leaping bodies; and, finally, fierce, black eyes. "I will have a strong, fearless husband. He will bring me wampum and white linen. The wife of a captain of a tribe." She saw, again, the black wolves frozen in power, and she recalled the ferocious lines of paint. She remembered a thick scar across his shoulder, a mark of pride from battle.

Dirt swished behind her. She pivoted. Out from the darkness of a tree appeared a tall and wide shadow. It rose in strength and flowed with power. Flight surged in Wind Maiden then plunged to her feet like rocks.

Black Wolf walked toward her with a long, confident gait. Her mouth fell open. She could not breathe.

"A wolf ... long and full of power," she thought. "My husband." Her mouth closed; her body fell back into the water and floated upon the swelling tide.

She felt young as the glossy blades of grass yet old as the dirt beneath them. Wind Maiden turned to meet Black Wolf.

He reached out his hands to her shoulders and looked down upon her. The hands were hard and heavy.

"Lovely!" His voice rolled easily from his mouth.

A yellow, shimmering numbness crept over Wind Maiden. She looked up to welcome him.

His mouth, though smiling, pressed harsh lines into his face. His eyes glared a demand; her body responded with yielding submission.

The hands of Black Wolf slid heavily along her arms. He squeezed her waist with both his hands, his fingers pressing painfully into her flesh. Wind Maiden gasped. A long ago scene of a fawn flashed through her mind: it poised, motionless, in the forest while a hunter aimed at its chest.

Black Wolf chuckled then released Wind Maiden, rubbing his hands along her thighs before dropping her arms to his sides.

"Soon ... but not here," he whispered. "I shall come again." He laughed — just once more.

"When you play your flute for me?" The voice of Wind Maiden was like the soft patter of a squirrel as it scurries along the ground. She was trembling now.

Black Wolf smiled.

"Yes," she thought, "when he plays his flute for me." Her mind flashed golden; she smiled back.

The gold-edged sunlight in the forest streamed vibrating flames across the path. "Fire," thought Wind Maiden, "like Grandfather Fire." She was walking back to her village, the half-filled carrying bag rocking against her back. She stepped through the airy flames. "Hot — like fire. Glowing with the promise of my hunter. Mighty hunter. Black Wolf — husband." Looking down upon her moccasined feet, she slid them along the path; a hum, rising from deep in her throat, guided the rhythm of her movements. Finally, Goschachgunk appeared, clamoring against the silence of the forest.

Wind Maiden stopped. "So — we call ourselves the Tribe of the Turtle. The Great Spirit-Turtle who protects us did not make us crawl upon our bellies like the turtle. My people are foolish. They do not hear the new voices of the spirits."

She gazed along the straight path of the village to where the second path crossed it. A cross — copied from Beautiful Spring, the village of the Quaekel White Men and their praying lenno. Beside the paths, huts and cabins sprouted in stiff rows — copied, too, from Beautiful Spring.

Wind Maiden grunted. Five moons before, in Squalle Gischuch, the time when frogs begin to croak, the Lenni Lenape, the True Man, left Kekelemukpechunk because the Quaekel White teachers at Beautiful Spring and their lenno who had believed the lie were growing big and spreading wide. The True Man had crawled upon his belly to light a new fire here, Goschachgunk.

"The Lenni Lenape is free. He should dig his fire pit and build his hut wherever he chooses. He is not a White Man who must huddle in rows inside fences. Why does the Lenni Lenape obey and imitate his enemy? Does he become his enemy?"

Wind Maiden renewed her sliding gait. She would not become her own enemy. She would take what she wanted. She would not step into the footprints of the White Man. She would not hear the slow scrapings of the turtle.

"I have Black Wolf. I laugh at the white-headed ways of my mother."

Laughing One was crouching outside her hut. Wind Maiden passed by and noticed the figure arise. "The twisting green snake," she sighed. "it sputters painless warnings."

Laughing One circled behind her, snarling, "Long-legged pup, biting its own tail." She stepped sideways, snagging the foot of Wind Maiden on her own. Wind Maiden toppled, her carrying bag clattering against her back. She yanked it aside, rolled, and stood.

She spun to face Laughing One. She examined her opponent, noticing her height — short; her build — large-boned; her weight — much heavier than Wind Maiden's. And Laughing One was older; she had fought more.

Wind Maiden squinted against the sunlight. "Move fast," she determined, "escape strength; tire her." She despised this contest. She bent forward.

Small boys, wearing only breech clouts, scampered up; men laughed and strolled toward them; several women dropped their weaving and stood at a distance.

"They watch the dogs snap at each other's throats." Wind Maiden detested them.

Laughing One stood, poised: "Puppy!" The words slid through her teeth: "Go sit in a corner and scratch fleas." She lunged.

Wind Maiden turned; Laughing One stumbled, evaded by her enemy. The men roared. Wind Maiden spoke, her mouth drawn back: "You are clumsy. No one trips you. No one needs to." She felt confident now.

Laughing One squealed, stepped, and swung her arm in a rapid arc at Wind Maiden's neck. Wind Maiden jumped back but a thump struck her chest. She coiled and gasped. Laughing One fell upon her, nails digging like claws into the arm of Wind Maiden. Wind Maiden twisted and kicked. They became one writhing creature. She felt that long moment when their struggles suspended ... and they were falling. The weight of her adversary crushed Wind Maiden against the earth. Her mind screamed; her body squirmed and thrust. Puffs of dirt strangled her and stung her eyes. She was a doe crushed by the resounding impact of a bullet, kicking upon its side.

Laughing One perched upon her prize, pinning with her legs the arms of Wind Maiden against her sides. Wind Maiden saw a glistening object move from Laughing One's waist to her mouth. For an instant, her body relaxed and she looked up ... a knife! The screaming in her mind gave way to a deep, red stillness. Her body surged; her legs fought against the earth.

The knife slid from mouth to hand, accompanied by a hard yank of Wind Maiden's hair. As Laughing One bent to cut the mass, Wind Maiden jerked sideways and chomped her wrist, holding in the death grip of a frantic animal.

The howl of Laughing One rushed relief to Wind Maiden's mind. She rolled to extricate herself, yet the detested and persistent mass rolled with her. Wind Maiden felt hope arise and walk away. She pushed against the remounted adversary who retrieved the knife and regained the thick cluster of hair.

Laughing One leaned forward again, now back from the jaws of Wind Maiden. A slash of the knife ... and a dark, shining, arm-long mass of hair was swung aloft. Laughing One leaped up with a whoop to the screams and howls of the crowd.

Wind Maiden lay upon the ground. "Why?" Her bruised mind stirred. "I am dirt, crushed by the foot." She pulled her body forward. The jeers of the crowd and of Laughing One pulsed with the thump of her heart. Her hair tumbled about her face and shoulders — the only covering in her shame. She fingered the shredded edges. Her blue stroud, the one she had worn the day she first became a woman, was torn and dust-covered. She sat looking at it. "Why? I am a woman. Shame does not crush a woman."

A hand stroked her hair back from her face. "Black Wolf," her mind cried. She looked up at Eagle-with-White-Head. He placed his hands under her arms and lifted her feeble body.

In the evening, Wind Maiden sat in darkness in the hut. She faced the fire pit where burnt logs lay amidst smoldering ashes. Star-at-Dawning sat upon

26

her bench near the door. The drum beat its invitation into the night. Wind Maiden listened. She felt her hair, trimmed by her mother. It was pulled back and bound ... unnaturally short. She dropped her hand below to where her hair once lay.

"The dance begins. You are going?" Star-at-Dawning whispered.

"No ..." Wind Maiden saw, again, the sneering face of Laughing One and the cheering men as the hair whirled against the sky. "No," she repeated.

Star-at-Dawning arose and stood at the door of the hut, looking out. Wind Maiden watched the roundness of her body silhouetted against the glow of the village fires. Finally, she returned to her seat.

"This warrior — he causes this." She leaned forward and tapped the hair of Wind Maiden.

"No, Mother, he does not cause it."

Star-at-Dawning hesitated — "Go to the dance." Wind Maiden looked away. "You are not a bird that flies only in darkness and hides in the day. Go to the dance."

"No, Mother." The voice of Wind Maiden rose — "They laugh at me."

"Go to the dance. We do not care for their laughs. If they laugh, they will make you strong. Will they stop laughing if you do not go? No! If you do not hear their laughs, you will become weak like an infant. But hear their laughs and see their faces ... Then! You will truly become a woman."

"Tomorrow, Mother, I shall go tomorrow."

Star-at-Dawning shifted in her seat: "Tomorrow."

~ ~ ~

The moon was high and round and orange in the black sky. Fish-of-the-Deep-Water was outside in the blackness, his voice humming around the droning voice of another member of the council. Wind Maiden rolled over on her mat to watch the opening of the hut. From far away, the beats and the thumps and the whoops of the dance floated through the hollow darkness.

Wind Maiden saw Star-at-Dawning arise from her bench and pass silently to the opposite side of the door where she spread the mat of her husband upon his bench. She crept back to her place to wait.

The voices unwove themselves and stopped. Fish-of-the-Deep-Water passed through the door and stared about the hut.

"Where are Red Face and Eagle-With-White-Head?" He spoke into the darkness.

"At the dance," Star-at-Dawning whispered.

Wind Maiden pretended to sleep; she did not want to talk tonight, not *this* night."

"And that one," he growled, "why is she not at the dance?"

Star-at-Dawning sighed, "Tomorrow she goes."

"You! Little scalped one!" His voice rumbled.

Wind Maiden rolled onto her back.

"I sat in the council tonight. They talked of the two fighting dogs and how one chomped off the tail of the other." He crossed to her and stood over her bench. "So. The wounded animal hides."

Wind Maiden stared up at him. She was an injured animal, licking its wounds, crouching in a hidden crevice.

"I am tired, Father." Her voice sounded to her like the voice of her mother.

"Tired from running." He walked to his bench and sat. He rested his arms upon his legs ... long like those of Wind Maiden.

"Tomorrow, you will walk through the village when the sun is high in the sky. You will sneer at their laughs." He looked away. Fish-of-the-Deep-Water had spoken. It would be as he said.

Wind Maiden lay upon her back, listening to the throbbings of the dance and envisioning the leaps of Black Wolf about the pulsing fire. "Tomorrow," she thought.

The drum stopped and, with it, the victorious cries. Soon, muffled voices and footfalls dispersed through the village. The dance was over.

Wind Maiden watched the door opening. Eagle-with-White-Head would tell her of Black Wolf. Did he dance? Did he dance for Laughing One?

When her brother entered the hut, Wind Maiden lifted herself upon her elbow and waited for Eagle-with-White-Head to look at her. She did not want the others to hear her question. She waited. She did not call him.

Eagle-with-White-Head greeted his father and mother. He walked to his bench at the rear of the hut and looked across his shoulder at Wind Maiden.

Wind Maiden raised her eyebrows and whispered, "Was he ..."

"No! "

Wind Maiden slid back onto her mat. "No." Did Black Wolf celebrate with Laughing One, or did he mourn with her? "No" settled upon and suffocated her mind.

Eagle-with-White-Head spoke to Fish-of-the-Deep-Water: "Does the council talk war with the Big Knife?" He leaned forward.

"Yes." The voice of Fish-of-the-Deep-Water filled the hut. Even the air was heavier and harder to breathe when he spoke. "The Saggenash from beyond the Great Salt Sea invites the True Man to stand with him and to sink his hatchet into the skull of the Big Knife, the disobedient child, who inhabits our land and kills our buck and takes the land for his own."

"Do we fight, Father?" asked Eagle-with-White-Head.

"No."

Red Face appeared in the door. "No, we do not fight!" He crept inside. "Chief Netawatwes and Captain White Eyes love the White Man more than they love the True Man. The black-coated teachers at Beautiful Spring smothered us at Kekelemukpechunk. We retreated here to Goschachgunk and, now, Netawatwes invites those teachers to build another fire upon our land and to draw us unto a manito that our grandfathers did not know."

Fish-of-the-Deep-Water sighed, "Yes ... is true. Netawatwes forgets the ways of the True Man. He pants after a new spirit. He licks the feet of the Black Coat."

A hollow note broke apart the conversation. Next, a second ... and a third. A flute.

Wind Maiden slipped from her bench. Black Wolf.

Star-at-Dawning glanced at Fish-of-the-Deep-Water. Her cocked head asked, "Does she go?"

Fish-of-the-Deep-Water frowned. Yes.

Star-at-Dawning arose. "Walk slowly," she admonished. "Remember the turtle."

As Wind Maiden left the hut, she glanced back at Eagle-with-White-Head, but he did not look at her.

The night breathed freshness onto her body; she inhaled. Her hair thumped against her shoulders, but with each step, she felt growth from each root of hair. She walked with slowness behind the hut, subduing the feet that wanted to run. She soared with the hawk; she was free again.

She approached the dark form which now stood to greet her. She moved nearer. She gazed at the legs, the arms, the face of ... One-Who-Runs.

"Oh." Her voice was hollow. She was black inside.

"I did not know if you would come." One-Who-Runs smiled upon her. "I heard ..." he hesitated, "... about the ... the ... morning. When you did not come to dance, I thought you would now hear my flute instead of the flute of ... another."

"Yes," said Wind Maiden, watching his nose. She had heard but had not heard what he had said.

His body was light; the muscles were developed but not large and powerful. From boyhood, he had been trained to become a runner, to bear messages from fire to fire. He could run many miles quickly and could carry long speeches in his mind. But he was not a hunter, and he was not a warrior.

The voice of One-Who-Runs rose, "I select you for my wife."

Wind Maiden listened, now, to the words of Black Wolf in the mouth of One-Who-Runs. "One-Who-Runs is a boy, the friend of my brothers. He shot his first arrow with them from the small bow carved for children and rode his pony with them through the woods and across the streams." She smiled at him. "Just a boy," she thought.

The sun burned high in the sky when Wind Maiden walked through Goschachgunk. Her hair was bound back, but the cloth hung high so that it would not hide the open wound. She would show her scar of battle with pride.

Women and men paused to watch her, some to laugh. "Their eyes are flies buzzing to my wound. I grab them from the air and squash them in my hand." Her thoughts fed her strength to walk on. "Black Wolf will see me today. The snake loses him. Then I shall laugh."

South-Wind-Blowing strolled toward her. Her mouth hung in a half-smile. She beckoned to Wind Maiden to walk with her.

South-Wind-Blowing spoke low, rolling in her mouth each word: "Laughing One will share the hut of Black Wolf."

Wind Maiden reeled. The words would not fit together but hung apart like a disjointed animal.

She heard the voice of South-Wind-Blowing rise, and, like a hatchet, pound each word into her skull: "Laughing one marries Black Wolf."

Her skull split open. The blood dripped in warm rivulets through her hair and down her face. From far away, she watched and felt nothing. She saw, again, the fire nourished in the forest and gazed into its flames. "Why?" she asked her manito.

The fire blazed, unheeding. The heat of its burning chilled her. It mocked her with its dark, blazing light.

The days passed, unwoven into one another. When South-Wind-Blowing carried the message to the hut of Wind Maiden that One-Who-Runs asked to marry her, Wind Maiden shrugged and her mother and her father grunted, "Yes."

They led her to the family hut of One-Who-Runs; she bowed and entered.

4
AUGUST 14, 1775 – SEPTEMBER 9, 1775

"... Twenty-two days, Brother Voss, in good weather," Brother Zundel was saying while he and Brother Voss adjusted the tethering ropes of the three pack horses. "Brother Zeisberger is even now returned to Schoenbrunn. I would wish that we had left with him in July. Yet ..." Brother Zundel yanked a rope and stood erect.

"Yet now he has a wife and cannot run at his pace but must await mine," concluded Sarah to herself. She clutched to her chest a small bundle wrapped in dark blue yarn and waited behind him.

Both Brother Zundel and Brother Voss wore black coats and breeches, white linsey shirts and leggings. Brother Zundel removed his wide-brimmed, black hat and wiped sweat from his forehead with a handkerchief. His eye caught the skirt of Sarah. He glanced around.

"So softly you approach," he said, then smiled. His eyes lowered to her fidgeting hands. "Another bundle?"

"It is small," murmured Sarah.

"Each one has been small." He frowned.

"Linen ... flax thread ... they are needful." Her voice rose.

"Needful ..." repeated Brother Zundel.

"... for curtains, table covers ..." She felt like a whining child. "... and a hand loom — I ... I knew we could not spare room for a large loom after I tried disassembling it ... it was ..." The tips of her fingers ached for the rough touch of the loom. Whom could she serve without her wheel and loom?

"... too large, yes," concluded Brother Zundel. He watched her, still frowning.

Reaching forth, he touched her hands with his as he took from her the package. "Linen, hand loom ... Remember, Sister Sarah, we ride into the wilderness." He raised his brows before looking away. She had wearied him. He worked the bundle into a pack and readjusted the horse's load.

Sarah reached beneath her chin to rub the blue ribbon of the married woman and watched him and Brother Voss retrieve the three riding horses. Wide shoulders, muscular shoulders — what did she know of Christoph Zundel? Forty-two days they had known each other. What could she learn on daily strolls? Most of the time, he had spoken only of his plans for the Indians.

"... and the Delaware Reading and Spelling Book," he had said, "the Mission Board has agreed to print it." His hands had moved with restlessness through the air. "We can teach them to read in their own language. And, with the hymns and scripture passages already translated into the Unami dialect of the Delaware Nation, they can begin to edify one another. The gospel will spread unhindered."

He had looked to her to share his enthusiasm. She had said nothing.

And July — Brother David Zeisberger had returned to the Ohio country in July. Brother Zundel had wanted to depart then. But Sarah had known him only fifteen days; and, although she had argued that she wanted to give her parents time to receive her summons and to attend her marriage, her real reason for postponement was terror. Moreover, she had known her parents would not respond. Confusion prevailed in the colonies. The English were relinquishing governmental posts and fleeing. Rumors moved along the roads faster than did messages, and messages were scattered. They were married one month after the departure of Brother Zeisberger. The waiting had been unnecessary ... wasteful. And the terror had not abated with time.

During the last two weeks, they had talked of more intimate matters.

"I am from Berthelsdorf in Saxony," he had said.

"My parents, too, are from Saxony. Herrnhut," she had replied. "They crossed over two years before my birth."

He had glanced away toward the river. "Your parents ..."

"Teachers from settlement to settlement, preaching the Word of God. I traveled with them until I was twelve. Then they sent me here to the Older Girls' Group. They have visited six times since." She had hoped she did not appear to lament. "The work is arduous, and their means are small, too small for unnecessary travel." How much she had talked! "Your parents?" she had asked.

"My mother died in childbirth when I was ten. My father ... he is of the Catholic Church of Rome, and ..." His voice had trailed off.

Sarah had rubbed her forehead and dropped her gaze. Her fingers had tapped against themselves in nervous jerks. He had sat several moments before continuing. And when he had spoken again, his hands had waved, his eyes had sparkled, his words had flowed. He had resumed an account of the mission among the Indians.

Whom had Sarah married five days ago and whom did she follow into the wilderness?

"God go with you to guide you into the mercies of our Saviour," called Deaconess Glaser. She and Sister Voss were walking toward Sarah.

Sarah avoided the gaze of the Deaconess. The meager training of these recent weeks in the dialects of the Delaware nation and in the habits of the heathen — they confirmed to her her inadequacy. Saviour! She needed His mercy.

Deaconess Glaser stood before her: "I shall pray for you."

"And I, too," said Sister Suzanne. She glanced toward Brother Voss: "And for my husband."

Brother Zundel and John Voss approached, pulling the riding horses by their reins.

Surely she ... fearful, incompetent ... could not be leaving.

"The roads are treacherous; the winters are severe in the mountains ..." began Sister Suzanne.

"I shall finish my survey for the Mission Board and return," interrupted her husband, "by November, perhaps October."

When the call came from the Mission Board for someone to accompany Brother and Sister Zundel to Schoenbrunn in the Ohio country and to return with letters and missionary reports, Brother Voss had petitioned first Suzanne and then the Board for the commission. Brother Voss would leave Bethlehem for adventure; and Brother Zundel would leave for his mission; but Sarah ... for what did she leave?

Brother Zundel led her to a speckled horse.

She contemplated the animal and its saddle, marveled at its height and at the distance from the ground of its stirrup. "He is larger than ..." she stammered, glancing up at Brother Zundel who stared down at her, waiting. "I ... mount poorly," she concluded.

Brother Zundel bent over her. He lifted her onto the saddle then looked up at her. His eyes were full of the clear, blue, August morning sky. Sarah looked back at him and bit her lip. Her eyes, cast down to the dirt below, surely reflected an uncertain brown.

Brother Zundel walked toward the pack horses. Sarah adjusted the skirt of her gown, trying to pull it down, down over her legs. But the moccasins which covered her ankles and lower legs still protruded. She wore them for the first time today — odd attire — to protect her from the bites of snakes frequently encountered on the trail.

"Brother Zundel, might I ride upon a sidesaddle?" she had begged the day before.

"Impossible," he had replied.

"My legs ... exposed ... why ..."

He had bowed his head, held his hands behind his back, and closed his eyes. "Sister," His words had come too patiently, "you cannot ride over narrow trails and mountain passages ..." He had looked up, blinked, and continued, "... sidesaddle upon a horse."

The men mounted. Brother Zundel rode to the front of the three pack horses, motioning Sarah behind him, while John Voss rode to the rear of the caravan.

The procession moved past brethren and sisters who had gathered along the street to watch them leave. Sarah's legs hung conspicuously; her hands fumbled with the reins.

Over the bridge and across the verdant valley of the Lehigh Rover they rode. As they climbed the hillside above Bethlehem, Sarah pivoted in her saddle. The community of grey stone buildings, square and erect, spread itself in orderly rows along wide, straight streets. Even the fruit trees grew in tidy columns beside the town. She wanted to grasp Bethlehem and drag it with them. She wanted to find her wheel and spin the flax into thread, sliding its coarse strands through her fingers. She rubbed the thick, solid rein which she clutched in her hand.

They rested that night at an inn beside a rock-laden stream. In the darkness, Sarah lay down beside Brother Zundel. She pulled her braid from her back and laid it across her shoulder. Covering her sleeping gown with the quilted coverlet, she stared up toward the ceiling.

"Do you sleep?" whispered Brother Zundel.

She was tempted to breathe a silent "Yes." She murmured, "No."

She felt the warmth of his body along her length. His hand stroked her braid.

"I had not realized such thick beauty lay hidden beneath a cap. "

Beauty? Sarah alone lay here beside him. He had seen this same braid these four nights before. And he only noticed it now? It pleased him! Was it tighter tonight, more smooth? Did he approve of her laying it across her shoulder? Tomorrow night, she could do it again.

She gazed back toward him in the darkness. The windows were small; she was glad for their meager light.

He pressed her to himself.

"I am unskilled in the ways of a man and a woman," she breathed. Her heart pounded against him.

"Yes, so you have told me these five nights." His arms pushed back from her. "Do I offend?"

"N ... no," she stuttered.

"Then forget your lack of skill."

She tried to forget ... but she remembered still.

~ ~ ~

Through Lititz, Lancaster, and Middletown they rode. Christian brethren welcomed them in each town. Their progress was slow and filled with many rests lest their unaccustomed bodies protest the strain of travel.

On the sixth day from Bethlehem, they left the last of the communities of brethren. Brother Zundel's gaze turned west, and the pace was no longer slow. That day, Saturday, after they crossed the Susquehanna at Harris's Ferry, the rain, first slow, began to fall. Sarah pulled up the hood of her black cape as faster and faster the rain fell. They rode without pausing toward Carlisle. The clouds smothered the earth in blue-grey dullness. Sarah peered out from within the darkness of her hood, against whose fibers the rain pat-patted with dull taps. She felt alone. Her lips trembled, and she let her face relax into weariness. She would fail the mission; she would fail Brother Zundel; she would fail God. She searched within herself, but she could not feel the stirrings of her Saviour's call.

Brother Zundel reined in his horse beside a stone dwelling on the edge of Carlisle.

"You are sore from riding?" he asked as he helped Sarah from her horse.

"Not very," she replied. She tried to stand upon crumbling legs. Would the confession of aching muscles on her back and thighs and calves lessen the pain? She could not trouble him with her foolish discomforts.

The wife of the innkeeper directed Sarah to a small room while the husband assisted Brother Zundel and Brother Voss with the bedding and feeding of the horses. She eased off her cape and outer garments then sat upon the bed and removed her leather moccasins, wet and clammy. She lay back upon the bed; its hardness contrasted with her soft feather bed in Bethlehem. If only she might sleep again upon that bed for but one night ...

Sarah rolled over and opened her eyes. Brother Zundel stood above her.

"Oh!" she gasped, sitting up. She pressed her arm across her camisole, her hand against her neck. Why did he not divert his gaze? She dropped her eyes. "Did I sleep long?" she murmured.

"No. We have just returned from the stable."

She fumbled with her gown and slid it on.

"Sister Sarah ..." he began.

Sarah looked up; he was shaking his head.

She displeased him. In the light, he had seen her ... and it displeased him. Too thin. She could eat ...

He paced toward the other corner of the room and turned to watch her. "Uh ... we cannot travel farther in this rain," he said. "We shall keep the Sabbath here tomorrow and resume our journey on Monday."

Some other utterance had lain behind the shaking of his head.

Brother Zundel wrapped his hands behind his back. "You are sore and tired?"

Would he forever ask this question? "Not very." She stood straight and pressed her lips together in feigned confidence. She wearied herself with pretension; it should not be so with a husband. But she feared losing him before she had even gained him.

"The wilderness begins west of the Ohio River." He stared at her. "The journey has not begun."

Did he worry that she might falter?

"Tell me when you need to rest." He swung his hands in front of him now. "I think of the mission and of our delay. I press forward, and I forget ..."

"... forget that he is shackled," thought Sarah. Though her bones rubbed through the flesh, as they seemed to have done already, she could not tell him. Not now.

"Sister ..." He stepped toward her and stopped. "I have known fellowship with God and brethren, both Indians and White Men. That has been sufficient." He gazed at Sarah. "I did not seek marriage."

Nor did she! Yet though she had not sought it, now she desired the fullness of their marriage. She rubbed her palms up and down along the skirt of her gown.

He pushed back his hair from his forehead. "I had seen you on occasion when you worked at your loom. I had passed you on the street and had observed you leaving chapel. I asked your name ... presumptuously, yes. Do I surprise you? I did not feel you were a stranger. You look so like my favorite sister who was born upon the deathbed of my mother ..."

He paused and Sarah knew he waited for her to speak, but she could neither open her mouth nor move.

"A man can be alone and not realize he is lonely. It is habit." He cleared his throat and coughed.

He made as though he would step nearer then rocked in place. "When the deacons suggested marriage and presented me the list of sisters, I saw your name. I was ... I was ... glad that you had offered yourself in marriage to me."

"But I ..." Sarah hesitated. She could not embarrass him by saying that she had not chosen him. Still, how brazen that would have been.

"I have ... a ... accepted my marriage to you," he said.

Accepted? How honorable. Surely he was a saint in the sight of God. And had she been chosen for her own merits or simply because she reminded him of his sister?

Sarah knew he awaited a like confession from her. Did she accept their marriage or did she yet struggle against its demands? Why, when once the call of the Lord had been so clear, could she falter now amidst doubts? "I endeavor," was all she could say. And not even she knew what she meant.

On the eighth day from Bethlehem, they resumed their journey. They traveled the highland trail, the route of the watershed. The land, never smooth, became more jagged and rocky. The trees loomed larger than their counterparts in Bethlehem; the forests grew denser; the settlements became rarer.

A long pack train of seventeen horses and three men emerged from the darkness ahead, passed, and disappeared into the stillness behind. Others like it traversed the trail.

Beyond Shippensburg, they lodged in a small wooden family dwelling. The beds, moldy-smelling and hay-crinkly, were lively with fleas and bedbugs.

On Tuesday, they crossed North Mountains. A decrepit hunter's cabin, nestled in the cleft of a rock, served as their lodging that night. The host was a melancholy little man, beyond the counting of years in age. He supplied no food, just space upon a dirt floor.

"Jess 'n me built this cabin afore White Men," the little man told them while they ate their bread and cheese. The German in Sarah's mind gave place to the English that he spoke. "Indian villages was in the valley. Elk, 'n deer, 'n buffalo ... yep, big, black buffalo ... 'n turkey, 'n skies full a grouse 'n quail. Gone ... shot up, moved on. White Men moved 'long this trail; animals moved on. 'N Jess is gone, killed by a rattler. 'N I'm too old ta hunt all day or ta move on."

The taste of the food mixed with the smell of his body and the close stench of the cabin. Sarah could not eat.

"The rattlers, they ain't good neighb'rs." The little man sniffed and spat onto the dirt behind him. "You, ma'am, in them skirts. Why you be wearin' 'em, I cain't see. Now them rattlers, they gets a-tangled up in them skirts, and then what ya goin' ta do?"

Brother Voss broke a piece of bread. It crumbled in his hand. "I kill rattlesnakes when they cross my path. Why should I fear them?"

"The Indian say the rattler is gran'pappy to him, that's what the Indian say. They's friends. The rattler don't bite no friend. Ya kill one, and the whole race knows it. They'll bite then. I killed rattlers for ma Jess. Then they goes on the warpath. But they should 'a killed me."

That night, Sarah snuggled down onto the sleeping mat beside Brother Zundel and whispered near, not touching, his ear, "How could snakes seek vengeance against man?"

"The Indian believes it. Snakes do not bite him," replied Brother Zundel. He turned toward her.

Sarah felt the rhythm of his breath against her face. "Do you kill rattlesnakes?" she asked.

"No," he said.

"Are you a White Man or an Indian?" she wanted to whisper but dared not, for she feared his reply.

On the afternoon of the following day, the horses began the stumbling ascent of the rock-strewn path of Sideling Hill. Rattlesnakes, yellow and black banded, slid off the path where they had lain in the sun. The horses paced nervously past them.

When the climb became too steep, they dismounted. Sarah slipped from the back of her horse down to where the snakes slithered.

In the nighttime, they built a tent of branches and of blankets and slept upon the ground beside the Raystown Branch of the Juniata River. The wolves howled; the owls hooted. Sarah scratched the nape of her neck and, again, her forehead. Fleas. She closed her eyes. She saw the sisters in Bethlehem kneeling, murmuring private prayers, reading passages of scripture before retiring. She saw the spinning wheels and the large, rectangular looms. Her hands twitched as she moved the shuttle through the warp threads.

In the morning on Saturday, August twenty-sixth, they were ferried across Stony Creek by canoe while the horses waded through the water. They rode through the Glades toward Laurel Hill, the next mountain of the Appalachian chain. That which was behind was still before. A new hindrance cluttered the trail on Laurel Hill: mountain laurel, an ivy-like vine. They dismounted to climb. The mind of Sarah was cluttered with rocks and vines and steep ascents. She recalled her walk along the Lehigh River and her eagerness in claiming for herself the promises of God. A memory without substance.

From Saturday night until Monday, they rested at Fort Ligonier, a town of about thirty log houses. Each night, Sarah fell down beside Brother Zundel upon the bumpy bed. She clung to herself and waited. He took her hand and held it between them. His arm was heavy over hers. Her arm grew numb. She did not move it; she might offend. They were in a separate room from Brother Voss, yet Brother Zundel did not take her to himself. Had he found so little pleasure in her that he had forsaken further attempts? Tears filled her eyes, but she dared not cry.

On Monday, they rode on.

"Tomorrow in Pittsburg," Brother Zundel said after they crossed the Laurel-hanne, the Middle Stream.

Across Chestnut Ridge they rode, the last of the mountains.

But the land beyond was still hilly, still rock-strewn, and always thick with wide, looming trees. The forest would not end, not westward.

Clouds covered the sky and impaired what pale light could penetrate to the forest floor. The rain oozed from the trees; it steamed up from the ground.

"Brother Zundel, I cannot," groaned Sarah when she saw the cabin where they must sleep.

Four other lodgers sat on a bench and drank their ale in a corner of the small room where they all would sleep. The toothless tavern-keeper tossed her, Brother Zundel, and Brother Voss filth-encrusted blankets. Fleas. Lice.

"Where else, Sister Sarah, can we stay?" he asked.

"In the forest ..." she began.

"In the rain and lightning? No," he concluded.

Brother Zundel settled down upon the floor like a child on a down-filled bed and slept. Sarah lay clothed on the floor beside him. She wanted to shake him awake.

The morning meal was a large bowl of bread and sour milk out of which all ate with dirty spoons. Brother Zundel reached and slurped with the other men. Brother Voss ate one bite and no more. Sarah could not eat at all.

After eating, they passed around a bottle of whiskey.

"Thank you. No," said Brother Zundel when it passed to him.

"You look and eat like one of us, not like your friend and your woman ... wife. But you do not drink with us," puzzled a man in German.

Brother Zundel chuckled and thumped the stocky man on his back.

"Where you heading?" asked the man.

"The country beyond the Ohio."

"Not traders ..."

"Teachers ... to the Indians. Christians."

"You are making trouble with them. What you want to teach them? Teach Whites. Indians cannot learn," said a dark-tanned man from the other end of the table.

"Ah, Karl! What you know?" yelled the stocky man. "Take your swig and pass it on." He looked back to Brother Zundel: "Why you doing this?"

Brother Zundel grinned. He did look like them. He wore no coat; his hat was off, flung somewhere. The sleeves of his shirt were rolled and pushed up above his elbows. His hair was only loosely bound back from his face. Sarah could not bear to look at him. She pivoted around and slid from the bench.

"My friend," she heard Brother Zundel say as she left the cabin, "Indians are men like us. They need ..."

"Savages!" interposed another voice.

"Ha," laughed the voice of Brother Zundel. "What is a savage? We have all seen ..."

Sarah stood outside. The sun dripped its idle rays down to the forest floor. She felt upon her chest the suffocating pressure of the humid air.

The cabin door opened behind her. She tensed and looked back.

"Pittsburg tonight," said Brother Voss.

"Yes," agreed Sarah. She had hoped for Brother Zundel.

"I have never ridden this far west." He stood beside her, barely taller than she.

"So far from ..." began Sarah. She almost said, "... God." God was in Bethlehem. The songs, the liturgy, the sermons.

"Far from home," concluded Brother Voss.

Yes. Home was Bethlehem. But Brother Zundel was running to his home among the Indians in the Ohio country. And as he hurried westward, Sarah trailed ever farther behind; for in her heart, she was yearning back to Bethlehem. Panic, like the dark oppression of the trees, enveloped her. Soon, would she lose sight of him and would she be lost and alone?

Brother Voss glanced at Sarah. "Your husband has just reminded those men about Daniel Greathouse and the ... um ... massacre of the family of Chief Logan. And the sour smell of the milk ... the sweet smell of the whiskey ... I decided to leave."

Brother Zundel appeared in the doorway. "We are ready?" he asked, almost chuckling.

He clasped the arm of Brother Voss. "Did you like my account?" he laughed. "Savages! All men are savages." He paused. A wave of anger swept across his face. "But for the Saviour," he murmured.

In the late afternoon, they entered Braddock's Field.

Sarah gazed around upon heaps of bones. Thousands of bones. Layer over layer, bone over bone.

Mountains of bones.

Sarah rode between Brother Zundel and Brother Voss.

"When did ..." began Brother Voss.

"Seventeen fifty-five," was the reply.

"Who heaped the bones?"

"A farmer."

"The bones are gnawed. The skulls ..."

"... scalped," concluded Brother Zundel.

Sarah could feel the eyes of Brother Zundel on her face. She held her gaze forward on the trail. A shivering began within her and spread outward to her arms and legs.

In Pittsburg, they stopped at a log tavern beside the Monongahela River.

"We got no room," explained the innkeeper, "on account of some from this commission from the Continental Congress to treat with the Indians already coming to town." He smiled. "Howsomever, you bein' a regular customer, Mister Zundel, I'll find you and your friends ... hum ... married? ... rooms."

The bed in the small room was high and plump. Feathers? Sarah hurried to the bed and eased herself upon it. It crunched.

"Hay," said Brother Zundel. "Clean. Feathers attract ..."

"Yes," interrupted Sarah. "Feathers attract bed bugs, fleas, and lice." What did that matter? She brought the fleas and lice with her.

She closed her eyes and saw herself easing down into a feather bed and pulling a feather tick up above her chin. She opened her eyes.

The mouth of Brother Zundel twitched upward. Did he stifle a laugh?

Her disappointment must not show. She scratched some bites upon her neck. "Can I get water and lye soap, Brother Zundel?"

~ ~ ~

A tall man with a deep scar under his chin gulped a mouthful of coffee and chomped a slab of venison: "English," he sneered, "and Indians ... all murderers."

Sarah prodded her venison. She glanced around the dark tavern. A plump woman across from her shoved a thick slice of greased bread into her mouth and winked.

Brother Zundel sat forward in his chair, a forkful of squash poised in the air. "The colonies might war with the English. But the Indians — Shawano, Delaware — will not take up the hatchet against the English or the colonists."

"When the delegates from the Continental Congress meet with the Indians in October, they will encourage them to stay neutral in the war," added Brother Voss.

"Encourage them with wampum and blankets, ya mean," grumbled the tall man. "But English'll en ... courage them with whiskey. They'll be en ... couraged, I'll tell ya!" He chuckled. "I know. I trade with them Indians."

"Whiskey?" Brother Zundel asked. "Then you are stabbing the colonists in the back, and you are taking their scalps."

"I ain't never stabbed no one ... not any White Man," muttered the trader.

"Killin' Ind'ns ain' murderin'," called out a younger man from the end of the table.

"And I ain't scalped no one, not even Indians!" The voice of the trader was rising.

"You sell the whiskey that makes the Indian wild enough to kill." Brother Zundel stood. He stomped from the eating room.

Sarah practically knocked over her plate trying to rise and follow him.

Brother Zundel paused for her. They walked through the village upstream toward the fort along the plain where the Monongahela and Allegheny Rivers merged. They sat, staring across the Monongahela at black ledges of coal on its opposite bank.

Finally, Brother Zundel said, "Man murders and calls it by another name." He glanced at Sarah then diverted his gaze. "Braddock's Field ..."

"I did not expect ..." Sarah faltered.

"And I did not know how to prepare you." He rubbed his fists up, down, up, down upon his breeches. "The French and Indians tortured and killed the English during the campaign against Braddock and his troops. And the frontier has not forgiven the Indians for the slaughter that followed throughout the settlements.

"When first I saw Braddock's Field, I was a missionary, twenty-four, and filled with zeal to save the heathen. But what man could overcome the hatred sown into the soil and stacked among the bones in the field? 'God!' I cried, 'I can do nothing.'

"I would have returned home, but I had neither home nor family."

Alone? In such a circumstance was Sarah. "Then the words of God came to me:

The hand of the Lord was upon me ... and set me down in the midst of the valley which was full of bones ... And he said onto me ... Prophesy upon these bones, and say unto them, O ye dry bones, hear the word of the Lord ... Behold, I will cause breath to enter into you, and ye shall live ... and ye shall know that I am the lord.'"

The eyes of Brother Zundel searched back and forth across the grass. "My God has promised. He will revive that which is dead and destroy the hatred that now spawns death. My Indians will survive through the salvation of God."

Brother Zundel gazed at Sarah. He could do it. He could follow the Saviour onto the fulfillment of this dream. And was she his help meet? Surely she could do nothing to bring to life those bones.

"My vision must become yours," he said.

Sarah Himmel — weaver.

"Perhaps, someday ..." she managed to say.

"Yes." His voice was low and dull.

~ ~ ~

Monday morning, September fourth, Sarah, Brother Zundel, and Brother Voss rode across the Allegheny River and along the path above the Ohio toward the Beaver River.

Giant trees mingled with each other in the distant sunlight. Gigantic grape vines twined among the upper branches of the trees, absorbing most of the remaining light. They rode beneath the heavy canopy in muted, silent light.

They arrived at Great Beaver Creek the following day. An Indian trading settlement sprawled along a wide plain where the Great Trail and lesser trails converged.

Almost-naked men ran to meet them. Their clothing was breech clouts and paint smeared on faces, chests, and arms. They even robbed their scalps of covering by pulling out the hair until only a single round and hanging lock remained.

Sarah fastened her gaze upon the women who lagged, with the children, behind the men. Their petticoats covered more flesh.

Brother Zundel dismounted and helped Sarah from her horse. For an instant, her hands pushed down upon his shoulders. Her palms slid down his chest. She stood upon the ground. She felt his hands press into her waist, and, then, he released her. She had not wanted him to let her go.

"This is Koquethagachton," said Brother Zundel to her and Brother Voss. "Called White Eyes ..."

Sarah stared into the bright eyes of an Indian not much taller than herself.

"... He is the principal war captain of the Delaware Nation."

Brother Zundel turned from her to White Eyes and began speaking with him in the Unami dialect of the Delaware Nation. Their staccato conversation was too rapid for Sarah to comprehend. He broke the interchange to wave in her direction and to say, "Sarah."

"Salah," said White Eyes, watching her. The Indian dialect provided no means to roll the German "r."

Brother Zundel said to Brother Voss in German, "Lenni Lenape ... the Delaware ... ride to Pittsburg to treat with the commissioners from the Congress of the colonies. They will discard the stroud of peacefulness and the hoe of harmlessness and will be the Woman no longer. They defy the Mengwe, the Five Nations, who say that the Woman cannot sign treaties with the White Man. They raise their rifles and cry, "The Lenni Lenape are men.""

Then Brother Zundel, with Brother Voss at his side, walked away with White Eyes.

He left Sarah behind.

Could he not glance at her, cast an encouraging smile, nod his head? He nodded his head ... at White Eyes. He smiled but not at her.

Sarah sat with the women all day. Earrings of wampum or silver dangled from most ears. The glistening black hair of the women was long, tied back with cloths. Their petticoats ... strouds ... were of red, blue, or black cloth. Bands of red, blue, or yellow were wound about the petticoats. Some women wore white shirts over the strouds. Upon these hung glittering silver buckles. Leggings of red or blue covered the legs to the feet. And upon the leggings, silk trimmed with coral bound the seams. Moccasins with beads of intricate design clothed the feet.

Sarah gazed into their faces. Round splotches of red paint colored many cheeks. Red darkened the eyelids, the foreheads, the ear-rims, the temples.

They stared back at her. Sarah's faded brown petticoat hung upon her, unadorned. Simplicity and modesty. Her only adornment was the blue ribbon tied under her chin. Even her hair was pressed into a bun against her head.

She ate pale yellow mush from a dirty bowl with a filthy spoon and tried to keep from thinking of the black and toothless mouths that had previously slurped from the spoon.

When the three rode out the next morning, Sarah carried the small, skin sack of bear's grease which the wife of White Eyes had given her.

"You will soon need that sack," said Brother Zundel.

"Not I," she thought. She was not an Indian, not yet.

The travelers often dismounted, stepping around or over huge, rotting trees that had fallen across the path. Mosquitoes and gnats buzzed upon faces and into eyes. First Brother Zundel and then Brother Voss smeared grease from the sack upon face, neck, and arms. The buzzings and the bites roused a frenzy in Sarah. Finally, she dipped her fingers into the slime and spread it across her face and arms. The gnats buzzed into the ointment and stuck.

Brother Zundel seemed to vibrate with restless tension. Even when they rested in their camp above the stream, he could not relax. In spirit, he had ridden on to Schoenbrunn.

"We can establish a Christian Indian state." Brother Zundel was thumping his knees with his palms. Brother Voss rested his chin into his hands, listening, almost sleeping. "Now that the colonies revolt; if the Indians remain neutral, they can wait and prepare. Already we, the teachers, sit around the council fire of the Lenni Lenape. They hear our voice. God moves. Our people will no longer be abused."

"Our people." His people. Sarah's people were yet in Bethlehem. Was the man she knew as her husband giving place to an Indian? Then what would remain of Christoph Zundel when at last they resided in Schoenbrunn? Sarah crossed her arms and clutched her shoulders.

They spread their mats upon bumpy earth beneath the heavy darkness of the forest night. Sarah's hand fumbled toward Brother Zundel, rustling, shifting at her side. Her palm pressed into the small of his back. She felt the muscles, tight though he slept, and she prayed that his strength and zeal might flow from him to her.

On the second day from the Indian settlement, Brother Schebosh and Brother Adam, forewarned of their approach by runners from the Beaver, rode out to meet them.

"We shore missed your husband in the fields this summer," Brother Schebosh said to Sarah in English. "Special since the famine bein' so big in the spring, was all could do to keep back seeds for plantin', the Indians needin' so much maize and grain from us. And now that we are buildin' that third mission town ...""

"Where?" broke in Brother Zundel.

"Netawatwes invitin' us near Goschachgunk. He's sayin' the Lenni Lenape and the Christian is one nation and he's a wantin' us close."

The third day from the Beaver and twenty-six days from Bethlehem, they crossed another stream. The horses bent their heads to drink, but Brother Zundel yanked his on and called them all to follow. He rode ahead upon the hill and disappeared. Sarah urged her horse at a steady clomp-clomp behind. She looked down into the plain. Faceless figures ran out from a village and swarmed around Brother Zundel. He swung down from his horse and disappeared into their midst. The village spread beyond, laid out in the shape of a cross, enclosed by a picket fence. Small, black cattle grazed in the wide clearing. The village wore the cloak of long shadows beneath a weary sun. Schoenbrunn ... the Beautiful Spring.

5
FEBRUARY 9, 1776 – APRIL 14, 1776

The cabin of the Chauchschisis, the Aged Woman, was grey in smoke and glowing in flames from the fire pit. Forms crouched upon the dirt floor; others sat cross-legged on benches. Upon a bench near the door opening sat the Story Teller.

He spoke into the fire tales which mingled with the flames. Wind Maiden watched the fire and listened to the voice, rising as from the mass of wood, writhing orange and gold.

She knelt on the floor near the wall of the cabin. One-Who-Runs sat upon a bench near his mother, the Aged Woman. She was white-headed, small. Her skin hung from her protruding bones. Brown, liquid eyes rolled around the room and floated over Wind Maiden who rocked onto her other leg when she felt the chilling gaze of the Aged Woman.

"The wordless river," thought Wind Maiden as the Aged Woman looked, again, at her. "It does not talk to the rocks or the banks that it flows against. It watches."

Wind Maiden turned toward the Story Teller whose wide hands were raised high into the smoke-hazed air, making alive the story of a hunt for the hairless bear, grandfather of all bears. "May the sun and the soil suck water from the wordless river." Wind Maiden closed her eyes: "May she die."

When Wind Maiden first came to live with One-Who-Runs, they had slept in the hut of the Aged Woman. Then One-Who-Runs had built a cabin for the Aged Woman, and they had lived with her until he had built a cabin of their own. One-Who-Runs had worked leaning upon the shoulder of slowness. He had laid aside the wood in the harvest month to carry flames of messages from the large council fire in Goschachgunk to the smaller fires of the True Man, the Lenni Lenape. He had put down the wood in the hunting

46

month to carry messages from the Fort Pitt of the Big Knife to Goschachgunk and to chase buck for meat and pelts. But the words he had run with from Fort Pitt were heavy, and he had returned many times for new loads so that he had hunted seldom and had returned with few pelts for trade and little flesh for meat. So their cabin was not finished until snow had covered the ground. And Wind Maiden had lived alone many nights with the Aged Woman who could not speak, who watched her with pools of fluid brown eyes chiseled into bony grooves.

The Story Teller was bowing his head, chanting the first words of another tale of the Lenni Lenape, how the True Man had crawled from his dark home beneath the earth to live in the land of light. Wind Maiden watched his golden face as he raised his head. The white of his eyes glowed in the firelight; his mouth slid in slow, wide circles around his words.

Wind Maiden thought of the toothless mouth of the Aged Woman which opened like the mouth of a fish and closed upon silence. Her eyes would roll; her mouth would open and close; her withered muscles would tighten. The mouth without teeth must be fed — mush of maize or beans or dried, powdered meat. Water would slide from the side of the mouth in a rivulet down her jaw.

One-Who-Runs would be gone bearing a message or a rifle so Wind Maiden would make food for the Aged Woman and build fires for her. When he would return, he would stroke the cheek of his mother, laugh, and tell her about council fires she had never seen. Wind Maiden would watch them together. She hated both the Aged Woman and One-Who-Runs.

On a night without a moon, Wind Maiden and One-Who-Runs had wrapped their kettle and straps and mats and blankets in bearskins and had moved to their new cabin. Wind Maiden had arranged the wood in their fire pit and, with fire borrowed from the pit of South-Wind-Blowing, not from the pit of the Aged Woman, she had begun the blaze which warmed and lit the cold, dark dwelling. A new fire in her own home. Wind Maiden had clutched the fire and its warmth, for they were hers. The eyes of the Aged Woman sat in another cabin and could not float over Wind Maiden here. But, now, Wind Maiden had to build and feed two flames; she had to wrap herself in blankets and trudge through the forest to find twice as much wood, pounding snow from twice as many logs.

"Gather the Aged Woman into your cabin until the Planting Time," Star-at-Dawning had advised her daughter. "One fire can feed three bodies. You do not need two fires."

Wind Maiden had thumped the ground with her fist and had pinched together her lips: No! The fluid eyes would not flow through her cabin.

Twice a day she carried mush to the Aged Woman; four times a day she fed and tended the fire. She bowed her head and would not watch the wordless rivers which flowed from the eyes of the Aged Woman.

One morning, Wind Maiden had thought of not carrying wood to the pit of the Aged Woman. She could see the warm embers of the night disappear and the Aged Woman, wrapped in her blanket, lying on her bench. The river was frozen and still. However, Wind Maiden had wrapped herself in her stroud and blankets that day and had hunted for wood to warm the river, to keep it flowing. She had not allowed the Aged Woman to freeze over, and she did not know why.

The ground hog, the Story Teller was saying, had stayed beneath the ground when the True Men and his brothers, the other animals, had climbed out. The Great Spirit had given the Lenape the entire earth over which to roam and hunt.

"I should be free," Wind Maiden thought. And an echo from long ago responded, "I am a woman now; I shall be free. I shall marry a hunter and a warrior ... like my father."

Wind Maiden looked past the other people in the cabin to One-Who-Runs who sat beside the Story Teller, watching the staccato movements of his flashing hands. One-Who-Runs had killed enough deer to fill the stomachs of his mother, Wind Maiden, and himself ... but not more. He did not bring back the skins of bucks to trade for the white linen, ribbons, and wampum Wind Maiden needed. Instead, her "hunter" had appeared with skins of does which were traded for three White Man's blankets.

In silence, Wind Maiden had scraped the skins and had cooked and dried the meat. She had not looked at One-Who-Runs because she had not wanted her eyes to say what her mouth would not, that One-Who-Runs was a scurrying rabbit. She yanked the ears of the rabbit that ate grass and leaves, and she wished for the wolf which ripped apart the flesh of its prey.

When they had first moved to their cabin, One-Who-Runs had sat beside Wind Maiden on the bearskin at night and had told her of the large council fire at Fort Pitt where the White Men from the Congress of the Big Knives and the Lenni Lenape had agreed to continue mingling their bloods as brothers. The Lenape had hidden his hatchet, for he had promised his brother that he would not pound it into the skull of either the demanding father or his offended son.

Wind Maiden had tried to not listen to One-Who-Runs; she had stared into the fire. Finally, his words had become fewer, like a stream drying in the drought of summer. Often, now, he would visit his mother who would watch with those eyes the words of his mouth. And Wind Maiden sat alone in their cabin and told herself that she did not care.

The Story Teller paused and looked around the glowing cabin. His gaze led; his head followed behind. The listeners waited. Wind Maiden heard her own breath rise and descend as if it were the breath of the cabin itself. The Story Teller bowed his white head; his long, loose hair fell forward, veiling his face.

"Tschipey Hacki, Tschipey Hacki, land of spirits, land of spirits." His words formed a song, flat and discordant, like the call of the cricket and the reply of the frog. He raised from his leather pouch a long string of wampum, white but for a band of black along its bottom. With slowness, his crooked fingers rubbed the top of the wampum — beads of sunlight in the grasp of a dead man.

He looked toward the ceiling of the cabin, lifting one arm: "From the star that sits in the sky, a rock in a stream, never moving, follow the path, the wide trail of the white buffalo ..." His hand, thumb, and first finger joined, traced an arc above his head: "... to Tschipey Hacki."

The hand of the Story Teller floated to his lap where he rubbed each row of beads in turn while reciting,

"Death! Spirit rises to the sky.
Steps upon the stars — stones upon the brook.
Hawks and eagles circle, specks below.
Fires of villages disappear beneath.
Through silence, through darkness, spirit walks.
Round sun rises, bright, hot,
Dries the brook, scatters the stones.
Spirit traveler hangs in sky, alone.
Sun calls, 'Come to me.'
Traveler climbs to sun, crawls in.
Stumbles along a glittering road,
Brightness singes sight.
Crawls into a golden hut.
Golden maize shimmers in a bowl.
Spirit sleeps upon a gold-woven mat.
Awakes and hears the call of voices
Rolling like warm wind through trees.
Runs outside, voices flee.
He wanders past a grazing herd of white buffalo.
White deer sleep beneath trees.
Village in the meadow —
Huts shine like yellow flowers in the Planting Time.
Men and women dance in a circle,
Clothed in white deerskin,
Flowers and vines mingle and sway.
Spirit dancer offers traveler bow and arrows,
Glowing like burning branches,
To hunt the white deer and buffalo.
Woman offers strawberries,
Large as apples, color of blood root.
He sits. He eats."

The hands of the Story Teller had traveled each row of the white beads on his wampum string. His fingers now touched the first of the black beads and stopped. He looked up. His eyes widened; he watched the firelight. Wind Maiden tracked his stare to where she thought she saw a spirit dancing in the orange smoke.

The fingers of the Story Teller began to move across the first row of the black beads. His voice obeyed the guidance of his hands; fingers and words moved faster, voice higher:

"Bad spirit, he who had sold lies,
He who had fought with brothers,
A stinging spider,
Hangs in a sky that is black — no stars.
Sun appears.
Sun does not call;
Bad spirit falls.
Bare-headed bird with black body snatches with claws,
Carries him to the dark land of Evil One ...
Machtandonwinck.
Evil one feeds the spirit roots and bark,
They eat the stomach —
He vomits.
Evil One, Machtando, changes spirit into a horse to ride,
Then a dog to kick.
Bad spirit whines and sits in a corner,
Scratching fleas."

No one moved while the Story Teller returned the wampum to his pouch. When he laid his wrinkled hands open upon his crossed legs, the listeners rose up like puffing smoke and left the cabin.

Wind Maiden huddled against the wall, one leg pulled close to her chest. "Machtandonwinck, Machtandonwinck: With the Evil One."

All left the cabin but the Story Teller, One-Who-Runs, the Aged Woman, and Wind Maiden.

One-Who-Runs arose. "Father! Your words have filled our minds like tender deer meat fills the stomach. My mother offers lodging, food, and fire to you."

"My fire," Wind Maiden thought. "I do not build it for the Story Teller!"

"Brother! I take your gift for this night."

One-Who-Runs assisted his mother from her bench. Wind Maiden crept from her corner and followed them through the door. She looked back at the fire, cracking and settling into the pit. She would not look upon the Story Teller.

Tonight, the flowing river would sleep in the cabin of Wind Maiden. "Only one night," Wind Maiden promised herself.

The evening air blew ice. No snow remained on the ground in the village except in small piles against the cabins. In the forest, clusters still cowered from the sun in the frozen shadows. It was the Time of Frogs.

"Machtandonwinck," thought Wind Maiden as she entered her cabin.

One-Who-Runs guided his mother to the back of the cabin where he spread a mat on a bench. Wind Maiden retrieved logs from a corner and crossed them over the sinking blaze. She knelt before it, watching sparks snap. Each glittered for an instant like a star in the sky.

"Trail of stars like stones in a brook," recalled Wind Maiden. Maybe she could crawl into the sun and dance in the meadows. She would pick the sun-sparkling flowers and slip them into her hair and into buckles on her shirt. She would find the other children ... children ...

"I follow ... to the land of spirits ... or ... I fall — to the Evil One." Her jaw quivered. The fire sparked; the star disappeared, and she was falling.

"My wife," One-Who-Runs whispered. "Come lie with me."

Wind Maiden crept to the bench of her husband and knelt beside it. One-Who-Runs lay there, watching her, his chest bare. She looked toward the Aged Woman who rested with eyes closed, a bearskin covering her withered body and brittle bones. Wind Maiden pulled her shirt over her head and slid beneath the bearskin beside One-Who-Runs.

He held her. His chest was warm against the coldness of her own. She closed her eyes: "I fall ... his arms, too weak to hold me. . . I fall."

One-Who-Runs stroked her hair. "He remembers my shame and laughs at me. My hair — gone — a dog without its tail ... I fall."

One-Who-Runs murmured, "You are a rabbit who runs. Why? Why do you run from me?"

"I do not run," she lied.

"He is the rabbit," she thought. "I do not want the rabbit."

"You do not smile and laugh as you did when Eagle-with-White-Head, Red Face, and I would wrestle or ride our ponies."

"He is a boy, not a real warrior. He can only play games," Wind Maiden thought.

"I am no longer a child," she said, snapping back her head so that she, too, would heed what she said.

"I have seen chiefs and captains of the White Men and of the Lenni Lenape laugh," persisted One-Who-Runs.

Wind Maiden thought, "He watches the wolves from his burrow but does not join them for the hunt."

She did not answer.

One-Who-Runs pushed Wind Maiden from him and looked down into her face. He rubbed her fragile chin. "What can I do to please you?"

"Pelts, many pelts to trade for wampum and ribbons and cloth," replied Wind Maiden. Yes! Bright, red cloth to hang down her back to cover the scar of her shame.

Her eyes looked up into his then fell to his full nose. Could this runner become a hunter? She did not think so.

The eyes of One-Who-Runs covered her face: "I shall try for you," he said finally. "But we hunt for bear this moon, and they do not want the skin of bears, the traders."

"I know," murmured Wind Maiden.

"But they will take fox and beaver skin. I shall hunt for these for you."

One-Who-Runs pulled her back against himself. His hands, with soft strokes, smoothed down the tight muscles of her neck and back. Her body relaxed against him. He pressed upon her. His legs, his stomach, his chest, his arms, they melted into her flesh.

"He is no hunter," thought Wind Maiden. Her muscles tightened, again.

~ ~ ~

The next days, Wind Maiden prepared the food One-Who-Runs would carry on the winter hunt. She packed tassmanane — dried and pounded sweet maize mixed with sap from the stone tree — into a prepared pouch. She strengthened his heavy moccasins with thick straps of hide. The Aged Woman had returned to her own cabin; Wind Maiden fed her and tended her fire. She thought of the hunt. She did not think of the Aged Woman. All the young men of the village were preparing to kill the bear whose homes in hollows of trees, in caves, and in thickets they had already found while hunting deer after the Harvest Time. They would drive the bear from its den and shoot it. One-Who-Runs would also carry traps to set for the beaver, traps made by White Men.

As she worked, Wind Maiden thought of hunters that stalked their prey like wolves ... black wolves.

Black Wolf. She would not think of him. He had taken his wife on the hunt after the harvest, and they had not returned. South-Wind-Blowing had said they were living among a tribe of the Turkey along the Beautiful River. Wind Maiden had said she did not care where the wolf lodged. But he was a hunter and a warrior, and she knew One-Who-Runs was not.

On the third night, One-Who-Runs stood in the door of the cabin with his rifle in his arm. "Tomorrow, I shall leave."

Wind Maiden wrinkled her brow and said, "Much beaver skin and bear flesh."

"With the help of the Great Spirit," said One-Who-Runs. "And if the big spirits of the beaver and bear permit."

"They permit. We do not care about them." Wind Maiden saw her small fire in the forest, fed by tobacco, burning a promise. Grandfather Fire – he did not care. He was like a White Man who says, "Yes," and does, "No." Same with the spirits of the beaver and bear. She rubbed down her hair to the blood-encrusted stub.

One-Who-Runs laid aside his gun and approached Wind Maiden, who stood before the fire pit. "If the spirit of the beaver says, 'No,' the trap will not catch a pelt or the flesh in the trap will be eaten by maggots."

"No!" exclaimed Wind Maiden. The mocking blaze of Grandfather Fire burned in her mind. "The spirits do not care. They fight us. You must fight back." The fire in her mind was consuming the trees of the forest. It ignited her slashed stub of hair and burned toward her scalp. She wrapped her hand around her hair to suffocate the blaze.

One-Who-Runs watched her, his dark eyes on her face. When he spoke, his voice was calm. "Your words will anger the spirits who will hide from me all pelts. Bury your words beneath the ground and cover the spot with leaves and branches."

Wind Maiden would not bury the words. Though this husband cringed and quaked, she would be the warrior. Charred and smoking remains of trees filled her mind. The spirits did not care.

~ ~ ~

The day One-Who-Runs left with Eagle-with-White-Head, Red Face, and other young men for the hunt, Wind Maiden gathered her hemp and partially-made carrying strap and visited her mother. Star-at-Dawning sat near the door of her newly-built cabin, crushing dry maize in a mortar. The bearskin on the door opening was pulled back so air could float into the smoky cabin. Wind Maiden crept through the opening.

"Mother ..." She felt the contentment of a fawn settling near its dam. "... I shall work with you today."

Star-at-Dawning smiled a tired, tooth-worn greeting. Wind Maiden knelt near her and began to weave the hemp through succeeding rows of her strap. The stone in the hand of Star-at-Dawning thumped and ground against the sides and bottom of her mortar. Her wrists were strong, her movements patient and slow.

Had Star-at-Dawning ever tried to flee from the grinding, constant grinding, or from the endless weaving? Wind Maiden wanted to rip apart the hemp of her strap and fling it into the fire. The fire would lap up the hemp and spark into a large fire beneath the black sky around which men and women would dance. Wind Maiden would dance round and round, thumping faster, faster. Her damp hair would cling to her face and sweat would drip from beneath her hair. She would stomp her heels into the earth. Her calves would ache, but she would never stop.

In and out she wove the hemp. Rub – thud ... rub – thud ... rub – thud droned the stone in the hands of her mother.

Finally, Star-at-Dawning asked, "One-Who-Runs begins the hunt today?"

"Yes," replied Wind Maiden. She thought, "Long hunt, few pelts." She looked into the sputtering fire pit.

"Good hunter, much bear flesh," said Star-at-Dawning.

Wind Maiden turned and looked into small eyes made smaller by layers of flesh and darker by the low-fluttering light of the room. She said, "One-Who-Runs is not like my father. He is a small, black-bellied fish, not like the Fish-of-the-Deep-Water."

"No, not like the Fish-of-the-Deep-Water," Star-at-Dawning agreed. "But he is a hunter. He piled high the pelts in our hut when he claimed you as his wife."

The words of her mother were flies buzzing in the air. "Yes. Pelts. For you and for his mother. Not for me. And ... and buckles, yes. For South-Wind-Blowing when she spoke for him to me. But no buckles for me!" Her words snapped like sparks.

Star-at-Dawning watched her daughter and spoke more slowly, "He is a hunter."

"A hunter who returns without buck pelts ..." Wind Maiden's voice slid to the half-whine of a child. "... for wampum and linen." Her mother did not know this man who had no pelts. Why did she refuse to know?

Star-at-Dawning stared at her daughter, and her silence said, "He is a hunter."

~ ~ ~

In the Shad Moon, as the days became warmer but the nights remained cool, the women prepared for sweet sap gathering from the stone tree. Sap would run now that the trees were thawing. The women took up their kettles and troughs and moved to low, moist soil among the stone trees. Some of the men paused from the hunt to construct bark hunting huts in which the women would dwell while they gathered their sap.

Wind Maiden abandoned her chores for the Aged Woman whose fire would be tended by other older women who remained in Goschachgunk. She filled her pack and lifted her kettle and followed to the sap-gathering camp. One-Who-Runs was still on the hunt. She was free.

Star-at-Dawning, Wind Maiden, and As-the-Water-Flows, the sister to her mother, constructed their hut in the early evening on the first day in camp. As-the-Water-Flows was a short, fat woman, younger than Star-at-Dawning. Star-at-Dawning sometimes called her the Snowfall because her words fell quickly and soon covered everything. Near their dwelling, South-Wind-Blowing shared a bark hut with two other women and a girl.

Wind Maiden had one large kettle of her own for gathering the drippings. She had borrowed two smaller kettles from her mother in which to boil sap. However, Star-at-Dawning could not share her wooden troughs used for collecting sap so Wind Maiden constructed simple troughs from bark. She selected a stone tree with several scars from previous tappings. When little sap flowed, she hatcheted through the bark of another tree. Again, the sap would not flow. Star-at-Dawning and As-the-Water-Flows already had sap to boil, but she could not even make a tree to drip.

She pounded into another.

The sap dripped. It dripped by day and slowed by night. When no more sap drained from one tree, she cut an oblong gash in a new one. Above a small fire, Wind Maiden boiled the sap in smaller kettles. When the sugar was boiled down, she formed it into small cakes which, when cooled, she stored in a carrying bag.

But the cakes tumbled over each other in the carrying bag. They broke and crumbled. The cakes of her mother were always round and flat, and they never crumbled. Wind Maiden knew what to do; she had watched her mother many times. Why could she not force the knowing into her hands?

The women talked as they worked gathering sap, finding wood for the fires, boiling, shaping cakes of sugar.

South-Wind-Blowing was crouching before her fire: "My new husband gives me eighty buck pelts," she said. "I shall trade them for ribbons and buckles." She smiled at Wind Maiden who stood near her fire, listening. "Maybe I shall keep this husband." The face of South-Wind-Blowing was angular and sharp, accentuated by shining eyes and full lips.

Wind Maiden frowned and sighed, "One-Who-Runs does not hunt. He is a rabbit."

South-Wind-Blowing looked up and tilted her head: "Leave the rabbit," she said. "Take another husband."

The heart of Wind Maiden beat like the heart of a fawn discovered in the bushes. "Maybe I shall leave him," she said. She did want the wolf. She hated One-Who-Runs ... rabbit! But she cowered like a fawn when she thought of leaving him.

"Leave the rabbit," repeated South-Wind-Blowing. "I am older and I know more."

The fawn crouched farther back into the bushes and licked its stubbed tail.

At night, Wind Maiden, Star-at-Dawning, As-the-Water-Flows, and others sat around the fire built outside their huts. Tonight, as on all nights, As-the-Water-Flows was talking. "The witch flies at night inside the body of an owl." She nodded her round head: "I have seen ... many times."

A small girl chirped, eyes wide, "Kill the owl."

"Yes, but it flies swiftly, and it is wise," explained As-the-Water-Flows. She appeared thoughtful for a moment then continued, "My husband killed two witch-owls. Fat, with much blood. When they died, feathers fell off and they were women, again. Their bodies dried slow in the sun. We were afraid, so we did not touch them to bury."

Star-at-Dawning whispered to Wind Maiden, "Snow falls." She arose and crawled into her hut.

Wind Maiden followed.

When they were seated upon woven mats of wild hemp, Wind Maiden said, "South-Wind-Blowing says, 'Take a new husband ... a hunter.'" She wanted to hear the words of her mother. She looked full at Star-at-Dawning.

Star-at-Dawning breathed in. The air in the dark hut tightened like the heavy stillness of a forest before a storm. The words of Star-at-Dawning were soft and slow: "Do not heed South-Wind-Blowing. Her voice arises from poisonous roots."

"She has a hunter and ribbons and buckles," stressed Wind Maiden. "I do not."

"I have known One-Who-Runs since he was first wrapped in a carrying bag and carried upon the back of the Aged Woman. After the passage of three harvests, I saw him run with Eagle-with-White-Head. His strides ... long, full like a powerful pony."

"He runs, yes! A rabbit, not a ..." Wind Maiden thought wolf; she said, "... panther."

"He runs more quickly than the panther. He remembers long messages, recited on strings and belts of wampum." Star-at-Dawning chided her daughter, "Search. You will find many hunters, many warriors in our village but few runners who carry messages among council fires."

Wind Maiden did not respond. This runner, a pony now, she would have to watch. She hid the words of South-Wind-Blowing and of Star-at-Dawning in hollow logs so she could take them out and look at them later.

~ ~ ~

The hunters returned to Goschachgunk soon after the women had finished gathering sugar. One-Who-Runs found Wind Maiden tending the fire of the Aged Woman, her back to the liquid eyes, damming up the constant, wordless stare. The river flowed over the buried thoughts of Wind Maiden who hid her own eyes from its course.

One-Who-Runs did not speak. Wind Maiden arose; he watched her. He went to his mother, knelt, and squeezed her hands. Then, he left the cabin; Wind Maiden followed.

In front of their cabin lay a large bearskin and several smaller animal skins. One-Who-Runs passed these and entered the cabin. Wind Maiden paused to glance at the pelts. Where was the beaver? She went into the dark dwelling.

She prepared a stew of beans and roots, placed it before her husband, crouched and waited. Where was the beaver?

He ate his food without looking up. His body smelled of dirt, smoke, and dried blood. His shirt was torn on one shoulder. She watched him eat. Where was the beaver?

One-Who-Runs put aside his bowl and looked at her: "One bear slept in the hollow of a tree. We hatcheted the tree; I killed the bear. It lies outside. I killed another bear. An old man stood beside me with his rifle lifted so I gave him the bear. I did not see a fox. I saw only tracks."

"And beaver?" The voice of Wind Maiden rumbled. He did not have beaver.

"The traps of the White Man caught only two. The beaver are gone, taken in White Men's traps by Lenape for pelts to sell to traders. Large villages of the beaver, our brothers, who built their huts on creeks, are gone. We have killed many for pelts. The spirit of the beaver must be angry." One-Who-Runs looked at the dirt floor of the cabin. "I buried the two beaver along the creek where the traps killed them. Their spirits can roam through the water." He looked at Wind Maiden: "I shall kill beaver no longer."

They stared at each other. The lower lip of Wind Maiden rolled out.

"My wife." The hands of One-Who-Runs reached out to the fists of Wind Maiden. "I remember when you found the ground hog who had chewed off his paw to escape the jaw of the trap. I sat beside you while you held him in your lap. You cried when he died. When we buried him, Red Face mocked and shouted, "Take the skin!" You sneered at him. Are you less wise now than the child was then?"

Wind Maiden glanced away, but she did not pull free her hands. The child was dead, and she was a woman. Less wise? No. But she needed ... she needed ... something that she had not needed then. She could drape bright cloth and ribbons over the need and then she would be happy again. South-Wind-Blowing said Wind Maiden must have pelts. Laughing One had pelts. The child cried for the ground hog, but Wind Maiden would never cry again.

She crouched with her head bowed and did not answer him.

~ ~ ~

It was the Planting Time, but the women waited to plant because the ground was not yet warm enough for seeds. The men had finished their winter hunt. They sat around fires and puffed pipes. They talked about the council fire at Fort Pitt where Koquethagachton, called White Eyes by the Big Knife, had raised his voice for the Lenape. The Seneca — Maechachtinni — of the Mengwe had scolded White Eyes for forgetting that the Lenni Lenape were women who could not speak for themselves but must obey the commands of the men ... the Mengwe.

White Eyes had thundered, "Women! Yes, you say that you conquered me, that you cut off my legs, put a stroud on me, and gave me a hoe and maize-pounder in my hands, saying, 'Now, woman, your business henceforward shall be to plant, hoe and pound maize for us who are men and warriors!' Look at my legs. If, as you assert, you cut them off, they have grown again to their proper size. The stroud I have thrown away and have put on my own dress; the maize-hoe and pounder I have exchanged for these firearms; and I declare that I am a man. Yes, all the country on the other side of the river is mine!"

The Lenni Lenape refused to be compelled by the Mengwe to raise the hatchet for the Saggenash against the Big Knife. The wood of his hatchet would rot and the blade would dull before the Lenni Lenape meddled in the family argument of the White Man. This was what White Eyes had said.

But that was not what Maker-of-Daylight, called Captain Pipe, had said. He was of the Wolf Tribe, a powerful captain. "The foolish words of White Eyes make the Mengwe howl in rage. The Mengwe will strike and they will kill the Lenape."

So Captain Pipe and his warriors from the Wolf Tribe now wandered among the Lenape whispering that White Eyes and Netawatwes had smoked a pipe in secret with the Big Knives. They would run together to slay all the youth who might rebel among the Lenape.

But Captain Pipe would save the nation from its enemies. And he would lead the Lenni Lenape back onto the path given to them by the Great Spirit. "Why," he asked, "do you follow those Black Coats onto the longer and steeper path made for the White Man? The White Man is a liar and he is an evil being so the Great Spirit gave him a trail that would break him. The Lenape sit beneath the cooling shadow of the Great Spirit and should walk the old and easy path."

Netawatwes could not hear these words. He was saying, "If the believing ones will live near me, I will be strong. They will make me strong against the disobedient." He invited the black-coated Zeisberger, whom the Lenape called On-the-Pumpkin, and his believing lenno to build a new village near Goschachgunk.

"Good!" many grunted as they sat around their fires and talked, "Our arm will grow wide and firm when linked through the strong arm of the praying lenno."

Fish-of-the-Deep-Water objected, "And do we forsake the path of our fathers, and do we paint our flesh white as have those believing lenno who once were our brothers?"

Then others puffed their pipes and asked, "Do you rise up to follow Captain Pipe?"

"No!" roared Fish-of-the-Deep-Water. "I whoop because my stroud is now ripped off. It caught on branches and clung to my legs. I am a man, and I shall fight. I shall fight the Big Knife and I shall fight the Saggenash!"

These were the words which the men passed around as they sat before their fires and which the women echoed as, together, they pounded and wove. These were the words which One-Who-Runs repeated to Wind Maiden. He had heard the speech of White Eyes and had carried it from Fort Pitt through the forest to Netawatwes and to the council of the Lenni

Lenape. He had recited it to Wind Maiden, and she had watched him sit back and smile, filled with the flesh of words. Often, he retrieved the words from the hidden place inside him. Wind Maiden would see him gaze into the fire and smile. She would know that he was remembering, but she would look away because she did not care.

During the Planting Time, while the pipes were still warm and smoke still rose from the fires of whisperings, Zeisberger – with three other White teachers and with the believing lenno – came from Beautiful Spring to spread out their village along the Elk's Eye near Goschachgunk. The Lenape rose from their fires to watch them chop trees and build huts.

Wind Maiden saw One-Who-Runs rise up. She knew he would go, for his ears itched to hear and his eyes burned to see any new thing that he could remember and repeat. That night, he recited all to Wind Maiden. She pinched together her lips and rolled her eyes. She scraped their bowls and prodded the fire. Her body told him that she did not want to hear, but she listened.

"They recited many chants about the chief who died but lives again. Listen ..."

He chanted a song of smooth, round words and continued, "Glikkikan, the Gun Sight, is there. He laid down his hatchet when I approached and hatcheted words into me about the Saviour whose blood cleanses away death."

One-Who-Runs was a messenger. These words were the only flesh he would bear through the forest. "I shall starve," moaned Wind Maiden, "if words are all I can eat."

Upon the rising of the sun the next morning, all Goschachgunk hurried through the forest to hear these believing lenno and their White teachers make their first speech at their new village. One-Who-Runs led Wind Maiden along the trail to the strange fire. When she saw the village, her feet dragged and fell behind. She paused and waited for them.

She wandered into the newly chopped clearing. A jagged stump of a sycamore blocked her path. It would not let her walk around so she stopped. She stretched out her arms upon it. Its width was wider than she could reach. She patted its rough flesh, still strong in death.

"Did they burn tobacco to your manito, aged sycamore? Or did they chop you without consent? I shall mourn your death."

She leaned against the sycamore and gazed toward the huts.

Beside a high and wide wooden bench stood the wife of Glikkikan and next to her stood a short, skinny woman. A White woman. She wore a long, grey stroud. Against a pale face were the wide eyes of a fawn. Her hair was pulled back and hidden beneath a white head covering. Wind Maiden watched her pull a white cloth over mounds of food on a bench, plunk down rocks, and smooth the cloth. She watched her lift her head and gaze out toward Wind Maiden. The narrow mouth of the White woman stretched into a long, thin smile.

6
APRIL 14, 1776 – MAY 5, 1776

"The ... the ... Schmierkaes ..." Sarah broke from the Unami into the German word for the curdled milk, "... is sour."

She sighed and looked up from the crock at Sister Anna Benigna. She could have spoken English; this sister would have comprehended it. But she wanted to be like the other sisters; she wanted to speak Unami. Anna Benigna smiled. Seven months and, still, the sisters laughed at her clumsiness when she spoke.

The milk was poured; the bread was baked; the wild berry jam was spooned into dishes.

"The butter ..."

"Churned," assured Anna Benigna.

"Good," thought Sarah. Good that the butter was churned and good that Anna Benigna had said it because Sarah had not remembered that word, either. Why could she not remember words used every day?

The plank upon which the food lay was one of five set out in the newly-cleared street of their newborn village, Lichtenau.

She tapped her chin with her forefinger.

"We shall call it Lichtenau ... Pasture of Light," Brother Zundel had told her when he had returned from the meeting in February with Chief Netawatwes in Goschachgunk, the new capital of the Delaware Nation. He had pushed his coarse hair back from his face. "A pasture aglow with the Light of Jesus Christ."

"It will be wonderful for ..." Sarah had begun.

"Yes," he had agreed. "Two and one half miles downstream from Goschachgunk on the Muskingum. Netawatwes wants us near him so the gospel can spread throughout the entire Delaware Nation. The disobedient will be subdued to him and to Christ."

He had enclosed her in a quick hug. She had gazed down in embarrassment. Oh, not at this intimacy, for they were alone in their own cabin. She was ashamed because she could only pretend to share his excitement.

"Sarah. My vision takes on substance."

"Who will go to the new village?" she had asked, trying to make her voice sound interested, not anxious.

"Why — Brother David Zeisberger, Brother Heckewelder, and we, of course. Brother David might not remain long."

And we.

She had stared across toward their bed. The unevenly-stuffed straw was covered by a red and white diamond-patterned coverlet. Upon the chest at the foot of the bed was draped her floral quilt. When they had arrived in Schoenbrunn, the brethren had just completed the cabin for them. Brother Zundel had previously slept in the Brethren's cabin. Their new dwelling was barren. She had laid out the embroidered linen and the towels upon the back of the door. She had cut and sewn the cloth into curtains. She had begun the rag rug to cover the drafty and rough plank floor. Certainly, a rag carpet would take long to complete when even rags could find better uses.

To leave now, when she had done so much, and to move near the heathen … Oh! And to part from Sister Jungmann. Sarah would be alone.

"I have not learned enough from Sister Jungmann to instruct the women and younger children without her aid," Sarah had objected.

"I shall be there," Brother Zundel had replied, still smiling.

Yes, he would be there. Hair unbound like the Indians'. Linsey shirt tied loosely at his waist. Leggings strapped high upon his legs. Moccasins upon his feet.

Sister Jungmann was not a man. She was not an Indian. Brother Zundel was a man. And he was an … an …

Sarah had folded and stored her coverlet and quilt and linen towels. Sleeping mats upon the dirt did not need coverlets. And what could easily hang upon the inner bark wall of a hut? She had given the rag carpet to Sister Jungmann. A carpet could not subdue dirt.

Lichtenau was newborn. Sarah rubbed her palms across her apron. The motion of her hands stopped. Her palms pushed into her stomach. Soon, would something else be newborn, too?

How could she be certain? Of whom could she ask her questions? She could talk to a White woman, but an Indian thought differently and spoke strangely. She glanced sideways at Anna Benigna. She had been a White woman, but she was an Indian now. Neither Sarah nor Anna Benigna had even tried to converse in anything but Unami.

Indians from Goschachgunk were roaming through the day-old clearing. Sarah heard the laugh of Brother Zundel before she saw him.

"Ah. Friend! Do you come for the ..." Sarah lost these words, "... or for the food?"

She followed his voice to where she saw him standing at the edge of the just-cleared street, thumping a tall, fat Indian on the shoulders. More gathered around them. Some roamed toward her.

They were bald but for oval scalp locks high on their crowns. Blankets, called match-coats, of black, red, and white or yellow, green, and blue were draped across their dark, muscular arms and shoulders. Most were painted black or red with violent lines.

The women followed, jingling with buckles and arrayed with red, blue, yellow, green ribbons. They looked like bushes decorated with outrageous berries and blossoms. The Indian sisters had forsaken gaudy attire. They, like the women from Goschachgunk, still wore skirts and shirts, leggings and moccasins; but their clothing was not hung with such array. Their moccasins were not beaded; their hair was not draped with buckles and bound with cloth but was bound into thick knots of dark hair and enclosed in muslin caps tied with ribbons denoting their status. With modesty.

The brethren and the sisters were but eight families, thirty-five people.

"Enough food for all?" asked Anna Benigna.

"Enough for all Goschachgunk, if they come," replied Sarah.

"They will come," chuckled Anna Benigna. "Long speeches and food. These will fill the body and the head. Look." She motioned toward the open space encircled by trees where the Sunday morning service would soon be conducted. "My husband begins."

Isaac Glikkikan stood above two other Indian men, pounding his fists together, then pointing up and pounding again. The Indians cowered beneath the blows.

"He is ablaze for the Saviour." The edge of pride slid round her words. "I sobbed long ago for the scalps my husband once raised in battle. Now, I sometimes shiver with the men he slays with words."

Sarah watched Brother Isaac enact an elaborate drama whose sounds she could not hear. He wore a linen shirt and linsey-woolsey breeches, leather moccasins and leggings. Over his shoulder hung the match-coat. Upon his head, he wore a black hat, wide-brimmed like those of the teachers. If Sarah had approached him from behind, could she have distinguished him from Brother Zundel? Yes — Brother Zundel had removed his hat.

The Indians from Goschachgunk were swarming now. What could Sarah do? Serve the food, yes. And until the serving time, prepare. She spread a linsey-woolsey cloth over the food and secured the cloth with four rocks. All was done.

From the corner of her eye, she saw a form, immobile, near the edge of the newly-chopped clearing. She gazed to where a girl stood apart, leaning against the ragged stump of a tree. The girl was observing her with steady intensity. Sarah tried to smile.

The girl jerked her head. A frown carved itself like a scar into the softness of her face.

"Go to pray! Go to hear!" called out Brother Nathaniel, walking through the crowd.

They followed him to the clearing near the river where Brother David Zeisberger awaited them. The girl, like the stump itself, did not move; she did not avert her eyes. But the crowd cut across the path of her gaze and freed Sarah from her view.

Brother Zundel appeared beside Sarah. He had approached softly ... like an Indian. His smile broke wide against large, white teeth. That smile alone would redeem the Indian nations.

He led Sarah to the rising upon which Brother David waited and pulled her down beside him. Sarah stared sideways at her husband. He had not spoken to her; she was not sure he had really looked at her. She could have been a pebble, kicked along beneath his feet, pursued by habit.

"Rise up, shine; for your light is come, and the blazing brightness of the Only One is risen upon you," called Brother David, holding out the Bible as he read.

His arms moved through the air, Indian fashion. He was small and frail in appearance, only in appearance.

"... the day for all Lenape to be saved is here." His voice was firm. His eyes sparked with a flame from the same fire that ignited Brother Zundel.

Sarah wanted to reach out her hand to the wide hand of her husband. But he was not with her, not really with her.

"Does he think of me seated beside him as I think of him?" she wondered. "No, not here." She watched his hand, his arm, his crossed legs — near to touch and far away.

Sarah tried to follow the words of Brother David's discourse. She strung together the almost familiar Unami words but lost the meaning.

"You panic," had said Sister Jungmann who had remained with her husband in Schoenbrunn. "Do not try to catch each word you hear or you will be translating one word while ten more slip past you. Let the words flow over and around you; then enter into their meaning."

So Sarah would listen to an eagerly talking sister. She would nod and smile, nod and smile. The words would flow over and around her. She would nod and smile. The sister would intone a question, and Sarah would have to stare back at her and mumble, "Say again."

Then she would panic and she would hold one word, pulling out its translation, and she would lose the rest. Finally, Sister Jungmann would be summoned to translate for her.

She was improving, however. Or, else, the sisters were using only those words Sarah could comprehend. She was like a child to them, hardly their teacher.

Sister Jungmann had shown Sarah how to substitute ground maize for wheat when the wheat supply was low or where to find herbs she might use in place of those she once cultivated in Bethlehem but which had not yet been planted in her garden plot in the Ohio country.

Most important, Sister Jungmann had discussed the intimacies of women. Sarah could never converse with Brother Zundel about *those* things.

"Menstruation gives the woman power, the Indian believes," Sister Jungmann had explained. "She cannot eat from the bowls others eat from or sleep in the same hut. She must not look at anyone."

"But our women have been taught that this is foolishness," Sarah had exclaimed. Yet even she had seen sisters avoid her eyes and refuse to eat. They did not run away, as did the heathen, to filthy shacks; but, though they had been taught otherwise, that was where their hearts hid.

"Tradition is difficult to undo my dear," Sister Jungmann had replied. She had hesitated a moment and continued, "Uh — Sister Sarah, when your flow begins, hide the stainings and keep the secret. If some learn, separate yourself. Lest you offend those that are weak in the faith."

Why respect foolish beliefs? And ... hide the stainings? Sarah had had none to hide these recent weeks.

Sarah pressed the back of her hand against her abdomen. Two days from Schoenbrunn. Would that Sister Jungmann were near.

She glanced at the dark, the silently-waiting forest. Her eyes moved over the heads of the heathen. They paused upon an upturned face. The Delaware girl was watching her, the frown slashed across her face. Sarah looked away. The frown etched itself into her mind.

She dropped her gaze. The forefinger of Brother Zundel thumped upon the earth.

~ ~ ~

Sarah clutched to her chest the almost empty bowl of schmierkaes. After the meal, the visitors had dispersed into the clearing to talk and to smoke the pipe. She watched them from behind the plank table.

Once, her hands had known their trade. Her skill was worthless now. She could not weave words with ease.

Back from the river, toward the fields of promise, stood Brother Zundel. Three Indian men stood with him. His coat was cast aside; his sleeves were rolled above his elbows. His fists rested upon his hips. Watching him exhausted Sarah.

She slid the bowl down onto the table. Her hands were empty. She intertwined them.

She looked across the clearing toward the river's edge. Anna Benigna sat in the grass talking to the scowling girl.

The girl looked up. She pointed at Sarah. Anna Benigna turned and beckoned to Sarah.

Sarah approached, rubbing her hands against her apron. She was the wife of a missionary. Whom did she need to fear?

Fear? This was a child.

"I am happy to greet you," said Sarah. She knew these words well.

Anna Benigna smiled. She was forty-three years old. Her skin was rough and dry, weathered by many years of wind, rain, sun, and snow. Her blue eyes alone suggested her origin. She had been captured during the French and Indian War, twenty years before.

"This is the daughter of Fish-of-the-Deep-Water, a captain among the Lenni Lenape," she said. "Her father and my husband were friends. Together, they fought."

"Glikkikan, Gun Sight, no longer fights for his people." The girl's voice was dull, but her dark eyes stalked their prey.

"My husband fights for his people," objected Anna Benigna.

"Many ways of fight," said Sarah. The girl turned her sneer upon Sarah. "Glikkikan fight for Truth, lives for Saviour, not by kill." Sarah wished she knew the refinements of this language.

The frown deepened: "That is not the fighting of a warrior." She looked at Anna Benigna: "You know. You have seen the Gun Sight, the brave warrior."

Anna Benigna looked down. "Yes," she said, "I have seen the brave warrior, fearless and frightening in battle. I have seen blood smeared on his hands and his chest and the prizes of scalp locks dangling from sticks." She rubbed her brow: "The blood of the warrior does not bring happiness. The Saviour teaches us not to kill. There is no longer blood on the hands and chest of Glikkikan."

The girl pinched her lips into a tight line. She looked toward the river. When she looked back, the frown was reset upon her face. "No warrior should be ashamed of the blood and scalps of enemies who spill the blood of the Lenni Lenape." She blinked then concluded, "But my mouth closes. I honor the memory of the Gun Sight."

Did this girl know only anger and cruelty?

"Friends bear words: you are married," said Anna Benigna. She smiled.

Married? This child?

The girl did not answer. She watched. And, though she did not move, she seemed to retreat.

"Husband ... a warrior?" asked Sarah.

"No!" she snapped. Her eyes narrowed. She studied Sarah.

Sarah's fingers felt numb. The face of the girl was like the dark, silent nights of the forest. Sarah spun an imaginary thread between her fingertips.

"This ..." The girl clenched her fists. "... White Man's religion. It is not for the True Man." She was looking at Sarah.

Sarah felt the blue ribbon under her chin. "Saviour died for evil of all men."

The girl shook her head. "No! The White Man is evil; he needs the Saviour to die for him. The True Man is good; he is a friend of the Great Spirit. He takes the short path to the land of the Great Spirit."

Sarah looked to Anna Benigna, but Anna Benigna only smiled back. Sarah was the missionary. She was expected to know how to answer.

"Man goes no ..." She gulped. "No man finds path to Great Spirit. Saviour leads only."

"The True Man does not need a guide." The girl pronounced each sound of every word. Sarah was the child. "He finds the path because he knows the signs." She waved her hand as if casting away a useless twig: "The White Man always loses the path. He needs the Saviour."

"All men in dark. Need light to find path," Sarah stammered. She herself was in the dark; she needed light. "Saviour ... Light."

"No. The White Man teaches lies to the True Man. When the True Man says, 'I will not hear the words of the White Man,' *then* he does good." The girl lifted her chin. Was it triumph or defiance?

"Yes, some White Men teach lies," agreed Sarah. She felt defeated.

"And this Saviour — another lie of the White Man. The True Man does not need a Saviour."

"No. Truth!" asserted Sarah. "You walk in dark; need Light – Saviour."

The girl jumped up. "No! Am I a fool that I should walk in darkness?" She stared down at Sarah.

Sarah arose. They faced each other. The girl was a half-head taller than she.

The girl stepped back: "I have heard the story; I know. The True Man did not kill the Saviour. The White Man killed him. The White Man killed the one who came to lead him out of darkness to the Great Spirit. The White Man is evil." She backed away, her eyes set upon Sarah as if Sarah might leap upon her. "The True Man would honor the Saviour, the Son of the Great Spirit." She turned and hurried toward the forest.

Sarah felt like running, too ... the other way. To where? She felt like crying, but where could she flee where none would hear?

"Sister Anna, what is her name?" she asked.

"Wind Maiden, wife of One-Who-Runs," was the reply.

~ ~ ~

The fires were dying orange-red as the sun set. Their crackling mingled with the hushed voices of the remnant of the visitors. Level land stretched far back from the river to where the hills began. Along a slight rise of the valley stood the temporary huts of branches and bark — a single row, parallel to the river, the shadow of the future Pasture of Light. Trees, predominantly sycamore, stood tall and virginal.

Sarah leaned against the trunk of a sycamore. She had wrapped her grey cloak about her and had pulled her hood over her head. She cupped her hands about her nose and mouth and breathed into them.

The trees needed buds, needed leaves to cloak the land. Schoenbrunn, a town of split-log cabins enclosed by rail fences, was as the summer compared to the spring of Lichtenau. And Bethlehem? Neither Schoenbrunn nor Lichtenau nor all the seasons of the year compared with Bethlehem.

Brother Voss had returned to Bethlehem five months before — November, early, before the deepest snows fell in the mountains. He had carried letters to Sister Glaser and to Sarah's parents, letters which Sarah had written those first lonely weeks in Schoenbrunn. She had not received replies. No one would travel through the mountains in winter.

"The forest is dark and silent," she had written. "Brother Zundel says when anyone first lives in the forest, he feels suffocated by it. He says it passes ..."

It had not passed. Sometimes, she could scream. Perhaps the cry would shatter the oppression.

Brother Zundel was kneeling with several Indians near one of the waning fires. They stood. The Indians might be Delaware, Shawano, Miami, or Nantikote. They all looked alike to Sarah. Five dark figures wrapped in blankets parted from one with a dark coat draped over a shoulder. Brother Zundel circled several fires, stopping briefly to speak at each. He moved with fluid rhythm. So easily. But Sarah stiffened and hid, afraid to enter the gentle sway of conversation.

He looked up and saw her. He did not often notice her these recent days in Lichtenau. She watched his long, careful strides, his strong, swaying body. He stood above her.

"Meet some of our visitors," he said, offering Sarah his hand.

The sun was almost set. The guests were departing.

"Netawatwes, Chief of the Delaware," said Brother Zundel as he led her to an old man who was readjusting his blanket before leaving.

"Brother!" said Netawatwes.

"Father!" replied Brother Zundel. He glanced at Sarah: "My wife."

"I heard on the wind that my brother had taken to himself a wife." The eyes of Netawatwes traveled down, then up Sarah.

She pressed her nails into the palms of her hands.

The old chief said, "She is a blade of grass in the youth of the year. She must grow and thicken before the snow descends."

Sarah sucked in her lower lip. Others discerned her weakness too easily.

Brother Zundel smiled. "Father, she has endured the snow. She is not a new blade."

Netawatwes nodded. "Kill much buck and give her the flesh and pelts."

"Thank you, Father. Your words are wisdom." Brother Zundel reached out and clasped the old man's hand.

"I shall come, again, tomorrow to watch my brothers build their village." Netawatwes grinned. "You must visit Goschachgunk. Bring your skinny wife."

"Yes," agreed Brother Zundel.

"Sit in council. Make your long speeches about the Saviour."

Brother Zundel squeezed and patted in both his hands the dark and wrinkled hand of Netawatwes.

The chief left with the last of the visitors.

Across the Muskingum, the sun set behind the hills.

Sarah was a pale green blade of tender grass.

"Indians prefer plumpness in their women," said Brother Zundel, watching her.

Sarah returned his gaze. "Perhaps he is correct, Brother Zundel," she said.

"But I do not prefer plumpness," he shrugged.

"Not outward thinness," she thought. "Inside, inside!" She wanted to cry it out, to expose the spindly blade.

"It is late, and you must be tired," he said. Already, the night was cloaking her husband's face in shadow.

She waited outside their hut while Brother Zundel retrieved an ember from the evening's blaze. Dark forms of sisters and brethren conversed and parted in the dying glow of the fires. They seemed shadowy dreams whose substances she could not know. Today was old. Tomorrow, in the light of day, Lord, she would try again.

Brother Zundel appeared with the smoldering stick. Sarah pulled back the blanket covering the entrance to their hut. The dwelling was dark and damp and cold.

He crouched before the pit to tend the fire. "How like an Indian," thought Sarah. She could retreat to her hut from the other Indians, but where could she hide from him?

She unrolled the matting and blankets which comprised their bedding — still damp. Soon, Brother Zundel would construct a temporary bed of hemp rope, forked branches pounded into the ground at the four corners, and other branches laid cross-wise for support. Beds of straw would, now, be to her like the beds of down in Bethlehem whose feel she could not recall. Would some day even this matting she now unrolled become a longed-for luxury? She shivered.

"You are cold," said Brother Zundel. "Pull the mat nearer the fire pit."

She settled down beside the still-cold pit. Brother Zundel opened a heavy, woolen, tri-colored blanket and laid it across her folded legs. He stood above her. For what did he wait? Surely, he was not shy. But, then, how could she know? What intimacy they had experienced upon their journey had vanished here in the wilderness. Oh — they lay down together; she would never deny him. But, even so, he restrained himself. Did she repulse him?

He settled beside her.

"I know …" he said. She could not see his face. "… this life is difficult."

"Oh …" exclaimed Sarah. She had begun to say, "Oh, no!" but such was a lie. Instead, the exclamation sounded like a confession.

Heaviness hovered over them. They did not know how to converse. Had they ever tried? Yes. Along the trail, he had tried. And she had responded … with fear, with judgment, with rejection.

Who was he? From whence came he? His father in Saxony, his favorite sister — he did not talk of these. And she did not inquire. She … she … she had brought the silence.

"Assuredly," his voice broke the silence, "it is a privilege to endure hardships for our Saviour's sake, He who has endured far more for us than we can repay."

Did he judge her for her weariness? Did she not also know that her depression was not justified?

His hand thumped down upon her knee. She wanted to pull away.

"The days will not grow easier. War is near. The Delaware stays neutral only because we missionaries sit in his council and preach peace. Too many preach war."

She did not answer. Battles enough raged within her. She could not contend with another war.

The fire lit and warmed their small room. She looked at him. His brows were furrowed. Again. She had brought the silence. She felt a soreness in her breasts and a fullness in her stomach. And how would she tell him of this?

~ ~ ~

The sun rose in the east toward Bethlehem. Sarah arose with it. She had not slept well these recent days. And the queasiness … "Father, not now. Soon, but not now. I am not prepared. And Brother Zundel …" She glanced over at him. His mouth was half open. His rough hands rested upon the blanket. What kind of a hindrance would this new burden be? His vision had not included a family.

She tied her hair beneath her cap, wrapped her cape about her, and left the hut.

She walked toward the river. Why did she fear? She stood above the Muskingum and watched its full and rapid flow. Be like the river, banked up by the Saviour. Only on one course could she, then, flow. Was she God? Should she chart her own course, dig out her own bed, erect her own bank? She had tried, and, always, the river overflowed. Like now. A course she could not control.

"Have your own way, then," she sighed. She had to yield. She had no choice.

From a small pile, she took sticks and branches already gathered for the morning fires. She re-entered the hut. Brother Zundel was pulling on his breeches. Sarah crouched over the pit and arranged the sticks. She avoided his eyes. She could not tell him.

"Arisen, again, so early, Sister Sarah."

Sarah glanced over her shoulder. "Oh, the river ..." She let her voice trail off, hoping he might infer the rest. She could not lie outright.

Brother Zundel waited, then said, "The river?"

She arose and turned. "Why, yes ..."

His shoulders were wide and thick beneath a linsey-woolsey shirt of blue and white checks. His blond hair hung in loose strands against his face. He smiled. "The river, then, Sister."

He wrapped his arms about her. Her stomach pressed against him. She would try, she must try to break the dam that blocked the flow between them. She laid her head against his chest. His arms slid tighter and held her within their clasp. She relaxed into his strength.

~ ~ ~

Sarah ladled the porridge into the bowls of the congregation. It was only the third hour of the day and, already, they had conducted the morning service and worked in the fields, clearing the low-lands for planting. As they had worked so they would eat – together.

The mixture of ground maize and water, flavored with maple sugar, slid from the ladle into the bowl of each person: Jonah, an assistant to the teachers, and his wife, Amelia; Judith, white-headed and revered by the Indians; Mark the Delaware; Christian, son of Jonah and Amelia, age eight, and his sister, Leah, seven; Isaac and Anna Benigna, his wife, and their son, Jacob, and daughter, Benigna; Martha, a widow, and her son, Thomas, age nine; Elizabeth, a widow, sister to Jonah; and others, eight families, thirty-one Indian brethren, sisters, and children.

Their faces were red from the wind; their lips were chapped. They paused before the kettle:

"The fire flames warm. Blessings, Sister."

"I pulled bushes and look! A rock." The small hand of Christian opened from around a smooth, grey stone.

"The wind smells of water. It rains today. I am grateful, Sister."

"I shall show you, today, the willow basket I made, Sister."

Sarah nodded and smiled, patted the open hand of Christian, promised to visit the hut of Elizabeth, and, yes, she would like to learn basket weaving.

But much more, she would like to sit before a large loom and adjust the pedals to produce a woven melody of colorful design.

Daily, the brethren cleared trees from the land, split the logs, and carried them to the site of the future mission house where they would worship until the church was built. First, the plantation must be cleared and seed must be sown. In the evenings, the congregation gathered for worship before retiring to their separate huts. Always, they had visitors from Goschachgunk. And day after day, Sarah prepared her speech for Brother Zundel. Each day she planned to recite it, and each day she could not.

The second week in Lichtenau, a messenger came from Goschachgunk. He was a slender young man. Sarah had often seen him speaking with Brother Isaac or Brother David or Brother Zundel. Sarah was on the plantation, bringing water, cheese and bread to the brethren. Brother Zundel spoke to the man then beckoned to Sarah.

"This is One-Who-Runs," he said in German, "a runner. He bears an invitation from Netawatwes for the teachers and helpers to visit his village tomorrow."

Sarah nodded. She stooped to gather into her apron chunks of bread and cheese.

"You must join us," he added.

Must?

Brother Zundel continued, "The night you met Netawatwes, he invited you. We must respect him."

"Bring your skinny wife." That was an invitation? She tried to look agreeable. She felt rebellious. She replied, "Of course."

Brother Zundel had already returned to plowing the field, his shirt sleeves rolled up on his arms.

Brother Zundel ... Brother Zundel ... Brother Zundel. They barely conversed. She turned away. Was it already time to milk the cows? Each day, she milked the cows, stored some milk, poured some into pails and skimmed the cream, churned the cream to butter, and made schmierkaes of the skimmed milk curds. She fed the chickens and gathered their eggs. She rendered fat and poured it into candles or stored it for making lye soap. She cooked dried meat many hours to make unsatisfactory imitations of

Bethlehem stews and baked breads Indian-fashion in the fire's hot ashes. Amidst all this, Sarah tried to train the Indian sisters in the chores and in the faith. With a small supply of words, with trembling ...

... What would she do in Goschachgunk?

Sarah walked, cradling her apron in her arms. She looked sideways to see the messenger walking near her. He stopped and looked back on the brethren and sisters plowing and hoeing the field. Sarah paused to watch him.

"The White Man is strange. Why does he work for no reason?" He pointed at the plots upon which Brother Zundel and Brother Heckewelder worked. "They plow all the earth. Why? Where do the worms and the friends of the food live if they plow all the earth? See how the Lenape plows a small spot and leaves a small spot for the worms to make their homes." His arm swung toward the Indian brethren and sisters who labored in small, separate patches, turning the earth for their gardens but leaving surrounding soil unturned. He lowered his arm. "The White Man always works harder. The Lenape prepares for the day and shakes his head at the work of the White Man. He says, 'The Great Spirit must be punishing the White Man with much work. But the Great Spirit loves the Lenape who rests all day and rises to kill when he is hungry.'"

He smiled across the wind-bent grasses at Sarah. His hair was plucked back to the scalp lock, but he wore no paint. His smile rose almost boyishly. One-Who-Runs. He turned toward Goschachgunk.

Sarah watched the workers in the field. She saw Brother Zundel take off his hat and wipe his brow with his arm. He glanced up. She heard his laugh. He tossed his hat toward Brother Heckewelder who snatched it as it twirled through the air and balanced it upon his own hat. Brother Zundel grabbed both from off the other's head, retrieved one for himself, and flung the other high.

He was not a stranger to others. Why to her?

Brother Heckewelder was tall and strong like Brother Zundel and of the same age. She heard him laugh. Had she and Brother Zundel ever laughed together? Brother Heckewelder called out, "Christoph ..."

Brother Zundel ... Brother Zundel ... Christoph.

She backed away. She was late to milk the cows. And she would have to assign extra chores if, tomorrow, she was to go to Goschachgunk. And would she encounter more hostile stares in this heathen village? She recalled a tall, slender girl whose scowl was fiercer than all the rest. One-Who-Runs. Yes! She had heard his name before. He was the husband of the scowling girl.

No, he was not a warrior.

They rowed by canoe the following day up the Muskingum to Goschachgunk — Sarah, Brother Zundel, Brother Zeisberger, Brother Isaac, and Brother Jonah in one large canoe. It was mid-morning. A parting fog hung over the water. With a covetous grasp, the dark forest clung to the river bank as if it were determined to engulf even this ribbon of water. Except for the swishing of the paddles in the slow-moving river, all things pulsed with silence.

Floating, swaying ... the salty saliva gushed into Sarah's mouth. She was going to be sick! She breathed in and bowed her head. Not here!

Was this pregnancy? To whom could she talk? What help could she find? She was the teacher, but about this, she must be taught.

Would she give birth, alone, in the wilderness? She floated with the current, and there was no paddle to dip into the water and no strong arm to pull her to shore.

She would retch. She would embarrass herself. So be it. Let them all know.

"Brother David, again we tell the Lenni Lenape to keep his hands clean from the blood of the White Man's argument," called Brother Zundel from behind Sarah where he paddled. He spoke in Unami and Sarah strained to concentrate upon his words and not upon the rolling waves of nausea.

"Again," agreed Brother David. "May the Mighty One melt their hearts." Brother David Zeisberger crouched in front of Sarah in the center of the canoe. He turned his head sideways as he spoke. His nose was narrow and long; his face was thin. He was the strength of the mission among the Indians and the source of the vision which Brother Zundel nurtured.

"Mengwe and Delamatteno kick the Lenni Lenape toward the Saggenash," warned Brother Isaac. He sat near Brother David. He thumped his fists together. "Captain Pipe takes the Wolf Tribe to the Mengwe. He whispers to the other Lenni Lenape about the gifts the Saggenash will give to its friends. The Big Knife gives no gifts."

The Saggenash ... the English, Sarah translated. What part need the Indians have in this dispute between the colonies and their mother nation? Certainly, this forsaken wilderness was far from that war.

"Netawatwes is old and weak, says Captain Pipe." Now Brother Jonah was calling from the front of the canoe where he leaned far forward with his paddle. He paused and added, "Captain Pipe pretends to tremble because Netawatwes refuses to follow the Mengwe into battle. But *he* will lead the Lenape to battle; *he* will protect the nation."

"How long will the White teachers be the strength of Netawatwes? How long will we keep the hatchet from the hands of the Lenape? Can we make enough speeches?" asked Brother Zundel.

"As many as the Saviour prepares, Brother Christoph," said Brother Zeisberger.

Brother Christoph ... Christoph. Sarah repeated the name to herself: "Christoph."

She could call out, "Christoph! Brother Christoph!" But she would shock herself, and she would shock him. She had made him become "Brother Zundel" to her. Could she find Christoph?

Who but she called him Brother Zundel?

Below the fork of the river where the Walhonding flowed into the Muskingum, Goschachgunk lay. Two main streets formed a cross, in design like Schoenbrunn. In the center was, not a church, but a large, two-storied log house, the home of Netawatwes.

A short, heavy woman and a younger and taller heavy woman sat on either side of Sarah in front of the house of Netawatwes while the men passed the pipe around the council fire.

The short woman said, "My husband is Fish-of-the-Deep-Water who sits beside Netawatwes." She pointed toward the council house within the darkness of which the fire cracked. Sarah looked toward where she waved, squinting as if she was obliged to see through the walls of the council house.

"My husband is Big Cat who sits in council beside Fish-of-the-Deep-Water and Netawatwes," said the other.

Sarah gazed out toward the large council house. She felt their eyes upon her. "My husband is Christoph Zundel. He sits beside fire," she murmured.

The other women of the village strolled past and stood to talk in clusters nearby. They did not glance at her while they walked; but when they stopped, they watched.

"The wife of Chief Netawatwes serves the meat. She cannot sit," said the short woman, the wife of Fish-of-the-Deep-Water. Sarah remembered hearing that name.

Sister Jungmann had warned her, "Never address an Indian by her name. It is an embarrassment. Use her name when she is not near. Call her friend; call her sister to her face."

So these women, they had no names.

And the heathen changed his name like garments to suit his mood or his new conception of himself. She might hear three names and not realize they belonged to one man.

In the Christian settlements, when an Indian was baptized, he acquired yet another name. Often, he chose the same name several other believing members of the congregation already possessed. Bible names. White Man names.

Like bulging tents, Sarah's attendants sat wrapped inside their blankets. Sarah slid her hands inside her cape and rubbed her knuckles across the coarse wool. She smelled the thick odor of the bodies of women. Would she be sick?

A woman appeared from the council house and motioned toward the cluster of women. The tall woman stood and walked toward the council house. Others followed.

"The lenno have finished eating," said the smaller attendant. "We shall eat."

Eat. Oh! She would be sick!

They lumbered toward her with the heavy, black kettle from the council house. Scooping out, they offered Sarah the first bowl. She clutched it in her hands. They tore off a slab of bread. She plopped that into her lap. She stared down at the stew.

The distance from the bowl to her mouth seemed ever so long; she was sure she could not make it.

Glancing sideways, she caught the penetrating eye of the wife of Fish-of-the-Deep-Water.

The stew smelled heavy and fat. Waves of queasiness flowed over her. She gulped and gulped, again.

"How long?" asked the short, fat woman.

How long? Sarah looked at her and breathed one long, deep breath. She swallowed.

"How long until you set down your load?" the woman asked.

"Eight, nine cycles of the moon," stammered Sarah. How could this Indian woman know she was pregnant? Sarah herself was not sure that even she knew.

The wife of Fish-of-the-Deep-Water slid the bowl from Sarah's grasp. She made signs with her hands, encircling her stomach, to the women who had gathered near to eat. Sarah heard them mumbling to each other.

"Your stomach will hold the bread," the taller woman said to Sarah. "It needs the work of fullness so it will not think of sickness."

Sarah took the bread from her lap and chomped a mouthful.

They watched her chew, and she felt them relax around her.

She heard their whisperings and the occasional word, "beson" ... medicine ... for what? She tried to smooth her features into the appearance of health. Whatever being pregnant looked like, she tried to look otherwise.

A woman whose bells jingled upon her ankles appeared with a steaming bowl. The wife of Fish-of-the-Deep-Water took the bowl, sniffed it, and passed it into the hands of Sarah.

"For the ..." She pointed with her forefinger to her stomach and then rotated her hand in a fast, small circle. Her eyes drooped in feigned sickness.

Sarah sniffed the hot brew. It smelled of mint. She glanced past the rim of the bowl to the woman.

"We gather the leaves near the river," said the other.

Sarah dropped her eyes to the bowl. Surely it could not harm her. She inhaled.

She sipped. It was a weak mint tea. She drank a portion. It was a very large bowl. She looked up and smiled, offering the bowl to the small woman.

The wife of Fish-of-the-Deep-Water shook her head. "All is better," she said.

Sarah did not desire better; she was content with less. She drank. A bloated stomach, not nausea, would afflict her now.

"We sit too much," said the short, fat woman when Sarah had gulped down the remains of the bowl. "Greet the village with me. "

They walked along the street toward the Muskingum, Sarah and her two attendants. The other women returned to their huts and cabins. In clusters, they wove baskets or straps. Some scraped hides. Hands busy, they watched her. Wolf-like dogs prowled the streets, sniffing in the dirt, chewing on scraps of food. Children, practically naked, scampered about and stopped to stare.

Small boys stood in the shallow water and shot small arrows from small bows into the river. The boys in Schoenbrunn and Lichtenau fished this way, too. One caught a fish and held it high on his arrow. Children. No paint smeared upon their faces; no hair yanked from their scalps.

She recalled a time, when she was no older than they, when another group of children waded into another river far away and swung small nets through the air and into the water, catching only each other's feet.

Suddenly, the boy gave a war whoop and leaped onto the land. The memory snapped apart. Sarah roamed through a village of wild, retreating savages.

They turned back toward the center of the village.

A young woman wearing buckles and beads on her blue stroud and bells upon her ankles stood along the street. Her cheeks were painted with bright red circles. Another woman, tall and slender, stood beside her. Her mouth waited to frown.

The short, heavy woman, the wife of Fish-of-the-Deep-Water, nodded toward the slender woman and said, "My daughter."

Yes. The Daughter of Fish-of-the-Deep-Water. How easily these names blended into a long list of fish and wolves and does and bucks and sun risings and sun settings which Sarah could not remember.

"I am happy to greet you," said Sarah. Wind Maiden frowned. "We spoke in Pasture of Light," continued Sarah.

"Yes," said Wind Maiden. Her eyes flashed sideways to the friend who stood beside her.

"I met your husband, and I meet your mother." Sarah smiled. She smiled at Wind Maiden; she smiled at the friend; she smiled at the short, fat woman, the mother; she smiled at the taller, fat woman.

"My husband visits this Pasture of Light much." The deepening frown said, "Too much."

The friend said, "I have heard that your Great Spirit sent his son to die for the True Man. The love of the Great Spirit is strange." She cast her eyes downward and across toward Wind Maiden.

"Yes, strange." Wind Maiden caught the look of her friend. "The story is like the tale of the great hairless bear we tell our naughty children."

Another dispute. "No tale." Sarah's voice wavered. "Truth. Friends of Son of Great Spirit put in scratchings what they see so we know."

"I do not know." Wind Maiden sounded like a scolding mother. "I cannot understand the bird scratches you say speak to you. I do not hear them speak." She glanced at her friend.

"Scratches — like pictures Lenape draw," explained Sarah. "We have school. You can learn what scratches say." And would Sarah teach this girl to read? They could only argue with one another.

The mouth of Wind Maiden opened, then closed. She said, "No! The Lenni Lenape do not need scratches."

The mother watched her daughter. The folds of skin encasing her eyes crinkled together. "I am old," she said. She looked back at Sarah. "I would learn to hear these markings if my eyes could hear more clearly."

Sarah rubbed her lips with her hand. Her other hand fumbled inside her cape. She pulled her handkerchief from her waist and rubbed the embroidered fringe with her fingers. She dabbed her mouth. She looked at Wind Maiden. The girl was watching the handkerchief. The face, unguarded for the moment, was that of a small child yearning after a trinket she could not have.

Sarah glanced at the handkerchief. Embroidered threads of blue, white, and gold encircled the white linen which was engraved with the initials in blue, "S.H."

Sarah reached the handkerchief toward Wind Maiden. "This is yours," she said.

Wind Maiden drew back, glanced at her friend, cast an accusing eye at Sarah, looked back at the handkerchief, and withdrew it from Sarah's hand.

~ ~ ~

"Brother Christoph! I am pregnant, and I thought you should learn from me before the entire village of Goschachgunk tells you." Sarah swished the shirt in the water and lathered it with lye soap. That was how she would tell him.

She, with the sisters, knelt at the river's edge. Warm and sunny, the days had rolled into May. Surely, the other sisters knew, too, though she did not show.

"Ho, Sister," called Sister Martha to Elizabeth, "another pounding and your shirt will be a cobweb floating in the water."

"I wash my shirt. Close your mouth and wash your own," mumbled Elizabeth.

"But you wash one shirt three times," laughed Martha. "Do you forget? And do you eat and sleep for three because you forget what you have done before? Do not whimper; I shall remind you. "

Elizabeth grunted at Martha.

"Sister, you wash tales in the water today," scolded Sister Amelia.

Martha glanced at the full belly of Amelia, pregnant with her third child. "Ah," chirped Martha, "I saw your hands waving a stroud in the air, rubbing and shaking it. Did you think you had reached the water? No ... but you could not see over the bundle on your belly."

"Brother Zundel, may I say, 'Christoph,' now that you will be a father of my ... um ... our child?" Sarah shook her head. She pounded the shirt with a flat rock.

"Foolish chatter," said Anna Benigna from beside Sarah. "A song will pull our gaze from earth to sky."

Sarah felt all eyes upon her. "I can sing in my words," she offered.

"Yes," agreed Anna Benigna. "I shall change the words, and we shall learn."

In Bethlehem, they would have sung, all together, all in rhythm to the hymn and to the pounding of the work. And in Bethlehem, they would tell her what to do.

"Oh, Brother Christoph, I bear a new burden. I am pregnant."

Her voice, small and light, began the song.

~ ~ ~

That night, Brother Zundel crouched in the dark hut. His hands, rough and dirt-worn, held a bowl of stew. His shirt was splotched with perspiration. He was tired. Perhaps she could wait until tomorrow.

How could she wait? Her head pounded with her secret.

"Can you help in the field tomorrow?" he asked.

She nodded. And would he not be surprised and embarrassed if the Indians from Goschachgunk told him first?

"Good," he said.

He chewed and added, "The fence now surrounds the northern slope of field."

She nodded.

She must try. She would burst unless she tried.

"Brother Zu ... Christoph!"

He lowered his bowl to the dirt. His head rose. A slow smile spread across his face. "Sarah."

"I do not want to offend. I ..." She gulped. "I ... yet ... how improper it must sound to not call you ... to not ... like everyone else ... when I ... we ... should ..." She would soon scream. ". . .a. . .a baby. "

His mouth formed into a circle. His head rose up, then down. "You are pregnant." Was he pronouncing a benediction over her condition? He watched her. He said, again, "You are pregnant." Was this consent? Could the baby now grow? "Sarah ..."

She was numb. She stared at him.

"Sarah. You are pregnant?"

A question. "Yes." She gulped the words and nodded.

He reached out and pulled her to him. The bowl of stew spilled onto the ground. "Sarah ..." He stroked her hair. He slid his hand down, down to her abdomen and pressed it there. "Do not ever again address me as 'Brother Zundel.' I detest the sound."

7
OCTOBER 23, 1776 – NOVEMBER 29, 1776

"Stand beside Netawatwes, your grandfather. He is old and must lean against you. Why do you build your fire here in this Pasture of Light when the light of Netawatwes dims because you have taken away your flame?" Red Face, his legs spread wide, his arms folded, scowled at Grey Bear.

Wind Maiden pressed her carved wooden bowl against her chest and stared along the street of Pasture of Light. This Salah ... this big-bellied Salah ... where did she hide?

"Friends." Grey Bear looked first at Red Face and then at One-Who-Runs. "My grandfather says I have chosen a wide field in which to build my fire where neither damp earth below nor rotting tree limbs above can disturb my blaze." He clasped the shoulder of One-Who-Runs. "You come here often so you should know. Here, we can hear the words of the Saviour who lifted from my back and bore for me the weight of sorrow for the scalps I have taken in battle. The Saviour removed the unquenchable thirst that burned in my throat and stomach for fire water. The water flowing from the Saviour fills me now."

He squeezed the shoulder of One-Who-Runs. Wind Maiden wanted to slap the mouth of Grey Bear.

"Bring your wife and mother. Give yourself to the Saviour and dwell here," urged Grey Bear.

"The Saviour of the White Man," snarled Wind Maiden to herself. "Let One-Who-Runs take the silent river to live among fools like himself. I can find a warrior, and I can become strong."

Red Face stepped forward: "The White Man enslaves the True Man with lies. Our Great Spirit spits vengeance toward all who wander from the paths of our fathers."

"Yes," grunted Wind Maiden. These were the words of Fish-of-the-Deep-Water in the mouth of Red Face.

One-Who-Runs clasped the hand of Grey Bear which still clutched his shoulder. "Friend. I must sip your words and roll them through my mouth before I can learn if they gush from a pure stream."

"A puppy ... pooh ..." murmured Wind Maiden.

"I warn you," continued One-Who-Runs, "that some True Men hate your Saviour. They will try to kill you."

"I have gone under the water and have come up a new lenno. I am John. I do not fear sorceries as once Grey Bear did. I shall cry out what the Saviour has done for me and what he can do for all men. This is the command of the Mighty One."

"Fool." Wind Maiden stepped backward, turned, and hurried between two cabins.

This White teacher, this Salah ... Only once since Salah had given her the linen with the braided edges had Wind Maiden seen her. One-Who-Runs had prodded Wind Maiden to Pasture of Light to hear more speeches. But Wind Maiden had not borne her gift then so she had not stopped to return the greeting which Salah had offered. Now she carried the gift.

Often, Wind Maiden slid her linen through a buckle upon her shirt. She wore it now. With a finger, she rubbed its rough edge. Salah had known that the cloth belonged to Wind Maiden, and Wind Maiden had taken it because linen, ribbon, bells, buckles ... they all belonged to her.

She looked across the field. Maize still stood to dry, but the other crops were almost harvested. Some women wandered through the rows of squash, gleaning the remnants. She waited.

From the hut of cackling hens appeared a woman, round like a fat-bellied bear. Wind Maiden hurried toward her.

"I am happy to greet you," said Salah as she stood straight, one hand pressed against her back, the other cradling a basket of eggs.

"Yes. And I greet you," replied Wind Maiden.

"Share eggs," offered Salah, reaching out the basket.

"No!" barked Wind Maiden. Would this White woman give, again, before Wind Maiden could give back to her? "I have brought these for you." She thrust out the bowl from her own chest and presented the grass and leaves and roots which she had gathered.

Salah gazed down into the brown, grey, green offering. "Yes ... What is ..." she began.

Wind Maiden frowned. "She is a puppy who has not learned the ways of the bitch when it bears young."

"This and this you must break," she said, pointing to the grass and leaves. "This you boil." Now she pointed to the roots. "And pour its juice over these," she concluded, indicating the grass and leaves.

"Yes ..." began Salah.

"Then you drink it." A foolish puppy. Must Wind Maiden even teach it how to drink? "It will take away pain and make your baby sleep inside you. Soon, he will kick in anger and scream to get out. But this will tell him to wait and sleep until your body pushes him out."

Wind Maiden had spoken wisely. "It is good," she thought, "that I have come to care for the foolish White woman."

"Oh ..." The mouth of Salah smiled, but clouds covered her eyes. "I am grateful."

Should Wind Maiden heed the words and the mouth, or should she heed the eyes? These White people, even these Quaekel Black Coats, could not be expected to both speak and look the truth. They were a mixed people and not pure like the True Man.

Why would Salah not be grateful? Wind Maiden squeezed small her eyes to think. No reason. Then Salah was glad.

So Wind Maiden said, "I shall boil the water so you can drink."

Wind Maiden gathered water gurgling through rocks from a rivulet. She poured the water into a small kettle and boiled it over the fire in the cabin of Salah. She dropped the roots into the bubbling water. Wind Maiden broke the leaves and grass into small pieces. They waited. Salah sat upon a stool, watching the fire.

The cabin ... it was large, larger than the newly-built cabin of Star-at-Dawning, and four slept there. Wind Maiden glanced down between her feet to the smooth, flat wood. She gazed up toward the fire.

"Why does the Quaekel build his fire against the wall and not in the center where all can sit around it and be warmed?" inquired Wind Maiden.

Salah looked up at Wind Maiden. She said, "We catch smoke in hole along wall and pull it out of cabin."

Wind Maiden raised her head. She liked that. Memories of burning eyes when the wind sealed the smoke in her cabin taught her that long holes to carry up the smoke could be of much use. But she would not say this. She said, "Better to build the fire in the center of the room where all can sit and sleep in warmth." She frowned and nodded and did not believe her own words.

"I hear wiseness in your words," said Salah.

Wind Maiden closed her eyes and sealed her mouth. "Yes," she thought, "very wise."

When Wind Maiden had prepared the beson in her bowl, she smelled its steaming contents and offered it to Salah. "The smell will whine, 'Do not drink me,'" she explained. "Do not listen. It does not like to share its secrets."

Salah took the bowl from the hands of Wind Maiden but did not draw it to herself. "I shall drink …"

"Now!" commanded Wind Maiden. "While it is hot. It speaks best through warmth."

Salah lifted the potion to her lips and drank twice. "The smell does tell me not to drink," she admitted. "Not easy to fight against the smell." She drank again, quickly now. She smiled and offered the bowl back to Wind Maiden.

"You leave some," observed Wind Maiden. "But you have taken enough; it is good."

They sat in silence. From outside, the voice of One-Who-Runs mingled with the voice of one of the Black Coats, the husband of Salah.

"… Two nights ago the runners returned," One-Who-Runs, the messenger, was saying.

The voice of the husband of Salah rumbled with muted sounds.

"Not good," One-Who-Runs replied, his voice crisp like a snapping twig. "The Delamatteno is a rash people."

"Rash!" thought Wind Maiden. "The rabbit calls them rash because they prepare to fight the Big Knife."

During the time when the earth was raised around the maize, the Delamatteno had said to the Lenni Lenape, "We advise our cousins to keep good shoes in readiness to join the warriors." But the Lenni Lenape refused to hear.

"The Lenape should no longer be the elder of the nations," decided Wind Maiden. "The Delamatteno should now bear the name of 'grandfather.'"

Wind Maiden closed her eyes. If she were a man, she would be a warrior. She would be free and she would fear no one.

"Water?" offered Salah.

"Yes," replied Wind Maiden, looking up.

She watched Salah rise and waddle, pour from a jug, and waddle back.

"How long?" asked Wind Maiden, sipping from the cup and watching from behind its rim.

"Two moons longer," said Salah.

"… The Lenni Lenape cries, 'Peace!'" One-Who-Runs was saying.

Peace with the White Man? The Lenni Lenape would never gain peace until the White Man fled from this land or died, decided Wind Maiden.

She gazed, again, over the rim at Salah. White woman. Dwelling on the land of the Lenape. Was she the enemy? Salah was pushing loose strands of hair back under her white cap. She rubbed her eye and almost yawned. Could a pregnant puppy be an enemy? Wind Maiden did not know.

"Eggs?" offered Salah.

Wind Maiden looked away. Another gift to return.

Silently, they sat. Wind Maiden watched the White woman rub her back, leaning forward on her stool.

"Yes, tonight," One-Who-Runs continued.

"Who will catch your little one when he falls?" asked Wind Maiden.

"Falls? Um ... Anna Benigna, the wife of Isaac Glikkikan will ... catch," answered Salah.

Wind Maiden watched her press her hand against the side of her belly. "The wife of Glikkikan, she would know, but these other women ..." Wind Maiden waved her hand to include all of the Pasture of Light, "... Do they know?" She leaned forward: "Star-at-Dawning, she can help. So can her sister, As-the-Water-Flows." Wind Maiden did not really believe that As-the-Water-Flows knew much, but she would tell stories. Salah would not even remember the pain after As-the-Water-Flows finished speaking.

The eyes of Salah opened like the eyes of an owl.

"Send a runner when the time comes," advised Wind Maiden, rising. She glanced toward the table where the basket of eggs lay. "I can take eggs now," she said.

In the street, Wind Maiden found One-Who-Runs still talking to the husband of Salah. Red Face was gone. Impatient with the dronings of the White teacher, he would have hurried away.

Wind Maiden glanced behind. Salah had accompanied her guest from the cabin.

One-Who-Runs saw them approach. "We go now," he said to Wind Maiden.

"Rest here for the evening meal and for the night meeting," suggested the husband of Salah.

"The Black Coat will always try to snare the weak rabbit," thought Wind Maiden.

"We shall light the council fire in Goschachgunk tonight to hear the messengers who return today from the land of the Delamatteno. I must listen and remember."

One-Who-Runs looked down at the bowl in the hands of Wind Maiden. "We are grateful for the eggs," he said, smiling at Salah.

"Grateful? We do not need to be grateful to the White woman. I shall return the gift," thought Wind Maiden.

"Your wife is generous with me," answered Salah. "My gift is small and I am grateful."

Wind Maiden gazed at this White woman. Salah could not be the enemy.

~ ~ ~

"I shall leave him soon," whispered South-Wind-Blowing. "The next moon, perhaps. I shall find a better hunter. More beads." She jingled the beads around her neck, smiling. "Leave the rabbit. More wampum and beads," she coaxed.

"Yes," Wind Maiden agreed. "Soon." And part of her said, "No. Now!" But she replied softly, "Soon."

Wind Maiden and South-Wind-Blowing knelt together beneath a window opening of the council house. Other women stood or crouched near them. They waited to hear.

Inside the council house, the fire was lit. Fish-of-the-Deep-Water would sit in the circle of the councilors. One-Who-Runs would stand to hear.

"Brothers. You sent us to the Sandusky country to say to our grandchildren, 'Sit down. Reflect on the misery you have brought upon yourselves by taking up the hatchet in the last war between the Saggenash and the French.'" The women listened to the voice of Captain White Eyes and pretended not to hear.

"Brothers!" cried White Eyes. "We laid the heavy burden of this message at the feet of our grandchild, the Delamatteno, but he cast us out toward Fort Detroit of the Saggenash to offer our burden.

"Brother!" The voice of White Eyes rose toward weeping. "The chief of the council at Fort Detroit chopped up our peace belts which we offered him. He threw them at our feet. Brothers! He nicked us like dogs and warned us to leave quickly or bear the guilt for more kickings. He spat insults into my face and warned me to leave lest I lose my scalp. Brothers! They mocked our words of peace."

"The peace messengers are waddling women whose tongues were tied with twine because they spoke like children." Wind Maiden leaned her head against the rough wood of the cabin. "White Eyes, brave war captain of the Lenape. May his sighs shame us toward battle."

Wind Maiden saw proud warriors crouching in shadows, waiting for the enemy. She could not see the enemy. Who was he?

~ ~ ~

Wind Maiden was pushing a stick through the ashes of the fire of the Aged Woman when One-Who-Runs returned from the thick-puffing council fire. She watched him wrap the blanket around the Aged Woman who glanced up from her son, her eyes flowing across the face of Wind Maiden. The cold, flowing river washed away the moss of Wind Maiden's pond and exposed the deep, hidden, crawling things. Wind Maiden clutched her arms around herself and shivered in her nakedness.

When One-Who-Runs left, Wind Maiden flung her stick into the fire and hurried after him. Outside, she regrew the moss and hid the murky depths. She floated upon the pond with stillness, for already the stench rose up; and she did not want to stir what hid below.

Inside their cabin, One-Who-Runs said, "White Eyes, the peace messengers, and Chief Netawatwes will carry, tomorrow, the burden of our insult to the council fire at Fort Pitt where our friends ..."

"Big Knives ... friends?" mocked Wind Maiden to herself.

"... will hear of the betrayal of the Delamatteno."

"Betrayal. Who betrays?" wondered Wind Maiden, sitting, legs folded, upon her bench.

"I shall run before the messengers to Fort Pitt." One-Who-Runs lay his carrying bag below the bench of Wind Maiden. "Pack tassmanane and dry meat for my journey."

"He will bring back only words from Fort Pitt," thought Wind Maiden. "Nothing that jingles and shines. Let someone else run. "

She said aloud, "You must return by the Hunting Time. Much buck skin ..."

"Yes. The Hunting Time," replied One-Who-Runs.

He pulled his moccasins from off his feet and sat down upon her bench. "Do not frown," he said, placing his hands on her waist. "Your face is like the rock fish when you frown."

Wind Maiden pushed her mouth into a deeper scowl. "Rock fish, no," she thought. "I will not be caught in a net and eaten." She tried to pull away, but his hands held her.

"Why do you coil?" he inquired, his mouth quivering.

"Rabbit," thought Wind Maiden. She said, "I want wampum and beads. South-Wind-Blowing wears bright beads and buckles and ribbons."

"You have buckles, beads, and ribbons," said One-Who-Runs.

"Not enough," she moaned.

"I shall trade my blanket for beads in Fort Pitt," he promised.

"Not enough," she thought.

"And perhaps the Great Spirit will allow me to kill many bucks in the Hunting Time," concluded One-Who-Runs.

Wind Maiden had heard him speak those words before.

One-Who-Runs stroked her hair and stared into her eyes. She looked back. His gaze was unsettled like a pond whose muddy waters were stirred. His pond hid no crawling things. She felt blackness coat her inside, and she did not hate him. She hated herself.

~ ~ ~

Netawatwes and the messengers had been gone sixteen nights when the runner from Fort Pitt cried through the streets, "Netawatwes is no more!"

Wind Maiden heard from the hut of her separation, for her time had come and she bled. She heard the wails of the old women as they walked through the streets: "Aooooo ... He is no more! Our chief is no more!"

He had died upon the soft, bearskin-covered mat of an aged man. Netawatwes was dead.

But had he not died long ago, spread out upon the wide and long mat of weakness because he sniveled in peace instead of whooping in war? His body was dead. Wind Maiden did not care. His spirit had departed long before.

She rocked on the dirt floor, a tattered blanket wrapped about her. She wanted to run to the cabin of Star-at-Dawning, sit on a bench, and watch in the light of the fire the round body with its sagging breasts.

She ate the bread and water left outside her hut by her mother, but she did not see her mother. She waited. Maybe the body of Netawatwes would appear from Fort Pitt after the redness had ceased to flow. Then she could walk and howl and watch his body slide beneath the earth ... and receive trinkets and linen from his family.

But, in two nights, the box bearing Netawatwes appeared for the burying, and the redness still flowed.

"Grandfather Fire and all the spirits laugh at me," she told herself. "They say, 'She is a green leaf, fallen early from a tree. Let us lift her upon the wind and fling her through the air.'" These words and many others Wind Maiden wove into a carrying bag of bitterness, filled the bag with anger, and bowed beneath its load.

Wind Maiden crouched at the door opening of her hut to watch the burial; but, staring from the dirt, what could she see? She knew that One-Who-Runs had returned, but she would not see him until her stream was dry. She flicked her hand and shook her shoulders because she did not care.

When the stomps and the rustlings, the moans and the wails had moved through Goschachgunk toward the field, Wind Maiden scurried after.

Two Black Coats from Pasture of Light and four True Men carried the box upon their shoulders. Chiefs and captains followed, then the other men, and, finally, the women. With the women rose the wails.

Cries snapped in the air as four women grabbed the body, commanding it to rise up and come back to them. But it said no, it would lie where it was. So they lowered the wooden box beneath the earth and covered it with soil and placed a carved wooden marker above its head whose curves said that a great chief lay there beneath the earth. The people groaned.

Then she saw him. He moved among the men like a pacing panther. She could see only his back ... the wide, wide shoulders, the muscles.

Far away, beneath a tree, hidden like a fawn in shadow, she quivered. Her head filled with dizziness. Her cheeks flamed. Slowly, she crept back toward Goschachgunk. Black Wolf had returned.

"Friend!" called a voice from her side.

Wind Maiden snapped her body sideways. The foolish White woman waddled toward her. "Get away," murmured Wind Maiden. "I bleed."

The White woman smiled and walked closer. Could she not hear? Or hearing, could she not understand?

"Go!" croaked Wind Maiden. "Because of the power."

Salah hesitated. "I do not fear power." She glanced back toward the field of burying. "I sat to rest ... I could not follow ..." She raised her brows. She bit her lip.

Silly full-bellied Salah. "You are foolish and do not understand." Could Wind Maiden be angry with an ignorant child? "The power can drain strength from the legs of hunters and boldness from the hearts of warriors and ..." She paused and stared at the belly full of baby, "... life from the big belly of a woman. Go." Why could she not understand?

Salah stopped. "I do not fear power. I honor you," she said.

Wind Maiden turned and fled.

Upon the day following the burial of Netawatwes, Wind Maiden arose from her hut of separation. She cast aside the stroud of filth and washed the dirt of her shame from herself. She pulled over her shivering body another shirt and stroud and returned to her own cabin. One-Who-Runs sat before the door. He arose and led her inside.

"I am glad to return to you," he said.

Wind Maiden knew he waited for her greeting, but she hid it from him. She was not glad that he had returned.

"I gathered wood for the fire," he said.

"I shall prepare the meal," she replied, for that was what she was supposed to say.

When she placed before him his bowl, he put into her hands his gifts. "Buckles, ribbons, beads," he said. "For my blanket. I told them the blanket had cost me much in pelts, but they laughed and said that a smart trader had stolen pelts from a foolish Indian. They would give me no more than these." He looked at the gifts which Wind Maiden had spread out before her.

"I am grateful," she said, and she was.

She smiled as she placed the ribbons onto her shirt and rolled the beads in her hands. "I shall place them on a strand and tie it around my neck," she said.

Then she thought. One-Who-Runs had joined the burial procession. Had he taken gifts from Netawatwes? The family and friends would keep nothing he had owned, and Netawatwes had owned much.

She spoke without looking up. She did not wish to see the face of her husband. "You took gifts from his family?" She did not speak the name of the dead chief. It would stir the mind and spark sadness.

One-Who-Runs did not speak. Wind Maiden lifted her head. His eyes stared beyond her. His mouth was pressed together.

He looked at her and said, "I could not take any gifts. I would see them and remember. I wish to forget the pain."

"But I would feel no pain," she thought. Her mind was dark against her husband. She gazed at the gifts. They looked small and very few. "Nuts stored by a squirrel," her mind said. She pushed the nuts onto the bench and stood.

She knew that he watched her and that his eyes grew small and his mouth fell open, but she did not turn to look at him. She heard him arise and leave the cabin. She did not watch him go. Her mind ran through the forest to escape from him. But, always, she heard his slow, sad steps pursuing her.

~ ~ ~

The new treaty had been signed at Fort Pitt. The Lenni Lenape would clothe himself in the stroud of peace and would urge his grandchildren to dress as he dressed.

Then the despised word arose and the True Man recoiled from the Big Knife. Those who sat at Fort Pitt had chosen a new chief for the nation. They said that the True Man would weep less if the new chief would speedily guide the people from the burial ground of sorrow. They pointed to Gelelemend, a grandson of Netawatwes.

"The chiefs of the Wolf Tribe and of the Turkey Tribe have not chosen him!" cried the people. "He is not our chief." For they knew that Gelelemend was weak and that this pleased the Big Knife. So they had no chief. And the sorrow of the nation was very great.

War parties of Delamatteno who had betrayed the word of the grandfather and war parties of Mengwe, to whom the Lenni Lenape was not the grandfather and who could never be trusted, roamed near the land of the Lenape.

The Big Knife at Fort Pitt advised all White Men to leave the land beyond the Ohio. The traders disappeared from among the villages. Only the Black Coats remained at Pasture of Light, Huts of Grace, and Beautiful Spring. They were Quaekels and not Big Knives.

The Munsee, the tribe of the Wolf, whispered of departing from the words of the dead and of washing the land with the blood of the Big Knife. Many believed that these words were first lifted into the air and set on wing by Captain Pipe who lit his fire nearby along the Walhonding. But his mouth was closed and his hands were hidden. Therefore, few knew what his hands said in secret.

Once, Wind Maiden sat in the dwelling of Fish-of-the-Deep-Water and heard his words to Red Face and Eagle-with-White-Head. She sat beside her mother. Fish-of-the-Deep-Water said, "The True Man must never listen to the honey-dipped words of the White Man; for when the honey is licked away, the gun barrel appears. The Big Knife at Fort Pitt or the Saggenash at Detroit, they both dip their rifles in the same barrel of honey. The True Man must not fight for the Big Knife or the Saggenash. He must fight for himself."

"Yes," agreed Red Face.

Eagle-with-White-Head shook his head; he did not know.

Wind Maiden sealed her hands in fists and shouted, "Yes," inside herself. Only Star-at-Dawning heard and looked at her.

Another time, Wind Maiden listened to the words of One-Who-Runs and Eagle-with-White-Head as they sat outside her cabin eating sun-bright squash from its gourd which she had baked in the warm ashes of her fire.

"My brother," said One-Who-Runs, "I remember the words of our chief before he died. The words of a dying man flow upon the rivers of truth. He said, 'Follow peace. Be not led over the false path of promises. Learn the lesson of our weeping after the last war between White Men. They smoked the pipe of peace, and we licked our wounds alone. Hear our brothers, the Black Coats. They speak from hearts of love. They bring the good words about the Saviour, and they speak for peace. Their words are a straight path. Follow them.'"

Wind Maiden thought, "Netawatwes was like a tree that can no longer fight the wind but must break. He is dead. And One-Who-Runs is dead with dead man's words. I live."

"I do not know, my friend, what thoughts to hear," said Eagle-with-White-Head. "I shall carry them with me and listen to them often until I know their worth."

"The words of One-Who-Runs are roots of sleep," thought Wind Maiden.

Later, when she laid the bowl of ground, dried deer meat and beans before the Aged Woman, she was still mumbling about her husband who stored words in his head. She could not cook words for food to fill the stomach or trade words for blankets and linen. Words could not heat a cabin; and when planted, they did not grow and bear fruit.

Wind Maiden saw but would not see the eyes of the Aged Woman flowing over her face. "Water of filth," she thought. She knew the eyes and silent mouth were calling to her, but she would not hear. She turned her back to the gurgling stream and added wood to the fire. "You whirl in my ear," Wind Maiden thought. "Flow away!" Her mouth twitched, forced down on the sides by weights of hatred.

She hurried from the cabin of the Aged Woman. She would take hemp to the cabin of South-Wind-Blowing, she decided. They could sit together and laugh at garments of foolish words. The wind blew. She pulled her blanket around her body.

He stood where emptiness had stood a moment before ... Black Wolf. He watched her walking toward him. He did not move. She wanted to run away. She did not. She looked. His eyes said, "Follow." They said more that she could not understand.

She told her eyes to say, "Leave as you left before," but she did not think they obeyed. She told her feet to walk past. They did. She looked back; she had to. Black Wolf was gone.

Wind Maiden did not go to the cabin of South-Wind-Blowing. She lay in her own cabin. "I have a sickness," she thought. "Sorcery." Her hair throbbed and bled where Laughing One had slashed it. The blood drained from her body; she was dying.

When death betrayed her and did not come, she arose. Her mouth burned for water. She left the cabin and wandered toward the Elk's Eye. She felt his gaze. When she looked, no one was there. She saw him where he was not, and, always, his eyes called her.

Wind Maiden held the water in her hands and lifted it to her mouth. As she drank, her eyes searched the land. She was a hunted fawn, fleeing from the wolf. The fawn was uncertain in its flight, running from but ever nearer its enemy.

~ ~ ~

"Prepare food," said One-Who-Runs that evening. "I shall leave tomorrow to hunt deer."

Wind Maiden breathed quickly. The cabin held no air. She did not want him to leave.

She said, "The traders hide beyond the Beautiful River. Will you go there to trade?"

"We shall eat the flesh and prepare the skins. Then we shall wait until the traders return," replied One-Who-Runs.

Wind Maiden closed her eyes. They pulsed red inside.

One-Who-Runs continued, "I shall not roam far. We must watch the land, for many snakes slide over it now."

He laid his blanket on the dirt floor of the cabin. He took Wind Maiden's hand and urged her near him. "Tonight ..." he whispered.

Wind Maiden said nothing but bent to her knees. She pleaded with him inside herself: "Become a hunter and a warrior. I must have a hunter. Destroy the rabbit. I run. Do not let me fall."

They slid their bodies smoothly beside each other. "Become the wolf," she pleaded.

8
DECEMBER 8, 1776 – DECEMBER 9, 1776

It was the Hunting Time. One-Who-Runs had left eight nights before. And the Wolf hunted, too, or had returned to his lair, for his print was not seen upon the streets of Goschachgunk.

"Good," Wind Maiden murmured. "I spit upon the wolf." She said these words again and told herself it was good that she had spoken them.

Tonight, the sky was a forest of clouds which chased away the stars and banished the moon. It would rain. Wind Maiden had piled wood along the inside wall of her cabin. She had not carried wood to a dry place for the Aged Woman. Smoking wood for one who did not gather her own was wood enough for her.

Wind Maiden ate her stew of fish and beans from a brown gourd. Maybe she would visit South-Wind-Blowing and hear whispered words about the Lenape village on the Walhonding. Some built fires there who had once lit blazes in Goschachgunk. She did not think the names, but the feeling moved in her body that Black Wolf and Laughing One dwelt there.

Something rustled outside her cabin. Wind Maiden clunked down her gourd. Jonah, a believing lenno from Pasture of Light, appeared at the door opening.

She heard him before he spoke. "Sister Salah," he panted.

Wind Maiden grabbed her carrying bag and blanket. As she passed Jonah, she said, "We come."

She hurried first to the cabin of As-the-Water-Flows because As-the-Water-Flows would be asleep and rise slowly and store a heavy bag of words upon her back which would take much time to pack and carry.

"The time for Salah," said Wind Maiden when she roused her.

As-the-Water-Flows spoke before she awoke. "The winds spoke to me yesterday and said ..."

"The time for Salah," repeated Wind Maiden.

As-the-Water-Flows looked up at Wind Maiden: "The time for Salah," she repeated. "Once, I saw three ... no, four small ones slide from between a mother's legs. It was the snow of the black ..."

"Throw away your words," scolded Wind Maiden, "or you will not see this small one fall."

"Let As-the-Water-Flows choke upon her mouthful of words," thought Wind Maiden as she left.

"The time for Salah," said Wind Maiden to her mother when she found her in the cabin of another woman old as she.

Slowly, Star-at-Dawning arose and shuffled through the village. From her cabin, she gathered leaves, grass, roots, and food and packed them into the bag of Wind Maiden.

Wind Maiden watched the movements of her mother — careful and patient. On other nights, those movements spoke rest to Wind Maiden's body. Tonight, they made her jump inside.

"I shall run before," she said, lifting the bag. She could be standing over Salah before Star-at-Dawning had even waddled through Goschachgunk.

"No, walk with me," advised her mother.

"The baby may not wait for us," argued Wind Maiden, adjusting the strap upon her forehead. She had told Salah that she would help. The burden was hers. And Salah was weak ... and foolish ...

"What will you do when you get there?" Her mother grunted as she leaned over to take another blanket from her bench. "Why must you run when you have never followed this trail?"

The lower lip of Wind Maiden rolled out.

Star-at-Dawning wrapped the blanket about herself. "It will wait. It will wait until you no longer want to wait." She patted the chest of her daughter. "Walk with me."

"Does the Snowfall come?" asked Star-at-Dawning as Wind Maiden led her through the village.

"I do not know," snapped Wind Maiden. "Let her follow if she can. Her words are wild horses. Let them drag her through the forest."

They had not yet reached the narrowing of the trail when they heard behind them the chipmunk chatter of a voice.

The shuffling steps of Star-at-Dawning ceased. "I do not need to stop," Wind Maiden told herself. But her feet did not heed her; they waited.

"An elm tree bowed and greeted me — there, beside the river," said As-the-Water-Flows when she saw them. "He invited me to sit beneath his branches and talk. 'An elm among sycamores grows lonely,' he lamented." She shook her legs and smiled at Star-at-Dawning.

"A winding tale. I shall not follow it," thought Wind Maiden. She leaned forward and resumed the journey.

The footsteps of Star-at-Dawning followed, pursued by the light, pattering step of As-the-Water-Flows. Vining through all steps was the story of the elm tree, then the tale of how the Snowfall had learned tree language during the time of the big wind.

Ten lenno sat around a fire near the Elk's Eye at Pasture of Light. "We are praying for our sister and the baby," said a woman, not Lenape but Mahicanni, Wind Maiden decided. "We are made glad by your arrival," they all said.

The wife of Glikkikan met them at the cabin door. "The pains are not often," she said.

Smoking fires in hanging pots lit the cabin in hazy light. The husband of Salah sat beside her on their high, wide, sleeping bench.

"No men. Leave," Wind Maiden mumbled.

Salah lifted herself onto her elbows. "I am glad to see you," she murmured. Her face looked pale against dark hair pulled back into a thick braid. She wore a linen shirt, not the grey stroud that always before Wind Maiden had seen. Beneath a blanket lay the mound of stomach. Small and weak. Salah — no enemy.

Star-at-Dawning approached the bed. She stood beside it, saying nothing. Wind Maiden watched from the shadows. Even As-the-Water-Flows dammed her mouth.

"The thumping of the heart is stilled because you come," said the husband.

He took the hand of Salah and spoke to her the blunted words of his people. Salah nodded and smiled. He left.

Star-at-Dawning leaned forward and placed her hand on the stomach of Salah. With her fingers, she listened. Soon, the stomach jumped and Salah groaned. Star-at-Dawning grunted. "The small one awaits the sunrising before he will abandon his warm home," she said to Salah. "He is wise. He knows sorrows lie in wait for him."

Wind Maiden crouched against the wall. She was cold inside. She had never seen a woman bear her young. She had seen a black-speckled bitch bring forth its puppies ... alone. It cleaned each pup and ate the cord. No one had helped it, and it bore eight. A woman dropped only one, not many. Why could not Salah bear and clean her own alone?

"Fill the kettle with water," said Star-at-Dawning to Wind Maiden.

When Wind Maiden re-entered the cabin, she heard, first, the voice of As-the-Water-Flows. The dam had burst. The water would flood the cabin.

"Four young," jabbered As-the-Water-Flows to the wife of Glikkikan. "She had four young that night. I walked across the frozen river to help. Took each child, washed it, wrapped it in rabbit fur. One died. It gazed at me before it died and said, "Why should I live when I can follow the shortest path of all to the land of the Great Spirit?"

Wind Maiden rolled her eyes. As-the-Water-Flows was supposed to chop off pain from Salah with her tales. Her aim was bad. She chopped into the skull of Wind Maiden, instead.

Wind Maiden laid the kettle near the fire and looked at Salah. Could a White woman, even a Quaekel, become "friend"? She backed toward the wall.

Through the night, the words of As-the-Water-Flows buzzed around the head and in the ears of Wind Maiden. Why did the wife of Glikkikan laugh? Her laughter swatted As-the-Water-Flows into more frenzied flight. The rain fell before the sun rose, thumping against the bark roof of the cabin. Wind Maiden tried to heed the whisperings of the rain and ignore the words of As-the-Water-Flows .

Sometimes, Salah mumbled in the language of her people. Wind Maiden watched the fire and the ceiling to spy the one who listened and understood. Would the fire speak back in flames or demand tobacco? Was Salah speaking sorceries?

"Tired," whispered Salah to Star-at-Dawning. The spasms tumbled one upon the other now. "Tired," she repeated. The strange mumblings rolled from her mouth, again.

When light pressed through the clouds of the eastern darkness, the husband appeared at the door. "Is she strong?" he asked Star-at-Dawning.

"I do well," rasped Salah, turning her drained face to him.

"Soon," assured Star-at-Dawning.

The husband walked to the bed and clasped the hand of Salah. He spoke in their grinding tongue. Water from his hooded cloak dripped to the floor.

"Leave," scolded Star-at-Dawning.

"Quaekels know little," thought Wind Maiden. "The infant will not crawl out while he is here."

The husband disappeared into the rain.

Like waves on the river in a storm, the pains increased. The face of Salah flashed red. The wife of Glikkikan arose and joined Star-at-Dawning by the bed. As-the-Water-Flows slept, her head bowed to her chest.

Why did not Salah squat and let the bundle tumble out? Was she too weak to rise?

Wind Maiden slid along the wall toward Salah. She dipped her linen cloth, the cloth Salah had given her, into a bowl of water. She squeezed it out and stroked the sweating forehead of her ... friend.

Salah glanced up, fumbled for and tapped her hand.

Salah gasped. She cried out and yanked the cords tied to posts above her head. The small one began its journey through the opening. Star-at-Dawning and the wife of Glikkikan moved and bowed together.

Wind Maiden scrambled back against the wall.

She rubbed her hand across the valley of her belly. No baby would ever make a hill grow there.

Water beaded and dripped from the forehead of Salah. She groaned and pushed.

A boy. They wrapped him in a white linen cloth and laid him in the arms of his mother.

The husband hurried in. He pulled aside a fold of the linen and gazed into the red, wrinkled face of his son. He stroked the wet forehead of Salah. She smiled.

When the sun climbed above the trees, Star-at-Dawning, As-the-Water-Flows, and Wind Maiden left. Salah slept. Her husband and the wife of Glikkikan sat and watched.

They pulled their blankets around themselves, for the wind blew though the rain had stopped. Over the muddy trail, they slushed. The voice of As-the-Water-Flows sputtered like a fly awakened in winter. Wind Maiden pulled her blanket over her head and ears. The fly buzzed far away.

Wind Maiden saw, again, the pale then red face of Salah and the small one sliding out. "Salah is foolish. She walks behind the heels of others. I shall be like the hunter and shall follow the trail to the buck." She was not a dog who bore puppies. No, she was not!

9
DECEMBER 9, 1776 – DECEMBER 21, 1776

"Christoph?" Sarah gazed down at him where he slept at the side of the bed, his head cradled in his arms.

He raised his head. "Sarah. How long have you been awake? Are you thirsty?"

"I just awakened ... No — I need nothing."

They stared at their son sleeping beside Sarah.

"Why do you sit on that stool? Come to bed."

"I thought I might harm ..." Christoph hesitated.

"You were awake all night?" she asked.

He rubbed his hand across his forehead: "I remembered my mother. She died in childbirth when I was ten. Last night, I became my father."

Sarah pushed his words into the numbness of her mind.

"I loved the child," continued Christoph, "but my father treated her as if she had caused the death and not ..."

"... not God," thought Sarah.

"I understood this morning," Christoph whispered. "If you had died, I could have hated our son."

"The grace of God ..." began Sarah.

"... prevented it." Christoph forced a smile across his face.

Even Sarah had rested more than he. "Come to bed." She reached toward him.

He stood. His hands combed through his hair. Was he embarrassed?

"I must ... The council at Goschachgunk has asked the brethren to write another letter for them to Fort Pitt. I ... I have to compose it."

"Brother David ..."

"He is visiting Gnadenhutten, and Brother Edwards only arrived in November. I cannot ask him."

Christoph turned to leave. "I should have sent it yesterday, but ..."

Sarah heard only mumblings for his last words.

"A moment," she pleaded. She glanced down at their baby. "He has no name." Before his birth, she had suggested they name him after Christoph's father. Christoph had replied, Perhaps ..." That was all. Sarah did not know the name of Christoph's father.

Christoph returned to her bedside. "I have thought to name him David after Brother Zeisberger."

"And on behalf of the vision," thought Sarah.

"A good name," she said aloud. "David ... Christoph."

Christoph watched their son. "Yes."

"David Christoph Zundel," concluded Sarah. His arms flailed. His nose wrinkled. She tucked tighter the linen wrapping. He settled back into sleep.

"I shall send Sister Anna," Christoph said before leaving.

Sarah leaned over the tiny, red-faced David Christoph and stroked his head. She lay back onto the matting.

Christoph ... she did not deceive herself ... he cared. They could become a family here — in Lichtenau.

She had borne an infant in the wilderness. Indians had assisted her. She had not needed the sisters of Bethlehem. What could be too difficult for her now?

She closed her eyes and remembered the faces of the night before: Anna Benigna, Star-at-Dawning. She felt, again, the cool strokes of the hand of Wind Maiden.

~ ~ ~

"No, Christoph," Sarah laughed. She was sitting on the edge of their bed watching Christoph fit a moccasin onto the foot of David who lay, wide-eyed, in his cradle beside the big bed. "Try both feet. Or perhaps you could slide all of him into it."

Christoph looked up. He smirked. He lifted David. "He is lighter than the moccasin," he said, seating himself beside Sarah on the bed. "True — they do not fit him now. But next week ..." He glanced sideways at Sarah.

Sarah wanted to hug Christoph.

"Sooner, probably," she agreed. They were joking with one another in the same manner that Christoph often jested with the brethren. She yearned to hold the moment and not let it pass.

David clenched his fists and exploded in a sharp wail. She opened her bodice. "He eats voraciously. In three weeks, the moccasins will be too small." She took him from Christoph and nestled him in her arms, his warm face pressed against her breast.

Christoph watched. She tried to pull the bodice around herself. She heard, or felt, Christoph grunt. He stood and walked to his cloak.

Awkwardness took the place of joy. She had thrown away the moment with her modesty.

"Another letter to write," he murmured as he slid on his cloak.

"Christoph ..." She wanted to regain intimacy. "Are you the voice of the Delaware council?" She had managed to sound merely peevish.

He paused. "Yes." He looked back at her. "They want me to report to Fort Pitt that war parties of the Delamatteno and the Mengwe roam near the valley of the Muskingum." He scratched the back of his neck where the coarse wool of his cloak rubbed. "I do not like to write these letters. I am a teacher of the gospel, not a ... spy for the colonies. Brother Heckewelder, he enjoys composing such reports, for his loyalty is with the colonies. Would that he were here and not in Schoenbrunn where the words of the council do not quickly travel.

He scratched his head and pulled up his hood. "Can the Lenni Lenape remain neutral and correspond thus?"

"Christoph ..."

"Sarah, I must go."

"But you could write here." She felt as small as the infant in her arms.

He sighed. "I could not concentrate." His voice inched down into controlled patience. "David cries and you ..." He shook his head and gazed at her.

He disappeared.

Sarah sucked in her lips. She had repulsed Christoph. Yet they had also laughed together. Some things were better than before.

David, milk dripping from his mouth, was dozing in her arms. She pulled him from her and resealed her gown. Raising him against her shoulder, she walked toward the small, high window which faced the street. She looked out. Flurries drifted from a heavy, grey sky. Several brethren, sealed in blankets, wandered toward the fields. She rubbed her son's back.

She walked to her chair near the fire and sat, staring into the crackling flames. She should read her Bible, she knew, but she could not concentrate.

The door clicked open. Wind Maiden stood in the opening.

"Friend." Sarah stood. "Come near. By the fire."

Wind Maiden moved toward her, her blanket sliding from her head to her shoulders and down her back. She settled onto a stool. Sarah pulled her chair nearer.

"I have come to see him," said Wind Maiden, watching Sarah.

Sarah pulled her son from her shoulder and laid him down upon her lap for Wind Maiden to see. "He grows ... twelve nights."

Wind Maiden leaned forward and looked. She cocked her head sideways and stared back at Sarah. "He grows," she repeated.

They sat and did not speak. Sarah snuggled David in her arms. "I am grateful for your help," she said, finally.

"Yes," said Wind Maiden. She turned her head from the fire to watch Sarah.

Sarah squirmed.

A tap upon the door broke the tension. Sarah opened the door. Anna Benigna smiled at her from within her blanket cloak. "Sister. Come in. Our friend is here." Sarah looked back toward Wind Maiden who was frowning past her at Anna Benigna.

"Maize bread," said Anna Benigna, offering Sarah a round, golden loaf.

"Thank you, Sister. Will you share?" She glanced at Anna Benigna and Wind Maiden in turn.

Anna Benigna shook her head, and Wind Maiden looked away.

Had Sarah offended?

"Sit with us," she said to Anna Benigna.

She placed the bread upon the table, laid David in his cradle, and joined Anna Benigna and Wind Maiden beside the fire.

Three now sat in silence.

"Your husband returns from the hunt?" asked Sarah of Wind Maiden.

"Soon," replied Wind Maiden, frowning still. "He is not a hunter and will not return with many pelts."

"He is wise and he is a rememberer," said Anna Benigna. "He is better than a hunter."

"No! The man who cannot hunt is never better than a hunter and a warrior," scolded Wind Maiden. "Are we cattle? Do we eat grass? The hunter brings flesh and makes us strong." Her eyes narrowed. "If he can hunt, then he can hunt the enemy who slays our women and children. Is there another path to honor? No. Other trails are scampered on by frightened women."

Sarah sealed her mouth. She hoped Wind Maiden could not argue with silence.

"The hatchet pounds death into the skull of the Lenni Lenape," said Anna Benigna.

"No! Can the wife of Glikkikan speak such words? You have seen the pride of the great warrior in the face of the Gun Sight. Must I scold an old woman whom I should honor?" Wind Maiden puffed out her words.

"I have seen the pride of the warrior," agreed Anna Benigna. She closed her eyes. Looking up, she asked, "Will you hear a story?"

"Snow begins to fall," replied Wind Maiden. "The time for the storyteller is near. I will hear."

Sarah's face felt warm from the fire's glow. She could easily sleep.

Anna Benigna stared into the eyes of Wind Maiden and began, "Before your eyes beheld the world, the True Man ran beside his father, the French, against the Big Knife village beyond the Beautiful River toward the sun rising. A White woman watched a warrior split open the skull of her husband. She wrapped her infant in her arms, the first child from her body. She fled to the forest.

"But the blood-red hand of a warrior snatched her ... a beaver in a trap. The baby cried. The warrior shoved them toward the other warriors and their captives. She clutched her child to her chest.

"Along narrow trails they ran to escape the Big Knife avengers. The woman stumbled; the baby cried. She pressed him to her cheek, clucked into his ear. He wailed. The warriors shook her and hissed whisperings she could not understand. They pressed their hands across the mouth of her baby until he thrashed in suffocation. She understood — he must not weep.

"She sang hushed chants to him, rocking him in her arms. Her murmurings were sharp with fear; her rockings were frantic. He cried. The warriors argued. They waved their arms at her. The mind of the mother flamed with frenzy. She could not stop the cries.

"She wrapped him in the folds of her stroud, rolled up from her legs. Panting, she ran on. The baby wept; the stroud could not muffle the wailing.

"The warriors stopped. One tall warrior, wider shouldered than the rest and painted with wide, red lines on face and neck, argued with a French brother who pointed at the crying one.

"Her baby, her own flesh, she pressed against herself.

"The warrior stood above the woman and watched the wailing bundle. His hands moved toward it. She lurched back. He bent and yanked her baby from the folds of stroud and from her clutching grasp.

"She screamed.

"He lifted the infant over his head. And hurled. Her son struck a wide tree and slid into silence on the ground. With an empty wail, the mother clutched mute death to her breast."

Anna Benigna bowed her head.

"What woman could endure such suffering?" thought Sarah. She could not. Never.

"The warrior must stop the wail of an infant," said Wind Maiden.

Sarah looked at her.

Wind Maiden sat rigid. She sucked air through her open mouth. "The Big Knife would follow the cry and kill the warriors," she snorted. Her chin quivered a moment before her jaw snapped shut.

Did Wind Maiden struggle to believe her own words?

Anna Benigna raised a tired gaze to Wind Maiden. "They must kill a baby to save the warriors."

"Yes," agreed Wind Maiden, her eyes widening.

Sarah envisioned a brown sparrow fluttering across the ground, trying to soar, holding in its beak a dry crust of bread that was twice its size. Wind Maiden.

Wind Maiden huffed, "We do not care for the life of a small one who cannot lift the hatchet or rifle like a warrior for his people."

Anna Benigna leaned close to Wind Maiden, breathing into her face. "I care," she whispered as if she were the warrior fleeing the enemy. "Glikkikan was the warrior. I was the woman."

10
APRIL 28, 1777 – AUGUST 6, 1777

Slowly, Sister Jungmann arose from the edge of Sarah's bed and reseated herself at the table. She smiled. "Dear Sister," she said, "forgive me. I am wearied from our flight from Schoenbrunn. Such a loss!"

"Her face is pale," thought Sarah as she poured tea and offered sweet bread to her guest. She envisioned the squared-timber cabins of Schoenbrunn, the fields enclosed by rail fences, the fruit trees, the gardens, the cool spring water. Lost now, perhaps forever. Schoenbrunn was overrun by Monsey warriors, and the faithful remnant had retreated with their teachers to Lichtenau.

She glanced down at David Christoph who slept in a low cradle at the foot of the big bed. His cheeks were full; his hair, blond like his father's. A brightly-quilted coverlet lay upon his small, round body. "David," she thought, "Peaceful, ignorant ..."

"These are the days, my dear, when the powers of darkness lay siege upon the kingdom of God," said Sister Jungmann. "They cannot prevail, not for long." She stirred her tea, sipped, and looked over the cup at Sarah.

Sarah glanced up and nodded. Her fingers felt moist; she rubbed them together.

Sister Jungmann continued, "Did I tell you we razed our lovely chapel? Yes, why I am sure I did. But five days ago. So the warriors might not desecrate it. They took the whole village. Why, some of our own brethren ..." She shook her head and stirred her tea.

Sarah shook her head with her sister. She bit her lip. She thought of hideously painted warriors, naked to the waist, running through Schoenbrunn. Schoenbrunn! But Lichtenau was secure. Christoph and Brother David were united and wise; they had not succumbed to rivalry in Lichtenau as had

Brothers Heckewelder and Jungmann in Schoenbrunn. Moreover, they were safe here in the shadow of the Delaware capital, Goschachgunk, the protector of the Brethren. Schoenbrunn, perhaps, but not Lichtenau.

"You must stay with us in our cabin, you and Brother Jungmann, until the brethren can complete your cabin," said Sarah. She allowed herself a slight smile to suggest willingness in having her sister. But she was not willing, not at all. One year before, she would have clutched the hand of her sister and begged her to stay. Now, she was jealous ... how shameful ... of her privacy with Christoph and David. Only here could their small family be alone.

Each day, they arose with the sun. Because the men and most of the women were preparing the fields for planting, Christoph rushed to the plantation after the morning scripture reading while she joined the women in preparing the morning meal. After the meal, the men and women hurried back to the fields. In the afternoon, Christoph usually assisted Brother David in instructing the children at the school. And, tomorrow, Sarah would oversee the soap making. Then, after the evening service, they retreated to their cabin. Christoph read his Bible and jotted notes to organize into messages. She mended Christoph's breeches and played with David. They were alone. He might lay aside his quill to swing David into the air. David would giggle until he hiccuped. Later, Christoph often disclosed to her the revelations he had gleaned from the Epistle of Paul to the Philippians or to the Galatians. She would sit, immobile, lest any twitch of muscle or shift of eye might discourage him from confiding. She hoped that, soon, she might presume to ask him questions on a text.

But, now, they would not be alone.

"Why, our own Brother Augustin ..." Sister Jungmann spoke, staring into her tea. She looked up. "Augustin Newallike. He was a Monsey chief before he came among us. You know this? He gave himself to Christ Jesus, was baptized. Mind this, Sister, a brother!"

Sarah frowned. Augustin Newallike had spread discord among the Schoenbrunn brethren and had encouraged many to flee among the Delamatteno in the Sandusky country.

Of course Brother and Sister Jungmann must stay here with them. How great their suffering had been. And in one week, maybe two, their own cabin would be completed.

"He finally left but many remained, seething with his words — poison," continued Sister Jungmann. "They opposed my husband and denied Him who had redeemed them." She opened her hands in a gesture of helplessness. "What could we do? They who lived among us were no longer our brethren. They plotted to take Schoenbrunn, they and the Monsey warriors, their friends." She looked at Sarah: "What could we do, Sister?"

"God have mercy on their souls," murmured Sarah. They had strayed, heeding the call of the hireling.

105

"Yes, God have mercy on their souls," agreed Sister Jungmann. "And on ours, my dear."

~ ~ ~

"Oh-oh," groaned Sister Elizabeth as she leaned over a large, steaming kettle suspended over an outdoor fire. "It smells like ..." Her nose twitched as she looked around at her sisters, "... like a pool of green slime where the flies buzz." She grinned.

"Phew!" agreed Sister Martha. "Its smell says to me that it cannot clean." She looked at Sarah.

Sarah rubbed her finger between her ribbon and her chin to relieve the stickiness of perspiration. "Scoop the slime off the top of the water."

"Slime, yes," agreed Sister Elizabeth as she lifted a gourd ladle. She shuffled toward the steaming kettle. Her small, fat nose wrinkled. She stepped back and huffed.

Martha thumped her legs and chortled, "Puffing dog. Does your fat hang so heavily on you that a nose twitch makes you pant?"

Sister Elizabeth's small eyes grew round; her lower lip shot forward. "Tongue," she sneered at Sister Martha.

"Sisters!" scolded Sarah. She sucked in her lips to hold back a smile and looked at Martha: "Sin falls from your mouth with foolish words."

Martha lifted her head and dropped her eyes.

"Close your ears to silly prattle," said Sarah to Elizabeth.

Elizabeth bared her teeth at Martha who gazed sideways away.

Sarah smiled. "Dear Sisters, let us finish this making of soap."

As she bent to retrieve the gourd which had fallen from Elizabeth's hand, she saw Wind Maiden watching from beneath the shade of a tree beside the clearing where the three worked.

Wind Maiden emerged from the shadows.

"Silent mouse," murmured Martha as she stirred the fire with a long stick.

Wind Maiden looked at Martha and Elizabeth. Her face was stone.

"Will you talk?" asked Wind Maiden, turning now to Sarah.

Sarah glanced about for a place to sit.

"Not here." Wind Maiden retreated toward the trees.

Sarah looked at each sister, smiled, made stirring movements with her hands, and waved them toward the kettle.

She followed Wind Maiden to a large maple within the darkness of the forest. Its gnarled roots extended their bony bodies across the flesh of the soil. Wind Maiden perched upon an arched root and motioned Sarah to an adjacent seat.

"Those ..." Wind Maiden motioned back toward where Martha and Elizabeth still worked. "They are hollow heads."

Sarah's smile formed and grew. "No," she laughed, "the work empties their heads; teasings and grumblings fill them up, again." Were these the words of a missionary? Sarah gulped; she felt her face redden.

Wind Maiden started to smile then shook her head: "I have come to show you signs; this is not a time to fill gourds with games."

Sarah looked at the girl then at the enclosing forest. Was not this child playing a game?

Wind Maiden's eyes searched the shadows among the trees. Finally, she looked at Sarah but did not speak.

Sarah diverted her eyes. Games. She touched the black soil beside the root. It was cold and moist against her fingers. Even the frowns which Wind Maiden put on were deceptive attire. What emotions did she truly wear? Sarah looked at her.

"We often see One-Who-Runs in the evenings when we sing," said Sarah, breaking the encircling silence. "You do not come with him."

Wind Maiden spoke with flat tones: "I do not know where he goes."

"He is your husband," blurted Sarah.

"Maybe. I only live with him."

Sarah stared at Wind Maiden who frowned and looked past her. "She cares nothing for him?" wondered Sarah. "Then she is a cruel girl and selfish, indeed."

Sarah rustled her skirts and made as if to arise. But Wind Maiden said, "This night past, warriors from Sandusky, ten warriors, pounced upon Goschachgunk. They cried for food, and we did not say, 'No.' They laid out wampum that invited us to fight the Big Knife." She watched Sarah: "I said ... but not to them ... 'Yes! We shall fight.' However, I am a woman and no one hears my voice. My people said, 'No' to the words of the wampum and returned it to the hands of the warriors."

Her smooth features wrinkled into ridges. "The warriors shook the wampum in the face of the Lenape and warned that if we did not take up the hatchet soon, they would mix our blood with the blood of our white-skinned teachers whose scalps would soon ride on sticks to the Detroit of the Saggenash."

Sarah tried to smile. She said, "We hear many warnings."

"It will be as it has been before — rumors, nothing more," she told herself.

"We live among friends," Sarah continued, her smile set upon her face. And Schoenbrunn, was not that town nearby? They had believed themselves among friends as well. "We have nothing to fear from people far away who are not as strong as the Lenni Lenape," she forced herself to conclude.

Wind Maiden thumped the stump with her hands. "The Saggenash are stronger than all. They do not want you among us. They hear whisperings that you persuade the Lenni Lenape against lifting the hatchet." She lowered her voice: "The whisperings are true. You must leave or die." The eyes of Wind Maiden gleamed with the light from a solitary ray of sunshine which pulsed beside Sarah's shoulder.

"Why do you speak to me these words?" asked Sarah. Wind Maiden wanted to slay the colonists, did she not? Why should she care for the lives of a few "white-skinned" teachers?

Wind Maiden replied, "You must leave ... now."

Sarah rubbed the ridge of her cap. "Why should I heed this child? Do not her own words betray her?" she thought. Crass words would not set fear in her heart, draw her from Lichtenau, send her in flight back to Bethlehem.

She looked at Wind Maiden: "You said, 'Yes' to the call of the warriors to kill White Men. Our skin is white. Why do you care what we do?"

Wind Maiden spoke slowly. Was she restraining anger? "The Big Knives kill us, snatch our land, and push us always farther from the land of the rising sun, the home of our fathers. You, Quaekels, are foolish, silly people. You are not Big Knives." Her tone changed and her mouth dropped. "I helped with the child; I brought my mother and her sister to help. You are more foolish than most, and I must watch you so you do not slide into the sinking mud." She looked away from Sarah.

It was not anger but hurt that Wind Maiden hid. Sarah said, her voice small in her throat, "Forgive me, friend. Your words are true; I am foolish. I did not want to hear you so I heard a lie."

Wind Maiden raised her head cocking it sideways, studying Sarah. "Yes," she said. Then, "You will leave now?"

"Oh!" exclaimed Sarah. Wind Maiden was in earnest, certainly. But overly emotional, perhaps. Past warnings had dispersed without fulfillment. Why should not this one? Besides — she, Christoph, they were needed here. And young David? There could not, must not, be danger.

"We cannot leave now," she answered. "The maize, the trees with fruit ... and our people ... we cannot ..."

"Their skin is the color of my skin; their hair is dark, like mine. They will not be killed. You will be killed. The sky will pour rain upon the maize and the earth will push it up. Trees will give fruit; that is what they must do. They do not wait for your word to grow. Go!" Wind Maiden thrust her hands toward Sarah.

"No," thought Sarah. She surprised herself. Did she not want to return to the security of Bethlehem? She could bundle up David and retreat. No one would judge her for it. And she could compel Christoph, not with urgings but with necessity, to accompany them. Why did she panic at Wind Maiden's suggestion?

Why? Because this was her home — her home, Christoph's home, and David's.

She said, "This is not a thing I can say, 'Yes' to. I shall hear the words of my husband."

"You tell him all I have spoken," urged Wind Maiden.

"Yes, all your words," agreed Sarah. She looked around the forest, dense in color — green merging into black — and dense in smell – leaves and stumps and branches decaying into earth. Fight to stay here? God had brought her here. Let Him do what He would.

"The Great One will tell us what to do," she said.

Wind Maiden inhaled. "I know what you must do. I tell you. Go!"

"I must wait," replied Sarah. "Much to decide."

"Do not wait long," warned Wind Maiden as she arose. "Tell your 'Great One' to speak quickly." She turned to leave, murmuring, "If he will speak at all."

"Oh, but He will speak to us," Sarah said, rising. "You will see. We belong to the Saviour."

"I HAVE seen," said Wind Maiden as she slid into the shadows. "The Great Spirit — I only hear him laugh."

Sarah brushed the leaves and bark from her skirt and watched until Wind Maiden disappeared. Lichtenau was secure; why need she worry? She squeezed her hands together. Her breasts felt full; David Christoph would want to nurse. First, the soap making. Sarah hurried back toward the clearing.

"Sister Salah says that you must put your hand to the slime," Sister Elizabeth's voice whined.

"Whew! My nose! She hurts and may fall off. Sister Salah would weep if my nose fell off," the voice of Sister Martha chirped in reply.

"But my nose ..." Sister Elizabeth began.

"... is a fine, fat nose," replied Martha. "It has smelled many foul things. It will smell nicely. Here."

Sarah came upon them as Martha was thrusting a stick into Elizabeth's resisting hands. She could never leave; she was needed ... here.

~ ~ ~

Sarah lifted David from a mat beside Sister Amelia who sat outside her cabin, weaving another mat.

"Your son, he is a good child," said Sister Amelia. "They, they are the small ones that must be watched by this hawk." She laughed, nodding toward six children playing at the river's edge.

David puckered his face. He cried.

"He will eat." Sarah turned toward her cabin.

She stopped. Sister Jungmann had been sickly these past days since her departure from Schoenbrunn. She would be in the cabin, resting. Where, then, could Sarah rest alone? And if she rested, who would churn the butter and set the schmierkaes to curdle? Christoph said that the Indian sisters could do these things if she would find and remind them. But her garden behind their cabin, that was hers. Only she would tend it. And she had hoped to plant herbs today.

Who would harvest what she planted? The warnings of Wind Maiden returned. She wanted Christoph.

Bouncing David against her hip, Sarah hurried toward the school. She pushed in the schoolhouse door.

Boys and girls sat on long benches along the two side walls, facing writing boards extended from the walls. Brother David was leaning over one youth, reading to him a letter in the Unami dialect and showing him the corresponding written symbols. This was Brother David's common practice. His Indian students wrote letters to him in their language, and he corrected those letters and wrote responses.

Brother David glanced up.

"Christoph ..." Sarah mouthed.

He shook his head.

Sarah closed the door.

David was huffing toward a wail. "Patience," she whispered. She walked toward the Muskingum, not its edge where men and boys fished, but above where willows formed a canopy.

She snuggled down upon the ground where she could watch the water flow. As David sucked, his eyes closed; his small head nestled against her. She wrapped a blanket around herself and him.

"You would not take this away," she prayed. "You sent me here, and You have given me the desire to remain." She was of use to the congregation. And here, in the wilderness, she and Christoph were finding love. Love. She did not often admit that to herself, certainly never to him.

"Sarah? You are looking for me?"

Sarah startled from her reverie. Christoph was leaning over her.

"Brother David told me," he said.

"How could you know to look for me here?" she asked.

Almost, Christoph seemed to smile. "Sister, you often come here."

He sat beside her, stretching out his long legs.

David slept. Sarah pulled closed her bodice. Often come here, indeed! How smug he was in his knowledge of her.

"Wind Maiden, wife of One-Who-Runs, came to me today," she said. "She warned of grave dangers to the White teachers." Sarah watched Christoph's face; its composure did not alter. "She claimed that Delamatteno will kill and scalp us. She said the English resent our influence here."

"We have heard such warnings in the past. We remain safe," said Christoph.

"So I say, Brother." Sarah pulled her knees up to support the weight of David.

"Still," continued Christoph, "the colonies are at war with the English. And the Indians of the Lake country fight on behalf of the English." He looked into her eyes: "In war, who can know the dangers?"

"What does this have to do with us? We are neutral." Sarah gazed up at him.

His eyes dropped. "Are we neutral? Do I ... we uphold neutrality?"

"Of course we do, Christoph." She could not understand him when he lapsed into these introspective broodings.

"Then God is for us!" Christoph smiled.

Was he confident? The war was not their concern. The Delaware would hold steadfast to their commitment. He should be confident.

If she were bold, she might say, "Christoph, those letters the council at Goschachgunk asks you to write to Fort Pitt about the prowlings of the heathen — lives are saved thereby. Would you have people die for the sake of your neutrality?"

She was not bold. She could say nothing.

"I finished planting apple trees today," said Christoph, "in the newly-cleared southern field. More peach and cherry trees will fill the space remaining."

Sarah rubbed her hand along her skirt. She wanted to rub it across his arm. "I saw the hazelnut in bloom," she offered. "Will you plant the maize?" The blossoms of the hazelnut announced the propitious time to plant maize.

"In one day, maybe two," he replied.

Sarah clutched David in one arm and pushed aside her skirt. "I must not detain you. You take your turn at the school?"

"Yes," he replied, standing now and taking her arm.

"Sisters Martha and Elizabeth are making soap. Am I not brave to trust them alone?"

Christoph smiled. He pulled her up beside him. "Brave? Sister — you are a martyr."

Martyr ... that she would never be. She tried to laugh, to capture the joy that was sometimes their own. "I do not bring them together. They will not stay apart."

Christoph chuckled and shook his head. He grasped her shoulders. His presence enveloped her.

"See the vision, Sarah," he commanded. "They are our flesh and our blood. We shall multiply to the glory of God. A war cannot hinder our Saviour."

The vision. Yes. With longing, with determination, Sarah nodded.

The fields turned from brown to green. The maize stalks, dark green in the summer sun, grew past the knees of their tenders. Again, the war belt was offered to the Delaware nation; again, it refused. Again, Wind Maiden scolded Sarah and stomped her feet and flailed her hands, trying to scare away the White teachers. Sarah insisted that rumors must not scare away the teachers although she knew that more than rumors traveled through the forest. Red-faced and -chested warriors with tufts of hair on balded heads passed near the villages. Not many, just a few.

It was early in July; the heat of the summer sun beat upon the earth. The morning's chores — the hoeing, the milking, the mending, the building — had been completed. Some brethren, carrying nets and baskets, went fishing. Sarah was in her small family garden, harvesting herbs. David crawled beside her between the rows.

"Too hot to work beneath the searing sun," the voice of Wind Maiden warned from behind.

Sarah turned. "Friend. The flowers bloom. I am late. The leaves are bitter soon. The sun will not stop, and I must not."

"Why do you plant what you do not need? Why do you work in the great heat? Your people fight with the earth, fight with the sun. In the forest, from which the sun flees, leaves and roots grow which my lenno use as you use these. That is where you should go." Wind Maiden crossed her arms.

Sarah readjusted her cap. "I hear your words. Our Saviour gives fruit in its time; He moves the sun with His Word. Why do I fight with the sun when He gives all?"

"You will learn," replied Wind Maiden, smiling. She started to turn. "So I will take you to the forest. We look for sweet leaves and roots." She looked back at Sarah. "We shall walk a little more and find some fruit still hiding in cool and dark places."

"Oh ..." Sarah glanced around at her plants. She was willing to agree with the words of her friend, but she could not follow in the meaning of those words, could she? She had a garden to tend. Yet could she say one thing and do another?

"Do not be afraid," comforted Wind Maiden, misunderstanding Sarah's hesitation. The forest hides dark things, but I am brave and I shall protect you."

"I can seem foolish," thought Sarah, "but I must not appear a hypocrite." How, then, could Wind Maiden trust her?

"Let us go," said Sarah, lifting David into her arms. Henceforth, she would not agree with Wind Maiden until she had considered what agreeing meant.

They wandered through the forest near the river. Sunlight penetrated there. They picked herbs and pulled roots which Wind Maiden chose. She explained their healing properties, tying each addition upon a long string which she hung over her shoulder. They crushed some leaves between their fingers, smelled, and tasted.

Sarah, balancing David in a linen scarf against her waist, rolled a narrow leaf in her hand and sniffed it. "Like thyme," she said, using the German word for the herb.

"Yes, like," agreed Wind Maiden, staring at the leaf with interest.

They hunted, too, for wild berries, especially the sweet cherry of which Sarah was fond. The season was late for berries; they searched far for them.

Sarah felt like a child, losing herself in play. A cloud of adult caution overshadowed her, but she ran out from under it and was a child, again.

"Here," exclaimed Sarah, pushing back the branches of a thick bush. Ripe cherries lay hidden beneath the layers of leaves. Sarah placed David upon the ground and assisted in filling the small basket Wind Maiden carried.

David wailed. Sarah turned. A tall Indian, not Lenape, leaned over the infant; two others stood beside. A scream rose within Sarah: "David!" Her mind rushed to him. The cry never escaped from her mouth. She walked toward the Indians and lifted David into her arms.

"Mengwe," whispered Wind Maiden from beside her. "Warriors," she added.

Sarah stepped back. She clutched the screaming David in her arms. "God help us," she murmured.

The faces of the warriors were streaked with vermillion, each line accentuating fierceness. Brutal enactments of murders and scalpings were etched upon their chests. Feathers protruded from the locks of hair upon their scalps. Two held rifles in dark, thick hands. The third swung a hatchet in the air.

The forest was silent.

Sarah's mouth was dry; her tongue swelled. Her mouth formed words without utterance. One Indian raised his arm toward them. Sarah said with slurring tongue, "What do you want? We are Quaekels, Black Coats," searching for words they would understand, "teachers ..." and concluding in German, "... Christians."

Wind Maiden grabbed her arm and pulled her back. "Shut your mouth." Wind Maiden took one long step forward and stopped, her legs apart and her hands on her hips.

The one with the hatchet spoke to Wind Maiden, his voice gruff, gesturing with his free hand and with his hatchet. Sarah's mind was transfixed by the hatchet.

Wind Maiden lifted the basket of cherries toward the speaker, but he sneered and pushed it aside. She looked at Sarah. "They want food. Meat. Food for warriors, weakened by the blood of battle." Her voice lowered, "They do not want us. They want our food. More come with prisoners."

"Oh!" whispered Sarah in a voice without breath. "We cannot give the Lord's food to warriors — murderers!"

"You do not give, then they will take," cautioned Wind Maiden. "They will kill your black cattle, hogs, chicken; they will trample your fields. They claim as friends. Do you want enemies?"

"We shall speak this to our people," Sarah said to the warriors, nodding, smiling, nodding.

The speaker hit his rifle against the ground and raved with gestures and deep, quick words. Sarah recognized some of the sounds as similar to Delamatteno she had heard but so much rougher and twisted in sound that she could not gain their meanings.

"They sleep here tonight with their people. They will wait for food," said Wind Maiden.

They ran back to Lichtenau. Did the warriors follow, and did the shadowed forest protect them from Sarah's view?

"Love them and do not fear," a voice whispered within.

"Murderers? Blood-stained?" her mind reeled in reply.

"Love them," the voice repeated.

"They would kill my David and our people."

The voice concluded, "And do not fear."

The string of herbs swung from Wind Maiden's shoulder; the basket bumped against her side.

They hurried through Lichtenau, gasping the news to sisters who ran beside them. Sarah slipped David into the arms of Sister Martha.

They found Christoph splitting logs for fences.

"Warriors demand our food," she panted in German. "We, Wind Maiden and I, encountered three with rifles and hatchet ..." The hatchet swung in circles through her mind. "... in the forest." She sucked in air: "What must we do?"

Christoph leaned his axe against a tree stump and stood erect. His actions were smooth and slow.

"We must call together the teachers and assistants," he said, looking first at Sarah, then at Wind Maiden. "Where do the warriors wait?"

Sarah rubbed her forehead. "Two, two and one half miles east ... I ... I am not certain." She turned to Wind Maiden and repeated the question in Unami.

"Yes," agreed Wind Maiden, "toward the rising of the sun." She looked around her at the congregating cluster. "Warriors." She sneered when she said the word. "They want food; give food. Do not play stupid games."

"We must take food?" asked Sarah in Unami as they hurried toward the village.

"Yes," replied Christoph. He said no more.

They collected smoked hog flesh, fish, milk, and cheese. Brother David chose Christoph, Jonah, and Mark to bear the food. Wind Maiden would lead.

"I go with you," said Sarah.

"No," objected Wind Maiden. "Weak, white-skinned women should hide from warriors."

"I go," persisted Sarah, "to comfort the prisoners."

They found the warriors where Sarah and Wind Maiden had left them, near the bushes of cherries. Ten Indians, all in war paint, took the food from the hands of the brethren. Several sticks, scalps hanging from them, leaned against a tree. Beside the tree sat two White women, a man, and a little girl, her blond hair hanging in tangles down her back. Their legs were secured beneath wooden stakes, their arms tied. Dirt-stained and listless, they slumped and stared.

"Brother!" exclaimed Sarah. She pulled upon Christoph's arm. "Four prisoners. A child." She hurried toward them.

One Indian stretched an arm before her. The White people looked up.

Christoph stepped beside Sarah. "We give them food," he said to the Indian, imitating eating with his hands. The warrior dropped his arm with a shrug.

"Where are you from?" asked Christoph in German.

The man shook his head and spoke in English: "Who are you? Are you their friends?" He cast his gaze toward the warriors.

"No, we are not friends," answered Christoph in English. "We are Unity of Brethren, living with peaceful, Christian Indians. We bring food." He paused, then asked, "Where are you from?"

"Fort Pitt ... south from the fort," said one of the women.

"My husband, three sons — dead," said the other woman.

"Did you see Mother?" the little girl asked of Sarah. Her face was round, her mouth small and open.

"Dead, too," the second woman said.

Sarah stroked the cheek and hair of the girl.

They fed them. Christoph and Jonah pleaded for the release of the prisoners. The warriors refused. Christoph offered cattle, pigs, geese. The warriors smiled and indicated that these Quaekels were crazy, wanting prisoners they could not use. Their smiles grew — but THEY could use these prisoners.

The Indians became restless and commanded them to leave. Sarah shook her head. "No!" She looked at the girl.

"The women and child will live," said Wind Maiden into her ear. "If the man is strong, he will live. The Mengwe will sell them to the Saggenash for the water that burns and does not take away thirst."

Christoph took Sarah's arm and turned her toward him. "We shall bring more food tomorrow morning and plead for them."

However, the next day, the warriors were gone.

~ ~ ~

Summer days, once marked by growing fruit and laden vines, by harvests and by baking and drying, were now marred by wandering bands of painted savages, growing in numbers like weeds in the field, demanding food ... insatiable. The prisoners – Sarah remembered every one. She kept a list of dates and names, of descriptions and origins. She preserved their memory for one day ... some day.

The summer sun blazed and the certainty ripened that the teachers must leave.

"Have we eyes throughout the forest or arms that can grab back the striking hatchet when it is aimed at your skull," pleaded White Eyes, "or ears that can hear all plans of attack on Pasture of Light and Huts of Grace? The Lenni Lenape once said, 'Yes, we shall watch over our brothers.' We cannot longer watch. Our eyes droop from weariness. We are few; warriors many. Leave."

Wind Maiden, too, returned. "You are still at Pasture of Light ... Why? I warned you. Will you smear your blood upon my hands? When the warriors come to Goschachgunk to call us to battle, they waddle like fat ponies with bellies full of soft grass from the hillsides. They laugh and say that the Black Coat is a turkey, too foolish to run from the hunter. The turkey squawks and calls the hunter to the door of his nest. Who would not kill such a silly turkey and take its flesh and feathers for himself? They will kill you. I do not have words for such a foolish turkey."

And Sarah finally said, "We leave."

"Too late, too late," her mind echoed, "too late to mend the war-stained present or to keep the tide of bloodshed from spilling into the future. Too late."

"You will come back," Wind Maiden promised, "later, when we have pushed back the Big Knife. The warrior will be full of other flesh and will not chase the foolish turkey. You will see, yes! We shall live in peace with you then."

"Yes," agreed Sarah, but she did not think so.

On August third, they knew. Runners from Sandusky entered Goschachgunk to say the Half-King, Pomoacan, was coming to compel the Delaware nation to fight. Rumors of plans to slaughter the traitorous missionaries followed their words. In four days, maybe fewer, Pomoacan would arrive.

"How can we know what rumors are true and which are false?" Christoph lamented, rubbing his palm across his forehead. "Of course, you cannot remain ..." His voice trailed off as he stared at Sarah.

Would he stay, then, and send her and David to Bethlehem alone? Should she release him? Could she?

"Stay, Christoph, if you must. We can, David and I, go back ..."

"Sarah!" Why did he shout? He stiffened. Why? "You think I could abandon you?"

"Your vision of the Christian Indian state ... you cannot ... forsake ..." she stammered. Did Christoph want to go with her, or did duty demand the sacrifice of his plan?

"The vision." He slouched then pulled himself erect. "The timing is God's; it is not mine."

Brother and Sister Jungmann and Brother and Sister Zundel of Lichtenau, Brother and Sister Schmick of Gnadenhutten prepared to flee. Brother David Zeisberger and Brother Edwards remained with their flock although White Eyes had warned Brother David, "You, best of friends, you leave, too. Many thirst after your blood. You are the voice of the Black Coat, the voice that sits in the council and tells the Lenni Lenape to resist the hatchet. They will cut off that voice."

Now, on the eve of departure, Sarah longed to gaze once more into the face of Wind Maiden. What was Wind Maiden to Sarah? She was wild and, yet, loyal. She claimed Sarah for herself, but she required nothing. She was a friend. Sarah's friend did not appear.

The morning of August sixth was overcast and unseasonably cool. Sarah, Christoph, and Brother and Sister Jungmann mounted their horses. David was perched in front of Christoph, bound against him upon the saddle.

Sarah looked down on the knee-high moccasins she wore. Odd, indeed, that she should have once shuddered at their appearance.

The congregation stood in a quiet circle around the group while Brother David prayed. Sarah could not close her eyes. "You understand," she prayed. "Much to remember." She watched the face of Brother David, now in repose. Christoph carried in his pack a letter from him to the Mission Board in Bethlehem. It read,

"My heart does not allow me even so much as to think of leaving. Where the Christian Indians stay I will stay. It is impossible for me to forsake them. If Edwards and I were to go, they would be without a guide and would disperse. Our presence gives authority to us. He will not look upon our remaining here as foolhardiness. I make no pretensions to false heroism, but am, by nature, as timid as a dove. My trust is altogether in God. Never yet has He put me to shame, but always granted me the courage and comfort I need. I am about my duty; and even if I should be murdered, it will not be my loss, but my gain, for then will the fish return to his native element."

"Thus would Christoph say but for young David and for me," thought Sarah as she recalled the contents of the letter. She glanced over at Christoph's bowed head. He had spoken little the two days of preparation, had told Sarah to pack of his garments those she chose but had no heart for packing himself. From the distance, Sarah had watched him cultivating the plantation, working beside his Indian brethren, pausing to lay a hand upon their shoulders to talk, stopping to drink from a gourd of water and to talk, again. The fruit would never be fully harvested — not by Christoph.

Jonah and Amelia, Martha and Elizabeth ... Sarah smiled. Anna Benigna and Isaac, Christian, Leah ... passed upon her turning gaze, enwrapped in prayer. They stood upon a painted canvas, lifeless.

Finally, the travelers glided down the single street. The Muskingum River, the row of cabins, the church, the fields behind, all reclined in peace, promising eternal continuity.

False promises?

They entered the trail, the forest swallowing the silent company in dense twilight. Sarah saw, or sensed, she never knew, a figure beside a tree on her left. She turned her head and saw Wind Maiden, her slender shape blending into the shadows like a sapling in the shelter of the trees. She felt the joy of friendship acknowledged and the anguish of friendship wrenched away. She wanted to wave, to call out a farewell. But the forest and the solemn figure prohibited it. She nodded, saying with that movement a whisper of gratitude. The shadowy shape nodded in reply as if the wind had stirred it and it bent. This, for all her days to come, became the sight Sarah most remembered of her flight from Lichtenau.

11
MARCH 27, 1778 – APRIL 6, 1778

The White Men — M'Kee, Elliot, Girty — and the Big Knife warriors who had run with them from the Big Knife camp across the Beautiful River spread words of fire on tongues of bitterness through Goschachgunk.

"General Washington is dead," they cried.

"The Saggenash have stamped out the council fire of their disobedient children and have poured their blood upon the earth."

"The Big Knives who still hold blood in their veins rise, like the sun, from the east across the Beautiful River to kill women, children, friends, enemies ... all Lenape!"

"All Lenape!"

"All Lenape!"

"Women, children, friends, enemies!"

"All Lenape!"

"Lift tomahawk, knife, rifle into the air and run upon them, kill before they kill women, children, friends, enemies, before they kill you!"

The drum beat through the day and night: "Prepare! Prepare! Prepare to kill! Kill! Kill before they kill! Kill! Kill women, children, friends, enemies! You!"

"Now!" shouted Wind Maiden, crouching in the shadows of the night, listening to the warriors as they cried. "Now we fight!"

In the light of the new day, more warriors came — Captain Pipe and the men of strength of the Wolf Tribe from the Walhonding. And Black Wolf, dark and tall and strong.

And Captain Pipe cried, "Paint your faces with rage, red and black; wear the eagle plumes of courage. We fight!"

But White Eyes arose in the council of the nation. His voice did not throb with the beat of the drum. "Ten nights," he requested, "to wait for word of our friend, Tamanend, from the place of the treaty, Fort Pitt. Why do we now heed the words of Big Knife foxes that fled at night from their masters, foxes that smell of fire water and of lies? Can we not see the twisting of their tongues? Wait ten nights for the voice of our friend."

"An enemy! An enemy!" The drum beat again through the words of Captain Pipe as he stood up against the counsel of White Eyes. "The man who will try to hide the hatchet is an enemy of the Lenape!" The voice of Captain Pipe settled like darkness upon the words of White Eyes. "He will see women and children die and will laugh!"

The assembly waited. Wind Maiden crouched outside the council house. Her ears throbbed with the pulse of the drum: "White Eyes betrays the dark skin of the Lenni Lenape and slides out of it like a snake. His new skin is the color of the Big Knife. We have no ear to hear the voice of the snake. The wolf cries and we answer, 'Yes,'" she thought. Wind Maiden saw the wolf, the Black Wolf. She was cold and hot inside.

"If the Lenni Lenape will lift the hatchet against the Big Knife," continued the voice of White Eyes, "I shall run with you. I plead peace to save the nation from death. But if you say, 'Ho' to me and run to battle on the words of foxes, I run with you. Not like the bear hunter who sets dogs on the bear to be beaten about by its paws while the hunter keeps at a safe distance, no! I will lead you, run in front, be first to fall. I will not survive my nation, wailing because of the destruction of the brave Lenape who should have lived in greater honor."

Silence. The men within the council house, the women without ... silence.

Wind Maiden could not breathe or think.

Then a voice said, "I shall wait ten nights."

Another joined, "I wait ten nights."

"I wait."

"I wait."

"And I."

"And I."

"And I."

The chiefs, the captains slowly joined their voices to the vote, "I wait ten nights."

And some said, "I will follow only White Eyes in battle."

The words spread from mouth to mouth, beyond the council house, upon the lips of the women, to the cabins, the huts, to the children, the aged: "We wait. We follow White Eyes."

Wind Maiden curled her lips from off the words. She clutched her chest and pulled her body into a ball. Finally, she arose with the women to stand silently back while the councilors passed.

Captain Pipe walked first, followed by the warriors of the wolf. They alone had not said, "Wait."

Black Wolf walked beside Captain Pipe. His eyes beneath heavy lids searched the watching women.

Wind Maiden watched his eyes search toward her. She heard a voice plead, "Hide." The voice was far away, the body of Black Wolf near. She waited.

He saw her. His eyes opened and said, "Come to me." He walked past.

She did not leave with the women. She backed against a nearby cabin and waited in its shadow. One-Who-Runs would sit beside a fire with Eagle-with-White-Head or Red Face and would not know. They would talk and hide their heads inside their shells. But she was not a turtle. She would fight the enemy, and she would win.

The night covered her. She thought she heard the voice of One-Who-Runs say, "I wait for you." She answered, "Find me. I sit in darkness. You must find me." Her heart beat, "Black Wolf must not see me." Yet she did not move.

The steps, almost no steps, the breathing, almost none, moved above her and bent over her. The face and hands of Black Wolf, stone, reached out toward her. His hands clutched her shoulders and pulled her up. Pain traveled through her arms. He said, "Follow," and turned toward the forest, darker still than night.

She counted his steps — ten. They broke like rods against her chest. She followed him. A rope hung heavily from her neck and was sealed in the hand of Black Wolf. Her head bowed low beneath the weight. She shuffled her feet and followed.

He stopped beside a tree whose brown and dead leaves covered the ground. He laid his blanket upon them. She ran from him to the fire of her cabin, but, still, her feet shuffled toward him.

She stood below the hunter and looked up. She was the fawn, the sacrifice. He took her blanket from her shoulders and laid it beside his on the ground. Without a word, he pushed her down before him.

He was hard and rough and his hands that slid across her stomach and engulfed her breasts were heavy, not like the hands of ... the other one. She tried to pursue him, but she fell behind, panting, her side aching. But he was a warrior and that was how a warrior fought.

He left her, shivering, wounded beneath the tree. She wrapped her body inside the blanket and covered the wound, hiding slashes no one but she could see. She arose and returned to Goschachgunk alone.

Day upon day and night upon night, the men prepared themselves by day and danced the war dance by night. And Wind Maiden followed Black Wolf when he called.

The men sat beside their cabins, plucking hair from their scalps, greasing their locks, practicing fierce designs with paints. Each selected the white plume of the eagle and laid it aside for the day of battle, for boldness in battle.

At night, they came to dance for war, beneath a ceiling of bark upheld by posts. A painted post of red and black stood in the center: the enemy.

And in the deepest blackness, where the moon would not shine, Wind Maiden fell before Black Wolf. No longer did the wounds sting, no more did she cower from darkness. He sucked the blood from her body and breath from her mouth. She clenched her teeth and dug her hands into the muscles of his shoulders. She stifled screams and subdued them into gasps. Surging, she fought in the arms of her warrior.

The women, the aged men, and the men who had not lifted the hatchet for war sat and watched the dance of the men. Captain Pipe led, hatchet held high, body painted for battle. He shouted and taunted and leaped and attacked the painted post, the enemy. The warriors of the Wolf Tribe followed, swinging clubs, knives, rifles, hatchets at the enemy. Black Wolf lifted his rifle above his head, held high with both his hands. He howled.

Each word was a command as he drew her to him or pushed her away, each touch a breaking of flesh and bone. She yielded. The warrior — Black Wolf.

Men of the Turkey and men of the Turtle arose to dance. Each step, each turn, each cry said, Yes! they would fight the Big Knife. One-Who-Runs sat beside Gelemend. He would not dance.

"Why do you move in silence?" he asked her one day. "And when I touch you, you jump back."

"You will not fight. You are not a warrior," she replied.

"You did not save me," she thought. "I wandered; I was lost. Now, I am not your wife."

One-Who-Runs said, "Many times I have heard songs of birds, carried by the wind. These birds that carry this new song are birds of death that eat the flesh of the dead. The Lenni Lenape never listen to birds. I do not prepare for war with such chirping in my ears. I will follow White Eyes into battle, but my feet will be heavy. I do not prepare for war ... yet."

Wind Maiden cried, "You will not be ready for war! Your muscles will be soft; and when you lift the hatchet, your arm will shake. Your tongue will fear to taste the thick and salty blood, so your hatchet will not draw blood from the skull of your enemy. Your ears will be dull from listening to droning voices, so you will not be able to turn against the sound of the rifle. You will run!"

"And you are not a warrior. You are not Black Wolf! You are not Black Wolf!" she screamed inside. But the screaming was a weeping in the dark and cold and hollow place within.

He shook her arm, and the pain was no pain. "You speak like this? I am your husband!" His face was first red then pale. "You do not honor my word or trust my actions. I am your husband!" He turned, took his rifle, and left.

She wept in a corner of the cabin. She hated One-Who-Runs, the rabbit. Black Wolf would be her husband — a hunter and a warrior. She buried the rabbit in a deep hole. She was free. Alone, she wept.

He did not return that night. She followed Black Wolf into the forest. He would be her husband: a hunter and a warrior. She was free. Bound in chains of darkness, smothered by the commands of her warrior, darkness grew inside of her until she could feel only a rotting hole. She searched the crevices of her hole and shuddered. She was free.

One-Who-Runs looked at her across the thrashing dancers. She looked away; she did not see him. The drum beat, and the pulse of the Lenni Lenape throbbed for war.

Seven, eight times the darkness enveloped Goschachgunk. The ninth day of light banished the darkness for a time. The darkness, then the tenth light would come. The waiting would be over; the Lenape would rise for war.

While the ninth day was still young, while the ice of night still clung to the air, the Black Coat, Heckewelder, and a believing Mahicanni rode upon horses, from the Elk's Eye, along the long street of Goschachgunk.

Everyone stood to watch them pass. A White Man, an enemy. This White Man had been sent back across the Beautiful River in the last Youth of the Year. He came, now, from Fort Pitt. He came from the Big Knife, the enemy who would kill women and children. "Go away!" she thought. "You bring lies." She burned like a fire, not red but black.

They rode to White Eyes who stood near the council house. The Black Coat slid from his horse. He offered the hand of friendship. Captain White Eyes stepped back. He offered the hand to another and another and another. None returned the grasp of a friend.

"Brother!" cried the Black Coat. "Does no man offer his hand to a friend?"

Captain White Eyes stepped forward.

"Stand back, fool!" thought Wind Maiden. "Do not talk. Fight!"

"We have been told that we have no friends among White Men who ride from across the Beautiful River. Other White Men who fled from the ravings at Fort Pitt tell us that all are enemies there and any who come from there speak lies to ensnare the Lenape and lull him to sleep so he will not hear the approach of the enemy."

"This is not true," replied the Black Coat. "If I were not a friend, I would not stand here now."

The voice of White Eyes was loud so that all the village could hear: "Then you will tell us the truth about what I state to you."

"Yes. The truth," said the Black Coat.

"Lies. Only lies," Wind Maiden murmured. Something was sliding from her and she could not grab it back. Almost, she wanted it to go, but she must have it back although it was cold and slimy and red, almost black.

White Eyes continued, "Are the Big Knife warriors all cut to pieces by the Saggenash? Is Captain Washington killed? Is there no more congress, and have the Saggenash hung some of them, and taken the rest to the land across the Great Salt Lake to hang them there? Is the whole country beyond the mountains in the hand of the Saggenash, and are the few thousand Big Knives who have escaped them now preparing on this side of the mountains to kill all Lenape in this country, even our women and children? Now do not deceive us, but speak the truth. Is this all true what I have said to you?"

"No word of this is true," answered the Black Coat. He took sheets of white, the White Man's voice of scratches, and called the drummer to beat the drum to call the council to hear the scratches of friendship from beyond the Beautiful River.

White Eyes called, "Shall we, my friends and relatives, listen once more to those who call us their brothers?"

The village with one loud voice answered, "Yes!"

The drum beat a different call, not arousing but subduing. The Lenape walked upon the words of the drum toward the council house.

But Captain Pipe and the Wolf Tribe and Black Wolf ... and Wind Maiden ... walked slower than the rest because the compelling sound of another drumbeat echoed within their breasts.

The war that never began ended.

But Black Wolf brought the Laughing One and their dark-eyed son and lived among the Lenape at Goschachgunk. So Wind Maiden went when he called and lay where he beckoned and heard the sound of the war drum once again in the strong, binding, breaking arms of her warrior.

12
AUGUST 10, 1778 – SEPTEMBER 24, 1778

The earth was opened; the seed of maize fell and was covered. The maize grew, was in the milk, now ready to eat. Wind Maiden planted her love for Black Wolf deep inside the dark place. The seed sprouted and grew. The fruit was in the milk, tender, ready to eat. She waited for him to take her as his wife. Her fruit was ripe; she could not wait longer. It was the moon of Win Gischuch.

She came to him when he called. He did not speak so she asked when he would take her as wife. He laughed. She asked again. He answered, "Soon," and would not talk more.

Soon. Was soon tomorrow or the new moon? Soon. Was it before or after the long chase? Soon all would know she was his wife.

Some knew already so she could not walk near them or look at them or speak to them. Star-at-Dawning knew; her eyes, deep within their caves, were grey and black. They watched. Wind Maiden had planted her seeds in a different place this year so she would not feel the staring of Star-at-Dawning. But her stomach turned and turned because she could not watch the slow, calm movements of her mother or feel the soft flesh of her arm rubbing against Wind Maiden's shoulder. Yet Wind Maiden was a woman now and a woman did not need a mother.

The Aged Woman knew. Her chilling stream washed against the face of Wind Maiden and took the breath, the smell, the taste, the sight. Wind Maiden carried food, water, and wood but never stayed and seldom looked. The river of filth could never say what she knew so Wind Maiden told herself she should not fear the silent, shriveled thing. But she did fear her and could not answer why.

Who else knew? She did not know but spoke to few and kept her eyes low.

When she passed Laughing One, she told Laughing One with sneers and words inside her head how she now wrapped herself within the body of Black Wolf and stole him from Laughing One like Laughing One once stole her pride, her hair and her life, from Wind Maiden. One day, Black Wolf would build a cabin for Wind Maiden and unroll his mat beside hers in the sight of Goschachgunk. He would pile his skins outside her door, and she would trade them for ribbons and buckles which would prove that she was the wife of a great hunter and warrior. And she would spit on Laughing One.

One-Who-Runs did not know. She wanted to scratch out his eyes which said, "Love me. Do not wound me now." She hated him, the rabbit! But she did not want him to hear, to see, and to know.

She often sat beside South-Wind-Blowing outside the cabin of the new husband. She would watch South-Wind-Blowing wave her head and chatter of skins and beads. South-Wind-Blowing would shake her legs and jingle the bells on her ankles. She would tell Wind Maiden to wear bells, too, so that men would look up when she passed. But Wind Maiden did not want bells; she hid herself and would be seen of none.

On days when the air was heavy with sunlight and heat, when the work was done and the village whispered lazily, Wind Maiden wandered in the forest. She had no one to whisper to. She wished that Black Wolf would find her and stroll beside her and talk to her about where they would build their cabin and when, together, they could leave for the hunt. But he only found her when he wanted her; and, when she spoke, he seldom replied.

"Do you prefer the blabbering messenger?" she chided herself. "Ha! No! Not One-Who-Runs!"

A warrior was silent and strong. He knew everything and would not heed a woman's chatter. And could a hunter drop his rifle and run each time a silly woman called?

So, alone, she walked near the Elk's Eye and often shuffled near the Pasture of Light. Sometimes, she watched the believing lenno working in the village and fields. Often, she came when she knew they would be inside their meeting house, singing to their Great Spirit. That was when she would sit near the edge of the forest, but always within shadows, and listen. The songs told of the death that made gladness. They promised peace made from a brew of sorrow. Her mind could not hold these things; they spoke confusion. But, when she heard the songs, the blackness in her chest would lift and she would breathe again.

She knew that One-Who-Runs sat at times inside the meeting house at Pasture of Light; she hated him for that. At first, he asked her to go with him to hear, but she would not because she was Lenni Lenape and would not heed the White Man's tales. Finally, he no longer asked. So she sat outside alone.

She would lean her head against a tree and think of Salah. She would wonder where Salah built her fire and in what village she now dwelt. Was she still foolish? Did she remember Wind Maiden?

She would return to Goschachgunk and sit in her dark cabin, waiting for the scratch on the wall which was the call of Black Wolf.

During the moon of Winn Gischuch, the warriors of the Delamatteno and the Mengwe appeared again, sent by the Saggenash. They brought a new war belt which shouted that the Lenni Lenape must join in war. But the word of peace cried louder from the mouth of Captain White Eyes and the Quaekel, Zeisberger.

So, alone, Wind Maiden fought the war with rage in the secret arms of her warrior.

In the Harvest time, White Eyes and the councilors of the Lenni Lenape followed the trail to Fort Pitt to make a new treaty with the Big Knife. One-Who-Runs was called to follow on their heels, to hear and to remember.

The day he left, he told Wind Maiden, "When I return, we shall go hunting. Together, we shall build our hunting fire."

Wind Maiden would not answer. She looked at him and handed him his pack of dried meat and ground maize. "When you come back, I shall not go with you," she thought. She would wait for Black Wolf to come for her and take her to his own camp.

One-Who-Runs bent over her; his long hands rubbed against her arms. An echo of a sob from long ago rose in the blackness that was now Wind Maiden. She strangled it with a frown. "Return," begged One-Who-Runs. "You live far from me. I wait for you to return."

She could not speak because the sob pushed against the frown. She shrugged her head sideways and looked down.

She felt his hand upon her dark, small head. "I wait for you," he whispered and was gone.

Wind Maiden fell where she had stood. "I hate the rabbit," she sobbed.

Now One-Who-Runs was gone, so Wind Maiden saw Black Wolf both days and nights in the forest and once inside her cabin.

"When?" she asked. She pressed her palms across the muscular hills toward the valley of his back.

"Soon," he said, pulling up her hips and leaning into her.

"When the Lenape kills ..."

"Be quiet!" he hissed.

On one day, they lay in the forest. The air hung heavily beneath barren clouds that held back their rain. Wind Maiden heard a rustle above her head. She rolled and turned. She saw the dark, retreating shape of a leg through the foliage of the forest.

Black Wolf pulled her down beside him.

"Someone!" she gasped.

"A rabbit or a squirrel," he shrugged.

"No, no! It was someone!" She wanted to sink beneath the earth, its cold, dark, suffocating dirt consuming her.

She looked at Black Wolf. He sighed, rolled upon his back, and smiled.

She searched far for wood that day. She gathered nuts she knew were too green to eat. She sat like a fawn in the high brush. Finally, she circled and circled toward home.

Everyone in Goschachgunk was the one whose leg she saw. She said she did not care because she was now the wife of Black Wolf. She was a woman and proud. She passed the cabin of Star-at-Dawning but never entered. However, she remembered the long ago laughter when she and Star-at-Dawning had danced together and she remembered the smell of the skin of her mother.

She dropped the food for the Aged Woman inside her cabin and fled. The Aged Woman mocked with silent sounds. She was a rock covered with green slime and crawling things. Wind Maiden could not breathe inside the cabin of the Aged Woman.

The third night after Wind Maiden saw ... someone, Eagle-with-White-Head entered her cabin. He stood at the door; she looked up, then down again, stirring a small fire with a stick.

"Are the whispers true?" he asked. His voice, like sand, rubbed against the ear.

She did not answer, for the darkness was moving into her throat.

He came near. "Are they true?" he snarled, yanking her arm and pulling her down upon the dirt.

"What do they say?" she asked, telling her voice to sound proud and fierce. It was the voice of a frightened fawn.

"You are the bitch of Black Wolf."

"No! No!" She pulled herself up near his crouching side. "I shall be the wife of Black Wolf," she said with the voice of a child. "I *am* the wife of Black Wolf!"

Eagle-with-White-Head leaned back from her. His face was twisted. "You are a crawling dog and a fool!"

"No! Do not say this," she begged.

He pulled farther back. "Laughing One cuts your hair short with her words. Again, the village laughs at you. Fool!"

The retreating leg took on the shape of Laughing One. "I shall laugh at Laughing One. I shall take Black Wolf," Wind Maiden yelped. Eagle-with-White-Head had to know that this was good.

"You are the wife of One-Who-Runs. Does the fool forget?"

"I am not his wife. He is a rabbit. Black Wolf is a hunter and a warrior. I am the wife of Black Wolf." This was true; this was what she had told herself so it must be true.

"You are a bitch," said Eagle-with-White-Head as he arose to leave.

Wind Maiden stood with him. "Will you tell of this?"

He looked back at her as he left. "I do not need to tell. Only One-Who-Runs does not know."

Black Wolf came to her more often than before. He laughed low and hollow when Wind Maiden tried to speak of the whispers. She was glad he did not care. He let all Goschachgunk know. Did that mean he took her as his wife? Yet he did not come to her as husband ... Why?

Many whispered, but no one knew. The words flowed from the mouth of Laughing One, and the source of the words was not known to be pure. The hair of Wind Maiden throbbed as she walked the streets. She spoke to no one, not even South-Wind-Blowing.

Six nights after the whispers began to flow, One-Who-Runs returned, bearing the words of the treaty with the Big Knives. She did not tell him; he would hear. She held her insides tight within her. She wanted him to learn. Then she would be free with Black Wolf.

One-Who-Runs slept and arose two nights and said nothing.

She lay with Black Wolf two, then three times.

She hated One-Who-Runs and loved Black Wolf. The blackness grew until it covered her eyes. She lay with Black Wolf and knew that the blackness was spreading over her head and, soon, she would be dead.

The third time, she sank into the arms of Black Wolf. He clawed at and unbound her stroud. She shook with fear. Where fled desire? He fell onto his knees and pulled her by her waist down, his mouth rubbing up her body as she fell.

She saw him standing over them, his mouth wide and black inside. She saw him stare and gulp and quake.

"You! You!" stammered One-Who-Runs, shaking his head, staring at Wind Maiden. His eyes and face were red. His hands flexed like claws.

Black Wolf jumped up. Wind Maiden crawled to her stroud, clutched it round her, and stood. This was what she wanted ... death to the rabbit! But where was the victory? Where were the whoops for the battle won? She felt nothing.

From far away, she saw the shape of One-Who-Runs fly against the dark, tall tree that was Black Wolf. Black Wolf growled an animal sound in his throat and broke One-Who-Runs as though he were a sapling and flung him against the ground.

One-Who-Runs pushed himself up and stumbled sideways toward Black Wolf. Black Wolf, his mouth curled into a snarl, kicked the leg of One-Who-

Runs. He buckled like a lame pony, huffed, then hurled himself into Black Wolf.

Black Wolf staggered back. He yowled. He clutched his hands together like a hatchet and chopped them into the neck of One-Who-Runs. The sapling fell, his face crashing into the dirt.

Wind Maiden looked up at her warrior. She wanted to run from him and hide and protect what remained of breath and life. "Now," she murmured, "I am your wife."

He looked at her. His eyes widened into deep wells of eternal blackness. A smile slowly spread over teeth that gleamed white. The teeth grew long and pointed. He raised his head and laughed a howl that was no laugh. He turned and left.

One-Who-Runs was rousing. She could not look upon him, for he would see in her the putrid decay. Silently, she crept deeper into the forest.

She slept that night, curled between the roots of a tree. She slept without thought or feeling and awoke with none.

She shivered from the damp, misty dew of morning but did not care. Beside a spring of frigid water, Wind Maiden crouched and washed. She tried to make her mind tell her where to go, but it would not. She bent her head and waited.

Black Wolf – husband? No. He slew the fawn, ate its heart, and drank its blood. He cast its bones away. The hunter had slain, the warrior had scalped its prey. A long ago voice of a child said, "... a hunter and a warrior ... like my father." Who was that child?

One-Who-Runs ... Now she would not hate his soft touch on her mangled arm or his gentle gaze upon her bloodied face.

"But I can never go back to Goschachgunk," she whispered. "They will mock. They will laugh."

Another voice said, "So! The wounded animal hides. Tomorrow, you will walk through the village when the sun is high in the sky. You will sneer at their laughs!" It was the voice of Fish-of-the-Deep-Water, speaking amidst the echoes, long ago.

Wind Maiden arose and said to the shadows, "I go."

From the edge of the village near the Elk's Eye, she walked, step after step, thrusting up her head. Flicking her eyes sideways, she saw the door of the cabin of Black Wolf closed, a block of wood leaning against the entrance. They were gone – Laughing One, Black Wolf, and their son. She walked on.

The women watched. They whispered. The men nodded. Wind Maiden did not glance across her shoulders but looked ahead. Her hair was chopped, high, into the scalp. The warm, red blood oozed over her face and down her back.

She could not feel the stabs of gazes; the watchers did not live.

No, she did not live.

South-Wind-Blowing ran forward between two cabins. Wind Maiden sighed. South-Wind-Blowing would speak to her and help her breathe once more. But South-Wind-Blowing stopped, leaned against a cabin, and spit.

"Stupid dog," her look said. "Were you caught in the trap? You played with a dangerous toy."

Wind Maiden winced and groaned.

Her feet remembered only one place to go. She would run the gauntlet until she fell or until she crawled into the hut of despair.

She crept into her cabin. Empty. She looked around. More than empty. The rifle, knife, and hatchet of One-Who-Runs were gone. His mat and blanket and furs ... taken. His bench was overturned, the fire scattered. One-Who-Runs had left.

No! No! This was wrong! This could not happen. One-Who-Runs could not be gone.

Where to run? The blood beat against her eyes. No breath, no air, no air, anywhere! The blackness flowed from her nose and mouth and engulfed the cabin. No air!

She backed into the street and turned. "Mother!" her thoughts cried. Soft arms and full, round breasts. She ran. She did not care who saw. She was dead. No, they were. No, she.

"Mother!" she called as she stepped inside the cabin.

The fat, soft face looked up. Then slowly, slowly, the body turned away. And a voice from far away said, "I have no daughter. Go!"

Wind Maiden stumbled back and out. "Where to?" she sighed, but only blackness replied. She was a curse, and she was without honor, the bungling warrior who had lost the last battle and the war.

One-Who-Runs! One-Who-Runs! Toward the cabin of the Aged Woman she ran. She stopped outside the cabin and grabbed a long, rattling breath. The flowing rivers might cover Wind Maiden's grave and complete her doom. She entered.

The Aged Woman sat alone. But the furs and blankets of One-Who-Runs lay beside her.

"Where is he?" demanded Wind Maiden, her voice hoarse.

The wrinkled hand wavered high into the air and motioned far away.

Wind Maiden followed the wrinkled hand down to the bony arm and across to the shriveled face. Large, silent tears from the pools of liquid eyes rolled across the ridges of the ancient cheeks. Two weak and shaking arms opened wide — aching remnants, beckoning from long ago.

Down into the arms of the Aged Woman fell Wind Maiden. Dry sobs from the chasm of darkness rose. Within the shielding arms, the sobs broke.

13
SEPTEMBER 30, 1778 – APRIL 6, 1780

September 30, 1778

"Spin and weave, compelled by love; Sew and work with fervor."
The sisters sang their tune; the wheels spun; the looms clanked. Sarah's fingers rubbed evenly over the wool fibers whose threads she fed into the spindle of the spinning wheel.

"Warfare, death, disease," she thought. "Never an end." The hospital of the continental forces had been removed, but the stench of death lingered in and near the Brethren's House. In the trenches dug into the hillside beyond Bethlehem, cartloads of unnumbered soldiers, dead from the putrid fever, were dumped. Without name, without prayer uttered. Their entangled bones would remain interred in the Lehigh valley. Always.

Christoph labored over the hill and across the valley upon a plantation. The Single Sisters cared for David in the Little Boys' Group, but only while she spun. They would not take him from her for long.

"If we were in Lichtenau," she thought, "we would not be scattered as we are here." The war brought confusion. The Brethren tried to maintain order, but their order compelled tidy divisions into groups. It had not been so in Lichtenau.

They had been fortunate to obtain a single small room in the Family House. They squeezed past brethren in the halls and heard one another through the walls.

Last evening, Christoph had sat huddled over paper at the eating table, the only table. The candle had burned low. Sarah had leaned above to change it. He had startled.

"Another sermon?" she had asked, embarrassed for her intrusion. He composed them nightly though no one asked him to deliver a message. Anyway — he wrote for Indians, and Indians were not here.

"No," he had answered, tapping the tip of his quill. "My sister ... in Saxony ... I thought to write to her. My father, my brothers, and my sisters ... I wonder if they live. She wrote once. She might, again." Christoph had watched the feather as he bounced it in his hand.

"The sister who looks like me?" Sarah had asked. She had spoken softly, afraid he might disdain her if she probed.

He had raised his head. "Did I tell you that? Yes ... her." He had looked away, rubbing his leg with his hand. "I was young. I ... should have explained my faith differently. Not with rage. God will give me another chance. Perhaps she will reply before we return to Lichtenau."

He always trusted that they would go back.

"Is your father ..." she had begun. Thumps from the floor above stifled her words.

Christoph had clasped his hands to his head. David had squirmed and groaned in his bed. "Can anyone concentrate here?" he had lamented.

Then he had taken Sarah's hand and smiled up at her: "I constantly think about Lichtenau. Even our cabin, our dark, little cabin." He had squeezed her hand until it had ached. "We shall return. And when the believing Indians multiply and enlarge their orchards and plantations and settlements, we shall subdue the people and the land."

She had knelt beside his chair. She longed for the ringing silence of the forest. Was that possible? Yes. The turmoil in Bethlehem exhausted her. She longed, too, for the joy which they had known for only moments in Lichtenau; she clung to the ache of its memory.

He had slid his arm around her shoulders. In the pause, they had heard conversations through the walls.

"Is the western border open?" she had asked.

"The Seneca attack. The settlers flee east. The route is not safe ... yet," he had said.

Today, in the banging, clanging, spinning room, Sarah's hands and mind sang, not the spinning song, but the lament, "I would go back."

She shifted the weight on her legs. Her fingers stretched the thread.

September 30, 1778 (same day)

"One-Who-Runs sends me." Jonah of the Pasture of Light stood at the opening of the cabin.

Wind Maiden arose. "He comes back," she whispered. She sucked in smoke-air. She would follow him in the hunt. He would feed her deer's flesh. They would run from Goschachgunk where all eyes and mouths laughed and scolded and asked, "Who is Wind Maiden? We do not know the meaning of the words, 'Wind Maiden'."

"No. He is gone," answered Jonah.

The air turned to ashes in the throat of Wind Maiden.

Jonah looked toward the fire. "Five nights ago, he came to me and took a promise from my lips." The Aged Woman sat behind Wind Maiden. Jonah looked down at her. "He asked me to take the Aged Woman to Pasture of Light, to call her, 'Mother.' I come for her now."

"No!" Wind Maiden stood between his eyes and the Aged woman. "She is mine!" The only life she felt flowed from the eyes and hands of the Aged Woman. "I feed her, build her fire. She is mine."

Jonah shook his head. "You are a woman with no man. No man in Goschachgunk will share his flesh with you because you are no more. You cannot feed the Aged Woman. I shall take her to Pasture of Light."

"No!" cried Wind Maiden. But she felt the stinging truth of his words. She slid her foot back until she felt the roughness of the blanket of the Aged Woman. She looked up at Jonah, and she was the child pleading with Eagle-with-White-Head to take her with him into the forest on his pony. "I shall take the Aged Woman to Pasture of Light," she said in a soft, small voice.

The arms of Jonah hung at his sides. He looked at Wind Maiden, then around her at the shadowy figure of the Aged Woman. "This is your wish?" he asked of the silent form.

The gnarled hand patted the leg of Wind Maiden and the head nodded.

"Prepare your blankets and skins. I shall come again soon," said Jonah, turning to leave.

"We are ready." Wind Maiden gathered a bundle of pelts. She was dead to Goschachgunk. She would live no longer upon piles of dry bones. She handed the pelts to Jonah, turned back, and lifted the fragile body of the Aged Woman.

~ ~ ~

December 24, 1778

"Baby!" announced David as he caressed the small, carved infant Jesus, lying in its wooden manger.

Sarah lifted him in her arms so that he might see the entire Christmas Pitz arranged upon the bed of dry moss on the table of their one-room dwelling. "His mother, Mary; Joseph, her husband ..." She pointed to the figures within the stable and beyond, "... the shepherds, their sheep, the angels, the Magi." She rocked David in her arms. "And, next year, we shall add the town of Bethlehem." Sarah looked over her shoulder at Christoph.

Christoph arose from his chair. He took his hat in his hand. "You cannot remember, David, but I carved that lamb and those angels when we lived with the Indians. You were just born then."

"You tried to eat the angel," said Sarah.

"Eat cookies!" cried David, squirming to get down.

"Our son has another vision altogether," laughed Sarah, easing her son to the ground.

Christoph stared down at David. He did not seem to hear. "To the Watch Service, then," he said, taking the hand of David.

"No. More!" David demanded, pointing to a tray of marzipan candies molded into flowers and pears and apples.

"Too much already fills you," observed Christoph, poking his son's belly. "A finer thing and holier awaits: a beeswax candle for you to hold and watch. Its flame will burn like the flame of love that burns from Jesus for you."

"No. More!" persisted David.

December 24, 1778 (same day)

Wind Maiden laid the bearskin along the side wall of the meeting house of the White Man's Great Spirit. She took the bony shoulders of the Aged Woman and lowered her upon the fur. Wind Maiden crouched beside her.

"Sit here, on this bench," said the wife of Glikkikan.

Wind Maiden looked past her, for she would not hear.

The always-green branches of forest trees hung like snakes across the walls and ceiling. A small hunter's hut lay on a bench, crowded with carved people: manitos serving the Great Spirit, Wind Maiden decided, nodding her head. Fires burned from long, thin, wax sticks which twinkled like stars on a cold, dark night.

Wind Maiden dropped her eyes and watched from beneath lowered lids the people in the meeting house.

"Stupid fawn," she chided herself. "Why do you sit in the house of the White Man? Will his words burn your ears like they burn and make deaf the ears of these lenno?"

Many days she had stayed in the hut in the woods with the Aged Woman. She took food from Pasture of Light, but she would not eat it there. No! She was of the True Man, the tribe of the Turtle. Now they knew and understood, and she was glad. She would never live with them – lenno who painted their skins white.

"Safe, now, to come and watch their special feast," she told herself. She had heard from outside but had never sat among them as she did this night. Now she would see what this "Great Spirit" would do. Wind Maiden folded her arms, frowned, and waited.

Women in white strouds ... Wind Maiden grunted ... served baskets full of honey-dipped breads. Wind Maiden grabbed one, two, three for herself, paused, and grabbed one, two, three, four for the Aged Woman. She lowered her head, ate quickly, sealed the breads in the hand of the Aged woman, and watched her eat.

She grabbed two clanging drinking bowls filled with steaming brown water. Stone-tree sweet and warm, it flowed into her chest and stomach. She held the other bowl to the lips of the Aged Woman who drank and smiled.

Songs of the baby, the one who saves ..."What can a little one save?" she thought ... mingled with a story of his birth in a poor hut. That hunting lodge was the hut.

"... And he became the Mighty One, the son of the Great One," proclaimed the teacher, Zeisberger. "He lives today."

Wind Maiden looked around the meeting house.

"The flame of his love burns like wax sticks in the hearts of all who love him."

She looked at the bright, warm, flickering fires of the sticks, and the cold darkness inside of her seemed colder and darker than before.

She looked at the Aged Woman, rubbed the sticky bread from the wrinkled face, and sighed.

~ ~ ~

April 6, 1779

"Test Act! Taxes!" Sister Suzanne Voss rocked her new infant in her arms as she spoke. "John says the brethren should not obey the Test Act and take the oath of allegiance. We should be loyal but swearing our loyalty to the new government is borne of evil. Christ himself said that. John says, British or Colonial rule, we serve the one that Providence ordains victor."

Sarah stood beside Suzanne in the kitchen of the family house, kneading and turning a large lump of dough. "Certainly, Sister ..." she began.

"Yet John supports the giving of taxes although the weight of the militia burden is grievous," interrupted Suzanne.

"If we did not pay the taxes, they would recruit our men. Paying is better than fighting and killing," observed Sarah, tapping the dough with her finger. She pushed her hand into her side against a gnawing pain. "Moreover, Christoph says ..."

"John says the same and gives the forfeiture, if not joyfully, then at least willingly."

Sarah stretched the dough and cut it with a long knife into four segments. She paused, took the first of the segments, and began kneading. She counted the beats and turns of the dough. Suzanne rocked silently.

"Christoph says that it matters little whether we give our 'yea' to the Test Act," said Sarah. "He says that the Continental forces rule most assuredly now and a 'yea' is not an oath but a willingness to serve the powers that be over us."

"Add anise to that lump," suggested Suzanne.

"We shall bake much these coming days," said Sarah, pondering her sister's suggestion. "Cool days are good days for baking." Their cabin in Lichtenau of the wilderness was often filled with the smoke and the heat of baking. How her Indian sisters would have gasped in amazement to behold this large, high-ceilinged kitchen with its deep, stone fireplace and large, enclosed oven. She envisioned Sister Martha trotting the floor, scolding and directing her other sisters.

"More than I fancy to bake," confided Sister Suzanne. "Bishop Reichel probably enjoyed much diversity of pastries in Europe where they are not experiencing the privations of this war."

Sarah smiled. "We shall do well although modestly." She thought and decided, "I think not anise today."

"When do they arrive?" asked Suzanne.

"Brother De Schweinitz has been gone these six days. Perhaps, in a fortnight, he will lead them into Bethlehem."

Sarah paused. She bowed her head. Those cramps again. Two months often passed before her flow would begin. And, then, the cramps would gnaw as they did today. What would Wind Maiden concoct for them? And would she make them go away?

She folded the dough into a loaf and set it aside. Bishop John Friedrich Reichel, his wife, his family, and others, many others, sent by the Unity of the Brethren's Elders' Conference in Europe, would uplift its war-afflicted settlements in America. All would bake, prepare, pray, consult, organize, and organize again during his protracted visit to Bethlehem. Such labor! Would it be fruitful?

"Remember the simplicity of Lichtenau?" Sarah asked herself. They had labored for the barest needs and had taught only the kernel of truth.

In their clearing, in their cabins, what did they now?

April 6, 1779 (same day)

"I go to the trap." Wind Maiden crouched over the Aged woman in their round, dark hut and closed the blanket across the bony chest.

The old woman smiled a hollow-cheeked grin.

"Will you go to Pasture of Light with me? They leave this day — Zeisberger, Edwards, and their people."

The Aged Woman thumped her legs and shook her head. The brittle bones would not carry her down the path today.

"I shall tell you all I see," promised Wind Maiden, rising to leave. The gourd of cooked and mashed roots was beyond the grasp of the Aged Woman. Wind Maiden nudged it nearer.

"My Aged Woman," thought Wind Maiden as she wandered among the trees. "Mother of One-Who-Runs," she whispered. He would come back; he was hunting. "Too long in hunting," she warned. She snapped a dead branch from a tree. No more would he come back.

She knelt at a spring of clear water. It was her spring. She had found it under the flat rock. She filled her cupped hands and drank. One-Who-Runs ... long of legs, slender. The water dripped down her chin. It was like the touch of the hand of her husband, he who was once her husband. The water froze; the hand trembled, for she had wounded it. The dark face of the wolf loomed before her eyes. The pit of darkness filled with black, slimy liquid.

The raccoon trap of logs and sticks was empty. Wind Maiden turned toward Pasture of Light.

She walked along the Elk's Eye to where the trees stood back from the village. Many of the Lenni Lenape, some Mahicanni, some Shawano were carrying packs from cabins and huts. Some would follow Zeisberger back to the Beautiful Spring to build a new fire there; others would follow the twig-thin one to Huts of Grace to take back the cabins they had left empty and to rebuild the fire in the cold fire pit. Some would stay in Pasture of Light with Heckewelder, he who had smothered the beat of war when it had throbbed in Goschachgunk in the Youth of the last year.

"My youth," Wind Maiden thought. Her bones were old and brittle now; she was the Aged Woman.

She sat on a log — moss covered, wet. The coldness of the wood crept along her flesh.

"Those who stay, will they leave on a night when I cannot know?" she wondered.

She liked to watch them when they did not see her. But words, no! She did not wish to share words with them. "I am a branch of this sleeping tree. I do not move because I am cold and stiff like my mother below me. They will not see a woman, for I am a tree." Her eyes moved along the streets of the village, eyes hidden by leaves of hair.

"Will the rest leave me? Salah left me. But, no — I sent her away. Back to the place of the rising sun."

Glikkikan, called Isaac, led a horse, white-speckled brown, to a post in the street. The warrior. His battle cry had died upon his lips. Had its death settled into his heart as with her? Did he still eat the bitterness of death and did it sour his stomach and eat his stomach through? She could not ask him, she the tree.

The one named Amelia carried blankets from a cabin. She stopped. She looked toward the Elk's Eye. She saw the log, its branch. She waved her hand and walked toward the mossy one.

"No, no! No living thing is here! You cannot see the woman," Wind Maiden scolded in her head. The branch jumped up and fled.

~ ~ ~

January 14, 1780

The small, brown-mitted hand reached up from beneath a brown, hooded cloak and grasped the hand of Sarah. "Step high, little David," Sarah laughed, looking down at the woolen mound pushing its way through the white, sparkling, newly-fallen snow.

David stretched his other hand down and scooped the snow into his mitt. He held it near his face, pebbles of snow, sticking to the woolen ridges.

They entered God's Acre and met other footsteps in the snow. David jumped from step to step, slid upon one long stride, and fell. He dangled from Sarah's arm. She pulled him up, brushed him off, pulled his hood back over his head.

"Big hole," he groaned.

The land and the grave markers were draped in white. Sarah looked up; the sky was grey. Where it bent to touch the earth, it lightened with the snow's glow.

Beyond a fork in the path, Sister Naomi walked with her two children. Sarah nodded blessings and turned down the other path.

"Days upon days, weeks upon weeks, all similar," she thought. "Days to spin and days to weave, and days to spin again."

David trod ahead to a low-hanging branch of an oak.

"Once, I would have been content. Now ..." She paused to watch David try to climb the slippery side of the tree. His round arms clutched the limb as he swung his short legs up. She strained with him in his exertions.

"Come, David," she called. "Your father might be waiting for us at the end of the path."

She had begged Christoph to meet her after the midday meal: "If you must eat with the workers, then walk with us afterward."

"I could not every day," he had protested.

"Just tomorrow," she had begged.

"I shall try," he had grunted. "But this winter is hard on the cattle. We constantly attend them and, still, they collapse."

Must Christoph always have a mission? Was he, now, called to save the cattle?

"Christoph!" she called to the black-coated figure turned away from her. He was facing the tree they had sat under when first they met. He turned.

"Do I take you from important chores?" she asked.

"The cattle and the horses cannot find open ground for grazing," he replied. "There is always much to do."

David tromped around the legs of his father. "Climb the tree," he begged.

Christoph lifted him up the bark. David scrambled toward a limb. He perched above, clinging to the arm of Christoph.

Sarah bit her lip. "Our tree," she said. "Do you remember?"

He cocked his head sideways and gazed at her.

How foolish she was to be sentimental. She rubbed her foot across the snow.

"Must you ask, Sarah?"

She shrugged. She looked up at David.

Christoph swung David down. David stumbled into the snow, stood, and stumbled again.

Christoph stared at her. "I could not forget this tree." He grabbed her fidgeting hand. "I remember our first stroll more keenly with the passing time, for more unites us now than then."

They watched David jumping into smooth, virgin snow. David united them; he was both of them.

Christoph continued, "You and I share the fervor of my vision."

That was the bond? Anything more?

"And David ..." she mumbled.

"Always David!" he exclaimed. "Soon, we shall return." He bowed over her: "I accomplish nothing in Bethlehem ..."

"And my service is just spinning ... here," she echoed.

"The war is abating. Be patient, Sarah."

Could their union ever stand apart from their commitment, together, to the mission? If one dissolved, would the other be destroyed as well?

They watched David run between the grave markers.

"He will like it there," she said.

"Sarah, he cannot return to the Ohio country with us."

Sarah pulled her hand free from his.

Christoph grabbed her arm. "It is a time of war. He could not be safe there."

She wanted to cry, "Do not say that!" She remembered the nights she had lain on a child's bed in the older girls' building in Bethlehem. In the darkness of her room, she would draw in her mind the face of each parent. She would make them smile at her and tell her that they loved her. She would ask God to tell them that she missed them and wanted them to return soon — before the snows, before the harvest, before ...

"He is too young to be separated from us," she protested. "And to be housed with the Young Boys' Group, oh, it is a lonely life. The sisters are kind, but there are many boys and energy fails. It is not for David. We cannot leave him."

She had been twelve. He would be far younger than she had been. She had no parents. Strangers had begotten her. It would not be so with David.

Christoph sighed. "I shall speak with the Mission Board," he said.

As Sarah reached for his hands, he raised them, palms facing her: "Expect nothing, for their regulations are explicit: children shall not travel to the mission posts during these perilous times." He shook his head, his eyes solemn. "There is a war, Sarah."

Christoph would persuade them. They would return. All of them.

January 14, 1780 (same day)

Rain. It clung, was ice on trees, on snow-crusted ground, on bark hut. Wind Maiden built the fire high in the hut. The Aged Woman shivered. Under blankets, pelts, somewhere lay the Aged Woman. Why did she still shake?

Feet from Pasture of Light had cracked the ice and brought stew, hot, for the Aged Woman. They wanted to take her to their village. But Wind Maiden said her old woman should not go. The ice would freeze upon her bones, and she would crack like the snow. They brought dry wood; then Wind Maiden made them leave.

She scooped the brown, steaming liquid into a gourd. She held the shaking head of the Aged Woman and tapped the dry, cracked lips with her finger. "Drink, Ancient One." The lips did not open; the eyes did not flutter.

Wind Maiden placed the gourd to the closed lips. Warm liquid flowed down the creased chin.

Wind Maiden crouched beside the Aged Woman's bench. She reached beneath the blankets and took the fingers of cold bones. "My Aged Woman," she whispered. The bones shook; she squeezed them.

The bones squeezed back once, twice.

"Do not shake, silent river. Rain cannot fall on you here. I build a large fire. And look! Many blankets and pelts. I keep you warm." Her voice fell; she pleaded, "Do not shake." She was a small girl on a cold night, huddled against the roots of a cold tree: "I keep you warm."

The shaking stopped. "Good Aged Woman," whispered Wind Maiden.

She waited. Cold, cold lay the Aged Woman. Frozen lay the body. Ice the bones became. Frozen roots enclosed the hand of Wind Maiden.

Ice spread up from the bones of the Aged Woman and flowed through the blood and the bones of Wind Maiden. Dead was the hand of the Aged Woman, and dead was the hand, the arm, the head, the chest, the body of Wind Maiden.

"Owwww! Owwww! Owwww!" Moans rolled upon moans.

"Owwwwwwwwwwwww!" Only echoing groans remained and rose from the chest of Wind Maiden.

April 6, 1780

"You would not return, would you?" An elderly sister whispered across the table in the large dining hall of the Family House.

"Of course, Sister Rachel," replied Sarah. "Soon. May, perhaps. Is it not so, Brother Christoph?"

Christoph was piling sauerkraut over his mashed potatoes. "Is not what so?" he asked without looking up.

"We shall return to the Ohio country. May, perhaps. Sister Rachel was inquiring ..."

"Yes," he said, smiling with a mouth full of chicken and onion at Sister Rachel.

"The Indian incursion on the frontier settlements — is that not a hindrance?" asked a masculine voice on Christoph's left.

Christoph paused. "Certainly. But not as severe a danger as it was in these two years past. Since Colonel Brodhead's expedition against the Seneca in the fall of seventy-nine forced the warring tribes to flee north to Niagara, we have more liberty to take the western trails."

Sister Rachel leaned forward. "Men can easily endure such dangers. You, Sister Sarah ..." She shrugged and gave a knowing sidelong glance at Sarah.

"Yes," said Sarah, fixing her eyes on those of her sister. She looked down on her slender wrists, white and smooth. She was a woman, and, more, she was a ... how would Sister Rachel express it? ... she was a "delicate" woman.

"I fear the warring Indians," she conceded to her sister. She envisioned scalps and prisoners and brutal, paint-smeared faces. "I have seen such men," she continued. Sarah veiled the faces from her mind. "I should not return if my memory contained but that." She smiled. "We have brethren and sisters who need us. Them I remember and forget the other."

Her mind amended, "Usually I forget." There were nights when she would see in the darkness names, endless names of prisoners she could not redeem. She could never see faces and wished she could. Names had no life.

She drank some milk.

"We are, indeed, needed in the Ohio country," explained Christoph, addressing his brother. "The mission at Lichtenau has dispersed into three settlements. Teachers, especially women, are being requested by Brother Zeisberger. We, Brother and Sister Senseman, perhaps others will fulfill this call."

Sarah watched his hand move as he spoke. That hand, that face — made prominent by hair pulled tightly back — were pale; they needed the dampness of the forest and the sun and the wind on the mission plantations to revive the dark roughness of life to them.

"If the call of the Lord is upon you," Sister Rachel was speaking again, "then you can be content knowing that your son will be well cared for here in Bethlehem in the Young Boys' Group."

Sarah followed her gaze to David who was perched beside Sarah. He was licking gooseberry preserves off a slice of bread, smiling up at Rachel. Sarah's heart beat in her throat. "But, of course, he is going with us," she replied.

The large room seemed suddenly silent as even Christoph turned to stare at her.

April 6, 1780 (same day)

Wind Maiden crouched outside her hut. She waited. She turned her ears to the sounds from Pasture of Light. They left today. Some up the Elk's Eye in canoes and others along the trails with horses and black cattle. Since the death of White Eyes, Goschachgunk was no longer a friend; the voice of the Quaekel was no longer heard. Chief Gelelemend listened, but his words were small and weak. Chiefs Machingive Pushis and Tetepachksi, who sat at the council fire, spoke louder words of love for the Saggenash and Delamatteno and Mengwe. They were heard.

So the Quaekel, Heckewelder, took his people to a new home, the place of Peace, Salem.

Wind Maiden slid her carrying strap upon her forehead and stood. She bent forward and balanced the weight of her pack on her back. She moved through the darkness of the forest toward the clearing and Pasture of Light. "Not yet," she told herself. She stopped.

Goschachgunk had come. Some lenno from the Pasture of Light were clasping hands with them. Others were loading canoes or leading cattle to the trail. The village behind was dead, its fire pit cold. Its meeting house for its Great Spirit was torn, its wooden bones scattered upon the ground. They took their Saviour with them.

"Now." She pulled in her breath and stood erect; the pack yanked back her neck. Her heart beat fast and told her to run, but her head told her feet to walk slowly and told her eyes to look at no one. She walked out toward where Goschachgunk stood.

Her eyes wanted to see her father, Fish-of-the-Deep-Water, who stood with the Lenape of the council. She would not let her eyes turn to look. Her eyes wished to look at Star-at-Dawning and to remember. She said, "No," but looked.

Her mother, small and wide, looked back. She raised her head; her small mouth opened. Her head turned ... away.

She was dead to Mother, Father, Goschachgunk ... dead. Wind Maiden walked past.

Another ache, deep inside where the death lay: Eagle-with-White-Head. She felt his eyes then saw his face. He did not turn away, but his face did not call her to him. A question burned her lips and tongue: "Brother, where is One-Who-Runs? Tell him I wait." The words slid down her throat before the air could carry them from her lips. They burned in her stomach. She called her feet to the trail.

Ahead, the last of the lenno from Pasture of Light turned into the black, sweet forest. Was there a place of peace? She would follow and see.

14
JUNE 16, 1780 – JUNE 30, 1789

"Days grew long in waiting for you," said Sister Anna Benigna. "Our faces crease; streams flow in sorrow from our eyes. You are here. The waters flow more slowly now."

"It is good," Sarah answered, forming the long-unused Unami words first in her mind, then on her tongue. She stretched her legs, cramped and tingling from the long ride. She smiled at each of her sisters: Anna Benigna, Amelia, Elizabeth, Martha, Hanna, others whom she did not know. Swinging her arms at her sides, she searched her mind for more of those elusive words.

"Sister! Your journey was not full of evil?" asked Elizabeth.

Sarah looked into Elizabeth's round face, darker, more worn than she remembered. "Not much evil ..." She recalled the stillness, unnatural and ominous, that hovered over every abandoned settlement; ragged, untended fields; burnt cabins; hastily painted signs on doors warning, "Indians on warpath. Massacre. Flee east. River." They had seen no one — not Indians, not White Men. She had rebuked the fears of another trip and had refused them entrance into her mind ... By the strength of God ...

"Across the Allegheny River beyond Fort Pitt," Sarah continued, "White Men shot into our camp. We thank ..."

"You rest now," consoled Martha, patting her shoulder. She shook her head: "White and bony! You need ..."

"Stop the flow," whispered Amelia. Louder she said, "We have built you a bark hut, not large ..."

"Sister. Such goodness," said Sarah.

Elizabeth patted Sarah's arm with her warm, moist palm and nodded toward another cluster of brethren and sisters. "She is second Salah?" she asked.

Sarah followed Elizabeth's gaze. Brother Heckewelder stood beside Sister Sarah Ohneberg of Bethlehem, his betrothed. She was tall, stocky, dark. Her hands were folded in front of her. Her head nodded in greeting to the Indian Brethren. Brother and Sister Senseman, Brother Adam Grube, all stood on the other side of Brother Heckewelder.

"Yes, the other Sarah," agreed Sarah. She motioned with her head, avoiding pointing: "Brother and Sister Senseman stay with you. Brother Grube goes back to Bethlehem."

"You stay ..." Martha rocked her head back and forth, "... with us?"

Sarah looked beyond her friends, beyond the cluster of horses to where Christoph stood with Brothers Isaac and Jonah on the edge of the village, surveying the plain on which Salem stood. Brother Jonah's outstretched arm waved toward a small, neat cluster of young stalks of maize. Christoph, hands on hips, legs apart, surveyed the plain — the grass, the trees, the crops. "I think ..." Sarah hesitated. Christoph was nodding his head. He now rested his large hand on Brother Isaac's shoulder. She concluded, "... no, we go to Huts of Grace."

She raised her brows and looked around at her sisters. "Brother Heckewelder, his new wife, Brother and Sister Senseman ..." Her voice rose; she hoped they would understand, "... they teach you here. We are too many. Huts of Grace is a greater need."

They stood in silence.

Children laughed, playing along the river.

Amelia called, "Leah! Do not splash water on little Mary!"

Mary. The age of David. Sarah blinked.

Amelia turned to her: "Where is your little one of three winters past," she asked, "the David you carried when I grew fat with that one, Mary?"

Sarah looked at Amelia. A voice pleaded, "No, Christoph! We must bring David with us."

She replied to Amelia, "He is in Bethlehem." She hoped her voice was calm. She could not tell; it spoke so far away.

Christoph had pressed her shoulders between his hands: "He cannot go, Sarah. You must understand. The dangers, the war ..."

Amelia grabbed Sarah's hand in both of hers. Her dark eyes looked into Sarah's faltering eyes. "You give the Saviour much."

Sarah dropped her gaze. Much? She fought her Lord till she was weak and only then gave Him what He asked.

Avoiding her sisters, she looked about the village, new, as Lichtenau once had been. A chapel of squared timber, bearing cupola and bell, stood in the center of the village. Permanent cabins and temporary huts of bark grew outward from the chapel.

"Beautiful village," murmured Sarah.

Anna Benigna nodded. "Peace fled from Pasture of Light and Goschachgunk. Not Delamatteno and not Mengwe only, but Lenape who once called themselves by the name, 'friend,' took horses and food from us and gave the new name of friend to the Mengwe warriors. Better are these huts of Peace than the cabins and trees of fruit in the Pasture once of light, now darkness."

"No friends in Goschachgunk?" asked Sarah. "Not ... Wind Maiden?" she thought.

"We have friends ... some," replied Anna Benigna.

Sarah rubbed her forehead. An enemy she had forgotten was watching her, breathing rhythmically and patiently beside her.

"I shall rest now," she said.

~ ~ ~

"Sarah?" Christoph was kneeling beside her on the dirt floor, shaking her shoulders.

She rolled onto her back and stared up toward his face, dark in the blackness of the hut. "Is it night?" she asked.

"Not yet. We are eating the evening meal."

Sarah sat up. "I had not thought to sleep." She pressed stray strands of brown hair beneath her cap. "I dreamt of David again." Christoph. How could he understand? She sighed to hold back the flow of more words.

Even in the darkness, Sarah sensed his impatience and could almost hear him say, "We have discussed these things before."

But he replied, "David is young. He will forget. And, when he is older, he will understand."

"Yes, I know ..." Sarah looked past his face. When her parents left her, she had not forgotten, and, for many years, she had not understood. She had been older, yes; that would make it harder, would it not?

He said, "He is loved. Brother John and Sister Suzanne will love him as their own."

"Yes," agreed Sarah. Her voice sounded weary.

Yet she could not really thank God. Sister Suzanne had three of her own children. She did not need the one, the only child of Sarah.

And Christoph did not seem to mourn their loss. This ... this vision had cost them their son. Had she thought it united them? No! It tore them apart.

But she was wrong; she was always wrong. "Do something, Lord," she pleaded. Do something with what? Herself? The vision? Or her sense of unutterable loss?

Christoph helped her to her feet.

The large, black pot of stew hung over an open fire. Long planks became tables for communal dining.

Sarah's eyes wandered past the congregation along the Muskingum toward the forest. A dark shape stood forward from the trees, still in the shadow of one. It quivered, turned, and vanished. Sarah's memory formed itself around another image of the same tall, slender form, hidden in the shadows, body rigid, face frowning.

Brother Heckewelder prayed the blessing upon the food. Christoph handed Sarah a bowl of stew and led her to a seat beside Brother and Sister Senseman.

Wind Maiden. She was here.

Anna Benigna sat across and down from Sarah. "Sister," Sarah said, raising her hand slightly. Should she have spoken in privacy? Yet she had not patience to wait.

Anna Benigna looked up.

"Wind Maiden," began Sarah, "from Goschachgunk ..."

"Near," nodded Anna Benigna.

Sarah ate the thick stew in silence. Wind Maiden here? Yet not ... here, not among them.

After the meal, while the congregation gathered for the evening worship in the new chapel, Sarah excused herself from Christoph and walked, not quickly, to Anna Benigna. She nodded at Sister Senseman and avoided the glance of Sister Martha.

"Sister," she began and hoped her voice betrayed no anxiety, "Wind Maiden, I saw her ... I believe I ... saw her, near the forest. There." She indicated the spot by the river's edge with a nod of her head.

"Yes," replied Anna Benigna. "My thoughts were to tell you. Tomorrow, the day that follows."

"She lives here?" asked Sarah. Where were her parents, then, or One-Who-Runs? Much was not as it once had been.

"Not here ..." Anna Benigna swayed her hands palms upward as she talked. "She is a silent one. She takes food like a wild squirrel and disappears. She lives in a hut in the wetness of the forest."

"Her husband, he lives with her?" Sarah felt an uneasiness rise from her stomach.

"He is gone. Some say he is dead because he did not come back when the Aged Woman froze in death." Sister Anna Benigna hesitated upon her words and looked about at the brethren who were now disappearing into the chapel. She continued, "The Lenni Lenape no longer look upon Wind Maiden. She ran after two husbands and lost both. She is a useless thing now. No man will share his meat with her. They think that she would bend the bullet so it would not fly straight."

Wind Maiden had always seemed a child. How old was she? Seventeen, eighteen perhaps? She was a woman, then. Sarah said, "I shall go to her, speak."

"This squirrel is wild," warned Anna Benigna.

"We are friends," explained Sarah.

"It makes no friends," Anna Benigna replied.

"I can help her!" Sarah exclaimed. How presumptuous she sounded. But she did understand suffering and loss. Even now she could feel the soft, smooth warmness of David's cheek pressed against her own, the touch of his small hand in hers. "You take food to her?" asked Sarah.

"Yes, at the rising of the sun or as it falls behind the hills. When we see her waiting ..." She looked to where Sarah had noticed the form of Wind Maiden. "... there."

"Tomorrow," said Sarah, "tell me when she waits. I shall take food."

The next morning, Sarah opened her eyes and stared at the bark overhead. She rolled onto her side. The bedding of straw softly crinkled. Finally, she lay on her back, staring into the parting darkness.

"Today," she thought, "Saturday. David will walk with Sister Suzanne and Brother John along the Lehigh. He will play with the other children. He might ..." She held her breath. She saw David throwing stones into the river. She wanted to gather him in her arms.

"Stop!" A sob pressed against her throat. She pursed her lips. "Lord," she prayed, "keep me from useless ..." Worse than useless, "... exhausting thoughts."

Sarah rolled to her side to look at the morning light which entered the hut through the low entrance. Her glance fell upon Christoph. He lay on his side, watching her.

"Have you been awake long?" asked Sarah, lifting herself on her elbow. Her face burned with embarrassment. She felt as if her thoughts had been whispered into the heavy air.

"No," he replied. His face was partly in shadow; the strong line of his chin was accentuated by the sharp contrast of light and darkness. "Did you sleep well?"

"Yes, better than on the journey." She had awakened often. Sounds, perhaps, or memories, or regrets had drawn her to the edge of wakefulness. Shadows under her eyes had always betrayed her to Christoph. She would not have told him had he not guessed.

He reached out his hand and took her waist. "Good. I believed that you would relax once here. Your regrets about our son might ..."

"I shall do well," she interjected lest his words should cause her thoughts to flow and her mouth should give them vent. "I know that the Lord has planned for us to be here."

She had been brazen to require provisions from God, but she would not go without them. "I cannot leave David in the Young Boys' Group, Father. You know my sufferings as a child; do not require the same of David. If you send us, prepare another home for him."

He had provided. Sister Suzanne came to her one day and asked to take David, to raise him as one of her own.

"As one of her own." Surely the Lord had made provision for Christoph and her to return.

And, yet, she could have refused to accompany Christoph to the mission. She could have forced him to stay with her and David. Then what had made her consent? The power of God? That vision? She could see it lying hidden in the recesses of Christoph's life. The vision — that was why he had married her and why she had married him. The vision, not the family, was her first commitment. The vision — she hated it.

However, did more than this lead her back to the Ohio settlements, something inside herself? But if she acknowledged it, then ... the guilt for leaving David would be her own.

Sarah arose to dress. She avoided the gaze of Christoph. What could she say to him? Her thoughts were of David, and Christoph surely had tired of them. Whenever she tried to reminisce, his jaw and face tightened. She knew her words were tedious to him. In Bethlehem, their anticipation of returning had bound them together, but the loss of David was now a wedge between them.

Sarah was tying under her chin the blue ribbon of her cap when the church bell rang for morning worship.

She sat beside Sister Senseman upon the first long bench in the sisters' side of the chapel. Christoph sat across with the men, his Bible and his message clutched in his hand, that message, composed through three years of waiting in Bethlehem. He could, again, pursue his plan for a Christian Indian State in this wilderness. But could she run with him?

Later, they ate their pottage of greens and roots outside the cabin of Sister Amelia and Brother Jonah. Christoph and Brother Jonah were huddled together discussing the new rows in the orchard, and Sarah was describing to Sister Amelia the organ in Bethlehem when Anna Benigna appeared from beside the cabin.

"The silent squirrel, she waits." She pointed to the river's edge where a solitary form stared toward the village.

Sarah arose. "I go," she said.

"That one will not speak," warned Amelia. "She is rock inside."

Sarah looked at Amelia: "She is my friend."

Amelia cast her eyes away from Sarah's. She looked at the remains of the pottage in the kettle. "Take this." She scooped out the soup with a gourd and offered it to Sarah.

Amelia turned her head sideways and caught Sarah's eyes with her own: "She will not speak," she repeated.

Sister Anna Benigna nodded her agreement.

Sarah looked back at Christoph who was walking toward the orchard with Jonah. She cradled the gourd in her hands and approached her friend.

"I am a tree; my greenness covers me," Wind Maiden whispered.

Sarah called, "Friend! I am happy to see you." Wind Maiden did not move. She looked stiff and lifeless. Did she not recognize Sarah? "I bring food." She paused ten feet from Wind Maiden and lifted the gourd out from her chest. Still Wind Maiden did not move.

"The tree remembers nothing," she told herself. "This ... White woman ... carries the face of something once known, no longer known. I shall take its food when it comes closer."

"You do not remember your friend?" asked Sarah.

Wind Maiden swayed her head. "The tree does not speak, silly woman," she thought. "It remembers that this was a foolish, a silly woman."

Sarah hesitated. A thin veil of skin covered the protruding bones of Wind Maiden's body. Her eyes stared from behind the arches of high cheekbones, eyes black, flitting back and forth. Hair, once shining and smooth, now dull and broken, was pulled back from her face and tied, accentuating the gentle chin, the slender neck, the skeleton face.

Sarah took one, two steps toward Wind Maiden.

Wind Maiden bowed forward, slid the gourd from Sarah's hands, and pressed it to her own chest.

She paused. "The tree almost remembers this woman. It went away before ..." She stiffened her body and rustled her head. "No! That hurts!" Wind Maiden turned and fled.

"I come again. Tomorrow," called Sarah.

Wind Maiden entered darkness ... her forest. She followed the path to her stump. She stopped, looked behind and around, then sat, lightly, a small, brown bird landing on a branch. She held the gourd near her mouth and scooped up the thick liquid with her fingers, into her mouth. She licked her fingers and rubbed them against her blue stroud.

"Salah," she said to the gnarled branch of a tree. "I once spoke, 'You will come back ... '" The mouth of Wind Maiden stopped, but words continued in her mind: "... later, when we have pushed back the Big Knife. The warrior will be full of other flesh and will not chase the foolish turkey. You will see, yes! We shall live in peace with you then."

Wind Maiden stood. The gourd fell. Her arms, dead branches, hung at her sides. "Spitting words," she told the trees. "The warrior is full of my flesh. I spoke the truth. But I did not know ... my flesh."

She walked her narrow path to her small bark hut. Its low opening awaited her. "Salah is here," she said, looking at the dark opening. She bent low and entered

She crouched on the dirt and waited for her sight to follow her inside. Very soon, she saw the fire pit. Behind it, against the bark of her hut, lay her net. Wind Maiden crawled over and lifted it.

She roamed through the trees toward the Elk's Eye. "One-Who-Runs — gone; Aged Woman — gone; Star-at-Dawning — gone;" she thought, "all gone, all dead, dead like Wind Maiden ... dead." She stopped at the edge of the river and looked over into the water. "The red-spotted salmon swims today; I can call him into my net." She paused before casting her net into the water: "But Salah is not dead."

She went to the village the next morning; the tree, not Wind Maiden, stood by the edge of the Elk's Eye. Salah had said she would come back; the tree would see. Salah came with food, but the tree pulled its branches around itself and would not answer when Salah spoke.

Later, Wind Maiden stood quietly, not even rustling, within her shadow of the forest to watch the people in the Place of Peace as they worked and talked and walked. One time, two times, she saw Salah.

The tree returned the next morning and the evening of the day following. Salah came to her again, and again.

On the fifth sun rising, Wind Maiden returned to the village of Peace to wait again, and Salah came.

"The clouds gather today," said Sarah as she reached forward, only slightly forward, a maize paste wrapped in a large, green leaf. Today, she would force Wind Maiden to approach nearer. "A frightened squirrel," thought Sarah. "You want your morsel? Come take it."

Wind Maiden did not move. "I can wait," decided Sarah.

"Come closer, White woman," thought the tree. "I must have you closer before I grab your food." The White woman did not move.

The tree swayed its head from side to side. This woman did not understand. The tree would have to break its roots and come nearer to this ... foolish woman. It ripped up roots, a wonderful pain, and walked to the White woman and looked into her face.

Sarah held her breath; she feared to move lest even the flick of her eye might stir flight in her friend. Wind Maiden reached forward two slender, long-fingered hands. Her dark skin rubbed against the pale skin of Sarah as she slid the rolled leaf from Sarah's hands.

"You said I would return." Sarah whispered. They stood close.

"You could not hear my words then," answered Wind Maiden. Her eyes fastened upon the face of Salah.

Sarah paused. She could count her own and Wind Maiden's breaths. "I remembered you in Bethlehem."

"Truly? I thought you forgot; everyone forgot."

Wind Maiden turned and walked away.

"Tomorrow?" called Sarah.

Wind Maiden looked back and nodded, once, then scurried among the trees.

She lay upon her bear's fur bedding that night and listened to the chatter of the trees. They never talked to her; they did not know her.

Salah remembered. She rolled herself into a ball on her side. Salah remembered.

Wind Maiden returned the next sun rising. Salah asked about her hut. Wind Maiden told her it was a small hole to sleep in; that was all.

That day, Wind Maiden called back words and sights from days when she had been alive. She saw Salah walking past Wind Maiden's hut in Goschachgunk. She saw Star-at-Dawning holding up the little, wrinkled one.

"Where is your son?" asked Wind Maiden the next morning.

"David," Sarah said and looked past Wind Maiden toward the river. Strength drained from her. "He is in Bethlehem." She looked at Wind Maiden. "He did not come with us."

"You left him alone!" Wind Maiden was the son of Salah, crying in the night for the soft smoothness of his mother. "You cannot feel! You do not know," she cried.

And fled.

Sarah stood for a long time with the bowl of stewed deer's meat in her hands, staring at the spot where Wind Maiden had disappeared into the forest. Finally, she slid onto the ground.

She had failed. Wind Maiden wept and David wailed. And she could not reach either one.

"God, it was you, was it not, who led me here? I believed. What shall I do if I was wrong?"

She returned to Salem; she had to. She had preparations for the marriage of Sister Sarah Ohneberg and Brother Heckewelder to complete, chores to do, sisters to counsel. But her thoughts traveled a mountainous journey back to Bethlehem.

The Mission Board had refused to consider their request to take David with them. "Shall we seek elsewhere for a brother and sister to teach the Indian brethren?" they had asked.

"Perhaps," Christoph had replied.

"I told them we would decide within two days," he had told Sarah that night.

Sarah had watched Christoph, her mind exploding. She could allow Christoph to return to the mission alone, or force him to forsake the work among the Indians, or ...

"Do not stare at me, stricken, Sarah." Christoph had leaned over and enclosed her nervous hands in his.

She had wanted to pull away from him; she did stiffen.

"God has prepared plans for us; we shall seek His guidance." Christoph was looking into her face, his own face solemn. "He can do all things. If our Lord chooses to separate us from David for a season, He will grant grace sufficient ..."

"How could you, Christoph. How could you speak so ..." Her voice had risen, faltered, then continued, "... unfeelingly about your son. To merely ..." Sarah had watched his thick brows rise. He had released her hands and sat back in his chair. She had concluded in her mind, "... merely apply reason to such rending suffering." But the words had crumbled before she could utter them. She had wanted Christoph to respond with anguish and rage. Yes! To strike out at God, at anyone who would deny their right to their possession of David. How dare anyone rip apart her very soul.

She had looked for words in the tight air about them. "I cannot choose the impossible," she had whispered.

"I ask nothing of you, Sarah, but to seek the Lord." Christoph's voice had sounded too patient. His eyes had stared not at Sarah but into her.

The Lord would ask the impossible; how could she go to Him? "What can He know of my agony?" she had asked.

"Much," Christoph had replied, rising.

Sarah had been defeated. She had known she was wrong, that her words had been less than foolish. She had wanted to be left alone — by Christoph, by God, by everyone. "Yes, much," she had echoed.

The next morning, Sarah had dressed David early and had taken him for a walk along the Lehigh River. They had left the last street and had walked across a small field to reach the river upstream from Bethlehem. The April breeze had stung her cheeks and fingertips. She had wound David's brown woolen scarf around his neck and had watched him run ahead in his eager, uncertain gait.

She had paused to watch the wind ripple the water: rhythmic laps along the bank. She had walked, rested, watched David cast stones into the water, observed the widening circles those pebbles formed, and shooed David from the edge of the water where he was trying to slide into the mud.

Peace had fled. She could not glean from all around her nor gain from within her heart the solution of God to her plight.

"What do you require of Me?" she had whispered. "Why do you allow me to suffer? You gave us David; would you so quickly take him away? Must David suffer as well? Why?"

Silence, thick and heavy, had rolled upon her. "Why are you so far from me?" Finally, she had beckoned David and hurried back to Bethlehem.

Sarah had remained in the church building that evening after the final hymn was sung, after the last chord of the organ had faded. Christoph had taken David with him and had nodded at her; he had understood. She had bowed her head until the sound of the last departing footstep had ceased, for she could not endure the raised brows or solicitous stares. Still, she had waited.

Finally, she had looked up. A few candles and lanterns continued to burn.

She had spoken into the twilight of the high-ceilinged room. "Here am I. My head aches from much thinking. I can reason no more. Do what you will."

"Do what you will."

Sarah had waited. She had thought she would be like the frightened bird, caught in a snare of omnipotent will, that could only wait. She was not. Her own will had been the snare.

Released from it, she could soar.

Had God ever given David to her? Had she not snatched him as a possession? Could Sarah choose the course most needful for David's soul? Never. God alone knew the road.

So she had relinquished David, relinquished Christoph, relinquished her own self and all that she had desired into the hands of the Saviour.

And she returned with Christoph.

She understood the fury of Wind Maiden, for she could not in her own self justify her abandonment of David. Yet God had required it. Only believing this could she find peace.

Sarah waited two, three, four days for Wind Maiden to return. Her time to reconcile was short; in one week, Brother Heckewelder would wed, and then she and Christoph would leave for Gnadenhutten.

On the fourth evening, Wind Maiden appeared, the sun setting in flames behind her.

"Why did you leave him?" she asked as soon as she could see the eyes of Salah.

"Our Saviour called us to come back. We cannot live here with David. Much danger."

"Your Saviour does not bruise or bleed ..." Wind Maiden saw tobacco flame to a manito. "... He is like a fire eating a forest. It does not care."

"No. He cares. That is why He sent us here."

Wind Maiden sneered, "Not for your son, your Saviour cares nothing for him."

"Can Salah not see the truth?" she thought. "This manito makes her blind."

She said aloud, "Alone. It is not good. I know this."

"Our son is not alone." Sarah pushed down frustration. And other feelings were rising with the accusations of Wind Maiden, accusations which hit the chords of her own still vibrating pain. "David is with a man, woman, children who love him. God did this for him."

"You are not there. You do not love him?" Wind Maiden watched the face and hands of Salah.

Sarah rubbed her chin with her fingertips. "I love him very much. God first."

"Your god demands the first love?" This was a powerful and selfish god.

"Yes. But he gives me the best love in return."

"This is the best love," Wind Maiden mocked, "to allow your son ..." She looked at the brown, tired eyes of Salah, "... and you to suffer? Why?"

"Why?" thought Sarah. She said, "He knows. I do not. He knows what must be done."

"So!" Wind Maiden would open to Salah her folly. "He makes suffering, but he does not suffer. Your god is powerful, yes. He is not loving."

"He suffered. He lived once, not like a chief or captain, but like you live. His friends ran from him. He was tortured — nails pounded into his hands and feet — and died ... for you. He sent me here to tell you."

"Yes?" asked Wind Maiden. She turned away. She had heard this before, but the words were always garbled in her head. She would listen to them again.

Wind Maiden lay in the darkness upon her fur. She told herself the words of Salah. Her eyes opened on blackness. Dead to mother, father, husband. Dead to Wind Maiden. A god lived that way? Died by torture? A manito would have more power; he would not die. So. This god was no god, or he lived and died because he wanted to. Then he was foolish. A god with no power or a foolish god ... he could not help Wind Maiden. A manito could lie, too; she knew this. It could lie to darken the eyes and dull the mind. Wind Maiden stretched her legs. She would learn about this god.

She arose before the sun pulled himself from beneath the earth; she wanted to greet him. The ground was wet with rain. Wind Maiden wrapped her blanket around herself, crouched, and waited. The sun hid its path behind a thick, grey cloud. "Not good," thought Wind Maiden. He will not listen. He knows I am dead."

Finally, the sun slid from behind the cloud. He stared at Wind Maiden with great boldness. She would be bold. She stood; her blanket fell to the ground.

"Grandfather," she called, "you know all ... all secrets. You stand in the pathway to the village of the blessed. You know who lives there. I hear stories about a god who lived the way I live here, in this hut." The sun crawled behind a cloud.

"Do not laugh at me. I laughed long ago, before ..." The sun peeked at her from the other side of the cloud. "I do not laugh now; I do not laugh at all."

"Grandfather, I must know this thing. Do you see this god? Does he live? Or does a mocking spirit lie?" The sun disappeared. "Do not flee. Speak to me what you know." Grey clouds floated together. The sky grew black; the earth grew dark.

The rain fell two days and two nights. Wind Maiden took food from Salah. They gave each other greetings, nothing more. The rain was a wide river words could not cross.

Wind Maiden sat in her hut; rain slipped under the bark and dripped puddles of mud. She did not seal the openings and force the rain to leave. She welcomed it and moved aside so it would have more room to drop. Its plop, plop spoke numbness to her mind.

The sun would not tell her about this god that is no god. Maybe the sun feared him; or maybe the sun would not answer foolish questions; or maybe he would not speak to her who was dead.

Salah had said this god had died, so maybe he would speak to Wind Maiden, the dead to the dead. How would she beckon him so he would speak? She did not have deer's flesh or bear's flesh to sacrifice to him. She did not have tobacco to throw into the fire. She could get maize, not her maize, but she would not tell him that.

Maize. She went in the rain on the second night, a hunter stalking his prey. It was not far, the village. The forest, black; the trees, dripping; the leaves, wet and slippery ... made the journey long. She heard rustles behind her. The brown wolf or the grey wild cat stalked ... her. Wind Maiden stopped. She listened, her eyes wide, her ears peering behind bushes and trees. Her heart pounded. The hunter.

The village was not covered with deep darkness like the forest. She would run, hide, scurry or they might see her on this clouded but too bright night. She crouched and scampered, low. Warriors ran that way.

She crept to the edge of the village, to a cabin with many wide openings on its sides. She slid through an opening near the ground and rolled onto a raised wooden floor. She could have crawled through the door, but the door looked toward the other huts. The maize of the last harvest, the maize of Pastures of Light, was stacked near the side and back of the cabin. Wind Maiden stood and breathed. She slipped forward and felt the maize ears with her hands, seeing each with her fingers. Her eyes saw mostly darkness. She lifted two off the top of a pile. A third rolled when she lifted the second. "That is mine now," she thought and groped in the darkness to find it. She hid the maize inside her stroud.

Going to the door, she looked out upon the village of Peace. Wind Maiden stood straight. She lifted her chin high. She saw no one nor the light of a fire. She heard not a sound. Through the door and along the outer wall of the cabin she slid until she reached its corner. She turned toward the forest and ran ... lightly.

Inside her hut, Wind Maiden lit a fire of dry twigs and small branches. She sat upon her mat and examined the ears of maize, first one, then the other, and the other. Good. Maize, her maize, to offer this god. She slid each ear into the hot ashes surrounding the fire. Lying upon her bearskin, she faced the sparkling fire, rested her head on her arm, and watched the flames, bursting bright and white, rising into blue, puffing into brown. She was smoke, rising through the smoke hole, into the air, past the clouds and stars, to the home of the god who once lived the way Wind Maiden lived.

Alone.

She closed her eyes, broke the heavy bonds, and floated free.

~ ~ ~

The sun shone high in the sky. Wind Maiden turned her back to him. "Grind, maize," she whispered to the yellow kernels she was rubbing between two large, flat rocks. She knelt over the rocks. Her hands and wrists moved round and round.

"Maize, wife of the Lenni Lenape, speak sweet words to the dead god. Grind small as dust, sparkle yellow as the sun." She brushed the yellow dust into a bowl carved from the hump of a root of a tree. She ground more kernels, hands and wrists moving round.

She parted leaves from a flat place between tall, white-skinned sycamore trees and laid her fire with care, twig upon twig, branch over branch. Long she rubbed her stick before she caught a spark to grow a fire. She would make a new flame, not an old one borne of an older fire.

What would please this god and make his mouth to whisper secrets about himself? She sat, legs crossed, the wooden bowl enclosed by her knees. She lowered her head. She had seen the people of this god bow their heads to speak to him — in murmurs, not shouts.

"God, once dead, now alive ..." The words, almost a breath, slipped through her mouth. "... who are you? Are you a god of White Men only and of Lenape who become White Men? Can you become my manito or am I dead to you? Dead. You died? Why?"

She looked into the fire and cast a handful of ground maize into its greedy mouth. The flames snapped. She listened, threw another handful, and listened.

In their meeting house, she had heard them sing. She stood. They did not dance for this manito so she hung her arms beside her straight body and swayed but did not dance. "God, dead yet alive," she chanted, "I call you." Wind Maiden could not make more words so she chanted the same words many times high and many times low.

She waited. She heard, saw, felt ... nothing. The fire smoked and died. She kicked it apart.

~ ~ ~

"Your god. He mocks. All manitos laugh and close their eyes. He is like all manitos."

It was the sun-setting. Wind Maiden crouched beside the Elk's Eye. She threw her gaze across the water and not at Salah.

"He is not a manito. He is the only God." Sarah leaned beside her, seeking to read the mind of Wind Maiden in the frown of her face.

"He is silent or he is dead and never lived again in the dead body."

"He is alive; I know." Sarah's back ached. She sat. "Why do you say he does not speak?"

"I laid a fire, twig upon twig, and rubbed a spark which flamed. I gave him maize ..." Wind Maiden glanced low and sideways. "... my maize, ground to sun-bright dust. I sang to him. I whispered to him. The smoke rose; it choked my throat and stung my eyes. He did not answer; he does not care." She rolled out her lower lip. The words of Salah could not cover hers.

Sarah bent forward to catch the eye of Wind Maiden. "My God, the only God, is not a manito who comes when called by maize and smoke. He made everything and needs nothing. You can give Him nothing."

"Ha! Then he does not care!" Wind Maiden grabbed her wrists with her hands and thumped her legs.

"He cares. He died. He comes down to you and takes you to Him. He will not answer your way. His way."

Wind Maiden rolled her head. "Words, words. No more will fill my head. I am full of words I do not understand. I shall soon spit up these words about your dead god. We shall forget him until the moon dies and the nights are black. I shall have consumed these words by then.

"Oh," said Sarah. "But I shall not be here then." She should have told her sooner but had waited for a better time which had not come. She bit her lip.

Wind Maiden looked at Salah then dropped her eyes. They ran away, all ran away. She should not have taken her feelings out of the deep, dark bag she had hidden them in. She gathered and resealed them with a light touch to ease the pain. She began to rise. She murmured, "It is nothing to me."

Sarah tapped Wind Maiden's arm with her fingertips — gently, lest she frighten her. "I do not go far. To Huts of Grace. Go with me."

Huts of Grace. Wind Maiden had seen that village many times. She walked near there gathering firewood and roots. It was close, not far.

"Go with me," repeated Sarah, holding Wind Maiden's arm more firmly.

Wind Maiden pulled free and stood. Huts of Grace. Mahicanni lived there. She was dead to the Lenni Lenape. They could see the dead no more. Would the Mahicanni see her? Here, the forest was silent. She did not like the roar of its silence in her head. The trunk of the tree was cold; its roots were dry and thirsty. "I shall go."

Sarah stood. She had gained a friend. "Five sun risings. First the marriage of Brother Heckewelder; we leave the next sun rising. You go then?"

"Too soon. Slowly," thought Wind Maiden. She backed away from Salah. "I go. Not then. When I come, you will see me."

15
JULY 11, 1780 – JULY 15, 1780

Wind Maiden stood tall beside Salah. They walked through the village of Huts of Grace.

"This is my friend," Sarah said to her sisters as, together, they passed.

A tall woman, not of the True Man and not Mahicanni, smiled at Wind Maiden. Another, ugly, opened her lips; words of greeting flowed over black teeth.

"This is my friend."

A young Mahicanni stopped. She lowered her clay jug of water. It swooshed and spilled onto the dirt. "The sun is high; my back is hot. For that I am unhappy. For you, I am happy to greet you today." Mahicanni, sister words to Unami, rolled from her mouth like chirps. She bore the age Wind Maiden would have carried if she were still alive: too old, not old enough.

"This is my friend."

A black-grey head looked up. The eyes of Star-at-Dawning, black eyes pushed deep into the flesh, looked into the eyes of Wind Maiden. Another face — thick-jawed, another mouth — thin-lipped, another body — tall, straight, joined themselves to the eyes. This was not mother. Wind Maiden wanted to hide in a black cave; she wanted to sit beside this woman and watch her scrape her raccoon skin, listen to her breathing, feel the warmth of her skin. Her desires were an opossum, tearing apart her dead flesh. She looked at Salah; they walked by.

"This is my friend."

Who was the friend of Salah? Wind Maiden? Wind Maiden was dead. And she had shining hair, smooth, oiled with bear fat. She wore new strouds, blue and red. Bells rang upon her slender ankles when she walked, light-stepped, in moccasins beaded bright. She who walked beside Salah had torn hair and a torn stroud smelling of firepit ash and body sweat. No bells; this one should not be heard; no brightly-beaded moccasins, this one should not be seen. Who was the friend of Salah?

Wind Maiden looked sideways at Salah.

"This is my friend." Sarah felt the gaze of Wind Maiden. Friend. Wind Maiden had helped with the birth of David; she had warned Sarah of the approach of the warrior. But what had happened to her friend? Almost, Sarah was angry with this young woman who, with bitterness and hatred, had destroyed the girl. Yet, hidden beneath the refuse, cowered Wind Maiden, the friend, sometimes peering at Sarah for a moment, quickly gone.

"This is the meeting house." Sarah stopped beside the small chapel, the heart of the village. The squared logs were smooth and even. Three oblong glass windows spaced themselves along one side of the building; three other sister windows repeated the austere design along the other side of the building. At the front of the meeting house, two doors, one on each side, narrow and erect, watched like sentinels over the house of God and opened themselves to sisters, here, to brethren, there.

"Forever uniform," thought Sarah. The simplicity of the structure spoke of simplicity of faith and of the symmetry of perfect balance and consistency in the law of God.

Wind Maiden looked at the meeting house. She wrinkled her nose and squinted. Rain would not drip through that roof; wind would not blow through those logs. Someone should live in it ... *She* would like to live in just a corner.

Sarah walked toward the left door.

The wood-planked floors made a hollow thump as they stepped into the empty room. Long benches lay one behind another on either side of an aisle, a straight path to the platform with a long table and chairs whereon the teachers and assistants sat during worship. Behind the platform loomed the fireplace.

"Oh. I could sleep in it," murmured Wind Maiden. It was wide and high, grey-stoned, strong. She despised her own fire pit and her own hut.

She gazed up at the woven mats that hung upon the walls. The designs were Mahicanni and not Lenape. Did she betray her own lenno by standing here? What lenno? Long ago she had betrayed them and they had abandoned her.

The soft voice of Salah filled the room: "We meet here in the morning, in the night."

They left the meeting house and walked to the bluff overlooking the Muskingum River. The bell in the cupola above the meeting house rang the hour in bright, shimmering tones.

~ ~ ~

The bell rang, hollow and muffled. Sarah looked up, over her head, toward where it rang.

She was sitting on the front bench in the chapel beside Sister Christiana, an assistant. Christoph sat in a high-backed chair upon the platform with Brother William Edwards and Brother Schebosh. The congregation was entering the building, beckoned by the bell.

The bell rang, low and trembling. It sighed long and far and tumbled lightly through the dark, dew-drenched forest to the ears of Wind Maiden. Everyone came to the bell. Their god came when it called, and he did powerful things for his lenno.

Wind Maiden wanted to hang the bell upon a branch in the forest and ring it forever. Would smiling faces follow its call to her? She wanted that bell, wanted to feel its hard coldness in her hands.

Would these lenno notice her and remember her? One-Who-Runs, mother, brothers, father, they all forgot. Or did they remember, remember and never forget and never forgive?

"Do forget," she whispered. She stopped and dug her toes into the packed dirt: "No! Do not forget!" She clutched her head and shook it.

She walked, feet shuffling in small and slow steps. Looking ahead, she saw the light of the clearing shining onto her trail.

The bell had stopped ringing. Wind Maiden roamed through Huts of Grace … in silence and alone.

She stood near the closed door of the meeting house. The sun had set twice; now she came again. Her sun-faded, dirt- and smoke- and ash-marred stroud was wet with forest dew. Wind Maiden looked down and remembered the blue, blue as the sky after the sunset before the sky enclosed itself in black, it once had been when she first pulled it around herself in Goschachgunk. Now, it was ugly. They would laugh. And her hair … she had tried to comb it smooth, but she had no fat. She patted it with her hand. She had splashed water onto her face. A shadowy shape without a face had scowled at her from the surface of the water.

They would laugh. Once, many lifetimes ago, Fish-of-the-Deep-Water had told Wind Maiden to sneer at laughs. She opened the door and slid inside.

She stood behind them. The woman she had seen before who gazed out through the Eyes-of-Mother whispered to Salah. Salah looked round. She smiled. Wind Maiden crouched against the wall.

The lenno stood and chanted. A Mahicanni sat at a wooden box and banged, not the thump of a drum but the jangling of many bells. The words of the chant filled her stomach but not her head. Wind Maiden closed her eyes, held her legs with her hands, and rocked.

163

Then the voices and the box fell silent, and the voice of the husband of Salah rose up.

"A man went out to plant. He threw out his seed. Some tumbled beside the path and were stomped upon. Large, black birds ate them all ..."

Wind Maiden looked up.

"Others fell into rock-soil. They, with quickness, grew ..."

"They die, too," thought Wind Maiden, puffing out her lip.

"... then withered because their roots found no water. Some fell into thorns ..."

"He has much seed to throw away," decided Wind Maiden. "This seed thrower is lazy and he is stupid."

"... and the thorns grew with the seed and choked them. Some fell on black soil, broken apart, moist and cool; they grew and made fruit, much fruit ...He that has ears to hear, let him hear."

"I have ears, but I do not think I can hear this tale." Wind Maiden pulled her fingers through the snarls of her hair.

"The Saviour spoke these words to the lenno who followed him," the yellow-haired husband of Salah said. "The seed is the word. When ears of a man hear the word, but he cannot know its meaning; then the wicked spirit snatches away the word that was planted upon his heart. This is the one who received the seed beside the path ..."

Wind Maiden squeezed her legs and buried her head upon her knees. Her heart pulsed naked beside the path. She saw the word glittering upon her heart. But when she reached out to clasp the seed, the wicked spirit snatched it.

"... the seed thrown on rocky soil," continued the husband. "This man receives the word with joy. But the root cannot grow deep. People laugh at him and steal from him. The root withers; the seed dies. Soon, that man runs from the word."

Yes! Wind Maiden was that man. She ran from the word. Deep inside her lay the cold rock, large and heavy. The root withered upon the hard rock. If she were alive that she could cry, she would cry. The rock had not moisture; she was dry inside.

"... thorns, he hears the word. But thorns of skins and kettles and deer flesh, bells and strouds, fire water, all fill his heart more than the sprouting seed which has no space and no light to grow. The sprouting seed bears no fruit — like grape vines in the dark forest —"

Skins, deer flesh, bells, strouds. That was Wind Maiden. That was why she died. Thorns squeezed and pricked and choked her so she died.

"The seed upon the black soil, broken apart, moist — this man hears the word, learns its meaning, grows in knowing, bears fruit."

Wind Maiden looked up. She was not this soil, not this seed. Why was she here? Why did she listen to words that would not grow inside of her?

Fool. The dead could not dwell near the living. Her stink would rise into their nostrils and choke their throats. They would bury her; that is what the living did to the dead. Bury ... in rock-soil. Rootless. Without water. She would die again ... and again.

She rolled herself forward upon soft, brown feet. Turning, pattering, scratching, she scurried from the meeting house.

Through the silent village, bright in the sunlight, she ran. She stumbled into the darkness of the forest, moist, silent like the village. No, heavier, thicker silence. Living silence. She tripped, plunged, and rolled then grabbed the ground on hands and knees and looked behind. Alone. She crawled backwards to a tree and leaned against it.

Wind Maiden cried. Dry tears flowed from deep inside, filled the edges of dry, unseeing eyes, and rolled down parched cheeks. Dry, heaving cries without tears rose and fell, more groans than cries. Alone. The dead ... alone among the living and among the dead.

~ ~ ~

"Christoph!" His large linsey shirt clung to his perspiring chest and arms. Sarah had caught him walking from the plantation.

"Sarah, I do not have much time now. Brother Schebosh waits. We must repair the fence north of the village. After the evening meal ..."

"After the evening meal, you will translate scripture or a hymn, always something." And someone always waited. She waited, too. What was going wrong between them? A whip was snapping across his back and driving him. Did the vision hold the whip in its hand? She was falling behind him, and he did not even look back. "God, is this your plan?"

He stopped and rubbed the sweat from his upper lip with the back of his hand. Did he glower at her?

But she would not be intimidated, not this time. "Did you see Wind Maiden after the meeting this morning? I looked for her, but ..." Sarah shook her head.

"She rushed out long before the end," replied Christoph. He rubbed the rim of his black hat. Its wide brim cast a shadow across his eyes. "She is like an animal," he added.

"She seems to be, yes, but she is not ... not really." Sarah looked up. He must understand! "She is lonely. I know she seeks God."

"Then she will find Him." He pulled off his hat. "But you cannot find Him for her."

"I do not wish to. It is enough that I should find Him for myself." Sarah's head ached. She rubbed her eyes. Could he not understand? "She is lonely," she repeated. "I have asked her to join us here."

"You know that is not possible!" Christoph boomed like an irate teacher. "She must acknowledge the Saviour first.

"She will." Sarah wished she was more certain of that.

"She has not, not yet." He waved his hat. "We have rules, remember. Our entire mission is governed by them."

"Rules took away my son," huffed Sarah. "They will not destroy my friend!"

"He is my son, too." The voice of Christoph was little above a whisper. "That is why the rules must work. Can you not see that?"

No, she could not, but she nodded her head.

~ ~ ~

"Dip, lift, over, down," laughed the Twittering-Brown-Bird. Wind Maiden remembered her: she was the talker, the age of Wind Maiden, who had greeted Wind Maiden when she walked as "friend" with Salah through Huts of Grace.

"Slow, Sister Rebecca," said Salah to the Twittering-Brown-Bird, "do not splash the fat."

Wind Maiden crouched in the high grass and watched them. The sun beat; the fire blazed; the fat bubbled. The foolish women sweated. Eyes-of-Mother, who had scraped the skin and had greeted the friend of Salah three long, long nights ago, shoved sticks into the fire.

"Here! I shall dip these," chirped the Twittering-Brown-Bird, grabbing at another stick of hanging strings.

"Wait, Sister," Salah said, "those candles are not cool."

"Look! They are cool," twittered the brown bird. Wind Maiden rose upon her knees to watch. The bird fluttered over the stick and landed upon a hanging string. "Oh," she said, "it is not cool."

Wind Maiden lay back in the grass and smiled. She stretched her legs. The white, dancing warriors in the blue sky shuffled above, clothed in white puffs of smoke.

The voice of Salah: "Sit down, Sister, we wait now," danced upon the light breeze.

"We wait." Yes. We wait because the dead can only wait. The cool, wet earth is pulled over the lifeless body. Wind Maiden searched with her fingers into the dark soil. She dug with her nails, deeper, deeper, until the earth spoke to her fingertips and its words rose upon her fingers, her arms, her chest, to her head, like water traveling through the roots and trunk of a thirsty tree.

"I am the mother of everything," said Grandmother Earth. "I carried the great-grandfather of all – of all ants, rabbits, deer, snakes, Lenape in my belly until they crawled out toward the sun. And all their great-grandchildren I have carried since. I bore you. Now I wait for you to return to me. I am born waiting and I die waiting."

"Do not speak more, Grandmother," said Wind Maiden through her chest, her arms, her fingers, to the earth.

"I wait, and, as I wait, I grow. You think because you walk upon me that I am the woman and you are the man. You forget your beginning; you forget your end. I am your beginning; I am your end. I wait."

"I am dead and you have not claimed me," argued Wind Maiden.

"I have taken your inside, and, soon, your outside will be mine. You are a tree, eaten from the inside and hollow. The winds will come, and you will fall. And, when you fall, you will fall to me. Slowly, slowly, I shall take you unto myself."

Wind Maiden wanted to pull her fingers from the soil. Fear said to her. "If you try to pull free and cannot, then you will know that your outside is now dead ... The wind has blown; you have fallen. But if you do not struggle, then you can still hope." Her heart rattled up her chest and into her throat.

"Spirit," she groaned, "you plant seed that Grandmother Earth does not sprout. Grow in me!"

A knife, cold and sharp, broke apart the stone inside and began to scrape it into powder. She would die, yes, she would die. She did not care. The dark, cold death was lifting. This new death would be better.

Suddenly, warm sap ... sap like from the sugar tree ... flowed from the stone now broken. Something lived!

A voice cried out in victory, "Earth! I plant a new seed inside this tree, a seed that never knew the darkness of your womb. Take the rotting trunk. It is dirt and it is yours. But the sprout belongs to me."

Wind Maiden was an eagle, flying high into the clouds. She could wrench her fingers free from the Grandmother's pull; she knew she could! She waited, though, to hear the ancient one reply to the booming cry. She listened with her fingers and dug them deeper, deeper. She felt the dead, damp silence of the soil; her fingers felt nothing more.

"Sister Christiana will stir the tallow ..." A voice from far away, many moons away, spoke — Salah. "... then you can dip the candles."

Wind Maiden wiggled her fingers free; the earth was dead and not alive. She sat forward.

Eyes-of-Mother was stirring the kettle of fat with a long stick. Twittering-Brown-Bird was fluttering over a stick of strings.

"Slowly, Sister," said Salah.

She ran through the forest, crouching low. She would not take the path today. All the way, all the way to her hut near Place of Peace, she ran.

In the night, she picked at and ate a fish she had caught in her net and had boiled that day. And when she ate, she was full. She had forgotten fullness. In the past, she had eaten, and the death had consumed her food in darkness and left her empty. Tonight, the fullness filled her stomach, her chest, and her body. She was warm; she was sleepy. She did not know who was with her, but she was not alone.

In her hut, near her fire pit, she stretched out long upon her mat. She belonged to a warrior who had fought the battle and had killed the enemy. She had nothing more to fear. She slept.

She arose early the next morning before the sun cast its light onto the ground beneath the thick, high trees of the forest.

Wind Maiden bowed over her spring and lapped cool water from her cupped hands. She walked back toward Huts of Grace, slowly, waiting for the light of the sun to chase away the deep darkness. The darkness never fled the forest. It hid behind the trees and waited; it sent its sister, shadow, between the trees and breathed its dusky gloom above and below.

Wind Maiden knew the hiding places of darkness. Burn or chop down the trees where he hides; then he must flee, and the sun will shine and there will be no place for darkness, or shadow, or gloom to hide. He will flee, deeper among the trees that remain and he will become darker, heavier than before.

Her mind rolled around the thought, "The sun will shine." When she had first died, the sun had fled. She feared the darkness, but he had received her when everything else refused the one who was dead. Now she was twice dead. The blackness within was broken open and a gleaming sun shone upon a clod of soil and a spindly sprout.

She stopped at an open spot. The sun was casting grey-silver shadows among the deeper shadows on leafy ground. She crouched and touched a cold, wet spot where a grey-silver shadow lay. "Friend," she whispered.

Lenno were walking among the cabins of Huts of Grace when Wind Maiden came to the edge of the forest. The morning sunlight shone brightly and boldly upon the village. Grandfather Sun — he was "friend" here.

She crept around behind the huts and cabins until she crouched behind the meeting house. Creeping, plunging from shadow to shadow, scurrying, she ran along the side of the meeting house, the side for the women, until she crouched at the corner, staring along the street again. When eyes had passed and she could see only backs, she slithered in front, pushed open the door, and rolled in.

Upon the last bench and in the corner, she sat.

"Speak again, Spirit; as you spoke to Grandmother Earth, speak again to me." She rumbled with the desire for His voice.

She heard a rubbing and a clomp. Turning, she saw Salah.

"Sister Rebecca saw you enter," said Sarah as she slid beside Wind Maiden.

"The Twittering-Brown-Bird! I did not look up to see what perched in the trees," thought Wind Maiden. She watched Salah.

"We ... I ..." stammered Sarah. Wind Maiden looked like a colt that might bolt, and Sarah did not know how to subdue her. "The village eats the morning meal. Are you hungry?" She raised her hand to touch the hand of Wind Maiden, but it froze in the air. Her friend's glance revealed contempt.

"No!" Wind Maiden lied. She was not a wolf who came only to steal. "I am listening."

"Listening?" Sarah drew back her hand. Why could she not touch Wind Maiden? Because she feared rejection. She wanted to put her arms around Wind Maiden and comfort her as she would a child, but she was a coward. Sarah's hand fell to her lap.

"Your Spirit, the one who plants seeds, he stabbed me ... inside ... deep in the darkness where the rock is. I died."

Sarah shook her head. She could not understand.

Did not Salah know about the darkness and the rock? Had she not seen it in the dead eyes of she who was once Wind Maiden? "Here." She hit her chest with her fist. "Blackness, coldness, death. Your Spirit. He broke apart the blackness. I died. It is better now."

Sarah opened her mouth, smiled and exclaimed, "Oh! You met Him!"

"Yes. Who is he?"

"He? The Saviour. He is the one who ..."

"Hush. You talk too much. I came to hear."

"She came to hear," thought Sarah, "and, yet, she will not listen to me?" She did not understand, not at all. Yet she could wait, too, for the Saviour. It was lonely, she knew, to wait alone.

The walls rang with quietness. Other times Wind Maiden had waited ... beside the fires and beneath Grandfather Sun. Fear whispered that the other spirits had not answered, and this spirit would not, either. They had mocked; so would he.

"No!" she cried inside, inside where once was only blackness and the rock. "He has spoken; He will again."

Fear replied, "But has he ever spoken to you?"

Wind Maiden shivered. She glanced at Salah sitting close beside like a mother, hand against her chin and rubbing, eyes roaming through the air. Salah waited with her. Wind Maiden felt her own hands fall open on her lap. She felt her muscles ease down and relax.

Then she knew that He spoke now and had not stopped since He first broke apart the stone. He filled her up as He talked and talked. Today she would learn the meaning of all He told.

When the sisters, brethren, and children entered the meeting house for morning worship, Sarah raised her brows and pursed her lips at the sisters who were about to speak. She hoped they would pass by. They did.

She laid Wind Maiden upon the altar of sacrifice. Staring through the crackling blaze, she saw in the glow the full cheeks and blond hair of David perched beside Wind Maiden.

The lenno stood. Wind Maiden stood. They sang, following the chant made by the box of many bells. The bells stopped. They bowed their heads and closed their eyes. Wind Maiden closed her own eyes. She looked with them inside to where the Spirit dwelt. The words lit a fire that soon was out. Yet the warmth remained.

The believing lenno sat; Wind Maiden sat. The husband of Salah stood. He opened the black box of scratchings in which the mysteries of the Spirit lay. Would not this Saviour speak from there? The teacher began,

"He is despised and kicked away by men; a man, many sorrows, who knows the face and voice of grief; and we hid our faces from him; he was despised, and we threw him away like an old, flea-eaten skin. He lifted our griefs upon his back, and carried our sorrows: but our eyes only wanted to see him struck and kicked, pounded onto his face in the dirt by God, and covered with wounds ..."

The eyes of Wind Maiden held tightly to the white face of the husband of Salah. She did not see him; she saw the words he spoke. They echoed in her head and fell down her throat where they drove back her breath and pounded upon her chest. She cried out inside, "What have we done? What *have* we done?" Then, more frantically, "What have I done?" She wanted to run and hide. Where could she hide? The terror was within.

The words pushed deeper:

"But he was wounded for our faults because we kicked dirt upon the council fire, he was bruised because we did evil: he took the blows of our punishment; and we are healed with the slashings which fell upon him. We all are sheep wandering away; we have each one followed his own path; and the one who is forever has made him to gather unto himself the evil of us all."

The words were a weight growing heavier and heavier. Wind Maiden saw herself wandering among trees upon the path she chose. She wanted her skins and her buckles and bells and had turned away her face from the tears she had made to flow. He — Who was he? — took the punishment for the evil she had made. Who was he? She saw him lying upon the ground, bleeding. She had stood in the line of people with a stick in her hand ready to beat him as he ran past. And she had beaten him until he fell by her feet with blue, swelling wounds, and blood flowing upon the dirt. He looked up to her now: "I fall here for you."

The pain! She closed her eyes tight, tight. The breaths fell heavier and heavier, rising from her chest with power, pushing the darkness and death higher and higher, burning and swelling, roaring. Sob tumbling over sob rode upon the breaths and broke through her mouth. She wept. Tears from the pool which once was dry fell in heavy drops like rain. Heaving, heaving, crying, moaning, harder, harder. "I struck him ... me ... I ..." The words were breaths which rattled from her throat.

Sarah watched, her own nails scratching at the palms of her hands. All other sounds had ceased; all eyes turned upon Wind Maiden. Sarah held her breath. The child-like face of Wind Maiden was red, drenched with tears, squeezed tight in anguish. She sat alone, shaking, wretched. Sarah tightened with every sob. She wanted to reach out, to touch ...

Sarah leaned forward and pulled the shaking Wind Maiden into her arms. They shared the heaving of the sobs. Sarah felt the muscles of Wind Maiden first tighten then slowly, slowly, relax. And the head of Wind Maiden nestled against Sarah's shoulder.

16
JULY 15, 1780 – JULY 21, 1780

They were sitting in the cabin of Sarah and Christoph, eating a paste of pounded maize mixed with milk and an ash-baked bread smeared with butter. Wind Maiden licked the butter off the bread and asked for more. She wanted milk, too; she did not want maize. Sarah, Christoph, and Sister Christiana watched. Only the requests of Wind Maiden for more butter or milk penetrated the silence. Finally, Wind Maiden looked up, laying aside her bowl and cup. Her eyes glistened black in the glow of the sooty blackbird.

"Who is He?" She looked at the husband of Salah.

"God?" Christoph asked.

"I know many gods, many manitos. They are all greedy. They laugh at me. But the one who planted His seed in me ... You said He plants the seeds, the seeds that sometimes do not grow."

"Yes. The Saviour plants the seeds. He is God."

"Too much!" moaned Wind Maiden. "Saviour. I know the meaning of that. He saved me from the first death. Yes. He is the Saviour."

"And He is God, maker of everything," added Christoph.

"No! I do not want to hear that. Not now!" Wind Maiden looked from the husband of Salah to the face of Eyes-of-Mother, then to Salah. Dark light flickered across their faces. The air was heavy with smoke. To sit outside would be better. But the sun was high over the village now, and she would ask her questions in darkness and not in light.

Sarah glanced at Christoph. She raised her brows. Could he not see that Wind Maiden feared God? Christoph half smiled back at her.

"Our Saviour. His name is Jesus. He loves you," said Sarah.

The voice of Salah was the voice that had wrenched the roots of the rotting tree from out of the soil of decay. Wind Maiden could hear these words.

Sarah continued, "He suffered and died to save you from all your evil deeds and from death."

"I killed Him. I stood in the line and hit Him with sticks. Speak no more. The hurt!" Wind Maiden clutched her chest.

"He forgives you ..." began Sister Christiana.

"Speak no more." Wind Maiden turned angry eyes upon Eyes-of-Mother. She looked down at her bowl. "More." She nodded toward a larger bowl of butter.

Sarah cut a slice of bread and would have smeared the butter upon it, but the warm hand of Wind Maiden tapped her own.

"No. In here," she said, lifting her bowl.

Sarah filled the bowl with butter.

Soon, Wind Maiden looked around at her companions. She licked her sticky fingers. "I want to live here." The words had not come easily to her lips, but she had spoken them quickly so that her thoughts would not hold them back.

"If you hold to the faith, you may stay here," said Christoph.

"I hold the faith. What is it?"

Christoph looked to Sarah. "The rules of the villages. Are they here?"

Sarah nodded. She arose from the bench and went to a corner of the cabin where a small, black box lay in the shadows of the corner. She retrieved several yellow papers from beneath a pile of similar sheets. She gave the papers to Christoph and, in passing, smiled at Wind Maiden. Could Wind Maiden accept these rules of residency, she who did not yet know the Lord in whom she seemed to believe?

"Obey these rules and live among us," said Christoph, turning the first of the papers toward the light of the sooty blackbird.

"Many rules," groaned Wind Maiden.

Christoph read,

"We will know no other God but the one only true God, who made us and all creatures, and came into this world in order to save sinners; to Him alone we will pray."

Sarah watched the eyes of Wind Maiden drop. Wind Maiden raised her hands, palms forward.

"That is our Saviour. We pray to Him alone," explained Sarah.

Christoph paused and nodded at Sarah. She half-nodded back, saying in her gesture, "I spoke out. Do not disapprove."

Wind Maiden lowered her hands and rocked her head. "Only He answers when I talk. Yes. I shall speak to Him and not to the other manitos. They do not answer." Christoph continued,

"We will rest from work on the Lord's Day, and attend public service."

Wind Maiden rolled out her lip and grunted, "Yes." She would rest from work whenever she was told to rest. It was the working that was hard and not the resting. These rules would be easy to hear.

Christoph again lifted the paper toward the light,

"We will honor father and mother, and when they grow old and needy we will do for them what we can."

The bench slid against the wood floor. Wind Maiden stood. "I leave now." She backed from them, turned to the door, and opened it. Light flooded in; she stepped back from its rays for a moment. Then she fled.

Like one person, Sarah, Christoph, and Christiana arose. Sarah started toward the door. Christoph grabbed her arm. She yanked it away and looked up at him. What was he becoming? A man following the letter of the law right down to the jot and the tittle? Must he compel the rest of them to follow him?

"Let her go," he said.

His voice was calm ... as usual. Its sound infuriated her.

"She did not understand," argued Sarah, plunging into German. "She thought we would condemn her for ... for ..."

"Then she should have stayed to learn, Sister," replied Christoph also in German, glancing now at Sister Christiana.

He would be embarrassed by this outbreak in front of another sister. Let him be angry. Sarah desired his anger.

"She is frightened!" She watched him as he walked into the light of the door. In his own strength, could he not understand weakness in others?

Christoph looked at Sister Christiana, then at Sarah. "I know, Sister." He spoke in what Sarah recognized as his patient-as-to-a-child fashion. He bowed his tall stature to go through the door.

"I must go to her." Sarah felt rebellious, but her voice sounded subdued.

Christoph stood and turned. "No," he said. "She must come to us. The Lord can bring her back." He paused, looked at Sarah, then said, "I must attend the meeting of the teachers. So must you." He glanced again at Christiana.

"Wait!" pleaded Sarah.

"Later, Sister," said Christoph. He left.

Sarah glanced at Christiana, bit her lip, and looked over at the papers lying upon the table. She turned from the door, retrieved the papers, and returned them to the box in the darkened corner of the room.

Sister Christiana spoke from behind: "Wind Maiden is not a child that you must run to her. She is a woman."

Sarah sighed. She looked around at Christiana. Surely her face was creased with the lines of frustration. She was glad it was hidden in shadow. "She is alone," she managed to explain.

"Must not every person be alone ... this day, tomorrow?" argued Sister Christiana.

"Much pain," replied Sarah. She would lessen suffering when she could. She could lessen suffering now.

"Without pain, some things are broken buckles, worth nothing," Sister Christiana said, walking toward the door with Sarah.

"Yes, the cost of following the Saviour ..." said Sarah. The cost was too great, the rewards too few. She tensed with rage. At whom?

They left the cabin and stood in the sunlight. "About Lenni Lenape, your husband is wise," said Sister Christiana. "It is a proud and rebellious lenno. Pride must be snapped to its knees before Lenni Lenape can bow before the Saviour. You run after her, you bind a healing splint to her pride. Your husband, he is wise. "

Sarah nodded her head. Must she be rebuked by a sister? Why did Sarah fear for Wind Maiden? Or did Sarah fear for herself?

And Christoph — of course he was wise. And she was the fool.

Sarah lifted her skirts and hurried through the dusty street to the meeting at the cabin of Brother Edwards. She was always running. But did she run toward something, or did she run away?

The following day was Sunday. Christoph worked at the table, hunched over his Bible in the sooty blackbird light, preparing the message for the evening meeting. Or was it the meeting a week or two or three hence? He had a supply for a lifetime.

"Listen, Sarah, to my translation of Isaiah 9:6: 'For to us a child is born, to us a son is given ... '" he read in Unami.

So! He was working on the Christmas message. He had little time; it was only five months away. Sarah glared at him.

"That is the same as the German," continued Christoph, his head bowed over the parchment, "but I cannot decide how to translate, '... the government shall be upon his shoulder.' Do I call it the feathers of the primary chief? That sounds cumbersome and it does not convey the extent of Christ's rulership."

Why did he ask her? He possessed wisdom; he possessed perception. She stood by the fire, rubbing the back of her neck, and did not answer.

He glanced up at her, his quill poised in the air. "Sarah? What is wrong? Are you ..."

"No!" she snapped. Pregnant? Sometimes, she had thought that herself. Her bleeding did not come regularly, but, eventually, it always flowed.

He plopped his quill into the inkwell. "Then what ..."

"What is wrong with you?" she asked. "You work fervently. Since we returned to the mission, you have forgotten me ... uh ... people," she corrected herself.

"Forget? How could I?" Christoph slid back his chair. "I work because I remember too well ... everything. I work for you, for everyone. I must complete it."

"Complete what?" asked Sarah.

"The Christian Indian state, of course," he said.

"Are you God's only emissary?" thought Sarah.

"Surely, you understand the urgency," he continued. "By forsaking ... others ..." he stammered, "... we ... God has promised to bless us a hundredfold."

"Yes, Christoph." She was defeated, for she did understand. Yet something was wrong. What?

She walked toward the door. Already, she could hear the scratchings of Christoph's quill against the parchment. She stood in the open doorway and looked toward the forest though she knew that she would see nothing.

~ ~ ~

On Monday, Sister Rebecca told Sarah that she had seen Wind Maiden build a small bark hut near Huts of Grace.

"She chattered to herself," said Rebecca. "She pretended that I did not watch her. I did watch her. I walked round ..." Sister Rebecca walked behind Sarah, peered around Sarah's shoulder, and gazed into Sarah's face. "Her face was upon my face." Rebecca placed her palm against her own face. "She snarled at me then walked past me to gather bark and sticks and gave to me her back until I left. I left."

"These words are pleasant to hear," Sarah said.

The eyes of Rebecca sparkled. "I shall take you there."

"No ..." Sarah hesitated.

"It is very near. And she will not see you." Rebecca's mouth widened into a broad grin.

"No," repeated Sarah. Perhaps if Rebecca had not brought the tidings, perhaps if someone less impetuous had told Sarah; then she might rush to the new hut with an eager greeting. However, she envisioned herself, standing in front of Christoph then peering at him from behind, all the while telling him how she had found Wind Maiden in the forest. He would see her as she now saw Rebecca – a frivolous, impetuous girl. She would wait.

By Tuesday, Sarah was done with patient waiting and was reduced to impatient waiting. By Wednesday, she was done with waiting altogether. Wind Maiden dwelt but a few footsteps into the forest. Sarah could easily wander in that direction.

Could she be impetuous? Christoph was impetuous concerning his vision. But he would call it diligence ... and zealousness.

Could not she be zealous, too?

Not while morning chores waited to be done.

"Sister Leah," she called to a slender young woman who was rushing from the Single Sisters' cabin.

The young woman stopped and walked toward Sarah who was standing in front of the meeting house, holding a birch broom in her hand. Sister Leah eyed the broom.

"I do not sweep today," she said as she approached.

"Sister Rebecca sweeps. Is she in the cabin?"

"No. I will not sweep the streets for her," whined Sister Leah. "I pull the garden behind the meeting house, not the streets. I shall clean the streets ..." she paused, "... when?"

"After two sun settings," replied Sarah.

"Yes. Sister Rebecca sweeps today," concluded Leah.

"Yes," agreed Sarah, "and you do not sweep today." The two women were of the same height. Sister Leah was perhaps sixteen, the daughter of a Monsey widow with no man to provide meat for even one. Leah had been a child of nine when her mother had brought her to the teachers and had left her among them without even a blanket or a skin.

Leah was turning to go.

"Sister," said Sarah.

Leah looked back. "And I shall not sweep for her."

"No." Sarah's intent had been to ask but one question: "Where is Sister Rebecca?"

"Oh ... I do not know," was the answer. Leah hurried away.

Surely Leah did know. Rebecca went nowhere without flourish.

Sarah watched Leah disappear into the forest. She was, after all, little more than a child. A lonely child.

Sarah recalled her child, David, stumbling ahead of her between rows of maize. The maize was not yet waist high, but he was in a forest of stalk and leaf. He slid between two stalks and wandered on until, suddenly, he stopped and looked around. He was not lost; she saw him well from above. But he saw only thick stalks. His face fell, and he called, "Mutter!" She was there. He clutched her as she held him in her arms.

If he called now, she could not answer. She could not see him to find him.

She laid aside the broom and pursued Leah.

"You are a stubborn horse," scolded a husky voice from among the trees.

"You twitter and chirp, say nothing. Give back my arm!" was the reply.

Rebecca pulled Wind Maiden from a small clearing onto the trail. Sister Leah strutted after, her hands behind her back.

"Sister!" called Rebecca, seeing Sarah, "I captured her ... stubborn horse. We fought until I tamed her. I am very weak. Do not worry for me."

"Twitterer!" snapped Wind Maiden. She looked up toward Sarah. "She could not have perched upon me unless I had said, 'Yes.'"

They stood before Sarah now, Rebecca still clinging to the arm of Wind Maiden, Leah still some steps behind.

"My arm is not a perch for your claw," warned Wind Maiden to Rebecca who looked past Wind Maiden to Sarah, exhibiting her captive.

"She will run away if I do not tie her here. She is a wild horse. I am bringing her; she would not come so I ..."

"Sister, let go ..." began Sarah.

Wind Maiden reeled upon Rebecca, squeezed with her own free hand the arm which held her then clawed the arm of Rebecca. Rebecca yelped, released the arm of Wind Maiden, and cradled her injury. Wind Maiden rubbed her own arm. She ignored Rebecca and watched Salah. "Whimpering dog," she thought.

Rebecca, glaring at Wind Maiden, displayed her injury to Sarah: four red welts.

"A punishment well deserved," thought Sarah. She said, "Wash. It is small."

"It is a big wound," replied Rebecca.

"Why does Salah heed the Twittering-Brown-Bird?" thought Wind Maiden. "I could have hurt her. I did not. She is a silly bird. I do not harm silly birds." She watched Salah to see what she would do.

"I am made glad in seeing you," said Sarah, smiling at Wind Maiden.

"She would not come. I was bringing her," stressed Rebecca who lifted her arm to reclaim her prize.

Wind Maiden glanced sideways at her. The Twitterer dropped her arm.

"I am cooking many questions," said Wind Maiden to Salah.

"We know the answers to many questions," chirped the Twittering-Brown-Bird.

Wind Maiden groaned. "I shall not talk to the Twitterer."

"Remember the sweeping, Sister?" asked Sarah.

Rebecca looked back at Leah, then to Sarah. "Yes, sweeping," she sighed. "I am working hard today. I hunt ..." She glanced at Wind Maiden, "... am wounded ... Yes ... Now I sweep for you ... for all lenno," she finished with the triumph of a storyteller.

"The cabin of Brother Edwards to the ending of the path above the Elk's Eye," directed Sarah.

"The cabin ..." murmured Rebecca, meandering up the path.

The Brown-Bird looked back again ... and again. Wind Maiden knew she would. Curious birds would fly back many times to try to grab their lost twigs or leaves or worms.

Leah mumbled, slid around Sarah, and hurried after Rebecca.

They both fluttered around the bend in the path.

It was cooler in the forest than in the village. The thick smell of mold and dirt hung over Wind Maiden and Sarah. They looked at one another.

Wind Maiden squeezed the leaves with her toes. Stillness floated upon the breathless air. An arrow of sun pierced through the trees down to the earth and struck behind Salah.

"I am dead to mother and father," said Wind Maiden. Her words were spoken from the kettle of a conversation with Salah she had brewed for two days.

"Dead?" asked Sarah.

"I did not honor them. I died."

"I have heard the story."

"Many ears have heard. It is not a story ... truth."

Neither spoke.

"Do I console?" thought Sarah. "How?"

Salah was silent. "She knows ... dead to the Lenni Lenape, all lenno, even the lenno at Huts of Grace." The many questions Wind Maiden had stirred into the kettle she would throw upon the ground now. Salah was silent. She knew that no hope remained. Wind Maiden turned to leave.

"We have not talked," exclaimed Sarah. "You have not questioned. Why do you go?"

"Questions?" Did Salah mock? "I am dead to you. The dead cannot ask questions."

"You are alive to the Saviour?"

"Yes." This Wind Maiden knew. "He planted His seed in me." She thumped her chest: "I live inside."

"Then you are alive to me ... to all who know the Saviour."

"Still, I cannot live in your village. I live, you say. Yet you bury me ... dead." Words without meaning. Words that fell back upon themselves. Lies. The words of the White Man all flowed from one river.

"You say you cannot live in Huts of Grace," said Sarah. "These are not my words."

"Not your words? I did not honor my parents." Wind Maiden stomped the ground with her foot. "Your rule!"

"You would honor them, now, that the Saviour grows inside?"

Wind Maiden looked close into the face of Salah. "I would give honor. They will not take honor. They do not know about the seed."

"The Saviour washes away the shame of all yesterdays. The rules are for today and for the wants the Saviour plants in us for tomorrow."

The muscles on the jaw of Wind Maiden eased around the bony contours.

"Then I can live in Huts of Grace!" Wind Maiden would go in one night, maybe two. Once, she belonged to the forest. Her own emptiness had mingled with the silent blackness of the forest. No longer.

"You did not hear the other rules," warned Sarah.

Wind Maiden searched the shadowed face of Salah for lines of lies, paths of deceit. "The rules are all this way: for tomorrow and today, not yesterday?" she asked and watched.

"No yesterday," assured Sarah.

"Then I say, 'Yes' to all. I can walk all tomorrows in them if I might not walk backwards into yesterday." The pipe was smoked. She watched.

"First say, 'Yes,' then you can live in Huts of Grace ..." Sarah decided she must add, "... if the teachers and assistants find truth in your heart."

These words sent Wind Maiden falling again, rolling and grabbing at tree roots. She followed once more the paths across the face of Salah and found the trails wide and smooth. The paths were straight; she would wait. She stirred the kettle of questions and dipped a gourd into the steaming stew.

"Much to ask," she said.

~ ~ ~

"You went to her." Christoph was standing beside the fireplace, shoving tobacco into his pipe, a narrow Indian pipe which young Brother Schebosh had given him while the brethren had squatted around an outdoor fire the night before.

"She was near and coming ..."

"Alone?" interjected Christoph.

Did he know her so well that he had to ask all the wrong questions? "Not alone ... Rebecca was dragging her ..."

"She did not come freely." Now he was an inquisitor.

"Of course she came freely!"

"When we read her the rules, how can we be certain that her commitment will be given with a willingness for total sacrifice?"

"Christoph, she came freely."

"Dragged?" he mocked. "Sarah, leave God's work to Him to perform."

"Like you do?" she thought. Speech was useless between them. "Stop scolding me," she said. "I am not a child."

"Then act mature." He did not shout. She wished he had. She would prefer it to the voice of stern paternity.

"Stop this, Christoph. Do you want an apology? I apologize."

"Sarah, try to ..." Christoph breathed in and stood erect. "You know that many Indians attempt to join us because of the security we offer, not because they truly obey the Saviour. Difficulties arise, and they will be the first to fall away. And ..." He raised a long stick and waved it: "... they will lead others astray." He leaned over and prodded the fire with the stick. "Wolves are abroad who would scatter the flock." He lit his pipe with the glowing tip of the stick.

Christoph was reasonable; his arguments were always logical. Since he was an Indian, he knew Indians well. Sarah wanted to yank the pipe from his mouth and throw it across the room. Would he then lecture her upon the waste of breakage?

"That is not Wind Maiden," objected Sarah.

"She is desperate," he observed, puffing the pipe.

"Yes," conceded Sarah, "but she has met the Saviour."

"Yes ..." puffed Christoph.

"Can we doubt her?" Was he God? Could he know the heart of man?

"No," he agreed, "I guess we cannot."

"Then can we present Wind Maiden's petition at the meeting of the teachers and helpers on Saturday?"

"She must accept the rules of fellowship." He rubbed his lips with his thumb.

"She will accept," murmured Sarah. "I shall review them with her."

~ ~ ~

"Yes, yes," said Wind Maiden, her voice snapping like a twig. She squirmed and looked around. They sat outside on the ground, still wet from the rain the day before, upon red and blue striped blankets. Wind Maiden stretched her hand over a red stripe and rubbed along its length.

"Hear the rules; then say, 'Yes,'" sighed Sarah. Wind Maiden had to understand her commitment. She must not fall back.

"I say, 'Yes,' before; I say, 'Yes,' after. Yes is yes." She dropped her eyes and glanced at Eyes-of-Mother. The hand that did not rub the redness slid nearer Eyes-of-Mother. Why did they sit under the sun? The lenno who passed watched her as if she were dead. Did they know? Twittering-Brown-Bird and her angry shadow — they walked by, then again ... and again. Wind Maiden would pinch the bird. She looked at Salah. Not now ... soon.

"Open your ears," pleaded Sarah. "Listen to the rules. Later, all the teachers and assistants will hear your answers and know if truth dwells in your heart." They had little time to prepare; the meeting with the brethren would be later that day. Sarah sighed and re-read the sixth rule:

"We will not take part in dances, sacrifices, heathenish festivals, or games."

Buckles and bells, shuffling feet, shouts and jumps: "Yes, yes," repeated Wind Maiden. She slid her fingers to the blue of the blanket and danced along its edge

~ ~ ~

"Why do you ask to live in Huts of Grace?" Christoph stared across the table at Wind Maiden. Sarah watched him. He did not appear ominous. His voice did not boom with pulpit authority.

The teachers and assistants — Christoph, Brother Edwards, Brother and Sister Schebosh, Brother John Martin, Brother Joshua, Sister Christiana, and

Sarah — sat, bowed over two candles, around the long table in the meeting house.

Wind Maiden, in their midst, pushed herself to the front of the bench, back arched almost backwards.

"Your Saviour planted the seed upon the rock He broke. You belong to Him. I belong to Him." The husband of Salah knew her answer; he had followed that path with her before. Did he watch to see if she remembered the way and would not follow a new trail that branched from the old?

"You will obey Him?" The husband of Salah leaned forward.

"Yes." She was dead. Wind Maiden had killed her who was once Wind Maiden. She would listen no longer to Wind Maiden.

"Not easy," he warned. "When other lenno who do not obey the Saviour bare their teeth at you, will you still obey?"

"Anger cannot wound the dead."

"They come, saying, 'Friend! Drink fire water with us. Put on bells. Dance,'" warned Eyes-of-Mother.

Wind Maiden looked sideways at her.

Eyes-of-Mother continued, "The enemy comes; we stand back, arms folded, legs apart. We are wary of the enemy. But the friend wraps himself in our arms and stabs us under the rib with his knife."

Wind Maiden gazed at a ray of light which glittered upon the shining wood floor near Eyes-of-Mother. She turned back to the husband of Salah and did not answer.

"You heard the rules?" he asked.

"I said them to her," replied Sarah. The answer popped out before thought. She bit her lip and fluttered her hands in mute apology.

"You accept?" continued Christoph.

"Yes, yes," answered Wind Maiden. Rules! Her ears ached from hearing them.

"Hear again," said the Maker-of-the-Bells.

The thin teacher, Edwards, shook white, crisp autumn leaves and read,

≈ *We will know no other God but the one only true God, who made us and all creatures and came into this world to save sinners; to Him alone we will pray.*

≈ *We will rest from work on the Lord's Day and attend public service.*

≈ *We will honor father and mother, and when they grow old and needy we will do for them what we can.*

≈ *No person shall get leave to dwell with us until our teachers have given their consent and the assistants have examined him.*

≈ *We will have nothing to do with thieves, murderers, whoremongers, adulterers, or drunkards.*

≈ *We will not take part in dances, sacrifices, heathenish festivals, or games.*

≈ *We will use no witchcraft when hunting.*

≈ *We will renounce and abhor all tricks, lies and deceits of Satan.*

≈ *We will be obedient to our teachers and to the assistants who are appointed to preserve order in our meetings in the towns and fields.*

≈ *We will not be idle, nor scold, nor beat one another, nor tell lies.*

≈ *Whoever injures the property of his neighbor shall make restitution.*

≈ *A man shall have but one wife — shall love her and provide for her and his children. A woman shall have but one husband, be obedient to him, care for her children, and be cleanly in all things.*

≈ *We will not admit rum or any other intoxicating liquor into our towns. If strangers or traders bring intoxicating liquor, the assistants shall take it from them and not restore it until the owners are ready to leave the place.*

≈ *No one shall contract debts with traders, or receive goods to sell for traders, unless the helpers give their consent.*

≈ *Whoever goes hunting or on a journey shall inform the teacher or assistants.*

≈ *Young persons shall not marry without the consent of their parents and the teacher.*

≈ *Whenever the assistants appoint a time to make fences or to perform other work for the public good, we will assist and do as we are bid.*

≈ *Whenever maize is needed to entertain strangers or sugar for love-feasts, we will freely contribute from our stores.*

≈ *We will not go to war and will not buy anything of warriors taken in war.*

When Brother Edwards finished the reading of the rules, he laid aside the papers upon the table and looked at Wind Maiden.

Wind Maiden watched his fingers root themselves together. She knew he waited. "... 'not be idle'? ... 'perform work'? ... I am Lenni Lenape and serve no man." Her mind had started arguing before "Yes, yes" could hush it. "The White Man takes slaves ... remember the black skins ... another trick to make a slave of me! Why should I cut my wings? I must fly. Stay free!"

"Free." She looked at Salah, at Eyes-of-Mother, at the husband of Salah. She did not look at the thin teacher or at the others. Free. Free to be the tree. Free to die, to fall, to crash, to crumble. Free to rot where no lenno can see. Free.

"Yes," she said to the rooting fingers of the skinny teacher.

"We welcome you here," said Christoph.

"Welcome. Welcome, Sister," said Brother Edwards.

Christoph arose with the brethren and hesitated above Sarah.

"When I lead Brother Grube back to Bethlehem, I can carry your letter to Saxony," said Brother Schebosh to Christoph.

"Uh ... yes," said Christoph, turning away with the brethren. He walked several steps before adding, "It is already written. And look through the mails in Bethlehem. Perhaps a letter from Friedrich Zundel ..."

Sarah strained to listen.

"Bring skins and blankets and sleep here tonight," suggested Eyes-of-Mother.

Sarah looked back to the women. She laid her hand on Wind Maiden's arm.

"The Single Sisters' cabin," suggested the wrinkled-faced wife of Schebosh.

"Yes," said Sarah.

"Single Sisters' cabin? I was married," mumbled Wind Maiden.

"You can live with the widows," said the wrinkled one.

"They are old," said Eyes-of-Mother. "Your husband is dead?"

"I do not know. Gone two winters. He will not take me back. If he is not dead, then, to him, I am dead." She tried to speak the words low and cold as she had spoken them before. But the something new that now lived inside rumbled up and cracked her voice.

"The Single Sisters' cabin?" asked Eyes-of-Mother of Salah.

"Yes," said Sarah. She stared at Wind Maiden. "Now?"

Along the wide path of the village they walked, Salah and Wind Maiden. "My village," thought Wind Maiden. "My lenno."

Salah stopped beside a large cabin. Twittering-Brown-Bird and Shadow sat outside. "Curious pecking birds," thought Wind Maiden. "Fly away, foolish birds."

"Sisters," said Sarah to Rebecca and Leah. "We welcome our new sister to Huts of Grace. She will sleep with you in the Single Sisters' cabin."

Twittering-Brown-Bird jumped up and recaptured the arm of her prey.

17
DECEMBER 8, 1780 – DECEMBER 14, 1780

Ruth slid the carrying strap from off her forehead and eased the firewood onto the ground.

"Good," said Sarah, smiling up at her across the steaming kettle while stirring, stirring the long-handled ladle through the heavy chunks of pork.

She looked at the slender form of Ruth, removing the blanket in which she was cloaked to crouch before the fire under the kettle, adding firewood to keep the fire ever-burning, the kettle ever-boiling.

Ruth. Why had she refused to tell Sarah the reason she had chosen Ruth for her Christian name?

"You are tired?" asked Sarah.

Ruth shook her head without looking up. Black hair glistened blue-black with bear's grease, smoother, cleaner, shinier with the passing months.

"Sister Leah needs wood for her fire ..." began Sarah.

"I shall stay with you, not work with ..." Ruth jerked her head backward toward Leah. Her jaw set firm and her eyes narrowed.

"I am thirsty. Will you bring us water? Then rest — here." Sarah indicated the stump of a tree.

Ruth took up her blanket and hurried toward the water pail.

The first Friday after the new moon came late this autumn for hog butchering day. Sarah looked along the wide street of Gnadenhutten. The men were still draining the blood, quartering and sectioning the carcasses, preparing the meat for boiling. Every kettle in Gnadenhutten was filled with boiling meat and tended by the women. They would store in lard, pickle in brine, and smoke slabs upon hooks in the smokehouse. This day.

Christoph, black coat thrown aside and sleeves rolled above his elbows though the air was cool and the wind sharp, was hauling a slab of pork to the smokehouse. Sarah listened to his low laugh. It was a good day, a blessed day; it was a day of fruitfulness.

She said this to Ruth when her friend returned with the water.

"Such fruit! Firewood and water, they are heavier than fruit," complained Ruth, rubbing her neck, strained by the weight of the wood she had carried in the carrying strap. "We are full of fruit. The White Man gathers and hides and stores like a squirrel. The Indian is a hunter and does not need to store."

They sat against the tree stump. Sarah folded her brown cape over her skirt; Ruth let her blanket hang in folds beside her stroud. Their shoulders almost touched.

Wind Maiden had been cut and burned. She had become a stump. "Into the death of Jesus I baptize you, in the name of the Father, and of the Son, and of the Holy Spirit." In Winu Gischuch, the time when maize is in its milk and ready to roast, the water had buried the body of Wind Maiden beneath its heavy flow. And Ruth had arisen from the water.

The Twitterer had mocked, "Why do you call yourself, 'Luth'? Speak it! You cannot speak it."

Ruth had answered, "Speak your name. You can better say, 'Twittering-Brown-Bird.' That is how you sound and that is what you are."

Anyway, she did not have to speak her name; she was her name. Others spoke it.

Salah had asked, "Why do you call yourself, 'Ruth?'" Why had Salah asked? She knew the story of Ruth, scratched in the Book of secrets: "My feet step into the prints your feet have made; I throw my bearskin beside the fire you sleep beside. Your people ... my people; your God ... my God."

Salah had carried the mangled fawn to Huts of Grace. She had not plugged her nostrils against the stench of death in Wind Maiden. Now Ruth ate the food of the harvest and the flesh of the hunt. She drank the juice of the blood of her Saviour. These were her people. She had found her God.

But if Wind Maiden was dead, why did Ruth remember?

"I am going back," she said to Salah.

"Back?" Sarah lowered her cup from her mouth.

"Star-at-Dawning, I see her ... here." Ruth tapped her forehead. "She saw me stab the knife into my heart when I ..." She raised her eyebrows to indicate the thing that had no words. Ruth continued, "She said, 'I have no daughter ... I *have* no daughter.'" The tears slid down her face. "Father, brothers, husband, friends ... I see them here." Her hand held her forehead, palm pressing hard. "They frown and turn. One-Who-Runs, I see his back; I do not see his face."

She leaned forward from the stump and looked into the eyes of Salah. "I must go, tell them ... about Wind Maiden."

Sarah glanced down and reached with her hand to that of Ruth. The movement was not natural. She dropped her eyes. She held the hand.

"Faces you see in your head and heart are stubborn and refuse to disappear. I know." She looked at Ruth then past her. "I see David, here ..." She tapped her forehead as Ruth had done.

When Brother Schebosh had returned from Bethlehem with Brother Jung three weeks previously, he had brought a letter from Suzanne Voss:

"Brother John and I know that Brother Christoph and you are eager to hear about David Christoph. He is red-cheeked and healthy. He laughs and plays with our children. Already we think of him as our own. Our older children are planning surprises for his birthday. The younger are preparing songs for him. I do suspect that our Anna believes herself to be his mother. Do not concern yourself about his welfare.

The war in the east subsides daily ..."

"Do not concern yourself ..." He would celebrate his fourth birthday. She could not kiss his cheek nor stroke his hair. She must not concern herself?

"But you did not the evil thing; I did the evil thing," stressed Ruth.

"I did not evil," Sarah agreed. "I thought, in other days ... maybe ... it was evil to leave David. It was not. I know this now. But the pain burned for him, still burns for me ..." For Christoph? She did not know.

When Christoph read the letter, he had said, "David is well. I am glad."

"But, Christoph, I am his mother; you are his father. He will not remember us." She had wanted him to share the agony of her loss.

Christoph had sunk his head into his hands. She had begun to think he was hiding his disgust at her selfishness or, worse, that he had fallen asleep in his indifference. But, then, he had looked up and said, "He belongs to God as do we. His happiness must content us. We cannot be selfish, Sarah."

Then he had raised his hand as if to touch her arm. But his hand had fallen and he had stood. Why could he not touch her? Did she disgust him?

"I did the evil thing," lamented Ruth. "In this I am alone."

"The Saviour covers your bad deeds with His blood," consoled Sarah.

"Covered, but the deeds are still done," Ruth replied. "I shall go back to Goschachgunk and try to reweave the strands that were broken."

Sarah gazed at the face of Ruth. She released her hand and said, "Yes, this is a good thing. It is of God."

"It is of God," repeated Ruth. Salah knew these things.

"I shall go with you," said Sarah. But she thought, "To Goschachgunk where Captain Pipe gains power for the warriors on behalf of the English?" She continued, "... and Brother Christoph should go ... and Brother Schebosh ..."

"No," interrupted Ruth. Salah did not know all things. "I shall go alone."

~ ~ ~

"I go to Goschachgunk with you," Twittering-Brown-Bird said as she folded tassmanane in a leaf. She handed it to Ruth.

187

"No." Ruth took the tassmanane. She spat her words upon the ground of the Sisters' cabin and did not look up. Her words would be those of the daughter of Fish-of-the-Deep-Water. Her eyes might speak the truth, that she wanted to walk through the forest with even the Twitterer, but the Fish-of-the-Deep-Water would say that she was a mouse. He would not recognize the mouse. She must go alone. She pushed the tassmanane into her bag and stood.

The Twitterer followed her out of the cabin. "I could go with you," she whispered. "You carry enough maize for me and you. And Goschachgunk has painted faces and beating drums ..." Her voice was thumping faster and faster and louder and louder: " ... I could ..."

"Hush! You wake the village." Ruth bared her teeth. The Twittering-Brown-Bird crept back onto her perch.

She had become tame after Ruth bit her in the hand — the soft place between the thumb and grasping finger. Bites are good when placed well, Ruth decided. This bite had been placed very well. The warm saltiness of the Twitterer's blood had mixed with the saliva of Ruth. After the two had joined together, peace began. Then, when the Shadow had seen the pact that was made with the blood and the water, she had followed in the peace ... because that was what shadows did.

The Shadow stumbled through the door, pulling her blanket around her. "I do not go with you." She rubbed her eyes and squatted beside the door.

"No one goes with me!" These were children who played games. She was old now; no games. Ruth turned and hurried through the village.

"Painted faces. Beating drums." She did not run to these sounds with the feet of the Twittering-Brown-Bird. Such noises were poison that made the heart so it throbbed with beating, the eyes so they could not see, the ears so they could hear only the rumble of the drums.

She stopped upon the path in the blackness of the forest. She pushed her carrying strap higher upon her forehead and tucked her blanket around her. Her steps continued more slowly now. Her feet followed the path toward the Place of Peace. They knew the way and did not need to ask her eyes to lead them.

She would not stop at Place of Peace. No. Questions would fall from mouths there. She did not want to catch the words that tumbled.

The third night was now passing since Ruth first laid the path toward Goschachgunk with Salah. Salah had said, "Schebosh, husband, we go ..." so Ruth followed the path before they could put on their moccasins.

She had to tell the Twitterer because the Twitterer had seen the packed bag of Ruth. But the Twittering-Brown-Bird did not know how to put on moccasins so she could not follow.

The feet stepped lightly over the trail.

Blackness pushed against Ruth and said, "You do not belong to me any longer. I do not want you here. Go back."

"No," she replied. "I pass through; I take nothing from you. You do not the honorable thing if you do not let me through."

Darkness stepped back but not far.

The sun had begun its vigil above the blackness when Ruth came to where the path stared across the Elk's Eye toward Place of Peace. She turned then onto the sister path that once hurried toward Pasture of Light but which now groped toward darkness.

She pattered upon her toes. All the day she walked. She crouched only one time to eat her tassmanane. If a warrior ate much, his courage would fall asleep because his body was full and drowsy.

"I shall tell you about the family of Wind Maiden," she whispered to the Saviour. She told Him about them while her moccasins moved along the trail and, later, while she wound herself inside the body of an old and broad tree to sleep. It held no other sleeper and no one else's fleas, for she looked and smelled before she laid her blanket.

She spoke about Star-at-Dawning and how her eyes sat deep within the flesh of her face. Her arm was soft and fat. She smelled sour and salty. Wind Maiden had liked to cuddle close to her and feel the rhythm of her mother.

Fish-of-the-Deep-Water was the warrior and the hunter. He carried rifles, and he bore the bodies of does in his carrying strap slung across his shoulder. He provided flesh and warmth for his family but not from his own body. Wind Maiden had not wanted to sit close to him.

Eagle-with-White-Head, brother. Wind Maiden had said she would someday be Eagle-with-White-Head. He smelled and felt like both mother and father. When Wind Maiden had been young ... Had Wind Maiden ever been young? ... she had run on foot to follow Eagle-with-White-Head when he had ridden his horse with ... with ... the Saviour knew whom with. Ruth could not speak the name of ... husband. They had seen her follow, and they had not scolded.

Ruth did not want to tell the Saviour about Red Face, brother. "He is his face," she said. "You ask about him; then I shall speak." He did not ask.

She told the Saviour about One-Who-Runs not with words but with sighs. She turned his face out toward the blackness of the sleepless night. He was dead. If he lived, he would have claimed the bones of the Aged Woman and wept above her grave. He was dead.

"Tell him," she whispered, "Ruth remembers and regrets." His spirit might hear though she could no longer heal the wounds upon his flesh.

Ruth asked the Saviour to hold her hand and sleep beside her. When they lay down together, his breath was sweet and warm. She slept.

She arose to greet Grandfather Sun the next morning. His cold-grey rays fell late between the trees. "Did you have to build a big fire to warm your creaking bones?" Ruth mocked. He did not answer.

Although they knew the way, her feet slid reluctantly down the path that day. Thoughts raced among the trees, darting like gusts of wind. Some, more frightening because of their boldness, lay across the path like narrow rays of sunlight. They said, "Captain Pipe struts through the streets of Goschachgunk. Black Wolf walks with him ..."

"Hush," she whispered; the darting rays cried louder. She stepped across them, but their light passed through her body with icy, sharp stabbings.

Moccasins thumped the earth. Ruth scurried from the path. She lay stretched out upon the cold shadow of a wide, rough-skinned tree. Her breaths were like the shallow rubbings of the limbs of trees.

She was near Goschachgunk.

Three hunters, not warriors, walked by, rifles hanging from their arms.

They passed. She stood — the hunter, darting among the trees upon the feet of a doe. Rays of fears pursued her, whispering, "Hunted!"

Goschachgunk — sleeping beneath the grey-stone sky. Ruth stood beneath the last trees before the clearing. A cluster of men threw dice, crouching in the earth near a fire, while a larger cluster stood above them watching, whispering, betting. The day was dark, good for the hunt. They did not hunt. Why? Smoke puffed from the centers of huts and cabins. Huts, new huts, leaned in toward the old village like lazy women. Ruth walked along the path of Goschachgunk toward the cabin of her mother and father.

Low doors opened into black huts and cabins where orange flames burst from black fire pits. Women sat around those pits. Ruth could not see them, yet she knew they watched.

Four blanketed women huddled around a smoking fire built from wet, soft firewood.

A wrinkled face looked up, black like the smoke. It puffed a pipe held in black jaws. "Lenni Lenape?" she asked through the sides of her mouth. Smoke puffed with the words.

Ruth forced her eyes to meet the eyes of each of the women. One she remembered. The others were not Unami.

"Caw!" croaked the Unami. She cackled in her throat and leaned forward into the circle croaking and laughing until all four cackled together.

She would pull their ash-heads; she would spit in their faces! They were ruder than children, as rude as White Men. But they croaked at Wind Maiden, and Ruth was not Wind Maiden so she walked past.

Toward her walked a woman leaning under the weight of firewood upon her back. The woman looked up. Wind Maiden would have recognized this woman. She was the Singing Sparrow, friend to sister of mother. The eyes narrowed, then widened. Singing Sparrow stopped and almost turned. Her hesitating body said, "Tell Star-at-Dawning? Not time." Singing Sparrow bowed, again, and walked, nodding with almost a greeting as she passed.

Smoke rose from the center of the cabin of the parents of Wind Maiden. Ruth stopped and watched it. She bowed and entered the blackness. Her heart screamed to be released to flee. She saw a form sitting upon dirt near the fire. The chin rested against a full, round chest. Small, square, plump hands lay in the lap. A flat rock where the hands had been grinding maize sat on the ground in front of the hands. She was a mound of sleeping grey clay.

Ruth stepped nearer. Her heart settled into a thick mat of memories. Ruth crouched beside the mound and whispered, "Mother."

Star-at-Dawning jerked her head up. Startled eyes, puckered mouth softened, softened into eager welcome. Yet where welcome should have moved the lips, silence formed. Ruth saw her mother struggle against gladness. Star-at-Dawning looked away.

But she did not say, "Go!"

Ruth murmured to the grey-black head, "Wind Maiden is dead; she killed herself. I buried the body." Star-at-Dawning did not move. Ruth continued, "I come to ask you to forgive the evil Wind Maiden made. She smeared shame upon your face, and she smothered herself in shame until she died."

Ruth wanted to sit beside her mother, but Star-at-Dawning had not offered a bearskin. Ruth stood. "I take no more from you. I know now ... Wind Maiden tried to take too much."

Star-at-Dawning looked up at Ruth: "I am glad to see you," she said. Her voice was weak and old, much older than the ears of Ruth remembered. "Sit." She pointed with a plump hand toward a bearskin upon the dirt.

Ruth settled upon its corner near her mother.

Star-at-Dawning reached forward and rubbed the arm of Ruth. The hand of Mother — soft, warm, moist. "Fat covers your bones," said Star-at-Dawning. She stroked the hair of her daughter: "Bear grease. You have meat. You are married?"

"Wind Maiden was married. I am not," replied Ruth.

"Who, then, can hunt for you and not lose bent bullets in tree and ground?"

"I live at Huts of Grace. I belong to the Sav..."

"Shush! I did not hear you! Do not tell me." Star-at-Dawning waved her hands in front of her face as if to scatter the words of Ruth before they reached her own ears.

Silence traveled between them. The fire crackled and settled lower in the fire pit.

"Father?" asked Ruth.

Star-at-Dawning snapped her head toward the open door. She watched it. "He hunts," she said. "He left before the rising of the sun." She looked at Ruth, into her eyes, deep, deep. "He will come back soon. They meet ..."

She rolled her head from side to side, "... and he will meet with them. You go soon before ..."

"Eagle-with-White-Head?" asked Ruth. Many questions. No time.

"Married," was the reply. "He is here."

"Red Face?"

"Dead!" spat out Star-at-Dawning upon frowning lips. "Lenni Lenape killing Lenni Lenape. The White Man ... oh, he is very clever to make Lenni Lenape fight Lenni Lenape."

Dead? Ruth had not known Red Face was dead. She would think many thoughts about him now ... now ... dead.

"And As-the-Water-Flows," continued her mother, face easing into weariness, "dead. The stream is dry. The water does not flow, and the snow will never fall again."

They shared a gourd of silence; each took long, deep drinks. Dead. Dead. Ruth knew death. It was not hard to die. Skin was thin and bones brittle. Blood flowed through rivers whose banks washed easily away. Dead. Aged Woman. Red Face. As-the-Water-Flows. Wind Maiden.

"One-Who-Runs. Dead, too?" she asked after her stomach was filled with the liquid of silence and the flesh of memory.

Star-at-Dawning spilled her gourd of silence on the ground with a short gasp. She looked at the eyes and mouth of Ruth. Then her own eyes darted to the fire where they searched among the embers. She said, "The answer. It is not mine to give you."

"He is dead," repeated Ruth, her voice weighted with certainty.

"The answer, it is not mine to give you," said her mother, looking at Ruth now. She flicked her hand through smoky air to nudge aside the question.

The light through the door went out. Black covered the mind of Ruth; black covered the cabin. Ruth saw the face of Star-at-Dawning, red toward the fire, shadowed on the side away. Star-at-Dawning stared with frozen face past Ruth. They were dead. Yes. Both dead together and buried. Ruth followed the gaze of her mother past her shoulder toward the darkened door.

Fish-of-the-Deep-Water stood, legs apart, rifle in hand. He watched Ruth. She could not speak; she could not swallow; she could not rise. She said, "I am happy to see you," but sound did not travel with the words.

Far, far, far behind her, the voice of Star-at-Dawning said, "The body of our daughter is buried. This woman dug the hole with her own hands. She comes to tell us. I have welcomed her beside our fire. Because of the memory of our daughter."

Fish-of-the-Deep-Water did not move. He watched Ruth. He did not speak. The fire cracked and dozed and slowly closed its fiery eyes to sleep.

Fish-of-the-Deep-Water bent and leaned his rifle against the wall in the shadows beside the door. He slipped his carrying strap from off his shoulder. He shook his muscular arms. He watched Ruth.

He had crossed to the fire pit, sat down beside it, and stared across its glowing red ashes. He said, "Your face is formed like the face of my daughter, but, no, you are not my daughter. My blood no longer flows through the veins of any Lenni Lenape. "

"Eagle-with-White-Head?" thought Ruth. "He lives." She glanced at her mother, but the face was carved from wood. No marks were scratched there that could tell Ruth the meaning of the words of Fish-of-the-Deep-Water.

"You are welcome," continued Fish-of-the-Deep-Water. "Eat flesh. Share warmth. Lie under the cover of my roof. If your blood is the color of my blood; if it flows where my blood flows; then I shall mingle my blood with your blood. I shall adopt you. "

Father ... Mother ... Lenni Lenape. Huts of Grace was a lifetime of footsteps away. Was Goschachgunk home?

Fish-of-the-Deep-Water looked at Star-at-Dawning: "I am hungry."

She arose and scooped boiled chunks of roots and deer flesh from the kettle over the fire. She handed him a steaming bowl and a bread of maize baked in the smoldering ashes.

"Eat my food," he said to Ruth.

Star-at-Dawning gave her a bowl of steaming, tender meat. Ruth held the bowl carved from the knob of a tree. She rubbed her palms along its uneven surface. She had eaten only tassmanane since she had left Huts of Grace. She had walked and slept like the hunter. The hunter would have been hungry, but she was not. Yet she ate, lifting the thick wooden spoon to her lips while watching the rhythmic, drumming sips of her father. To not eat would be to not accept his welcome.

He was not older but was darker and fiercer. Although he sat eating, his muscles were tight. He was a wolf, ready to spring. Ruth watched. Would he spring upon her?

Fish-of-the-Deep-Water ate one, two, three bowls of flesh. Star-at-Dawning did not eat. Ruth nibbled upon her meat like a doe upon tender leaves while Fish-of-the-Deep-Water watched her and she, beneath shadowed brows, watched him.

The light of the fire was now barely a glow beneath ashes. Star-at-Dawning did not rise to add firewood. Why? Soon Fish-of-the-Deep-Water would scold her as though she were a lazy child. Ruth recrossed her legs upon the bearskin. She scratched her ankle and looked sideways at her mother.

Star-at-Dawning stared toward the door, but her eyes did not see. She looked at Ruth but did not see Ruth looking back at her.

Ruth slid her bowl upon the dirt toward her mother. "I go for wood," she whispered.

"No!" Did the wolf spring? His voice shook the ground. "You are not daughter ... yet."

He looked at Star-at-Dawning. He would devour her! Like a turtle, her mother rose and gathered her blanket shell around herself. Her stroud rubbed against the back of Ruth as she passed.

They were alone. Fish-of-the-Deep-Water frowned toward the door then back at her. He rubbed his knee and stretched his deerskin legging tight and smooth. He shook his large, shaved head. He did not speak.

Star-at-Dawning returned and laid the wood in the fire pit. Ruth did not help. He watched.

The light through the door grew dimmer. Fish-of-the-Deep-Water rose. He took his pipe and pouch of tobacco. He walked past his carrying strap and lifted his rifle. He looked back. "Sleep there," he said, pointing to the bench that once had been Wind Maiden's. He was gone.

The fire burned a thick warmth. Ruth dropped her blanket from off her shoulders. She scraped with a stick hot, red chips of wood back into the pit. "You said Eagle-with-White-Head lives." She spoke into the fire.

"He lives."

"Fish-of-the-Deep-Water ..."

"He is dead to Fish-of-the-Deep-Water. The White Man is crafty. Lenni Lenape fighting Lenni Lenape." The voice of Star-at-Dawning heaved.

Ruth looked at her: "Do not play games with the child. I am not a child."

"No, you are not a child. I am barren. No child." Star-at-Dawning sealed her toothless mouth. She opened it to say, "Fish-of-the-Deep-Water will lift his hatchet for the Saggenash. Eagle-with-White-Head still lifts his hatchet for the Big Knife."

"Fish-of-the-Deep-Water would never fight for any White Man, not Saggenash, not Big Knife," objected Ruth.

"They put a spell on him, these White Men," mumbled Star-at-Dawning. "He thinks he fights with the bullets of the Saggenash and not for them. But the bullets of the White Man obey only their master."

Star-at-Dawning waved her hand: "Now they go to sit around the council fire, to smoke the pipe, to stomp the foot. The Lenni Lenape will choose for which White Man he will slice out his own heart."

"This night they choose?" asked Ruth.

"They choose every night. Long time to tear apart the body of the Lenni Lenape." Star-at-Dawning leaned toward her daughter: "Soon, the last bone will break; the last piece of flesh will tear; the Lenni Lenape will die." She scratched her greying head then pressed her palms against her eyes. "Sleep now," she murmured. "I am tired."

Ruth cast the bearskin onto the bench and lay upon it on her side. She watched the fire spark and the smoke rise. She heard above her head the quick, forced breaths of her mother ease into long, shallow sighs.

Had Ruth always slept here beside the fire pit? When had she first come? She felt the pressure of whispers she could not hear, of faces approaching she could not see. The fire flickered black and red, crackled ... and crackled again.

A tall form entered the cabin and fell upon the bench on the other side of the fire.

Father? Mother? Is this home? Ruth remembered a meeting house where bells and chants soothed the pulsing of the black, seeping wound and where many words once flowed over her parched lips and swollen tongue and filled with pleasant fullness her stomach and the dark, dark pit. "Salah ... Salah ... do not forget though I forget. Saviour? There is a Saviour, but He is not here ..."

Wind Maiden was buried deep beneath the frozen earth. She shivered and turned in her burying box. The air, cold and heavy and damp and filled with the stench of rotting flesh, pushed its greyness across her face and up her nostrils.

"No! I am not Wind Maiden! I am Ruth! She is dead; I live." Her head throbbed faster and faster.

"Help me!" she screamed. "I live! I live!"

Her eyes opened. Dark. Quiet. The fire was out. The outside air had crept inside. Star-at-Dawning, Fish-of-the-Deep-Water, they slept.

She sat up. "Ruth lives," she said to herself.

She gathered her blanket in her arms. "Salah gave this blanket to Ruth." Her lips formed the words over and over.

She arose in silence and left the cabin. A rustle told her that Fish-of-the-Deep-Water saw.

Ruth crouched near the door. She wrapped her blanket over her head and around her body. Her knees pulled close to her chest.

Her eyes watched from within the blanket cave. Thin puffs of smoke rose from the centers of some cabins and huts; others breathed no smoke at all. The rubbing sound of the village and the hollow sound of the forest surrounding it rode upon the back of the wind. Goschachgunk, smoldering and flickering, settled into its ashy-grey fire pit.

Whispers. She opened her eyes from sleepless sleep. Two Lenape passed her, carrying rifles. Hunters. They watched her as they passed.

Three times more the hunters passed. And one ... he walked between the huts with long strides and smooth. Muscles, many muscles, filled the blanket draped across his shoulder. His head was wide and dark and smooth. He walked in darkness. Black Wolf.

No!

He disappeared between the shadows of the huts.

Ruth shivered. She rubbed her legs, her arms, her face. The coldness settled deep inside. It was not Black Wolf, no!

195

Blood red, the light of the sun lightened the tips of naked trees across the icy Elk's Eye and pushed against the smoky clouds of night. Slowly, day forced itself into the sky.

Women crawled from huts to gather firewood. Smoke rose in thickening puffs to float, to hover, to burn the nostrils and the eyes.

Ruth heard them inside the cabin, rustling, rising. Fish-of-the-Deep-Water came out. He said, "My guest does not sit outside. She has a mat to sleep upon. Does she forget?"

He waited until Ruth stood. They passed each other as she went inside.

Star-at-Dawning was spreading the ashes in the fire pit for the fire of the new day.

"I shall go for wood," said Ruth, lifting her carrying strap.

Star-at-Dawning glanced toward the door. "No. I go."

After she returned and built the fire, they heated and ate the meat of the night before. They did not eat words until their bowls were empty. Then Ruth said, "Fish-of-the-Deep-Water ... gone?"

"Gone," agreed her mother.

"Eagle-with-White-Head ... gone?"

Star-at-Dawning puckered her lips and blew through her black-toothed mouth. She did not know or she would not say.

"I must find Eagle-with-White-Head." Ruth stood. Was she a mouse that she should hide in a hole? Eagle-with-White-Head could speak with a free tongue, he who once was brother. He could tell her about the death of ... the husband. And she could tell him about the death of Wind Maiden. She looked down at her mother.

Star-at-Dawning stood. "I shall walk with you; you must not walk alone. They will talk. My steps will say, 'We walk together, her feet and my feet.'"

"Fish-of-the-Deep-Water will rage?" asked Ruth.

"He will rage." Star-at-Dawning gathered her hair from her face and wound it back with scarlet cloth, spotted brown with dirt and torn, traded long ago when traders still floated down the Elk's Eye and traded in the villages for pelts.

She looked at Ruth but did not speak.

Finally, Star-at-Dawning breathed the words, "He is my son." And lower, with words upon the lips that only eyes could hear, "You are my daughter."

They walked together through Goschachgunk. Faces Ruth recalled, older now and ... more wild, watched them pass. Eyes said, "Fool! You are dead. Do you not know? The dead must not walk here."

They could not see; they were blind. Ruth lived in the body of Wind Maiden. She raised her chin. She heard the shuffling of her mother beside her. Mother. Star-at-Dawning had spoken with her lips, "Daughter." Mother. Star-at-Dawning was not blind; she saw. Let the faces cry their lies. The cries would crawl inward and choke the liars until they died.

When they came to a large hut, Ruth stood outside while Star-at-Dawning bent and went inside. She came back out. "Not here," she said.

At another hut, smaller, Star-at-Dawning looked out from inside and rocked her head one time. Ruth followed through the door.

A woman, old like her mother, sat by the fire. Ruth recalled this old one sitting with Star-at-Dawning and As-the-Water-Flows, weaving hemp into carrying straps.

Another woman, a tiny woman, sat nearby holding a baby wrapped in a blanket and pressed against her breast. The Fawn. Her legs had once been thin like twigs. Her face would flush red when the men walked by and she would struggle to force words to her lips when she spoke. The Fawn was now a Doe.

She looked at Ruth. The bones of her cheeks pushed against leaf-thin skin. Her mother, the old woman, said to Star-at-Dawning, "I am happy to greet you. Sit here beside me so I can see the moving of your eyes as you speak."

"Will Star-at-Dawning protect you from me, old woman?" thought Ruth. "My breath cannot float across your breath and smother you. It bears power no longer." Ruth crouched upon the dirt beside the door.

"My husband returns soon," the Doe said to Ruth.

Eagle-with-White-Head ... a husband and a father. Ruth looked at the cradled bundle. "Son?" she asked.

The Doe smiled.

They sat in silence until the Doe arose. She pulled her blanket around herself and her son. "We shall wait at my hut," she said.

Ruth walked behind the Doe. She made her shadow crawl close beside herself. She would not cast the shadow of shame upon the wife and son of Eagle-with-White-Head. Star-at-Dawning walked beside her daughter.

Inside the hut, the Doe gave her son to Star-at-Dawning while she stirred a pot of steaming beans for her husband. Ruth crouched near the door. Star-at-Dawning pulled back the blankets and Ruth saw a small, round head with straight black strands of hair. His eyes were open. His lips were puckered. Star-at-Dawning looked across the fire at Ruth.

Eagle-with-White-Head entered the hut. Ruth crept sideways into darkness. He looked at the Doe. "One buck," he said. He looked back through the door to where it lay. He propped his rifle near the door. "I am happy to see you," he said to Star-at-Dawning.

"I am happy to greet you," she replied. "I bring one who tells of the burying of bones." She looked past him to Ruth.

He turned.

Ruth stood, throwing aside the blanket of darkness from across her face. "I buried the bones of Wind Maiden deep within the earth. She is no more." She stepped forward. "I come now to soothe the ache of the pain she made."

Eagle-with-White-Head said, "Walk nearer."

Ruth stepped beside the fire pit.

He looked into her eyes. Did the rot of death still cling to them? Her eyes wanted to scurry across the dirt at his feet.

He said, "Your face is the face of Wind Maiden. But she was weighted down with pride too heavy to carry into Goschachgunk. Wind Maiden would never put down the weight and return. Yes, she is dead. I welcome you here."

They sat together and talked about the seasons that had passed — about the Planting moons, the moons of the Red Deer, the Harvest moons, the Hunting moons, the moons of Frogs.

Then Eagle-with-White-Head said, "Your blanket is not frayed; your moccasins are new-sewn. You do not live alone. You are married."

"No," Ruth said.

"A hunter kills your bucks and gives you flesh and skin." Eagle-with-White-Head leaned closer.

Ruth glanced across the fire at her mother. The head of Star-at-Dawning hung upon her chest. Ruth looked back. She said, her voice low, "I live at Huts of Grace. I belong to the Saviour."

"Shush!" hissed her mother, looking up, her eyes within their folds of skin widening, forcing back the heavy lids.

Eagle-with-White-Head did not shriek or slide away. He mumbled. Ruth thought she heard, "Sometimes, I wish to go ..."

He said aloud, "Do not speak these words in Goschachgunk. Many walk here who would kill the White teachers and burn their villages and rub war paint upon the faces of the men who live there. They raise their rifles for the Saggenash. They say the teachers warn the Big Knives at Fort Pitt when they attack." He stared into the fire.

Ruth looked at the Doe who rocked the son and watched her husband. The Doe frowned. Ruth frowned with her.

"You do not shoot the bullets of the Saggenash?" asked Ruth. She remembered the words of her mother.

Eagle-with-White-Head looked up. "No," he said. "The Lenni Lenape received the war belt first at Fort Pitt. Do I run to the Saggenash because their trinkets are shinier?"

"That is what One-Who-Runs would have said," decided Ruth.

"Have you seen the place where the earth covers the body of ..." His name pounded inside her but would not come out. She pushed her hands, hidden beneath her blanket, against her stomach and continued, "... the body of the husband of Wind Maiden?"

Eagle-with-White-Head pressed his hands upon his knees and leaned backward, his back straight, his arms stiff. He looked at Ruth then at Star-at-

Dawning. The shadows hid the meaning of his look. One-Who-Runs was dead, yes, and never buried. Scalped. His bones had been gnawed by wolves.

"You did not tell her?" Eagle-with-White-Head asked Star-at-Dawning.

The old woman swung her heavy head: "I have poured out my bag of sorrows and have no sorrows left to offer her. Some other voice must give ..." Her words sighed and vanished.

"Lean closer," said Eagle-with-White-Head, watching now the face, the mouth, the eyes of Ruth.

Ruth slid onto her knees. The fire burned one cheek; the other froze in greyness. For what did Eagle-with-White-Head search? She wanted to hide the weariness drooping from her eyes, but she looked back into his face, opening her eyes with boldness.

"Why do you ask for him?" asked Eagle-with-White-Head.

"He ... he ..." she stammered, glancing away. Wind Maiden, wife, she was dead so she could not ask. Ruth was without family among the Lenni Lenape. She could not claim the bones of the memory of One-Who-Runs.

She opened her eyes again up toward the face of Eagle-with-White-Head: "My stroud is stained with blood from the wound of One-Who-Runs. Wind Maiden is dead, but the blood will not wash out in the flowing water."

"He is here," said Eagle-with-White-Head. The words traveled over lips which did not move.

"Here? His spirit is restless? His death ... it was brutal?" The eyes of Ruth followed the flames rising from the fire pit to meet the cold air above.

"No. He builds his fire in Goschachgunk with warm hands of flesh," replied Eagle-with-White-Head.

"He lives," Ruth heard the words. Did she speak them? She was far away and could not feel the movement of her mouth. "He lives." That was spoken both farther away and closer. "He lives."

"Will he see me?" She said that. Her heart pounded.

"I do not know."

Ruth lay upon her bearskin that night in the cabin of Fish-of-the-Deep-Water. "Will he see me? ... I do not know ... I do not know ... I do not ... I do not ... I do not know."

~ ~ ~

Snow fell in the night and the next morning. Ruth walked in it though the icy snow melted into her deerskin moccasins and chilled her feet. She had arisen early but did not leave the cabin until Fish-of-the-Deep-Water had opened his eyes and could see that she was not casting shame upon him by wandering in the night.

She had not eaten; her insides were squeezed tight and would not open for food. Star-at-Dawning had watched. She had known why Ruth did not eat.

She knew much more, but she did not open her mouth to the one she called, "daughter."

Ruth shuffled through the snow. It fell like white ashes from off her moccasins, white, cold ashes hissing beneath a frozen fire. She looked up. Where was the fire? Hidden within its pit of clouds, it smothered and sparked and flamed ... coldness.

She walked near the Elk's Eye. The smoke of the icy fire puffed whiteness all around her.

When her toes called out their numbness, she returned to the fire pit of Fish-of-the-Deep-Water.

He did not take up his rifle. Star-at-Dawning watched him while she added sticks to the fire. One of the men from the council of the Lenni Lenape came to smoke his pipe with Fish-of-the-Deep-Water. The smoke from their pipes rose together. Fish-of-the-Deep-Water told his friend that the visitor had come to recite to them the story of the burial of his daughter.

"Do not sigh," he said. "The visitor will soon put on the stroud and shirt of 'daughter'."

Ruth rocked herself. Was she becoming the daughter? She belonged to the Saviour and not to Fish-of-the-Deep-Water. Was the blood of the Lenni Lenape hidden beneath her skin or did a different blood now flow there? What words would Salah speak?

Eagle-with-White-Head appeared while the pipes were still smoking and the men were still staring at the visitor.

Fish-of-the-Deep-Water looked up, then away. He puffed his pipe, his back rigid, his eyes two grey rocks.

"I am happy to see you, Father and Mother," said Eagle-with-White-Head. Star-at-Dawning glanced at her husband then nodded her head one time. Fish-of-the-Deep-Water did not hear him.

Eagle-with-White-Head said to Ruth, "I shall take you to him now; he waits."

Ruth stood upon numb legs, numbed not by sitting and not by freezing.

"Where do you go?" The low growl of Fish-of-the-Deep-Water threw the breath backward into the throat of Ruth.

She could not speak.

"I take her to One-Who-Runs, Father," said Eagle-with-White-Head.

"Where do you go?" repeated Fish-of-the-Deep-Water. The growl, still low, moved closer.

"To One-Who-Runs," she repeated.

"Yes, you must go," he said. "Show her the way," he said to Star-at-Dawning, waving her up with the hand that held the long-necked pipe.

Star-at-Dawning arose. Her movement swept both Ruth and Eagle-with-White-Head out of the cabin.

The snow had stopped falling. Blanket-wrapped Lenape shuffled past them. Ruth did not see their faces. She saw only the memory of one face.

They walked toward the edge of Goschachgunk. Star-at-Dawning stopped. She stepped backwards. "I shall wait here for you," she said.

Mother! Ruth wanted to cling to the soft warmness of her mother's arm. She clenched her fists and continued beside Eagle-with-White-Head.

A man, narrow-built like a sapling in a forest of grandfather trees, stood in front of a hunting lodge – not a hut that would push out the winds of cold nights and hold in the warmth of the fire. He walked toward them.

He limped. His right leg did not want to join the other but trailed beside its stronger brother.

Ruth watched him approach. Her body shook; it cried out the secret, but the part of her that shaped thinking would not take the truth and speak it.

He limped. He pulled his leg along beside him. His body slid into the shape of a memory. The memory did not limp.

Now he was twenty steps away from them. She did not think his name, for she knew him through all her flesh. And along her entire body and down to the tips of her fingers, she could feel the touch of his presence.

She held herself erect. The throb of his limping pulled her sobbing, sobbing, down inside. Then they stood before each other and he stared at her with a look she could not see. His face was blurred by the water she lay beneath. And she knew that she was crying. The wetness flooded her eyes and overflowed onto her cheeks. Oh, she wanted to see, but she could not see!

His arms wrapped tightly round her and her arms she wrapped around him.

18
DECEMBER 14, 1780 – DECEMBER 17, 1780

"Your face is full; your eyes glitter. You are lovely," he said, rubbing her cheek with his palm. He wiped out the wetness that was now cold upon the face of Ruth, but he did not speak about the tears. "Red and icy," he said wiping the other cheek, hand moving round.

"They were cold," said Ruth. "You have rubbed in warmness." The fire had gone out. He had rolled his stick upon the dry board; the board was warm; the fire almost blazed. Ruth squeezed her eyes closed to press out the tears and sniffed in the spring of flowing water until the spring was dry.

She looked at One-Who-Runs through eyes that now could see. Lines formed by smiles and frowns were scratched into his face. A small scar was carved into his brow. Had these marks always been there? Had she never seen before? Her memory had formed itself around a big nose. Eyes and mouth lay around the nose like rocks around a boulder. She had only seen the boulder, but now she saw much more. She looked. She knew she still stood in the dirt of Goschachgunk. Eyes would see them standing there and mouths would tell to ears what eyes had seen. However, she was a woman who had lost her way because she had never learned the marks of the path. She would learn so that she would remember and not be lost again.

She knew he would not take her back. "Do not hope," she warned herself. That was why she had to carve his features into her memory so that the memory would hold itself before her eyes like breathing flesh. One of his hands rested upon her shoulder; the other still rubbed her cheek. She leaned her face into the rubbing hand just a little so he would not notice.

He touched her. "No! Do not hope!"

"My hut is small but the fire is large. Let us trade words there," said One-Who-Runs.

Ruth looked around. Eagle-with-White-Head stood behind her. Was she "wife" that she should follow him alone?

"Shall I come with you?" asked Eagle-with-White-Head, watching Ruth.

"Come," said One-Who-Runs.

They walked. He limped. Ruth had almost forgotten that he limped. This man was much like One-Who-Runs, but One-Who-Runs did not limp. Secrets were hidden in that limp.

They sat together upon one bearskin: One-Who-Runs, Eagle-with-White-Head, Ruth between them. She felt like the little girl of their youth, hiding with them in secret places to wait for the bear. The shadow would become the bear; the wind would be his growl. They would attack and kill and she would watch. A bearskin, not a shadow, lay beneath them now and she was not a little girl and this was not a game.

"Wind Maiden is dead," said Ruth.

"Yes, I know. My eyes show me; my ears have heard," replied One-Who-Runs. "I grieve for the death of the past she walked through."

"The Aged Woman is dead." Ruth would bury all the words of sorrow so she could then shake her shirt and stroud free from the dirt of digging.

"I know this," he answered.

How had he heard? Wind Maiden had not wailed through Goschachgunk the cry for the death of the Aged Woman.

"I know that Wind Maiden fed her and warmed her flesh. Wind Maiden slept at her feet and was a daughter to her. And I know that Wind Maiden wept when she died."

Who had told him these things? He had not seen where the grave was dug nor laid his hands upon the beads and bells that had belonged to the Aged woman that he might give them away to her friends. She swallowed back words and gazed into his face. What more did he know?

He looked back. His eyes he opened wide: "You have built your fire and laid your sleeping mat in Huts of Grace since the time of the raising of the earth about the maize. Now you wonder from where I have gathered my story? It is spooned out of the mixture of a larger story."

One-Who-Runs rolled his head from side to side. He stretched his leg, the leg that limped. When he looked again at Ruth, the full lips of his mouth frowned and his eyes — shadowed eyes in darkness — saw far away and long ago. He had put on the face of the remembrancer of speeches, of the reciter of the long ago times of the Lenni Lenape when they still lived in the land toward the rising of the sun, of the runner bringing back to hearers the words of deeds from distant places.

"When I carried my rifle from the cabin of Wind Maiden, from the home of my mother, from the village of Goschachgunk, I laid it down in Fort Pitt at the feet of the Big Knives. We of the Lenni Lenape would run for the Big Knives and become their eyes among the trees, along the paths that led to the council fires of the Mengwe and of the Delamatteno who lived along the saltless sea at Sandusky and who painted their faces for the Saggenash.

"But the Big Knives ran like turtles. They were lazy. They crawled until they found a spot to dig a nest. They left men to guard the nest and crawled toward the head of the tide on the Elk's Eye to dig another nest, to lay their eggs.

"I had run ahead to the Elk's Eye to open the easiest path for the turtles. When I returned, I heard the cry, 'White Eyes is dead.' When I had left, he was stronger than a Big Knife; I returned and he had burned, sweated, and died with the sickness the White Man calls smallpox.

"I said to the Big Knife, 'Show me his body.'

"He answered, 'It is buried.'

"I said, 'Take me to where you covered his bones with dirt.'

"He answered, 'I do not remember where I dug the hole, and we cannot go back to search for it. We must hurry forward. First we build the fort; then I shall find the place where we dug the hole.'

"White Eyes was alive. Suddenly, he was dead, and I never saw the burying place.

"I did not lay my bearskin near the fire of the Big Knives. I slept with the other runners, and we kept our fire blazing and our eyes open in sleep. Because although the words of the Big Knives sounded like words of friendship, the smell of the words was foul.

"They built the fort against the warm bosom of the Elk's Eye. I watched water ripple over rocks while they slept. Their voice trembled and they said, 'Our warriors are hungry; our warriors are tired. We must march back to Fort Pitt.'

"'We were cutting a trail for you to follow toward the big fires of the Mengwe and the Delamatteno and farther to the resting place of the Saggenash at Fort Detroit!' cried the Lenape. 'The nations know that the Lenni Lenape have become the eyes of the Big Knives. They will stab out those eyes unless you stab first.'

"'We shall leave warriors here to protect the Lenni Lenape,' replied the Big Knives, 'but we must march back to Fort Pitt.'

"Lenni Lenape and other lenno had left their villages to watch the Big Knife warriors weep for fear. The Big Knife captain, McIntosh, called out to the gathering lenno that he would punish all who did not obey him. The lenno laughed and could not breathe for laughing. Was that the Big Knives' plan, to suffocate all lenno with laughter?

"So they ran back to Fort Pitt, each man finding his own path among the trees. Behind them, they left a huddling group of warriors to protect the Lenni Lenape against the laughing lenno.

"I crouched beside the Elk's Eye to watch while the laughter floated among the trees to warm the ears of the Shawano, Mengwe, and Delamatteno who ran to the commands of the Saggenash. Soon, they attacked the huddling nest and forced the turtles to crawl into their shelter. I watched the passing of days. The ground squirrels came out of their holes; then the frogs croaked; and, finally, the shad swam up the river. When the sun thawed the forest so that sap flowed from the stone tree, more warriors trickled through the forest to flow against the fort.

"I and other Lenni Lenape hunted in the darkness to find flesh to feed the hungry Big Knives who were protecting us. Flesh could not fill the bellies of these turtles.

"They sent me and two other runners to the first nest they had built along the Beaver River. I ran and puffed out the words that our protectors were weak and starving. The Big Knives marched heavy-footed toward the nest upon the Elk's Eye.

"Alone, I followed.

"A rifle cried from behind me, another, and another. Were the Big Knives hunting? Another cry ... I fell. What were they hunting? I lifted myself upon one leg; the other flowed red. I leaped and rolled among the shadows of the trees. I crawled between two fallen trunks and piled brown leaves upon me. They searched for their prey, these Big Knives, these White Men. They knew they had wounded it, for they found the warm blood. Its saltiness must have made water flow inside their mouths because they searched until darkness hid them from one another. Frightened because they could not hold the hand of each other, they crawled back to the nest that slept upon the Beaver.

"I dragged myself over leaves and branches through the blackness. I leaned against a tree and felt my swelling wound ... above the knee, into the bone. I had lost my bag and carrying strap. I had lost my rifle. I sweated; I shivered. I had not food nor covering for my body. I tore the sleeve of my shirt and wrapped it around my wound. I crawled farther from the trail.

"I awoke. Day had come; I did not know when. Voices whispered among the branches. Monsey. I called to them. They carried me to their canoe and up the Allegheny River to their village.

"The bullet in my leg gave me the name, 'Friend to Enemies of the Big Knife' so they laid leaves and healing paste upon the wound and bound the shattered bones until they grew together. I said that I was Lenni Lenape, once a runner; I did not say more."

One-Who-Runs paused and shifted his leg.

"The day is in its warmth," said Ruth. She watched his leg. "We can walk outside and build a fire, talk where we find space to stretch."

They sat beside a new-built fire near fields of maize now harvested. Ruth was again the young girl near a man she liked but whose nearness she feared. So she had asked with her eyes, and Eagle-with-White-Head had followed them.

One-Who-Runs ... the name would mock him now. One-Who-Runs was dead, too.

"I slept in the village of the Monsey during the planting and growing moons," continued One-Who-Runs. "When the maize was in the milk, my thoughts ran back to Goschachgunk and the Aged Woman. My thoughts were stronger than my leg so I waited. I would leave in the Harvest moon.

"In Winu Gischuch before I could lift my carrying strap upon my chest, the cry ran through the village, 'Flee! The Great Moon, Brodhead, leads Big Knives up the Allegheny! They burn our villages! They kill us!'

"We fled with Seneca and Monsey from the lower villages and with Ienno from the upper villages along the Allegheny River. Our maize, our squash, our beans we left behind.

"The Saggenash reached out his arm to pull us to himself in the land by the saltless sea of the Delamatteno. We crouched there and waited.

"We crouched there and many starved while maize lay upon frozen ground in abandoned villages, while snow fell and wind blew and wind blew and snow fell.

"Still my thoughts roamed through the forest toward Goschachgunk. I had not food to give me strength; I had not fur to cover my feet and body; I had not legs to climb through deepening snow ... I could not return to Goschachgunk. I would die in the land of the Mengwe among Ienno I did not know.

"I lived upon scraps thrown onto the ground by the Saggenash. The snow crept away; Grandmother Earth opened her hard-frozen eyes.

"When berries appeared upon leafing shrubs, I lifted my carrying strap and my bag and roamed back toward the Elk's Eye and Goschachgunk. My load was light: I did not have a rifle.

"I picked berries and speared black fish and buffalo fish. I slept wherever bank or hill would hide me from wind and rain. I was not the runner, but the walker and the rester.

"In Goschachgunk, I heard that Pasture of Light was called by a new name. New faces slept there. My friend ..." One-Who-Runs looked at Eagle-with-White-Head, "... spoke words of weeping about the death of the Aged Woman. He turned me toward the Place of Peace. 'There, you will hear the story from those whose eyes saw and whose ears heard and whose hands fed the dying one,' he said.

"In Place of Peace, the wife of Glikkikan sat with me and spoke until she had no more speaking to make. She told me how the Aged Woman had died and how Wind Maiden had fed her, warmed her, and then wept over her body when she died. She pointed along the trail toward Huts of Grace and said, 'Wind Maiden sleeps near the path that rolls toward Huts of Grace.'

"My eyes followed the trail; my feet did not. No voice had whispered to me, 'Wind Maiden is dead.' I call now to the spirit of the dead wife: The one who can no longer run is grateful that you were daughter to the Aged Woman after she had lost her son."

They inhaled silence. Ruth ate the words that One-Who-Runs had spoken. Much was sweet and much was bitter. Husband. Wife. Ruth could not claim the names and One-Who-Runs would not.

They stood and they did not speak. Ruth looked at Eagle-with-White-Head. He spoke with his eyes, but she could not understand. She glanced at One-Who-Runs. He waited. "You have placed before me joy and sorrow. The sorrow I must bury in the grave of Wind Maiden. I shall wrap myself in the joy: you live."

Still, he waited. "I bear the redness of the slashings that Wind Maiden once struck upon your body. You can no longer wear them," she continued. "I howl like a dog over the burying place of what could have been and what is not."

He waited. The eyes of Eagle-with-White-Head cried out.

They walked through snows of silence back to Goschachgunk, back to the hut of One-Who-Runs.

"The slashings healed long ago," he said to Ruth. He bowed and disappeared into his hut.

Ruth and Eagle-with-White-Head walked through the snow along the footprint path where other fur-covered feet had trod. Between huts and cabins, the snow sparkled a saltlick glitter.

As they approached the place where Star-at-Dawning had stepped aside, Ruth stopped. "I cannot hear the words that fly from your eyes," she said, with a voice that blew upon the whistling wind. Lenape watched them. "The ears that pass hear only wind," she decided.

"Are you blind that you cannot see? Maybe you are also deaf so that you cannot hear the words of my mouth." His voice did not whistle upon the wind. It stood like a wide tree, unbending.

"Yes. Maybe I am deaf, for I do not hear the reason for your answer." Ruth stood straight. She filled herself with the cold, wet air. She let it blow forth: "Wind Maiden is dead to One-Who-Runs. I no longer have a place to sleep in Goschachgunk ... not upon the bearskin of 'wife.'"

"Are you the fool? Or does the pride of Wind Maiden still live in you?"

"I must be the fool," she sighed with more cold air she had taken in and now pushed out. Its coldness stole warmth from her.

"Then, fool, I shall speak with simple sounds: Why do you not go to One-Who-Runs, cook his stews, sleep at his side?"

Was Eagle-with-White-Head the fool? "He does not want me."

"I did not hear these words from any mouth but yours."

Eagle-with-White-Head was cornering the frightened squirrel. Would he eat her so that only the pain remained?

207

"He did not go to Huts of Grace to take me. He knew I was there. He turned back to Goschachgunk." Her voice no longer rode upon the wind. It tumbled along the ground. She would cry out if he took a bite. "He does not want me."

Eagle-with-White-Head laid his hands upon her shoulders. He pulled her nearer the cabins. "Listen, little sister, and I shall train you as a mother trains her baby how to talk. Say the name of him who was the husband."

Ruth did not answer. The shame would fall like icy crystals from the air.

"Say the name," demanded Eagle-with-White-Head. His hands pressed upon her shoulders.

"One-Who-Runs," Ruth murmured. She choked. He was not the one who runs.

"Tell me the sayings of Wind Maiden about the runner."

He still clutched her shoulders. The metal trap had snapped around her. If she struggled, she would tear herself apart.

"She said the runner was not a hunter and a warrior. He did not bring pelts to trade for bells and buckles." Ruth looked up into the eyes of her brother: "But Wind Maiden is dead. Those thoughts are buried with her."

"Can he know who lives inside the flesh that once belonged to Wind Maiden?" Eagle-with-White-Head slid his hands from her shoulders. His eyes held her now. "Listen to me, little sister. I told him to wait in his hut while I brought you to him. But he stood outside. When he saw us, he limped toward you. He did not know whether you would lift a stick and strike him, laughing. He offered to your sight the limp and he did not know." The eyes of Eagle-with-White-Head were black coals, burning without light. "Think why. And think why he did not come to you in Huts of Grace."

Star-at-Dawning appeared from a cabin as they walked by. Eagle-with-White-Head greeted his mother, glanced at Ruth, and left. They walked on. They did not speak. In front of the cabin of Fish-of-the-Deep-Water, Ruth stopped and looked down at the round face of Star-at-Dawning.

"I must walk until I scatter many thoughts through the forest."

"How does a mother turn the eyes of her daughter from deep wounds and oozing blood?" asked Star-at-Dawning.

Ruth scattered the words of Eagle-with-White-Head in front of her then pressed them with her feet into the snow as she walked. The words pulsed life into her toes.

One-Who-Runs. What name should she give him? He was not the fox or wolf or bear ... no. He could no longer run upon the heels of his prey until it slowed and sobbed with panting. And he was not the dog who fed upon the putrid flesh of the kill of another. Was he the squirrel who gathered nuts or the rabbit who nibbled grass? He might eat with them the food of the shrubs and ground but he would not scamper with them when the enemy approached. No, he was not the squirrel or rabbit.

Perhaps he was the bellowing buffalo fish, gliding through the water. The fish was stupid while One-Who-Runs bore the wisdom of the grey-headed man. He did not bellow, either. His words alone, even whispered, would make hearts thump and heads turn.

Could he be the tree? Ruth looked around her until she found the highest, thickest, darkest tree. Yes. The tree. He, too, stood proud. His roots ran deep into earth. He did not lean upon another for support. But the tree was cold and though it did not take, it did not give, either. He was not the tree.

Some would say he was One-Who-Limps, and they would speak the truth. But he was not his limp. What was he? He was greyheaded wisdom, kindness greater than mother; he was love. Could she call him, "One-Who-Loves?" No. He could call himself that; she could not. Then he was the One-Who-is-Loved: the Beloved One. Yes. She spoke it to herself and then aloud, "The Beloved One."

His wood-carved eating bowl lay beside Fish-of-the-Deep-Water upon the packed dirt. Ruth saw it first after her sight had crept from the light outside to the darkness within. Her eyes crawled up the folded legs and up the chest to the face of Fish-of-the-Deep-Water.

"Sit and eat," he said.

She could no longer eat food cooked over the fire of Fish-of-the-Deep-Water when the fire of "husband" blazed nearby. Ruth crouched beside her father. She rolled her tongue inside a dry mouth. "I must, go to the fire of my husband."

"Husband!" he howled. "Who is your husband? One-Who-Cannot-Run … you call him, 'husband'?"

Ruth dropped her gaze. "Yes," she said. Fish-of-the-Deep-Water would kill her now. She opened sideways her neck so he could chomp the death bite.

"Then you are Wind Maiden and you lied when you said she had died, for he had been her husband."

He had not bitten! Ruth looked up. Her eyes found first her mother before they returned to Fish-of-the-Deep-Water. "Wind Maiden is dead. But I carry her burden on my back; I carry her love. I shall go to my husband if he will take me in her place."

"He is not a hunter and he is not a warrior!" This was the bellowing buffalo fish. These were the words that had once fallen from the mouth of Wind Maiden and had dribbled down her chin and stained her body in shame.

Ruth looked at her father: "That is the reply of Wind Maiden. I am not Wind Maiden."

"You must have food and fur." His voice dropped and became the snarling warning of a wolf: "And soon you must have the protection of a warrior."

Ruth rose and gathered her carrying strap and bag into her arms. She closed her eyes. Her lips trembled. She opened her eyes and turned back to the fire and her parents. Fish-of-the-Deep-Water had turned away his head. He was lighting his pipe. "I am grateful that you have fed and warmed my flesh. I want to call you, 'Mother' ... 'Father;' or, if those names are foul, I want to call you, 'friends' ... You are my friends."

Star-at-Dawning smiled a slow, heavy smile upon closed lips.

"I must go to him," Ruth said to the puffing head of Fish-of-the-Deep-Water.

He turned his head and almost looked at her. "No, you are not Wind Maiden. Wind Maiden would have stayed here." He was not the wolf and he was not the buffalo fish. He was a shriveled man, very, very old.

Ruth walked alone through Goschachgunk and she did not care if eyes clung to her. Her heart ran ahead so that she had to pull it back.

She stopped before the entrance to the hut of the Beloved One. A voice whispered, "He does not want you. Why will you let him kick shame into your face?" Her arms hung down. That voice, she knew its sound. It was the clicking of the bones of the dead one.

"Go, cry of death," she snarled at it.

Ruth bowed and crept inside.

She crouched beside the door opening and placed her carrying strap and bag in front of her. Her eyes searched for him.

He had been lying and was sitting up, leaning against an elbow.

"I have nothing to bring you but all that you see," Ruth said. "But I can build fires and cook stews and bake bread."

"I limp. I showed it to you that you might know," he said. "Where are the pelts of One-Who-Limps? Does the buck wait for him to limp up to it? Does the bear roll over on its back like a dog for him?"

They watched each other. She did not answer.

"Can One-Who-Limps carry messages through the forest while those who sent him pass him by?" he continued. "I cannot give you many pelts or bells or buckles. I cannot give you the cry of a warrior. "

"Can you give me love?" asked Ruth.

"Oh, yes," he sighed, "I can give you love."

"Then you are One-Who-Loves and you are my Beloved One."

He crept near her, took her bag and strap, and laid them in the corner.

~ ~ ~

"Saviour, speak," said Ruth as she wandered among the trees. The snow that had fallen four nights before had melted and sticks and branches waited to be gathered, dried, and burned. She bent and gathered two sticks; her carrying strap hung empty upon her shoulder. "You do not answer?"

She stretched. Goschachgunk, it was a dying village. Deer no longer wandered near; bear chose sleeping places far away. She bent, again, to scoop more sticks into her arms. And the sticks and branches and dead trunks were almost all gathered.

"I do not forget you. I do not forget that you died and live so that, although I die, I live. Hear? I remember. What more do I remember?" She thought. "This day is the day of resting." The bell would ring. The brothers and sisters would come to sing and to listen to the sounds of the shapes in the black Book. They would rest. They would eat. They would rest. Ruth stretched again.

"I am not with them ... you see where I walk ... and I cannot rest today. But, listen! I remember."

She looked about toward the distant place of Huts of Grace. "Saviour. I know you talk to Salah. Tell her what I tell you. I do not forget."

She spread a tattered blanket upon the ground and wrapped her sticks in it, breaking some so all would be the same size. She lifted the bundle upon her carrying strap and hung it on her back. She leaned forward. "Saviour. Take me back there. And take the Beloved One there, too." She hesitated. Did she ask much? "Take Star-at-Dawning, Eagle-with-White-Head the Doe, the tiny one ..."

She stopped, but the talk went on. The Saviour was walking with her. He talked of plans she could not understand. She did not ask the meaning of His words because He did not want to tell her now. She was the child. He taught her the sound of the music that He spoke. Someday, she would hear, again, the jingling and the thumping of the music and she would know the steps to dance. She knew that she would only dance this dance once. After it was over, she would understand the meaning of the music and of the dance.

Ruth crouched before the fire in the hut. "Make soft flakes of white ashes, oak sticks," she whispered. While the fire blazed, she shaped a small, flat loaf of maize bread. She placed water to boil over the fire pit and gathered up the few dried beans she had to drop into it.

"Is he here?" Eagle-with-White-Head crouched in the door opening of the hut.

"He hunts," answered Ruth. "I am happy to greet you. Sit beside the fire."

"I am happy to greet you," said Eagle-with-White-Head, bending, shuffling his feet to the place near the fire.

"I have not yet prepared food to offer you," said Ruth. She leaned over to scrape with a stick the hot ashes into a pile close by the heat of the fire.

"No food," answered her brother. "Today I have already filled myself ... not with food. This is not a time to eat. It is a time to crouch, to look around; not to sleep, not to eat."

Ruth slid the round, flat loaf of bread into the ashes and covered it with more white ashes. She did not wish to hear the mutterings behind the words of her brother. One-Who-Runs would eat bread with her and would not fill himself with the whisperings of Eagle-with-White-Head.

Eagle-with-White-Head stared into the fire. He crouched; he did not sit and rest.

"Where does he hunt?" he asked.

"He checks his trap near the Elk's Eye. And he fishes."

"He carries his rifle?" Eagle-with-White-Head looked up from the fire.

"Yes — his rifle."

Eagle-with-White-Head returned his gaze to the fire: "I would not find him quickly in the forest. I shall wait."

He waited like a tied dog waits. He rocked upon one leg, then the other. He almost stood; he crouched.

"My husband can find you when he returns," suggested Ruth. This dog must be loosed, she decided.

"No ... there is no place for him to meet me."

"The hut where the Doe and the little one ..."

Eagle-with-White-Head shook his head.

Ruth heard the rustlings of the Beloved One outside their hut. She pushed her hands flat upon the bearskin mat.

"It has happened? The council fire goes out?" the Beloved One asked when he saw Eagle-with-White-Head crouching inside.

Ruth slid over to him. She could not stand; the top of the hut was low. She took a short, wide, white perch from his hand. He gave it to her but his eyes held Eagle-with-White-Head.

"The council fire has gone out," agreed Eagle-with-White-Head.

The Beloved One knelt beside him. "Who stands above and who below?" he asked.

"Captain Pipe and Wingenund stand over all here in Goschachgunk."

Ruth thumped the baking bread and covered it with more hot ashes. She did not hear.

"Gelelemend?"

"Runners go to tell him that Goschachgunk and the Lenni Lenape lift the hatchet for the Saggenash. He will not return here."

The Beloved One laid his hand upon the shoulder of Eagle-with-White-Head. "What do you, my friend?"

"I go up the Beaver River with Welepachtschiechen and the other Lenape who have not crawled to the Saggenash for food and fire water and blankets and clothing."

"The Big Knife gives only promises," warned the Beloved. "He does not give food; he does not trade for pelts; he does not protect us, his friend."

Ruth glanced at his outstretched leg. "He gives bullets into the leg of him who serves as 'friend,'" she decided. She frowned.

Eagle-with-White-Head stiffened his back. Ruth saw his gaze fall, too, upon the leg. Again he bowed forward: "I hear and I see from where your words come. The Big Knife, he is cruel. But we do not lift the hatchet for the Big Knife only. The Yenglese who live toward the rising of the sun beside the great salt sea ..."

"Where once the Lenni Lenape roamed," thought Ruth.

"... and the Quaekel, they hold the hand of ally with the Big Knife. We took hold of the hand with them; we must not let go." He sighed and shook his head. "Can we find another hope? They promised the Lenni Lenape that he could build a huge council fire of his own and gather his brothers, his fathers, his uncles about it; and it would be like one of the thirteen in power. Is that not a promise worth many pelts and much food?"

The Beloved One was silent.

"You saw the scratches of these promises carved out in the White Man's fashion at Fort Pitt," urged Eagle-with-White-Head. "Is this not our only hope?"

"Our only hope," agreed the Beloved One. "Worth many pelts, and much more."

"But perhaps the hope has ended and we have lost the promise because the Lenni Lenape is a child who could not wait and hold tight the hand of the ally." The words of Eagle-with-White-Head were sharpened arrows. "I cannot waste more time on words. The friend of the Big Knife can no longer find a safe place to sleep along the Elk's Eye. I follow Welepachtschiechen up the Beaver to enlarge the fire at Gekelemuckpechunk and to wait for our chief, Gelelemend. The Doe now gathers blankets and pelts and will follow me with our son. I do not return to our hut; I do not return to Goschachgunk."

"Our parents!" Ruth threw the words before her brother. She had forgotten that she did not hear.

He looked at her with eyes that did not remember she was there. "They stay here."

Ruth sucked in the corners of her mouth. She saw her mother and father torn apart by brown and black wolves. "You could tell ..."

"I shared words with Fish-of-the-Deep-Water last night. He shared puffs upon his pipe and no words. They stay. I am here to say to you ..." He looked back at the Beloved. The words of Ruth had not belonged in the weaving of this conversation, "... run. Go with me."

"I am no longer the enemy of the Saggenash as you are so the friend of the Saggenash is not enemy to me. And I am no longer 'friend' to the Big

213

Knife so why should I ... walk ... to where the friend sleeps?" said the Beloved.

"Do you doze? Do you not understand? The Big Knife will turn the eye of his watchman toward the Elk's Eye. When he sees a new fire burning, built from logs carried down from Fort Detroit, he will hurry here to put out the fire. It blazes too near Fort Pitt and the fires of the Big Knife. Go with me."

The Beloved One looked from the fire to Ruth. They each held the eye of the other. Then Ruth leaned forward and nudged with sticks the bread from the ashes of the fire. She lifted the bread with the corner of her blanket and shook and dusted away the clinging white specks.

"I must eat the words you have spoken until I am full of the knowledge of what I must do," said the Beloved One.

Eagle-with-White-Head rose. "I cannot wait for you. Do not take long in eating before you follow me. The trail might become covered over and soon you will not be able to follow at all." He moved to leave.

"Thank you, my good friend, for the warning. You have been patient in giving it," said the Beloved.

"I can accept the waiting with patience if I know that the warning has not been spilled upon the ground and wasted," said Eagle-with-White-Head. He threw the words over his shoulder and left.

"Eat," said Ruth. "The bread is hot; the kettle boils."

The Beloved One looked at Ruth. He smiled. "I have eaten more than I would like to eat already," he said. "I must chew again and taste more slowly. You eat now; I wait."

Ruth gazed down at her warm loaf of maize bread; "I wait, too," she sighed.

Ruth stood outside and waited. She stood behind the hut and waited. She stood beside the hut and watched the street of Goschachgunk.

Lenape whispered in small groups then hurried on to stop and whisper in new groups. Some women carried heavy loads upon their backs and whooshed children ahead of them. Other women watched, frowning. The scurrying ones and the watchers nodded at each other but did not stop and stand and talk. The warnings of Eagle-with-White-Head gave meaning to the flutterings and gatherings of these birds. She knew to where they flew and from what they fled. The burning fire would soon ignite the brittle leaves and sticks and spread beyond the fire pit. It would spread through the forest and consume all things that did not flee before it.

"Lenni Lenape killing Lenni Lenape," her mother had said. They swung the death club at their own head. She sniffed and wiped her nose with the back of her hand.

"I should not care," she cried to herself. Goschachgunk had long ago cast Wind Maiden out among the dead. Should she grieve because now Goschachgunk built its own fire in the Place of Death? Ruth sniffed again.

To where would she and her Beloved One fly? Her nest was built at Huts of Grace; her flock would take her back to itself. Would he go?

She crawled into the hut. "Eat now?" she asked.

"Not now," he said.

She sat beside him. He stroked her hair. His hands had the strength of the warrior though their shape hid their power beneath a more gentle form. She felt the fingers rub across her head and down her back.

"Where is the place of rest for us?" he asked.

Did he ask to hear an answer? Ruth listened for more.

He stroked her hair and said, "Where do we go when neither for the Big Knife nor for the Saggenash we crawl?"

Again. Did he speak to her or did he speak to hear his words? However, a question thrown into the air would hang there until answered. She yanked the question from the air and said, "Those who belong to the Saviour refuse to lift the hatchet for any man but wear the peaceful stroud of the woman."

"Yes," he said. He put his hands to her waist and turned her: "I must send you there."

"I shall go with you. I shall not go alone." Two feet had walked the trail before; now she was the wife and she would only walk four.

"You must go there," insisted her husband. "I am not of them and cannot come."

"You can live there," said Ruth. She looked into his eyes to display confidence. The husband of Salah would speak for him. The Saviour would not turn away the Beloved One.

She rocked her eyes down and mumbled, "You must give yourself to the Saviour and to no manito." She heard, again, the rules, the many, many rules. They pounded themselves out to her, but she did not now need to make the sound of them. "There are some other rules," she murmured.

"The Saviour ... I remember the recitings about him. I used to go to hear the speeches of the teachers when ..." He did not say it; they both knew when. "I shall take you to them."

"Four feet upon the trail, yes," Ruth said. "When do we go?"

"Now," he said.

She lifted the bread. "We have food to eat along the path."

~ ~ ~

They walked together through Goschachgunk. Ruth slowed her step near the cabin of her parents and searched until she saw Star-at-Dawning standing with three other women, wrapped in whisperings.

"Go with us, Mother." Her mother came to her and to her husband who stood at her side. "We go to Huts of Grace. The Big Knife will kill you here."

Star-at-Dawning rocked her heavy body. "My husband stays. He is dying the death of the Lenni Lenape and I must watch and howl over him when he breathes no more." Her small face turned to the Beloved One and then to Ruth. "You both are young and can endure the pain. All my bones ache. I have no warmth of fighting left in me. I want to die."

Star-at-Dawning patted the blanketed shoulder of her daughter. "You are my daughter. Eagle-with-White-Head is my son," she said. "Fish-of-the-Deep-Water is my husband. We are Lenni Lenape. Do not forget!"

Ruth with her beloved, they turned toward the fork of the Elk's Eye and followed the winding trail away from Goschachgunk. And the going back was easy and the pain it did not hurt and the darkness it did not hinder but pushed them through. And the only thing that weighted the feet and dragged the stride was the knowledge that the mother was left behind.

19
APRIL 15, 1781 – MAY 6, 1781

Toward the east beyond the village they walked, toward the east where the sun arose, toward the east where God's Acre lay and where each grave marker turned its face toward the east ... toward the remembrance and the promise of resurrection.

They stood around the graves of those who had fallen asleep.

"Nolsittam nekti Getanittowitink, Wetochwink, Wequisink woak Welsit Mtschitschangunk ..." called out Brother Christoph. "I believe in the one only God, Father, Son, and Holy Spirit, who made from nothing all things through Jesus Christ, and was in Christ, bringing back the world into the embrace of friendship."

"Quawullakenimellenk Watochemellan ..." sang back the worshipers. "We thank you, Father, Ruler beyond the clouds and upon the earth, because You have hidden these things from the wise and careful, and have revealed them unto babies: even so, Father; for it seemed good to your sight."

"Wetochemellan ..." cried Christoph. "Father! Glorify Your name!"

"Ki Wetochemellenk talli epian Awossagame, Machelendasutsch Ktellewunsowagan ..." they chanted. "You our Father, dwelling there beyond the clouds, praised be your name ..."

"... Your kingdom appear; your thoughts come to pass, here all over the earth, the same as it is there beyond the clouds ..." The words of the Lord's Prayer passed over Sarah's lips and not even her mind clung to the German. She did have a thought, however, yet barely a thought, that David recited this same prayer this Easter morning; and she remembered yet tried not to recall how she had taught him the first words so very long ago in Bethlehem. But she did not hear his faltering voice blending into light chords upon the recitation here in Gnadenhutten; no, she did *not* hear it at all.

217

She did hear the voices of Christoph, of Brother Edwards, and of Brother Michael Jung who stood nearby.

Sarah glanced toward Sister Christiana at her side and toward Sister Schebosh on the other side.

She looked far to her right, toward the rising sun, to see Ruth. She could not hear her voice but watched her features, her swinging arms, her restless legs.

"... but keep us free from all evil; for you claim your kingdom and the superior power and all magnificence from now to always. So may it come to pass."

Ruth lifted herself up and down upon her toes to the rhythm of the chanting of the husband of Salah and to the pulsing of the reply of all around her.

"The Lord Jesus Christ will descend from above the clouds with a shout ..." he was saying.

She knew that shout would be more powerful than all the combined scalp yells of all warrior lenno. Her knees bounced.

"... with the voice of the most mighty messenger, and with the horn of God, to judge both the living and the dead ..."

Ruth wiggled her toes inside her moccasins.

"... This is my Lord, Who bought me ..."

Did he trade a pelt, ten pelts? No. He traded His blood. Her feet thumped the dance of the blood sacrifice of the Lord.

"... so that I should be His own, and live under Him and serve Him, forever in goodness, innocence, and happiness ..." the voice of the husband of Salah continued.

Ruth felt the drumming of his words, and she began to see the movement of the dance.

"I could dance the shape of the words," Ruth said to the Beloved One soon after the last "So may it come to pass" had settled to the ground. They sipped warm milk in the center of Huts of Grace where big fires blazed and heavy kettles bubbled and where the brothers and sisters gathered together to eat. "You could chant the meaning of my shufflings."

He bit into a round, small loaf of bread smeared with butter and crushed berries. Pushing the lump to the side of his mouth he said, "I would not know the meaning of your dance so I could not chant it. You must chant it."

"I do not know the meaning," she protested.

"If you did not know the meaning, your feet would not be able to trace the pattern on the earth."

"Oh," said Ruth.

"I could dance the shape of the words and you could speak the meaning of my shufflings," Ruth said to Salah after the Beloved One had wandered away to talk to Joshua, the thumper of the meeting house box of bells and while the women were smothering the fires with dirt and cooling and cleaning the kettles.

Sarah wiped her hands upon her apron. "How did you learn the dance?" she asked.

"The Saviour taught it to my legs and feet."

"And to your understanding?" asked Sarah.

Ruth rolled her lower lip out and in and said, "My husband says I know the meaning. But the Saviour did not tell me that I know it."

"Then you must wait," said Sarah, "until He does."

"How long to wait?" asked Ruth.

Salah knew all the secrets of the Book. The Saviour probably told her upon the scratched lines. "You wait from the planting of the seed until it cracks the earth with sprout," it would say. Or longer ... "until the flower opens or the bean ripens unto harvest" ... then He would reveal His secrets.

"How long?" wondered Sarah. In the day when God would finally reveal all secrets, would the questions be forgotten?

"I do not know," she said.

"Who is wise and can look ahead and will tell me what he sees?" Ruth persisted.

"The Saviour, He can see and He can tell," replied Sarah.

"But He will not tell!"

"Then wait. Waiting is better than knowing." That was scripture; it must be true.

"Gibberish," muttered Ruth. Louder she asked, "Is it better to be blind than to see?"

"The Saviour loves us?" asked Sarah.

"Yes, yes," mumbled Ruth. Salah could not answer; she made more questions.

"He gives us the good thing?"

"Yes, yes."

"He gives us blindness. Blindness must be the good thing, or He would give us sight."

"Backwards talking, tripping, falling ..." thought Ruth. She did not think even Salah understood herself. Ruth swayed. She clicked her tongue. "I shall dance; and when I dance, I shall listen; and when I listen, I shall learn. Then I shall grab the hand of Salah and I shall lead her.

"Sisters ..."

Sarah gasped. Christoph. Why could he always surprise her? She stepped back and looked at him with what she hoped was composure.

His lips curled up on their edges. Surely he did not startle her intentionally.

"Uncurdled milk for our visitors?" he requested.

"We gathered all the milk this morning and laid it on the planks," Sarah answered, looking past Christoph toward five Indian men, gulping down pottage, who were among the visitors from Goschachgunk.

Christoph smiled at Ruth, really smiled. "Did my wife tell you that, last night, the teachers and assistants gave one voice for Jacob?"

"No. We talked about dancing ... knowing ... waiting," replied Ruth.

Christoph looked about until he saw Jacob with Joshua. He called, "Brother!"

Jacob limped toward them.

"Listen!" the Beloved One had said to Ruth one day while the snow still covered the ground soon after they had dropped their carrying bags in Huts of Grace. "The teacher, Jung, he who limps, he told me this about the father of a mighty people who onced lived far away, but the same God was there who is here today. "

He had paused to gaze past Ruth. He had continued, "That man, the father, he fought with a messenger — a runner ..." The Beloved had nodded his head one time as he said, "runner." "... from the Great and Mighty God. They struggled through the night. With the lighting of the sky, the ... runner ... touched the hollow place below the thigh of the father and crippled him." The Beloved had smiled. "He limped. God, the One who lives beyond the clouds, He caused the limp.

"The father of the mighty people, his name was Jacob. The messenger called him 'Israel' after the struggle ended." The Beloved had turned over and over more thoughts in the hands of his mind before he had said, "Israel means, 'warrior of God.' I am not Israel. But I was crippled and I do limp. I shall be Jacob."

So, when the water had buried the body of One-Who-Limps, the new man, Jacob, had risen up.

Christoph, still smiling, reached out and laid his hand upon the shoulder of Jacob. "Brother!" exclaimed Christoph. "After seven nights, you will break the bread and sip the wine of our Saviour."

Why could not Christoph smile like that at Sarah? Or lay his hand upon her shoulder? Alone with her in their cabin, he talked but he did not converse. He paced the floor and studied his Bible long after Sarah had abandoned him to crawl into bed. If he could not see, he would labor until light dispelled blindness. But in finding sight, he would see only his vision.

~ ~ ~

In that nighttime, Sarah returned alone to the cabin after the evening worship. She stood in the threshold, the damp chill of the dark room greeting her cold across the face. Wrapping her cloak more tightly about her, she entered. With a long stick ignited from the glowing fire's ashes, she lit the wick of the sooty blackbird which hung from the beam overhead. She lit two candles and laid them on the table. Around them glowed a yellow light like the aura of resurrection victory proclaimed this Easter day.

She tried to rouse the fire. She poked. It groaned in its dying bed but would not stir. She was like these crackling ashes and not like the candle. She groaned with the fire. She nudged a log onto its side and piled sticks and dry bark beneath. The fire would not respond.

She was tired, always tired. Every joint ached. She prodded the stubborn embers.

The door opened. "I can do that," said Christoph as he entered.

Sarah stood. She stepped back.

He laid his Bible and sermon notes upon another pile of papers on the shelf along the wall, flung off his cape, and turned toward the fireplace. A sheet fluttered from the pile to the floor.

Sarah walked around the table, knelt, and picked it up. It was folded like a letter. She rubbed her finger along its brown and frayed and creased edge.

"A letter?" she asked, balancing it on the palm of her hand.

Christoph glanced back. His mouth flattened into a thin line. "Give it to me."

Sarah clutched her stomach beneath her cape. She walked toward him, dragging her heels like a naughty child. What had she done to deserve his wrath? She reached out to him the paper.

He snatched it from her. "Do you regularly rummage through my papers?" he snapped.

Rummage? Never. "It fell to the floor. I picked it up!"

She tried to snap her voice as he had.

He gazed at the paper and folded it again and again until it became a small, square wad. "A letter ..." he finally said, still watching the wad in his hand. "... from my sister in Saxony." He sealed it inside his hand. "Brother Jung brought it from Bethlehem." He turned and bowed toward the fire.

His only apology was the reward of civility. Sarah's hands tightened into fists. She wanted to pound his back. Her lips rolled into a pout. Brother Jung had arrived in Gnadenhutten almost six months ago. For six months, Christoph had unfolded and refolded that letter and had never told her. He never would have told her. And what had he now revealed? Nothing.

Later, when they lay in the darkness in bed, Christoph murmured near her ear, "The letter, it said that my father is dead."

Sarah turned to look at him, to say she was sorry, to fumble for his hand. But Christoph had already rolled over in the bed.

~ ~ ~

"I cannot countenance the recent conduct of certain brethren who themselves had helped to legislate the official neutrality of the believing Indian congregations," Christoph was saying in German. He leaned across the long table, his hand clenched and pushing into the smoothed surface of the wood. His fist turned red then whiter, whiter. Sarah wondered if he would pound the table. No, he would not, not Christoph.

Yet Christoph would not be bellowing at his brethren as he was now, either.

"I do not know words," he said now in Unami, "to open to you the weight I bear inside." His voice rose toward the rafters of the meeting house.

He looked around the table at the teachers and assistants. Michael Jung watched, eyes wide. Newly arrived to the mission, perhaps he did not know the history of the determined neutrality of the Brethren despite the threatenings of the English and the urgings of the Americans. The others — Brother Edwards, Brother Joshua, Brother John Martin, Sister Schebosh, Sister Christiana — they all had struggled to restrain the Christian Indians from joining the battle. Some, indeed, had fallen back to heathenish practices. Christoph, and the others, they all suffered the sense of failure for these losses.

"I ..." Christoph faltered. Sarah held her breath.

"Brothers. When Colonel Brodhead and the warriors from Fort Pitt called some of us to their camp these two days past, we went and heard their war plans against Goschachgunk. They asked for food; we gave it. So have we done with all warriors, both brown-skinned and white, who have camped nearby and asked for food."

His hand, still white, lay like a rock upon the table top.

"I did not know that Colonel Brodhead would take with him Chief Gelelemend and other Lenni Lenape to hatchet their own brothers in Goschachgunk and Indaochaie where once lay Pasture of Light." He lowered his head. "I did not know though I should have suspected."

He looked up. "Colonel Brodhead lost not one man to even a scratch. Do you hear? But Chief Gelelemend crossed the Elk's Eye, he and his warriors, and fought other warriors, Lenni Lenape, drunk with fire water. Much blood flowed. Death flowed with the blood."

Lines, shadowed by flickering candles, emerged upon Christoph's forehead. "Teachers and assistants from among us had heard these plans before the march and had added counsel to guide the feet of the warriors upon an even smoother path.

"Brothers. Are we, the believing body, truly neutral? Or do many of us take up the war cry of the Big Knife? Do we play games with man and God? How long will either God or man close his eyes to our mockery?"

"Brother Zeisberger would have held up the hand of neutrality," said Brother Joshua.

"Yes," agreed Christoph. "Must we rest upon the strength of Brother David? Have we not strength in our own arms? He will not return with Brother Schebosh from Bethlehem until summer. Where is wisdom now?

"Eyes have seen and legs will carry to the Saggenash at Detroit the story of the believing lenno who proclaim that they lift the hatchet for neither the Big Knife nor the Saggenash. But in the darkness, they stalk beside the Big Knife," said Brother John Martin.

"I have seen flesh slashed to the bone and I have smelled burning flesh," said Brother Joshua. "I do not shake in fear of them. Before my Saviour I stand. But I shall shake with fear when I see Him if out of my mouth has come both no and yes, I will not and I will." He leaned across the table and said to Christoph, "Brother, I ask with you, are the believing lenno truly neutral?"

"Some among us," confided Brother Jung, "hold to the Big Knife in our hearts."

"Hold it there but spread it no further," warned Christoph.

Sarah watched as he opened his clenched hand and rolled it palm up upon the table. "The Lenni Lenape who gave themselves to the Saggenash have fled from Goschachgunk to the land of the Delamatteno. Gelelemend and those who follow him in friendship with the Big Knife have gathered their blankets and go to build their fire near Fort Pitt and the home of their new father." He spread his hand flat upon the table. "Brothers, our three villages are now alone in the wilderness beyond the Ohio.

"Hear the sound of no one but ourselves."

Outside, spring crackled in the sunlight; the dew still lay in droplets upon the grass. It was the Youth of the Year, the Planting moon, yet the brethren were not in the fields; the sisters were not heating the morning meal. They had heard the message during the morning scripture reading of the attack against Goschachgunk and were waiting near the doors of the meeting house.

Sarah emerged from the grey light of the meeting house and gazed along the street of Gnadenhutten. Five days ago, they had celebrated victory over death. However, death, not resurrection, reigned today.

Ruth pushed herself from the side of the meeting house where she had been crouching. She tapped the elbow of Salah. "More whisperings," she said. "I must feed upon more whisperings about Goschachgunk."

"No more," answered Sarah. "An armful of warriors were killed; an armful of old men, women, children taken prisoners," she added, reciting all she had heard. God forgive her ... she dreaded learning more.

"An armful," said Ruth, circling one arm around the unseen load and clutching it to her chest; "an armful," she repeated, circling her other arm around another load. She flung her arms out. "Sticks without names. I must carry sticks with names." She scrutinized the ground where she had scattered the invisible burden.

"There!" she said, pointing. "Is that mother? There!" Another stick, another spot, "Is that my father?" She looked along her arms to the palms of her hands: "And where is my brother?" She watched the eyes of Salah; they did not hold the answer.

"Friend," said Sarah, "I do not know the names." She glanced along the dirt then up at the face of Ruth ... smooth, round, enclosed in a muslin cap with the blue ribbon of the married woman tied in a large bow beneath the strong jaw.

"I know nothing," she mouthed. She could not enlighten; she could not console. What could she do? Wait for an evil fate to overtake them all?

"Brother Christoph might learn more," she added. She glanced among the brethren to find the blond head of her husband. He and Brother Edwards stood with Brother John Martin and Brother Phillip between two cabins. He shook his head; he nodded. He left them and disappeared behind the cabins. They closed their circle and continued talking.

"Ask," demanded Ruth.

"The messengers still run. When they gather all they see and hear, they will bear it here," said a voice from behind Sarah. She turned to see Jacob.

"Can you wait until then?" he asked his wife.

"No!" answered Ruth. She gave him a frown and a sigh.

"Are these messengers squirrels," she wondered, "that gather their nuts and hide them but do not bring them back to break open and share?"

She did not speak these words because she was Ruth and Ruth did not say these things. But Ruth did not say, "No!" and frown, either, so she said, "The messengers, are they squirrels?" She turned her head sideways and looked back at the Beloved One.

"Squirrels," pondered Sarah. She looked at Ruth and Jacob then toward the spot where she had seen Christoph disappear. Never had she seen him give place to his anger as he had this morning. More lay hidden behind his words than she could comprehend.

Squirrels? She looked again at Ruth. She scratched her wrist.

Jacob seemed to understand his wife. His eyes became slits as he said, "Messengers carry heavy burdens which blow the stomach open when consumed and not shared like eating too much tassmanane. They can rest only when their food is consumed by others."

Ruth did not answer.

Sarah mumbled, "I must ..." but she could not determine, must ... what? She smiled, backed from them, and hurried away.

"You are a quiet, good wife," whispered the Beloved.

Ruth rolled her eyes from side to side; they did not settle upon her husband. "I must hear about my parents and my brother." She could be the messenger; she could run through the forest and gather words.

"Soon," he said. "Do not try to rush the gathering. You will sweep up dirt and sting your eyes."

"Soon? Today?" asked Ruth. If she did not have to wait, then she could wait.

"Today ... maybe," he replied.

Ruth threw away the "maybe." She could wait.

Sarah lifted her skirt and walked between the cabins where she had seen Christoph disappear. Some brethren were leaving the storage shed with hoes and rakes, but Christoph was not among them. To be with him, that was her desire.

She envisioned herself stroking his hair from his face. She would whisper, "Confide in me. I want to help you." He would thrust her hand away. He never confided in her. He did not want her help.

The dense and dark forest loomed around her. She began to suffocate as she had when first she settled in the wilderness. She, the believing lenno, Christoph ... alone.

She wanted Christoph. She wanted his arms around her. She wanted his assurance that she was not alone because he was with her.

Yet he was not with her. He had courted and married his vision. He pursued it with ... with lust.

And what could she say that would not be reduced to an argument? Whatever bindings had existed between them, she had long ago severed with the sharp edge of her own accusations and regrets. What was left?

When she found him, could she say, "Christoph, please, I want to be near you"? Was she a whimpering child? He would judge her for it.

She stopped upon the hill. She saw the men working in groups of two and three among the rows of future root crops of potatoes, turnips, onions. Some carried rocks to the rockpile. Christoph was not among them.

Sarah turned toward the orchard. She would go for a walk, then. And if she encountered Christoph, why ... why she would decide what to say to him then.

Between the rows of pear and peach trees she walked. The pear was hearty; it grew well and produced much fruit. The peach was a sickly, a coddled child that struggled to bud then lost its tender blossoms in a late frost. The apple — Sarah walked across to the neat rows of the apple orchard — was a treasured crop upon the plantation. The Indians, who coveted even the tart crabapple, relished the apple.

She rubbed her side. Again, these past three months, the time of menstruation had not come. And the pain, again, upon her side. Often, both in Bethlehem and here, the cramps had come after two, three months, cramps in her abdomen, legs and thighs. Then the blood had followed — thick, dark clots.

The cramps began; soon, the blood would follow.

225

She had forsaken hope that it might be otherwise. The blood would come tomorrow.

She strolled to the end of a row and turned east along the lane between the orchard, in tidy array, and the forest, in disarray. A lane? In Bethlehem it would be a lane. She would walk along the hillside and she would see the Lehigh River, the tall, stone Single Brethren's House and Single Sisters' House, the church, the other buildings that faced each other along the wide, smooth streets.

Here in the wilderness, they had cultivated civilization. The vision. Sometimes, she did believe in its fulfillment.

She squinted into the sun. She stopped. Christoph sat beside the lane, staring toward the apple orchard.

Christoph – his hair loose around his face, his legs in moccasins strapped over his breeches — was he the embodiment of the vision? He frightened her.

"I often wonder why our Indian brethren will snatch apples from the trees while they are still small and green," he said in German without looking up. Then he turned his head toward her: "Ah, but they will eat the mouth-puckering crabapple until their stomachs bloat, will they not?"

He smiled. "I surprised you? How can this be?" he joked.

"See, I am deep in thought. Come ... startle me." He looked back toward the orchard.

Sarah stood above him.

Glancing up, he clasped her hand. "Perhaps it is not in you to startle me. Sit beside me."

Not in her? Was she a window he peered through, no subtleties, no complexities? And Christoph — how unfair that he was a wall without windows at all. She sat where his nod indicated.

"You were ... vehement at the meeting today," she said. She had wanted to say, "distraught," but such a suggestion would intrude upon his privacy.

"I was angry," he replied. His eyes climbed the trees. "I must yet prune the two in this row and the four in the next. Some dead branches there ..." He waved his hand up. "... and those are unruly altogether." He pointed to two that stood above their brethren in the row.

Sarah gazed over the orchard. Her own thoughts when she saw the budding trees spoke to her of paring, cutting, coring, drying, cooking, boiling, stirring, stirring to make dried apples, applesauce, latwerg — apple butter ... that was what she saw.

She glanced at Christoph. His eyes drifted from the upper limbs of the trees to the sky above.

She composed in her mind, "Why were you angry? Some brethren have always assisted the Americans." She caught her breath at the imagined austerity of his gaze before he would reply. She said aloud, "I do not see pruning; I see apple butter."

"Apple butter," he repeated, nodding his head and watching her.

She widened her eyes in reply. Perhaps she could be as cryptic as he.

She gulped and asked, "Why were you angry? Some ..."

"Why?" he exclaimed. "I thought you would understand. Do we encourage Indians to fight Indians?"

"No. Why ... I ... it is horrible," she stammered. "But no brother advocated that the Indians should fight. That was instigated by the Americans and by Gelelemend. Some brethren ..."

"Some brethren support the Americans," he interrupted again. "They are **not** neutral."

A redness deepened beneath the tan of Christoph's face. Once, she had wanted him to explode in anger. But could he not choose a better adversary?

"When have certain brethren ever been neutral in this war? What is different now?"

He leaned toward her. "Everything. We approach the end."

The end. Sarah stared at him.

He dropped his head and pushed his fingers through his hair. "No, nothing is different," he amended. "They are wrong now; we were wrong then." He looked at her. His eyes were weary. He added, "Even I wrote letters warning the settlements of attacks."

"You were asked to do it by the peace chiefs at Goschachgunk," Sarah said.

"I could have, I should have refused." His brow wrinkled; his eyes tightened as though they ached.

Something was wrong with his perception. Sarah wanted to help him. But had he ever heeded her? "Women and children would have died if you had not warned them, Christoph."

"So they were prepared and they slew the warriors! Do you want me to decide who must live and who must die? And why did we not warn the women, children, and old men in Goschachgunk about the militia attack if we must consistently sacrifice warriors?"

"Why do you bellow at me?" Sarah stood. "Pretend this is the plan of God! Now, no heathen resides in this region of the wilderness. Only the Christian Indians are left! They can spread; they can multiply. You can fulfill **your** vision of the Christian state!"

She raised her skirts and hurried away. She could not look back. She had stabbed and she had wounded. And her intent had been to apply salve.

"Sarah, we were wrong," Christoph said when he found her in their cabin where she had retreated to mend torn shirts and breeches.

"We?" she thought. "Apologize for yourself," she wanted to say, "and leave my apologies to me."

But she chewed down her words and murmured, "Yes."

He did not reach across the table to her, and she did not come around it to him. He bowed toward the fireplace to light his pipe from the fire. She watched the back of his head and said nothing.

Before the evening meeting, the messenger appeared in Huts of Grace. He recited about the living and the dead, the warriors and the victims, the victors and the defeated. Eagle-with-White-Head had followed Chief Gelelemend to battle at Goschachgunk and had stained his hands with blood of Lenni Lenape and had carried scalps of Lenni Lenape back up the river. Eagle-with-White-Head, the Doe, and their son now followed Chief Gelelemend, weighted down with his household of warriors and friends, to Fort Pitt of the Big Knife where Colonel Brodhead had prepared for them a mat of safety.

Fish-of-the-Deep-Water and his wife, their fire had not been found burning in Goschachgunk. Long ago, they must have kicked apart the sticks and ashes and built a new fire beneath the roof of the Saggenash, beside the Sandusky River, where Captain Pipe gathered the Monsey and all lenno who heeded his voice.

Huts of Grace, Place of Peace, and Beautiful Spring — Colonel Brodhead beckoned them all to Fort Pitt where the wild creatures who now prowled through the forest along the valley of the Elk's Eye could not devour them.

The Saviour would protect the believing lenno. They would not go.

After the evening meeting, after all lenno had emerged from the candle-flickering meeting house into the dark star-glittering night, the street was quiet for a breath of time. They stood scattered along the street. Who but the believing lenno remained in the land beyond the Ohio? They would go now to huts and cabins to build fires and boil meals. The smoke would rise alone in a clear sky. Alone, they would close their eyes in sleep. They would arise and walk alone along the trails in search of roots and berries. They would hunt alone among the trees and the sound of their rifles would echo alone. They would plant and harvest and eat alone. They would live wrapped in the arms of the Saviour. They, with Him alone.

One resting day, the third Sabbath after the believing lenno had wrapped themselves in solitude in the valley of the Elk's Eye, warriors appeared, traveling from far to far to pound their hatchets into the skulls of the Big Knife. They were drooling men, filled with lust, and they could not hold back themselves from grasping after the believing lenno.

"Friends. Go with us," they crooned, "to a land where the Big Knife will never molest you and where you can rest beneath the shadow of the Saggenash."

"Do our friends truly love us as their words of syrup speak?" replied the believing lenno. "Then avoid our villages going out to hatchet and burn or returning with scalps and the smell of blood upon leggings and breech clouts. The smell of the warrior will bring the Big Knife along the war path to the home of the peaceful lenno.

"We cannot follow you. We are peaceful and in no danger. Besides, we are too heavy to rise up and go."

"If you pass safely through this war," one, Captain Pachgantschihilas, said, "and I see you all alive at the close of it, I will regret not to have joined your Mission."

Safe ... safe ... the believing lenno must be safe. Ruth hugged her blanket-wrapped body. The family of Wind Maiden was scattered. The memories were dying or dead. Ruth stood behind the Beloved as he stared from the edge of the clearing into the thickening blackness of the forest, listening to the footfalls of the warriors thump from Huts of Grace toward Place of Peace.

The spirit of One-Who-Runs hovered over the body of the Beloved. "You want to run?" she asked.

"To run," he said, "until the chest throbs and I cannot suck in enough air to push aside the rising stone within ... then, when I know that I will die unless I stop and fill myself with air and rub the chest that throbs; suddenly warmth comes and the cleansing breath and I know that I can run and run and never stop. And never wish to stop." He looked down at his crooked leg.

He turned and clasped the arm of Ruth above the elbow. His hand was warm and it was strong. "I am content. The body breaks with age or injury; this is ever so. I know it broke that I might learn about the things that never break before age not only breaks my body but also takes away my learning and my wanting to learn."

"Huts of Grace ... is it a thing that will never break?" asked Ruth.

"Yes, Huts of Grace will never break," he replied.

"Even when the warring lenno try to drive us away?"

"Even when they *do* drive us away," he said.

"Yes," she murmured, "it is part of the dance. But I do not understand."

Behind them glowed the dim lights of Huts of Grace.

In their cabin, beneath the hazy glow of a sooty blackbird, sat Sarah and Christoph. They sat at their small table, their faces glowing in the lesser light of a tallow taper.

"I was working in the field this morning," Christoph was saying, "planting potatoes. I heard a shout and looked up. Brother John Martin was running toward me; two warriors were fleeing. He told me that he had seen the two raise their rifles and point them at me. But for the Providence of God in bringing our brother, I would now be dead."

The salt-taste of nausea flooded Sarah's mouth.

"I do not fear for myself," Christoph continued. "My God will protect me as He has ever done." He looked at her. She tried to stare back. "I fear for you." He cleared his throat: "I am responsible for you."

"Responsible." Beneath the surface of the table, Sarah pressed her fingers against the slight swelling of her abdomen. She wanted to be many things to Christoph, but not a responsibility. Yet, now, most surely, that she soon would become.

"You are not safe here. I would return with you to Bethlehem, but ..."

"Then we shall stay," replied Sarah. Her fingers rubbed round and round. Two weeks of pain, and, still, no flow. Sarah knew what she would not admit before, that each time the clots had come, they had hidden a life lost and unmourned ... an error, a vessel poorly molded and recast upon the spinning wheel to be reformed.

"No. He shook his head. "You must go. Brother Zeisberger will return with Brother Schebosh from Bethlehem within two months. I shall then ask Brother Schebosh to accompany you back across the mountains.

Sarah stared at him ... through him ... past him. She could not travel. But she could not stay. How could she bear a child in the midst of such danger? How could he survive?

Her eyes focused upon Christoph.

"I cannot accompany you, Sarah. I must try ... I must try to save ..." He sighed and glanced down. Looking up, he continued, "God gave us the vision. If a man sins and betrays the calling, he must return to obedience. You understand, then, I must succeed ..." He rubbed and pinched his eyebrow.

"You have betrayed no one, certainly not God," exclaimed Sarah.

"I have not followed my calling. I contributed to the downfall of Goschachgunk." He paused. "I warned the white settlements; I should have warned the Indians. Or else I should have warned no one."

Sarah chewed her lip. Did God judge Christoph so harshly?

His hand slid forward along the table as if he were reaching toward her. It stopped. "God will redeem the vision. The communities of Christian Indians will survive."

And would Christoph be the saviour? Sarah shook her head.

"No, Sarah, do not try to argue. You will return to Bethlehem."

She rubbed her lower lip across her teeth. She formed the words: "I could not endure the traveling. I am pregnant."

His head fell back as if he had been struck. A burden, a responsibility. He struggled for the victory, and she wielded the weapon for his defeat.

"Yes," he said, looking into her face. "No, you could not safely make the journey."

Could he say no more?

"When?" he asked.

"October. Early November. I cannot know for certain. My flow, it was so irregular."

"Our Lord had planned it thus." His lips barely moved. "You must stay ... you and the baby."

Providence. He accepted her pregnancy with resignation.

"Christoph, I had not planned this." Sobs choked her breath as she spoke. Would she behave foolishly?

"These things are not ours to plan," he murmured.

Hers was the failure. Had there ever been success? She stood.

"Sarah." He arose. He slid his arms around her waist.

She felt the roughness of his muslin shirt.

"We shall raise our child here among our Indian brethren. This is our home; it will become his. You both will prosper," he whispered above her head.

Sarah closed her eyes. She smelled earth and fire.

"We shall pass safely through this war," he whispered. "And when it is over, we shall draw all Indians unto ourselves and unto our Saviour."

The vision. His arms enfolded her, their child, and the vision. She made room for it. She did not begrudge its looming presence, but she would not embrace it. The world was the smell and feel of Christoph and the baby growing within.

20
AUGUST 11, 1781 – AUGUST 18, 1781

"They are coming," thought Ruth. She stood in front of her cabin, listening. Her ears flowed with the Elk's Eye toward Place of Peace. The dull thump of horses' hooves, the shuffling of feet, the rubbing that was fuller than wind ... these told her: they were coming. Others stood along the street and in the fields of Huts of Grace, turning their ears toward Place of Peace. Upon the stillness of a warm and sunny day rose the heaviness of movement that was more, much more than their own.

Ruth knelt. She slid her hands along her stroud, onto the ground. Some lay flat, cheek and ear pressed against the packed dirt. Her fingers, only the tips, touched the warm earth. She felt the shiver of Grandmother Earth as the pound, pound, pound bruised her ancient face. Ruth eased her full palms against the ground and saw upon the quivering vibrations the warriors moving upon horse and on foot from Place of Peace where they had slept the night before to Huts of Grace where they would await the gathering of the teachers and the assistants from Huts of Grace, Place of Peace, and Beautiful Spring.

Since the time when the earth was raised around the maize, the wind had blown the warning that they would come. From Upper Sandusky, from Lower Sandusky, they would come, riding upon the command of the Saggenash to put out the last fires blazing along the Elk's Eye.

But the warning had been wind that chilled through skin to bone. She had shivered when it had first struck her, but then she had forgotten its touch. And, through these sunny days of planting, building, cooking, singing, praying, the only breeze she usually felt blew warm and caressed the cheek. It rolled around the head and scampered through the hair. It was a child that could only frolic so Ruth had danced in the arms of the breeze and had forgotten the battering of the wind. Until now.

Some sisters and brothers hurried away from the approaching rumble, carrying in their arms treasures wrapped in torn strouds or frayed blankets. They would bury these bundles in the forest and wait until the danger had blown past to dig them up again. Ruth glanced toward her cabin. Did she and the Beloved One have anything to bury? They did not even have an extra stroud or blanket to wrap their bundle in. They had enough, though. They had a cabin that their brothers had helped to build. Rain did not fall and wind did not blow inside their cabin. What could they bury? Themselves? Deep, where warriors could not find them. Deep, where they could suffocate. She stood.

Watch.

Wait.

Salah was walking toward Ruth. She stopped beside the Twittering-Brown-Bird and the Shadow. They went into their cabin; she walked on. Salah carried a bundle beneath her flesh, and it was buried but still it was seen. She spoke to Eyes-of-Mother who disappeared into her cabin and came out with a mixing bowl and a carved, long-handled spoon. They continued together. Sister Lovel, Sister Philipina, they tore their ears from the sound in the forest when Salah stopped to talk.

Ruth pretended that each footfall upon the trail in the forest was moving, step by step, farther and farther away.

She watched Salah shuffle toward her. She wanted Salah to ask her to hoe the garden with her. They would use hoes with metal mouths whose teeth tore apart weeds with sharp, quick bites. She had always before used the hoe whose mouth was the shoulder blade of a deer — walking beside Star-at-Dawning, ripping apart the weeds with dull grandmother-toothed blades. Today, she and Salah could work between rows of wheat and maize, and, later, they could grind wheat until it slid softly, smoothly through their fingers. They would make with it their love-feast bread and their small, heavy communion loaves. And the rustle along the trail would move ever farther away.

"I am happy to greet you," said Salah and said Eyes-of-Mother.

Ruth pulled the blue ribbon under her chin. Her white cap crushed the hairs on her head. "I am happy to greet you," she replied.

"The warriors will arrive when the sun sits at its height," said Eyes-of-Mother.

Ruth pinched her lips, dropped her eyes, and lifted them upon Eyes-of-Mother. "I know this," she muttered.

She raised her head and stared at Salah: "You hoe the garden? I can hoe with you."

"Forget the warriors," she wanted to say, "then they will go away."

"No," answered Sarah. "We must mix and bake. One Hundred-forty warriors march from Place of Peace. More come later. Bring your bowl. Stir with us."

Ruth frowned. Salah did not understand. She would summon the warriors with her preparations. Ruth tugged at the warm blanket of yesterday to cover her against the chill of today.

Where would she be safe? She glanced at her cabin. In that hot, dark hole, she would be trapped like a ground hog that had dug only one door. She looked southward toward the warriors. She looked northward toward the field where she could run and not be cornered.

"I must hoe."

Sarah watched the tall, slender, blue-strouded Ruth scurry between the cabins.

"Lenni Lenape — he is the man with the thrusting chest, grandfather and father among many nations," said Sister Christiana. "I am Mahicanni. Mahicanni is last and least and almost is no more. Mahicanni cannot uncover the pride of Lenni Lenape."

"She is not proud, not now," said Sarah.

Ruth was frightened as a squirrel, but Sarah could not stop to tame her. Those warriors, the emissaries of Satan, must be fed.

She would rather hoe the field with Ruth.

The baby pressed down inside her. She looked at Sister Christiana. Together, they proceeded through Gnadenhutten.

Ruth chopped with the metal hoe through the garden behind her cabin. She stabbed and broke apart the soil. She sliced and crumbled. The hoe clanked against a small rock. Ruth bent and picked it up. She threw it into the rock pile.

She hoed toward where she could see around the edges of the cabins to the end of the trail at the clearing.

The warriors appeared. Ruth hoed through a turnip root.

She could see their plucked heads and long scalp locks, their bare and smooth and painted chests. In the sun, red and black vibrated from off their bodies. They swung their rifles loose and low in sign of peace and friendship. Step by step, they opened wide into the clearing.

The lenno upon horses rode behind. In front would ride the Half-King, Pomoacan, chief among the Delamatteno. She could not see his face, but she knew the place of power. The red-coated, white-skinned Saggenash followed him. One lifted the red with blue and white flag of the nation of the Saggenash from across the salt sea.

Sisters hurried from cabins; brothers ran from fields. They stood together at the edge of the village.

Where could Ruth run?

A foot scraped across the ground behind her. The warrior! She clasped her hoe with both her hands. She turned.

The Beloved One walked toward her. His black hat covered seedlings of hair, no longer plucked, growing black and straight. His face was painted only in shadow from his wide brim. His chest was hidden by a loose shirt. His hands swung open at his sides.

"I saw you when I crossed the field," he said. He could watch much now because he could no longer run.

He watched too well. Ruth rolled out her lip and stood straight, her legs apart. She let the hoe slide from her grasp, hid her hands behind her back, and clasped and unclasped them. She knew he saw the hidden clenchings of her hands.

"Come," he said.

"No!" she exclaimed, pulling apart her fingers. "You can go to gape at the warriors. I must hoe."

"Why? The weeds do not grow high." He stomped a thistle and stared at her.

The lower lip of Ruth rolled out. "Why should I greet my shame?" she screamed inside. She did not say it. The Beloved knew why.

She squeezed her hands into fists, and swung them at her sides. She followed him toward the other lenno.

The Twitterer looked back with wide rock-eyes and bounced to her side.

Trapped.

Delamatteno, Mengwe, Shawano, Unami, and Monsey — Captain Pipe, Wingenund, and other captains and warriors rode or walked along the path, then veered from the path and moved toward the grassy level plain above the Elk's Eye.

Fish-of-the-Deep-Water was not riding with the captains. Thicker blood and redder than the blood of the strouded lenno awaited his hatchet.

Monsey swaggered past. They frowned and strutted and grasped their rifles against their chests. And one..

"Look," squeaked the Twitterer. "The big, dark one. Oh!"

Dark as night, his body sucked away the light of day. Black Wolf. The rabbit hopped frantically against the flesh-wall that caged it inside Ruth. She huddled near the Beloved.

The Twitterer chirped and fluttered near the ear of Ruth. Where could the rabbit hide? He had eaten Wind Maiden. She was not Wind Maiden, was she? Would he bare his fangs and crouch to spring at Ruth?

She flicked her head from side to side. The gaze of the Beloved followed Black Wolf. The mouth of the Beloved was quivering into a sneer. He would protect her.

She turned her head sideways and bowed it. The Wolf would not know that the white cap and the blue stroud concealed Wind Maiden.

235

No! Not Wind Maiden. The caged rabbit.

No! Ruth! Ruth!

"See his wide shoulders and the muscles on his back," whispered the Twitterer.

Ruth looked then. He walked away from her with slow, wide strides. She saw the back of his head, his scalp lock hanging to a wide neck. Darkness lingered where he had passed.

"He looked at me," chirped the Twitterer, her voice higher than Ruth had ever heard.

"Run from him," warned Ruth. "He is the wolf that tears apart and kills; and, still, its victim lives."

"You are a whimpering puppy because he did not look at you!" The eyes of the Twitterer glittered with a burning that ignited the memory of a fire whose ashes lay in a small heap that could burn no more.

The Twitterer glanced at the Beloved. She dropped her voice: "And you could only find a husband who ..." She paused and frowned.

Ruth stepped in front of her, a tall tree against a bending vine. She would grab her hair in two tight fists and yank apart. But that cap protected her hair. While Ruth pondered how to rip back the cap, her muscles loosened. She squashed the eyes of the Twitterer with her own gaze. Black Wolf had made her fight once before; he would not make her fight again. Ruth turned away from the very foolish bird.

She followed the Beloved One to their cabin.

"No new-cooked food to give you," she said. The pot was cold above a cold fire pit. She lifted bread from the day before. It crumbled.

"I did not come to eat," he said, taking the offered bread in his cupped hands. "I saw him."

"Yes," replied Ruth. She watched her husband eat. The Wolf would not come near her when the Beloved was here. She crouched beside him; he pulled her against his knee.

"Do not tremble, little rabbit."

Rabbit? She shrugged from his grasp.

He pulled her back and held her with his encircling arm. "He cannot take you unless you go."

"You stand between me and him." Ruth talked toward the ashes of the fire pit and leaned into the clasp of her husband.

"If you try to go, I shall step out of the way." The words of the Beloved crept along her back.

"No!" She glanced over her shoulder at him. Did not the Beloved know that the Black Wolf hung a heavy rope around the neck of its prey and pulled it wherever he wanted it to go? Ruth could hide far from him so that he could never tie the knot upon her neck. But did the rope still hang from the neck of Wind Maiden and the pulsing flesh of Ruth?

The hand of the Beloved One rubbed along the path his words had crept. "I give love," he said.

Ruth wrapped her arm around his leg. Love. She would hide behind and cling to that.

The Beloved arose. The arm of Ruth slid from his leg.

"Where do you go?" she yelped, jumping up beside him.

"The cabin of the teacher, Senseman. We are cutting and splitting logs. The warriors are nothing to us. We still work."

"I shall go with you."

"Will you be my puppy?" he asked, his hand heavy upon her shoulder.

She gazed back. Yes. She would pant at his heels.

"Can you split logs?"

"Yes!"

He stroked her arms. "You build fires and you cook. Above Huts of Grace, the warriors sit. Nothing changes here."

He walked toward the door.

He turned.

"Do not walk alone," he warned. "The warriors sway their bodies to the rhythm of 'peace', but that is only a dance. They are warriors. Look behind you and look in front and walk with a sister but do not walk alone."

"Nothing changes?" she mocked.

He smiled. "Inside, where we trust, it is the same."

She pretended to smile. He left. Warmth fled.

Nothing had changed.

The Wolf lurked near.

Nothing had changed.

She would practice the swayings the Saviour had given her. She bent her knees. She could almost feel a beat, but the thump seemed to rumble from the camp where the dark cloud hung. The Saviour would not move beneath the cloud. He would not sing about the slitherings there.

And if He did, she would refuse to hear.

She would not look toward the Saviour.

In the cabin of Salah, Ruth could stir thoughts, mold them into small, round heaps, and knead them in her head. Salah would protect her from the nothing she feared.

She dragged herself into the street. She glanced at the bluff. The blood-dipped flag of the Saggenash hung above, surrounded by half-built huts, rising like tree-men crouching beneath bark blankets. The Wolf hid there.

She slid into the cabin of Salah.

"You must help me plop bread onto the paddle and push it into the hot cave to bake," said the Twitterer, "but you must not burn yourself."

Ruth groaned. She had not pounced when the Twitterer had slashed with sharp words so the Twitterer had forgotten the throb of the bite. And Ruth was not Wind Maiden; she could not bite again.

Ruth bared her teeth and hoped that the Twitterer would not notice they were blunted.

"I cannot slide the bread alone," squawked the Twitterer.

"I shall slide you into the oven," thought Ruth, "and eat baked twitter-bird." She gulped. Those were the words of Wind Maiden.

"Work beside me," said Sarah.

Ruth stepped between Salah and Sister Philipina.

"Here, Sister," said Sarah, rolling dough from the clay bowl onto the table. "Flour is there." She pointed to a larger crock in front of Sister Lovel at the end of the table.

Ruth thrust her fingers into the dough.

Sister Christiana, from the other end of the table, shoved a pitcher of milk toward Sarah.

Sarah poured. More dough to mix. "Flour, Sister," she said to Sister Lovel who pushed the crock along the table to Sarah. Sarah rocked from one foot to another. She rubbed her lower back.

She glanced up at Anna Senseman who sat upon a stool across from Sarah. Sister Senseman approached the last month of her own pregnancy. "She has more strength than I," lamented Sarah to herself.

Sarah pulled a stool to the table. Sitting, she tried to balance the bowl upon her lap. "I am an over-stuffed feather bed," she thought as the bowl slid off her knees. She lifted it back onto the table.

"Already your baby spills his bowl," laughed Sister Philipina. She was short and fat. Having borne seven children, her stomach protruded in token of perpetual pregnancy though she had not brought forth in over five years.

"This one is bigger than ..." Sarah glanced around the table and folded her lips upon themselves in an attempt to smile. David lived again in her; she tried not to think about it.

"How much longer?" asked Sister Philipina.

"The passing of two moons," answered Sarah.

Sister Philipina looked sideways down at the round fullness. She shook her head.

Sarah stood and yanked her apron over the folds, what folds still remained, of her skirt. Was she wrong in her calculations?

Ruth glanced at the belly. Her own belly was flat and tight. Was flat and tight better? If the baby of the Beloved grew inside her, everyone would know that she belonged to him. Maybe salt had been hoed into the soil long ago by the other one. Nothing could grow in her then.

"He is a boy," said Sister Senseman, rubbing her own stomach. "He kicks hard, more hard than a girl."

"Me, I cannot guess," said Sarah, leaning over her bowl and stirring. She wanted a daughter, for a son would be David.

"Pish ... pish ... pish," thought Ruth. "Jabbering about squirming things inside. Do they have worms?"

"Go away," she wanted to say to Sister Senseman. "Huts of Grace is full of big bellies."

When Brother David had returned from beyond the mountains toward the rising sun, he had sent Brother and Sister Senseman here from Beautiful Spring and had taken away Brother Jung, the one who limps like husband.

"You carry him low. Boys are low," said Sister Senseman.

"You want a son, then watch boys play and close your eyes when girls run by. The baby will copy the seeing of your eyes," said Sister Philipina.

Ruth groaned. She would suffocate beneath these bulging bellies.

"No, Sister," corrected Sister Senseman. "God chooses, boy or girl."

"We help?" suggested Sister Philipina.

"We cannot help God," said Sarah. Then why was she struggling in the wilderness? She could leave and God could complete his work without her. But Christoph would plant and cultivate and he would harvest both men and crops with or without the help of God.

These three months since she told him she was pregnant, he tried to be teacher and pastor to her as he was to the other brethren and sisters. But she was his wife. His wife! When they lay in bed at night, who did he think lay beside him? A sheep in his flock? Why could he not confide in her? At least they no longer quarreled. How could they? Though near, he was far away.

"My breasts are full," murmured Sister Senseman. "They ache."

"My wider bodice, you can use it," offered Sarah.

"If you will drop your milk, I can milk you." Sister Philipina smirked.

"Oh, but if she is a sow and not a cow," objected Sarah, "who will offer to milk her then?"

The sisters yowled.

Sarah glanced at Sister Senseman who, mouth hanging open, stared back at Sarah.

Sarah bit small nibbles along her lip. She had spoken like an Indian. Often, she did not even think in German anymore. And she did not care.

She smiled at Sister Senseman.

Ruth watched Salah. Salah had confused the sow. Maybe it would go away. She punched her dough.

"That is ready for the loaf," said Sister Senseman, looking at the dough of Ruth.

"Is this the first time I make bread?" grumbled Ruth. She punched the bread again.

The tappings in the bowl of Salah stop. Ruth lowered her head to look at Salah.

The eyes of Salah said to Ruth, "Are you Wind Maiden? Where is Ruth?"

"I am Ruth!" proclaimed the voice inside. But it shook with the fear of Wind Maiden.

Ruth had fought down Wind Maiden when Wind Maiden had tried to rise up in Goschachgunk. She would win again. Against Black Wolf? He moved with power over her ... over something in her.

A wail rose from the shadows of the sleeping place.

"I hold her now," squeaked a high voice: Maria.

"No. I!" came a lower squawk: Benjamin.

"Do not pull on Naomi!" scolded Sister Lovel. "She is a sprout."

"Benjamin, give her to Maria," said Sister Philipina.

The bare feet of Benjamin thumped upon the wood floor. He trotted past the sisters.

"Where do you go, wounded bear?" asked Sister Philipina.

Benjamin stood at the door. He puffed out his chest beneath a loose muslin shirt.

"Why does he wear a shirt?" thought Ruth. The captains and warriors would say that a boy only needed a breech clout. They would mock the believing lenno.

"Will the sun freeze his skin?" they would sneer. "No! It will make his flesh glisten like polished metal. Does the teacher want the believing lenno's skin to turn pale like his own?"

"I go to Brother Christoph," whined Benjamin.

"He does not teach today," said Sarah. "The warriors ..."

"Not outside," admonished Sister Philipina. "Do not whimper or I shall punch your snout," she added to the grumbling child.

Benjamin plopped onto the floor by the door.

Ruth looked down at her stroud. She shook her covered head. She could not see the color of her flesh beneath the folds of White Man's cloth or the color of her hair beneath its cap. "You are Lenni Lenape. Do not forget," her mother had said.

"More warriors!" The voice of the Shadow preceded her into the cabin.

"Monsey warriors," she puffed, chest rising and falling.

Rebecca dropped her paddle and rushed toward Leah and the door.

"Slowly, Sister," directed Sarah. "We go together.

The Twitterer turned and grabbed the arm of Ruth. Ruth yanked away. She pushed the detestable bird. She would not be dragged into the mouth of the Wolf. The Twitterer fell into Salah.

"Sister," said Sarah, hurrying Rebecca past her and out the door. She walked to Ruth and laid her hand upon her arm.

Ruth shrugged off the hand. "Go away," she moaned, rubbing her hands up and down her arms.

Salah ...

Sarah hesitated. Not Ruth! Not Ruth rejecting her.

"Sister Sarah," called Sister Senseman from outside.

"Go," repeated Ruth, dropping her eyes. Too near. Salah might see what lurked inside.

"Friend ..." began Sarah. What could she say when she had no time? She turned away.

Ruth slumped over the table. Where could she hide? She looked into the bowl of Salah. She lifted the wooden spoon and stirred.

"They sit above us like vultures," groaned Sarah. She squeezed her eyes shut. It was still night-time within the cabin though Christoph was leaning, breeches pulled on, over the fireplace, stirring, spreading the ashes with an iron prod. He built the fire in the mornings now, now that Sarah arose with rollings and pushings.

She squirmed into the soft, feather-stuffed tick. In July, Sister Susan Zeisberger had brought her two bags of feathers when she had arrived, newly-married, from Bethlehem. Though not enough to fill two ticks that she might sleep nestled between the warm softness above and below or even enough to fill one tick into which to lie, still she could, using an underfilling of hay, line the top with feathers. Then, if she did not nestle too deeply, she could pretend that ...

Sarah felt the coarse rustle of hay. She rolled onto her side and pushed herself up.

"Why does Pomoacan delay the meeting that he himself demanded?" asked Sarah. "Brother David hurried from New Schoenbrunn and Brother Heckewelder from Salem — and Sister Heckewelder so recently having brought forth — to wait." She scratched her cheek.

Christoph laid dry logs upon the ashes. "I do not complain about the wait," he observed. "It gives me ... us ... time ..."

Did he think he could patch together the shredding present with threads of time? Sarah wanted him to patch together the vision so that it could cover and protect him. Or did she really want it to fall into shreds so that it could never be worn again? Saviour, forgive her. But if the Christian Indian state was the plan of God, why did Christoph struggle as if God was not involved?

"The Delamatteno, Shawano, the Lenni Lenape, and Captain Elliot of the Saggenash cannot agree upon what lies to tell us," Christoph continued. He was standing erect now, his voice calm and patient. He might have been speaking before the congregation instead of to Sarah in their cabin. "Pray for their confusion. The passing days make heavy the believing congregations. Soon, we shall be too heavy to budge."

"But we slaughter hogs and cattle. Our grain disappears. All to feed those warriors." That was what was happening to the believing ones ... now. Sarah thought of the warriors sitting within their wall-less huts, watching the brethren and sisters labor. She slid her legs onto the floor and pulled down her sleeping gown.

Christoph would think that she grumbled against them because of the provisions they took, provisions that were not her own but God's. "I do not begrudge the food or labor," she added. She rubbed her right temple with her fingers.

Christoph wiped his hands upon an old and worn shirt, now a cleaning rag. He threw down the rag and watched her. "You work hard," he said.

"No. No harder than the other sisters," Sarah answered. Walls of defense rose about her. She grabbed them for support. Why could he force her to stumble back when she could not budge him?

"Accompany Sister Senseman when she goes to New Schoenbrunn for the delivery of her child," said Christoph.

Leave Gnadenhutten? She could not.

Sarah knew her own capacity; she was not a child to be dictated to. She said, "Sister Senseman will give birth very soon, but I, why ... I have two months." Two months? Even now she felt the pushing of the baby down, down. Two months? "No, I do not need to go."

Sarah looked toward the fireplace. She felt Christoph's gaze upon her face. She rubbed her legs against the wood frame of the bed.

"Those warriors. They do not whoop through our street, but where they camp ..." She met the eyes of Christoph with her own. "Not even you can ignore the noise of their dances and ribaldry. And, Christoph, please prohibit our young men and women from going to their camp."

Christoph was shaking his head. Sarah added, "Our Rebecca strays toward the camp of the scavengers — harlots — who straggled after and camp near the warriors. She will not work; she ignores my scoldings. She says that I am not her protector or her ruler but she is mine."

And to where did Ruth disappear most days? Did she accompany Rebecca? Ruth's were wild animal eyes.

Christoph still shook his head. Sarah continued, "And our young men ..."

"I know," interrupted Christoph, his voice exploding, then silent. He looked into the fire and rubbed his lips with the back of his hand.

She had nagged him. She had deserved correction so why did he bury the anger that he surely felt?

Christoph gazed back at her, his mouth pulled into pulpit patience. Sarah wanted to grab his wide shoulders, shake off his condescension, and expose the rage and frustration she knew hid near the surface. Why did he climb back into the pious mold that had already been shattered? How patiently he must have glued together the pieces. Was it not better to shatter the mold than to crush the soul into an unnatural shape?

He said, "Restrict our people and the coiling warriors will hiss, 'Hear? You praying lenno are the groveling dogs of your teachers. You say that they have come to teach and serve you? Ah ... the White Man. He makes slaves of all who wear different colored flesh. Remember the black-skinned man. These teachers want to teach you to wear a rope around your neck!"

Christoph rubbed the back of his own neck. "Already they say this. We must prohibit nothing. Pray that God will restrain the arm of Satan."

Sarah nodded. "Yes," she whispered.

She wanted him to sit beside her, slide his arm around her full girth. She wanted to apologize for arguing. He did not move; she did not speak.

~ ~ ~

"You are an old woman," complained the Twitterer, leaning against her hoe.

"Close your beak," murmured Ruth, digging at the roots of weeds at the end of a row. She started up the next row between the wheat, away from the Twitterer. She looked at the Shadow who had stopped hoeing and was listening. Ruth frowned and bent toward the hoe.

"You do not leave Huts of Grace since they came." The Twitterer flicked her head toward the camp where the warriors waited. "This morning, you tell me that, yes, you will leave the path shadowed by our cabins if I will go with you. Yes, I said, I would go; I would take you to the camping place of their women. Or ..." She lowered her voice. "... if you were afraid, I would walk with you among the trees for I have found a place where we could hide and watch ..." She licked her lips. "... the warriors dance."

"Perching bird," thought Ruth. She had seen too many warriors dance.

"Instead, you take me by the hand and lead me behind the meeting house to hoe!" The Twitterer threw down the hoe.

Ruth did not blink her eyes; she watched the green weeds roll onto their backs and kick their roots up toward the sunlight to die.

"Old woman!" repeated the Twitterer.

Old woman? Yes, she would be an old woman if she would not see him. The blackness had not reappeared since seven days ago when it had spread past her with the warriors.

"Go with me now."

Ruth did not answer. She turned the soil and the weeds ... again, again.

"Look!" cried the Twitterer.

Ruth glanced up and followed the pointing of her outstretched hand toward the camp. Two men were emerging, darkness from deeper darkness, from the clustered huts. They swaggered, rifles swinging, toward the forest. Ruth watched the tall one.

"Eeee ... the dark, strong warrior," shrieked the Twitterer.

They stopped, looked around, and started toward the little garden.

"Quiet, fool!" mumbled Ruth. She would have torn the throat from the bird! Her legs bent to run, between the cabins, to the arms of the Beloved One. She heard in her memory the mocking laugh, deep-throated, of Black Wolf. He might spring upon her if she ran, and, in her flight, she could not bend and roll away from the strike. She bowed her head and dug with her hoe deep into the soil. He might not see her face and would not know ...

"Dig," she snarled at the Twitterer. She heard a sound of hoeing ahead of her; that was the Shadow.

Feet scampered up beside her. "They come here," croaked the Twitterer.

"Fool! Stand from me," murmured Ruth.

But the Twitterer was hopping all around, tapping at the back of Ruth, and would not hear.

Ruth tried to work to the end of the row, but the Twitterer danced behind. "Stand from me," pleaded Ruth. Her words fell off in weakness.

"Ha! Young One!" called a high voice whose sound she did not know. "Come with me to my camp. You are too frisky to stay here. Are you not bored by prayer and the words of the White Man?"

The Twitterer did not dance; she did not answer. Ruth lifted her hoe and walked away from them.

Something clutched her arm. Black Wolf? She yanked sideways and clawed at it with her free hand. The Twitterer squawked and pulled away her hand.

The eyes of Ruth flicked across the row of wheat toward Black Wolf. His eyes clamped upon her own; she was trapped. She turned again.

"Oh ... a wild one," laughed the high voice. "I shall tame you!"

"No, this is mine!" A dark, low voice rose from swirling blackness. A shadow rustled beside Ruth and stopped in front of her at the end of the row.

She looked up.

His tall, dark shape stood above her. He blocked the sunlight; he smothered her. Silence roared and pressed against her ears.

His mouth curled into a slow, wide smile. "I have tamed this one; it wears my mark," he said, watching Ruth. His eyes dropped down her body.

Ruth stood straight and stepped toward him. "Go away! I see death and rot. Your stench makes me vomit!"

He laughed, huffing through his nose.

She yanked together the heavy breath that sat inside her chest and thrust it out: "I spit upon you!"

He laughed! He raised his head, the howling wolf, and laughed!

Deep inside where only she could hear, Ruth groaned, long and slow. Step forward and he would suffocate her; move backward and she would fall. Fall, then he would pounce. She dropped her head; she stood; she watched.

Silence dripped from his lips. He became more ominous than before. With stalking step, he slid close. "Come with me," he muttered. "They ..." He jerked his head toward Huts of Grace. "... are dead. "

"My husband and the ..." began Ruth.

"Dead!" snarled Black Wolf. "The limper? Yes, I have heard. Dead! Your fire burns low; I shall rub life back."

Ruth looked up into his face. Deep within, she felt a stirring in a place that had lain hidden beneath the blackness that once had been. Wind Maiden was dead; what was this? She slid into it; it opened and spread. Was this life? No! Poisonous death.

"Death, not life," she said.

Black Wolf reached out and clutched her wrist. Pain surged from without and, breaking and rising, from within. Pull back, pull back and run!

He stared down at her. He frowned and wrinkled his brow. He, the hunter, gazed at her as if she were a strange animal he had found. "You are ..." he began.

"Friend!" called the high voice.

Black Wolf glanced up. His grasp eased. Ruth slid her hand away.

"Later," cautioned his friend.

Black Wolf slowly shook his rifle still clutched in his other hand.

Ruth watched him taste the animal with his eyes. Was its flesh tender and sweet? He opened his mouth as if to speak, but, instead, rubbed together his teeth.

He turned his back — she was not the enemy that he should fear her attack. He strode to his friend; Ruth did not move her feet but watched with her turning head. They walked toward the forest ... hunters ... and did not glance back. Their murmurs and their laughter alone turned back.

The Twitterer slid close to Ruth, but even she did not speak. The Shadow crept up behind.

"Talk about this and I shall bite into the bone, deep, so that the marks of my teeth shall never heal," warned Ruth, gazing first at the Twitterer and then at the Shadow. Her face felt cold and wet. Bite? She was toothless and ready to die. Would they believe her lie?

The Twitterer rolled her mouth into a circle. "No words," warned Ruth. "He thought I was another." Yes, another. Wind Maiden. She was Ruth. The Beloved One was her husband; the Saviour, her God. But the hidden thing was stirring yet, darker than blackness, colder than death.

Wind Maiden ... was she dead?

~ ~ ~

"More tea, sir?" asked Sarah, poising a steaming pot above the cup of Matthew Elliot.

245

"Mmm ... 'preciated," he replied. He reached for the bowl of maple sugar granules. "Ain't nary a woman in Detroit c'n cook vittles like yorn." He bit into a biscuit, nodding up at Sarah.

She lowered her eyes.

"Your biscuit bread eats good, ma'am," mumbled Alexander McCormick through a mouthful of crumbs.

"We are glad you join us tonight, sir," said Sarah to Mr. McCormick. "Captain Elliot brought your regrets other nights. We are glad Pomoacan releases you from your post tonight." Sarah had practiced that speech in English during the entire meal.

"Thank ya', ma'am," replied Mr. McCormick. He glanced at Captain Elliot. "They's ... uh ... allus taskin' me."

"Yup," agreed Captain Elliot. "And nary none gets out 'a camp lessen Pomoacan leaves 'im."

"No ... uh ... no," stammered Mr. McCormick.

Brother Heckewelder leaned his tall frame against the table. "Captain, tell us: why do you delay your meeting with us until Monday? We gathered in Gnadenhutten as appointed ..." He motioned with his hand around the table toward Christoph, Brother David, Brother Edwards, and Brother Senseman. "... to await your pleasure for a week and longer."

"Sa! I ain't delayin'!" exclaimed Captain Elliot. "I's ignorant of the doin's of th' Half King. An' ma *pleasure*, Sa, 's yournses safety. Be mindin' that the Half King hollered me ..." He glanced at Mr. McCorniick, "... and Mr. McCorimick into comin'. Comin' in peace, surely, I trow."

"In peace?" said Brother David. "Your warriors bear arms; you carry colors with you."

"Ma warriors? Not ma warriors," corrected Captain Elliot, "Youse slep' aside 'em longer 'n I'se. Ya know outen their rifle, they goes nowhar." He smiled around the table and took another biscuit.

"Butter?" he asked, indicating the dish in front of Mr. McCormick.

McCormick sliced a slab of butter for himself and slid the dish toward Captain Elliot.

"Hogs, chick'n, cow ..." enumerated Elliot, "... milk, butter ... You 'n yer Ind'ns is prosperin'."

He sat back in his chair and rubbed his stomach. He burped, "We's frien's many year, Mr. Zeisberger, Mr. Heckewelder, Mr. Zundel."

"We have been acquainted some years," replied Brother Heckewelder.

"Jes' acquainted?" exclaimed Elliot. "Ya ain't faultin' me, is ya, fer bein' mistook when Girty, McKee, an' me tol's 'em Lenape the Big Knife was warrin' agin 'em." He shrugged. "We wus lied to. I'se grateful fer correctin'." He flashed a smile at Brother Heckewelder. Bowing his head, he purred, "But I'se larned, I warn't wrong, jes' ahead a time."

"Because of your meddling," thought Sarah.

Even from where she stood beside the fireplace, pot still in hand, Sarah could see the disclaimer rise upon the lifting brows and opening mouth of Brother Heckewelder. He glanced at Brother David whose face she could not see. His mouth closed though his brows remained arched.

"Learned? What do you know?" asked Christoph from the head of the table, leaning into the candlelight.

Captain Elliot turned toward him. Had Sarah perceived a flash of animosity before his face sealed into bland amiability? No, certainly the candles alone cast the ominous shadow.

"Sa! I say agin': I'se ignorant. Th' Half King tells me nary nothin'." He pushed his chair back as if to rise. "I'se itchin' ta larn his min' with ya." He stood. "Today's Saturday. Y'll scratch yer itch come Monday."

He nodded to Mr. McCormick to arise. "C'n ya settle yerself 'til then? If yer itch is blisterin' ..." He looked around the table at the rising brethren. "... whyfor did ya refuse ta meet t'marra?" He waved his hand against protestations: "I ain't faultin' ya. Yer sabb'th." He smiled. "Th' Almighty 's makin' ya wait."

Captain Elliot turned toward the door. Sarah watched Mr. McCormick arise and place his hat upon the seat of his chair. He pushed it to the table. Some steps behind, he followed Elliot toward the door, arms folded behind his back.

"Much 'preciated, sa an' ma'am," said Captain Elliot, nodding toward Sarah and Christoph in one vague gesture.

Mr. McCormick mumbled and shrugged his thanks.

"God's blessing, Brother, Sister, and upon this house," said the brethren while departing.

The door closed. Sarah gazed at the chair. She cleared the tea cups from the table, slipping around the chair without touching it. She stacked the cups upon the cabinet and glanced at Christoph who was bending over the fireplace, pushing a twig into the glimmering ashes. He stood and lit his pipe with the glowing tip, puffing, puffing, concentrating.

They heard a tap, hardly a tap, upon the door. Christoph paused. He cocked his head and gazed at Sarah.

"Mr. McCormick," she said.

His mouth dropped open. He began to nod his head but paused and frowned.

Christoph cupped his hand over his pipe and strode to the door. When he opened it, Mr. McCormick stumbled in.

"Sa," he stammered, "I'se pressed. I'se makin' out like I'se forgot ma hat." He stepped farther in and waved toward the door with his hand near his chest.

Christoph closed the door.

"Cap'n Elliot, 'e's no frien'. 'E's a talkin' nice t' you-uns, but ..." He sighed and rubbed his palms against the side seams of his coat: "... 'e's the plottin' un, not 'em Ind'ns. 'E's aimin' ta ruin you-uns and ta scatter yer Ind'ns. 'E's full a venom, 'e is."

"We suspected this," said Christoph.

Mr. McCormicK clasped together his hands. "Then ya know ya don't dast disobedience 'im. 'E'll tak ya from yer towns. Ya best go. Else, youse'll die."

"Thank you," replied Christoph. He stared at Mr. McCormick. "I may repeat this to my brethren?"

"Thems who 'ere here t'night? Yes. None othern lest the Cap'n larns ..."

"You are safe?" asked Sarah.

"I'se not jeopardized, thank ya, ma'am," answered Mr. McCormick, glancing back toward her. "I'se pressed now. Suspectins ..." He murmured something under his breath while retrieving his hat from the seat of the chair.

Sarah grabbed the basket of remaining rolls, covered it with a napkin, and offered it to him.

"You are late in returning to camp because we have been talking of your wife and her sweet roll recipe, have we not?" asked Sarah. "You say that my rolls are as light as hers. I am pleased. I offer you these."

He took the basket and smiled down at Sarah. "Would that I could set at 'er table now, ma'am."

"But you could not warn us then, sir," said Sarah.

Christoph opened the door for the fidgeting Mr. McCormick. He stepped through the doorway, slipping his hat onto his head.

He looked back: "I reverence God, sa. I ain't discomfitin' no pastor!"

"You will not do that, sir," replied Christoph. "God's blessings on you."

Mr. McCormick nodded then hurried into the night.

Christoph closed the door and looked at Sarah. He scratched his head. He glanced at his pipe and returned to the fireplace to light it. From the fireplace, he looked back at her.

Sarah wanted to rush across the room and cling to him. Why was he watching her? She gathered the butter and preserves from the table. Could he not speak?

"Do we obey the demands of Captain Elliot?" She tried to sound calm.

Christoph was puffing his pipe. How could he appear so calm? "We have not heard the demands yet," he observed.

"You know they will try to drive us from here." Now he played games with her.

"Then God knows what we must do." Smoke floated up from his mouth.

Sarah sighed. She laid the food upon the cupboard and leaned against the wood. Simple answers would be less tiresome to hear. "Yet ..." she began.

"We cannot go willingly," Christoph said, "not to difficulties and starvation."

Sarah was very tired. "Not go? But we must go." Her voice droned in her own ears. God was sovereign. Their situation only appeared hopeless, only appeared.

Christoph laid his pipe upon the stone slab near the fireplace. He walked toward her and stopped before her. His hands rubbed her shoulders, just for a moment, then fell to his sides.

"You need rest," he said.

Yes, she did need rest. She could rest in the arms of her husband if he would allow her.

"I am sending you to Schoenbrunn with Sister Senseman," he continued.

"No!" exclaimed Sarah. She clasped her wrists, pulling, pulling herself up from smothering weariness. "I have two months. I ... I ..."

How could she tell him? The sisters needed her. Rebecca. Leah. Ruth. She could reach Ruth again if she had time. And without the sisters, how could she sustain ... sustain what? And leave Christoph? She was losing him while she yet saw him. How could she retain what was left if they were separated? She was clinging. She was panicking.

"The sisters. They fall back to heathenish thoughts. They need me." She stood as straight as her abdomen would allow and turned her head up toward his. She would be strong.

He merely stood above, watching her with furrowed brows that shadowed his impenetrable eyes.

"I am tired each night, yet I revive each day." She turned from him. She rattled the plates in front of her. She wanted him to rub her shoulders, her back, ease the achings of her body and mind. But she had turned from him. Hers was the fault. She would finish her work, and she would be strong.

The baby squirmed and kicked. She closed her eyes. "David," she thought, "are you so eager to get out?" David ... David ... She did not try to correct herself.

21
SEPTEMBER 2, 1781 – SEPTEMBER 3, 1781

S arah scooped stew from the steaming kettle in the fireplace.
A rifle boomed in the street of Gnadenhutten. More shots echoed and re-echoed. Cackles and howls rolled in the wake of the booms.

Those warriors, they killed more cattle and hogs. They danced their war dances around the carcasses and left the carcasses to bloat and rot in the street and fields. Who could stop them or even try to drag the dead from Gnadenhutten? Most kept to their cabins. And what did the warriors really want to kill? The teachers. Why did they delay?

Sarah wrapped her apron around the bowl and carried it to the table. She set it down beside Brother Edwards.

"This is a modest meal," she apologized. She glanced around the table at Brother David and Brother Heckewelder and at the assistants who had accompanied the teachers from New Schoenbrunn and Salem upon this third journey to Gnadenhutten in response to the call of the Half King, Pomoacan. "I had not time to prepare," she added.

And if she did have time, would she have strength? She felt her eyes droop and mouth sag.

Who could eat when, instead of the smell of stew, the stench of putrid flesh filled the nostrils? The soul of Gnadenhutten was rotting. Not even Christoph could preserve it.

He did try. Sarah glanced across the table at him. By what determination did he make alert his eyes and arch his brows? When he bowed his head, as often now he did, did his brows fall; did his gaze slip? She was sure they did.

Sarah sat at her place between Christoph and Brother Senseman.

She looked sideways at Brother Senseman. "Sister Anna ..." she whispered, afraid of being overheard by the other men.

He looked at her. His eyes were heavy, and he did not try to hide it. "Brother David assures me that she and our son are well. Three days old, Sister, and I have not seen him." His voice breathed out into a sigh.

"If we do say, 'Yes,' to their demand that we follow them to Sandusky," Brother David was saying to Brother Jonah, "our lenno might shake the fist at us when, in Sandusky, we starve. My Brother, listen ... we *shall* starve."

The eyes of Brother Senseman darted toward Brother David and back to Sarah. "I shall tell you more later," he said to her. His gaze fell upon Brother David.

Always. They speculated. They exchanged the same words and made the same prayers that they had made when first Pomoacan and the captains had demanded that the believing congregations abandon their homes and plantations and accompany the warriors to the home of the Delamatteno in Sandusky. Did the men never tire of groping over the same trail leading to the same destination? Could they not complete the journey? Perhaps there would at least be rest at the end ... Even death would be rest.

"We want to please our Uncle, Pomoacan, and all our friends," the assistants had responded to the warriors. "But, as you see, we could not go with you now. We are heavy and must have time. We shall keep and consider your words, and after the fields have been reaped, we shall reply."

Upon the first encounter, Pomoacan had been satisfied. But a hidden stick prodded the flesh of the Half King. Friendly warriors had assured the teachers that Elliot jabbed the stick. A second meeting was called; again Pomoacan had been satisfied. Yet the stick still pricked and prodded, for now the brethren waited upon the eve of the third meeting.

Ruth had scurried up to Sarah and warned, "Blood will soon flow from the body of Believers." Then she had fled.

Sarah had whined to Christoph, "Why can they not leave us alone? We harm no one."

"No one?" Christoph had replied. "The warriors suspect we warn Fort Pitt of their attacks. Are we harmless?"

"We are ... most of us are now," Sarah had objected. "When the Lenni Lenape were neutral, then we wrote letters to the White settlements for them. No longer. We remain neutral."

"Neutral?" Christoph had mocked.

"We serve neither side!" Sarah had exclaimed. She could see him enveloping himself in the warm blanket of martyrdom.

"Do we?" had been his reply.

They died daily, riding upon the back of speculation. They might as well march to Sandusky. In the march, they would regain momentum.

Momentum toward what?

Were they out of the will of God? Had they incurred His wrath? Was this their punishment?

Sarah, the only woman, sat at the table and listened to the teachers and assistants prepare the same response that twice before they had given.

"Go with me," Sister Anna Senseman had begged Sarah. "Even now we could gather your belongings. I can wait. Schoenbrunn is not host to warriors."

Sister Senseman, blankets wrapped about her, had leaned forward in the canoe, reaching toward Sarah.

"My time is not yet," Sarah had said. "They will depart before that. You must go; your time is soon." She had not believed her own words, none of them. But she could not leave. If her people must die, she must be present for the burying. If they were to live, then she must stay close lest she lose them.

Eleven days had passed since the departure of Sister Senseman. Gnadenhutten was overcome by the warriors. An end was near.

Sarah sipped broth from her spoon. The baby was pushing up into her stomach. Already she felt filled. She forced herself to eat — she counted them — five more bites of stew.

Warriors, howling like hungry wolves, ran past the cabin.

"Some of our own lenno," Brother Jonah was lamenting, "scheme with the warriors. They say, 'Take our White brothers prisoners to Sandusky. Then all the praying ones will follow.'"

"Yes," agreed Brother David. "Plottings from within ..."

"Rottings from within," thought Sarah.

"We must go," insisted Brother Jonah. "Go now. Fill our own packs. Hang them from our own chests, carried on our own backs. Should we wait for Pomoacan and Captain Pipe to pack them for us and lay them upon our backs? Are we horses that do not know when to do it for ourselves?"

"We follow the Saviour," insisted Christoph. "He built our fire here upon the Elk's Eye. The evil one would destroy what the Saviour builds. We wait; we trust. The evil one makes fear. We do not run in fear."

Did Christoph still trust in his vision? Or did he pursue redemption through martyrdom? Sarah wanted to hold him ... talk ... talk ...

"If we go to Sandusky, the Saviour will choose the moment. His arm is long; he can still grab us back," said Brother Heckewelder.

Grab them back, falling as they were? Those who fell willfully ... Rebecca, Leah ... would God, could God, take them back? What would Sarah do? Save them herself?

Was the promise of the Christian Indian state like the promise made to Abraham? Must they, too, wait four hundred years for the fulfillment of the vision? They would die, many generations would die, and those who inherited the promise would not even remember it. Or perhaps God had never provided the vision. Had Sarah and Christoph constructed their lives and offered their sacrifices upon delusion? Death would be an awakening from error.

Sarah bit her lip. No! She would not give up.

Where was Ruth? Why did she no longer come to Sarah? Their friendship had not been another delusion, had it? Ruth did belong to the Saviour, did she not?

"Pomoacan, his captains and his councilors, and Elliot, meet again tonight around their fire," said Brother David.

"Why ... again?" The voice of Sarah rose like a tired chirp above the deep rumble of the men.

They looked at her.

Outdoors, the smoke of the council fire rose slow and straight through windless air toward the star-blinking sky.

Cowering behind the Beloved, Ruth leaned against the back of their cabin and watched the smoke. It carried secrets to an evil being hidden inside the blackness of the sky.

"I am not a messenger who runs," sighed the Beloved. "I am not a warrior who hears and prepares. I watch the smoke and I wait."

"For whom would you run? Against whom would you fight?" asked Ruth.

He gazed back at her: "For the believing lenno, I would run. I would reveal the secrets that hide in the smoke."

"And fight ..." thought Ruth. She knew whom he would fight.

"The dark thing, if it attacks ..." Ruth swallowed her words. Black Wolf was already crouching, sniffing its prey, planning its feast.

The Beloved squeezed tight his fists. "I shall kill him. I shall cut out his heart. I shall kill him."

Her arms started shaking. She folded them against her chest.

He slid his arm around her shoulder and pulled her against him. "Do not be afraid," he whispered.

She did fear. She feared for herself. She feared for the Beloved. He could not kill the Wolf. The Wolf would devour him.

She clung to him. She wanted to tell the Beloved that Black Wolf was prowling near and that she was afraid of something ... something inside her. But her words would slay the Beloved.

She wanted to tell Salah, but the eyes and ears of Salah had turned inward. What could Salah see? How could she hear?

They watched puffs of smaller fires and heard whoops of warriors as they stomped the ground and encircled and stabbed the pole, their enemy. Boastings of scalpings and murders would ooze out of their mouths as they danced. The blood-words would dribble down their chins and onto their chests.

Behind Ruth and the Beloved, through the street of Huts of Grace, other warriors whooped and stomped. The believing lenno, they were the pole around which the warriors danced.

"If you were a runner, you would listen. You would not be here. And if you were a warrior, you would paint your face and pound your heels there, where the smoke rises. You would not be here. "

"I would be a runner and a warrior for you," he replied.

"What am I?" she asked. "Am I wife? My belly is flat. No children. Among the Lenni Lenape, you could find another wife who would grow fat with babies. That one you should protect. Not me."

"If the seed has rotted, it will never grow even when it is planted. I plant the seed. Is it rotten? You could leave me. You could find another husband who would plant dry, new seeds that grow," replied the Beloved.

Ruth wrapped her arms about him. "Do not say this."

"Among the believing lenno, husbands and wives do not abandon each other," concluded the Beloved.

Rifles banged in the field, then in the village.

"Back to our cabin," pleaded Ruth. She smelled the breath of the enemy.

"You hide inside our cabin from sun setting to sun setting. Why?" asked the Beloved. "Lenno, painted red and black for war, you have seen them before."

No, Ruth had not seen them before. And Wind Maiden had felt the slashings of the warrior, the spurtings of her own blood, the seeping of warmth from her body. She, Ruth, they both would hide.

"Danger is here," she said. She had seen it. Five sun settings ago, the Wolf had stalked through the street of Huts of Grace. She had smelled him before she had seen him ... the smell of dry blood floating through the open door of her cabin. Now, she was the grey rock lying upon the dirt floor. It might lie, covered by a shadow of a tree, and sleep and dream forever about nothing. She would wind her arms around her legs and pull in tight and round. The rock.

"The Saviour protects us from the enemy," said the Beloved.

Who was her enemy? The warriors? The black one? Herself?

The Saviour was chanting down, down, deep within and all about.

He beckoned, "Practice."

"No," she groaned, "I cannot dance into the blackness where you call." Another shuffle pounded louder and louder. It stomped its foot; it was stubborn.

"Obey me or freeze."

"I stay," she whimpered. "I am the rock."

The night had howled with evil. The powers of darkness enveloped the new day. Sarah was stirring her still-hot porridge. Christoph, chin in hand, stared past her.

She rubbed her eye and forehead with the palm of her hand. Tiredness settled upon her like blankets placed one over the other, piled ever higher. She smothered. Christoph glanced at her, but his eyes snapped away to stare.

"Talk, Christoph," Sarah wanted to say. "Remember me."

"The vision ..." she began. His eyes darted upon her. ". ..It is destroyed?"

"No!" he exclaimed. "Has this age ended? Has Christ returned?"

"No ..."

"We may die; that is God's decision. The vision cannot die. It cannot be destroyed."

Did he await death?

"But we have failed?" she asked.

"Yes, perhaps." He squeezed closed his eyes. "Not you," he corrected.

A knock.

Christoph rose to answer. Brother David entered with Brother John Martin.

"A warrior," said John Martin, "son to my brother, was at the council of Pomoacan last night. He says, 'Today, the teachers are prisoners; today they may die.'"

"Oh ..." breathed Sarah. She slid around the table and stood beside Christoph.

Christoph nodded his head.

"Flee to Fort Pitt," John Martin urged. "The believing lenno will help you."

"No," said Brother David.

"No," agreed Christoph. "Should we run? Are we ashamed? Are we afraid?" He looked at Sarah. "But you must go to Schoenbrum."

"Should I run?" she echoed. "Am I ashamed?" She could not echo, "Afraid." She was afraid.

"You are with child. It is different for you." replied Christoph. His eyes were a pale, pale blue.

"Sister Sabina and Sister Susanna are with child. Do they go, too?"

Sarah thought his eyes replied, "It is different with them. They are stronger than you."

She concluded, "It is no different with me than it is with them." She felt the poundings of fear against her temples.

"Not one of our villages is safe now," said Brother David to Christoph. "And if we sent her to Fort Pitt, she could not travel quickly. The warriors would overtake her. Our hope is God — alone."

Christoph gazed at Sarah. "I waited too long. I am sorry."

"I chose, not you," she said.

The jaw of Christoph quivered, for an instant, before he set it firm.

"Ring the bell for the eight o'clock service," Brother David said to John Martin.

Brother John Martin glanced at Christoph.

"Ring the bell," agreed Christoph.

In the street near warriors still sleeping or dozing where they had fallen the night before; close to the wandering warriors searching for food; beside the bloated, fly-buzzed black cows; in front of the cabin of Ruth and the Beloved, the Twittering-Brown-Bird stood.

"Go with me to find wood," pleaded the Bird.

"My husband goes," replied Ruth.

"But I have secrets to share."

"Secrets can fall anywhere. Must I hunt for them in the forest?" Ruth dropped her head and looked up.

"You hide from the big one." The Bird cocked its head and stared with beady eyes.

"I do not hide!" Ruth wanted to pluck the feathers of the Twitterer. "I can hear your secret here." She stepped into the door opening.

The Twitterer flicked her head from side to side, watching the street. "The Delamatteno, he will lead the believing lenno to a new home along the river in Sandusky," she whispered, leaning into the shadow of the door.

"Ah, wide ears, how have you heard? And where is your home? My home is here — the Elk's Eye. Are you Delamatteno?"

"No!" grunted the Twitterer. "I hear from a warrior, my warrior. "

"My warrior." The sound fell back three harvest times. Its pain fell forward into today.

"I shall not go with them." Ruth rubbed her fingers along the sides of her stroud. "You should not go with them."

"Pomoacan promises us food. Fish swim tail against tail in their streams; the deer do not startle and run when they hear a twig snap but sniff into the barrel of the rifle ... in Upper Sandusky of the Delamatteno where they will take us," whined the Twitterer.

"You believe their lies?" Ruth added, "Fool!" but not aloud. Shake this bird, and it might drop the morsel about Black Wolf it carried in its beak.

"We are not safe here." The lower lip of the Twitterer curled out. "Pomoacan calls us, 'cousin.' He says that two powerful spirits open wide their jaws to bite and swallow. We sit between them and shall be ripped apart and eaten." She leaned forward: "And you could have the warrior ..."

The bell rang. It rose to cover and to subdue all sound. It called the lenno to the meeting house.

Ruth tried to growl. She moaned. "Fly far from me," she murmured as she walked past the Twitterer into the morning light toward the meeting house. She was not safe in the light; she was not safe alone. In the meeting house, she would not be alone. She heard the scratchings of the Twitterer pursuing her. She hated the Twitterer! She hated her!

From cabins and huts, brothers and sisters emerged. Children clung to the hands and legs of their mothers.

The stench of foul spirits and of death hovered in the air.

In the meeting house, Ruth slid onto the edge of a bench three rows behind Salah. She wanted Salah to sit beside her and to ask, "Why are you afraid?"

Sarah turned and smiled, but the smile was a wince. Salah could not hear more whisperings of pain and Ruth could whisper only pain. Silence was better.

The Shadow sat beside Ruth. Ruth thumped her fists into her lap. She watched for the Beloved among the men.

Scowling warriors stomped in beside the brothers. Trading women and old men from the camp that squatted beside the huts of the warriors slid sideways in.

One, whose bells still jingled as they had long before, gazed up along the lines of benches. Ruth dropped her head and gazed out from between the shoulders of the other sisters sitting behind her. She peered out at South-Wind-Blowing.

They filled the meeting house; more pressed in. Others watched from the street through the open doors. The Beloved slid behind warriors and stood in the back.

Brother David called out a song. Ruth raised her feet onto their toes and bounced. The Saviour was beckoning her to the practice. Almost, she obeyed; but she recalled the camp on the hill from where she was sure chantings of the Saviour had come. Her heels banged flat onto the floor. She refused to follow Him there.

Brother David stood and made the speech of the believing lenno. He cried out that God had chosen for himself lenno who had once served the evil one. God might punish his lenno, but He would never leave them.

"We are a part of this chosen nation. And shall we who have been pulled from the darkness into the light, who have experienced the goodness of the Lord, and have seen His protecting hand over us, who have braved so many storms and the threatenings of the children of darkness, who have never yet been disappointed in our hopes — shall we forget this? Did we not frequently hear the same menaces? Were we not told, time and again, what would be done to us if we did not leave our habitations and live among the heathen? And did we obey? Or were we molested for not obeying? No! And why not? Because we put our trust in the Lord and depended upon His protection ...

... We are surrounded by a body of heathen, by enemies to the glorious Gospel, by those who threaten to take our lives if we do not go with them and make them our near neighbors. Nevertheless we trust in the Lord and submit to our fate. He will not forsake us. We will quietly await whatever He permits. We will not defend our lives by force of arms, for that would be putting ourselves on a level with the heathen, and we are the children of God. Neither will we hate our enemies. They know not what they do ...”

“Dance to the beat of the voice of the speaker,” commanded the Saviour.

“No. The dance is death.” Ruth covered her eyes with her hand. She could not hold. It ... everything ... was slipping away.

The door banged. Sarah gasped. The paddle tipped in her hands; the bread fell to the floor. Sarah crouched to retrieve the bread. She looked back toward the door.

The Half King, Captain Pipe, and three other captains stood at the door of the Brethren's House. They did not enter.

Sarah stood, clasping the bread in her apron.

“Seven nights ago, you asked for time to harvest,” said the Half King, peering into the room at Brother David, Brother Heckewelder, Brother Senseman, Brother Edwards, and Christoph. He scowled. “I say, 'No! We cannot hear your answer.' Answer, again, for we say one time more, 'Go with us as friend to the land of the Delamatteno.' Refuse and you raise the hatchet against yourself.”

The assistant, John Martin, looked at Brother David. His gaze pleaded that the brethren bend the reply they had prepared. Brother David stared past him at Pomoacan.

Finally, Brother John Martin said, “We have replied; we reply again: We cannot leave our villages at once. We ask for time to harvest.”

The captains turned. They disappeared.

Sarah looked at Christoph. She followed his gaze down to her hands where she was wiping, turning, wiping the bread with her apron.

“What else can we do?” asked Brother David.

“We cannot willingly forsake the call of God to trudge into privation,” said Christoph. “We must be consistent with what we believe even unto ...” He glanced at Sarah.

“... even unto death,” concluded Sarah to herself. He wrapped himself in death. Did he think it would warm him? She was bereft, and the one for whom she mourned still stood before her.

Sarah served the meal, but they ate, instead, the warnings of the brethren who tapped on their door and whispered, “Today, before night, you are prisoners.”

“Shall we stroll outside?” said Brother David to Heckewelder, Senseman, and Christoph.

“It is not wise,” Sarah cautioned.

“Do we make our own selves prisoners by hiding?” asked Christoph. “We trust God; we are not afraid. Our lenno must see.”

Sarah wanted to lay her head upon his chest. She wanted to feel his hand pressed against her abdomen. She wanted him to remember and to dream with her.

He squinted. He turned and left.

Sarah, with Brother Edwards, waited in the cabin.

~ ~ ~

"Prisoners," exclaimed the Turtle to the Beloved inside the cabin of Ruth.

"Death?" asked the Beloved.

"Maybe, but they fear the teachers. And what will the believing Ienno do if they kill the teachers? They wonder that."

Ruth crouched in the shadow. She whimpered.

She wrapped her arms around her legs and rocked. She was the rock. The rock knew how to wait. But she could not wait. Her legs flexed to run; her mouth twitched to howl. Yet her flesh was hard like rock.

~ ~ ~

Brother Edwards packed the fire to keep the smoldering ashes aglow although they did not need the fire's heat. The cabin was suffocatingly warm.

Sarah rubbed her fingers along the edge of her apron.

"Awooooooooooooo ..." The scalp yell.

Sarah tried to rise; she tried to walk to the door. She did not move.

"... Awooooooooooooo ... Awooooooooooooo ... Awooooooooooooo."

Four cries, four scalps.

"Sister?" Brother Edwards was leaning over her.

She looked up at him. She tried to say, "Is Christoph dead?" but she did not hear her own words.

She felt his arms around her. She pulled herself up upon them.

The door banged open. Five young brethren stood in the light, swinging hatchets in their hands. "Delamatteno took the teachers," they cried. "Stay inside. We guard your cabin." They pulled closed the door.

Rifles exploded from the direction of the Muskingum, one ... two ... three ... four times.

"Brother Edwards," murmured Sarah, "are the teachers dead?"

She had heard her own words, but Brother Edwards did not answer.

He walked toward the small window and peered out on the street. He looked back at her. "The scalp yell can count the scalps of the living or the dead. The rifle fire ... I do not know."

Oh ..." Sarah moaned. She felt herself moving toward the door.

"Warriors!" Brother Edwards exclaimed.

With screeches, with war whoops, they pounced through the village, pounding the blows of the gauntlet into the face of Gnadenhutten.

"Into the cellar!" cried Brother Edwards.

"They know we are here," Sarah said. "Why should we hide?"

Brother Edwards grabbed her arm.

They heard a scuffle beyond the closed door. Cries and grunts. The door burst open. Delamatteno exploded into the room.

Sarah and Brother Edwards stumbled against the wall.

The warriors swarmed past them, snatching bowls and pans and forks and knives from each other's hands. They stripped the coverlets and blankets from the beds, knived through the ticking, and took the cloth. They grabbed the food, even the partly-eaten loaf of bread. They snatched the clothing of the brethren. They poured out the coffee onto the floor and threw books and papers into the fireplace. What they did not want, they burned or smashed.

Their smell was alcohol and dirt and body filth.

Sarah and Brother Edwards cowered, unnoticed, against the wall.

A tall, slender warrior nudged Brother Edwards and led him and Sarah along the wall and out the door.

The shouting, squabbling Delamatteno consumed the cabin, oblivious to them.

"Go now, old man," the warrior said to Brother Edwards.

Brother Edwards pulled Sarah through the street.

She wanted to die.

He dragged her into a cabin. The cabin of John Martin.

They closed the door. Why? What was left to protect?

~ ~ ~

The Beloved rushed into his cabin, panting. He peered into the darkness until he found Ruth huddling in the shadows. "The death hallows were howled over the scalps of the teachers Zeisberger, Heckewelder, Senseman, Zundel," he whispered.

"Dead?" she asked.

"Alive," he replied.

"Salah ..." croaked the rock.

"She escapes to the cabin of Brother John Martin." He stepped toward Ruth. "Come out from the darkness."

If she came out, then she would be in greater darkness.

He crouched beside her. "The Saviour is here."

"He chants from the camp of the warriors. Why is He there?" She gazed up at him.

"What chant?"

"I told you in the Youth of the Year," she said. "But you could not show me the meaning of the dance."

He pulled her up from the floor. "Do not huddle here."

She clasped his hand. He held hers for a moment then pulled free. "I must watch." He backed toward the door.

"Watch Salah?"

"Yes," he said at the door.

"Will the warriors kill?"

"The warriors … you know the warriors," he said. He disappeared out the door.

Yes, she knew the warriors. Ruth slid back into the shadows.

~ ~ ~

Three rapid taps. The English attendant to Captain Elliot pushed in the door.

"Rev'rnd Edwards!" he panted. "Cap'n Elliot sends 'em other rev'rnds to the Delamatteno camp."

"They are dead?" asked Brother Edwards.

"I ain't sayin' no," he replied. "I c'n bring ya to 'em. You c'n see."

Brother Edwards nodded and started forward.

Sarah clutched her skirts and followed behind.

"No woman!" exclaimed the Englishman. "Dangerous."

"I am safe here?" Sarah exclaimed. She would die with Christoph, not exist in this nightmare.

The escort shrugged and led them through the door.

Across the field they ran. A pain stabbed Sarah's side. She crossed her arms over her stomach and pressed. The field was alive with Indians.

Inside the camp, long, low, and dark huts consumed the hillside. Warriors nudged past. Sarah gazed along the flickering line of Delamatteno fire pits.

A man crouched, naked but for a torn shirt, in the center of one hut. Sarah tripped, lifted her skirts, and ran toward him. "Christoph?" she called.

His hair fell loose about his face. He lifted his head. "You should not be here!"

Sarah bent into the hut. She stumbled upon the dirt and fell. Sharp jabs ran down her thighs. She pushed against the dirt. She could not get up. She crawled onto her hands and knees, pushed backwards, and, groaning, stood.

She collapsed into the arms of Christoph.

"The baby," he murmured.

"I … I had not thought," she gasped, pressing her abdomen.

"I am sorry, Sarah."

She clung to him. "I thought you were dead."

"I am," he said. He pushed her back.

Sarah saw his almost-naked body. She pulled herself against him.

Sobs rattled up her chest and over her throat. They broke across her lips.

"Sarah … Sarah …"

She felt him, but she could not find him.

"Where is God?" he asked.

She pressed her head against his chest. She clutched his shirt.

"Awoooooooooooo"

She glanced sideways to see the Delamatteno captain, Snip, grab the arm of Brother Edwards and drag him toward Sarah. Snip's bony hand clawed toward Sarah's shoulder and crunched the bones beneath her flesh.

She heard a high, shrill scream. It came from her.

Christoph struck the wrist of Snip who released his grasp of Sarah. She clung to the chest of Christoph.

Another Indian ran toward them.

"Christoph!" Sarah cried.

The Indian pounded him across the side of his neck. He staggered sideways. Sarah clutched at him.

Claws wrenched her away. Her mouth flew open. She could not scream.

"Awooooooooooo," yowled Snip from over her. His howl rose into a screech. It shattered her.

Her body sobbed through a thousand cracks.

"Brave captain," mocked Christoph from the ground. "You howl the scalp yell over the head of a woman full of child? Did she fight hard and long and did you win her scalp in battle?

Snip spat into the face of Christoph. "You do not want your scalp, White Man." He kicked Christoph in his ribs.

Christoph gasped and recoiled sideways. His long, bare legs scrambled in the dirt.

"Do not resist," sobbed Sarah.

Christoph's teeth clenched and his face contorted.

Brother Senseman was crawling toward Christoph. His one hand pulled down on the ragged shirt that only partly covered his naked body.

Sobs rattled in her throat and burned her eyes. Sarah diverted her eyes.

Snip thrust her toward the Indian who had struck Christoph. "Her scalp is yours," he growled. "Guard her in your hut."

The Indian, dark and small, pawed at her arm. He pushed her in front of him. She glanced back at Christoph.

"I am sorry ..." he was murmuring.

"Help me to pray," she called back to him.

She wept.

Sarah sat in the center of a hut, the small Indian crouching at her side. She looked through the opening. Between the droves of warriors that stampeded past with plunder, she could sometimes see into the wall-less hut where Christoph and Brother Senseman crouched, their arms wrapped around their legs.

Her back and thigh ached. Her leg was numb. The baby churned inside her. Christoph was looking toward her; she gazed back. She shook. She pushed her hands against the ground. What had happened?

"God ..." Her mind could not hold to the thought of Him.

22
SEPTEMBER 3, 1781 – SEPTEMBER 6, 1781

"Ooooo," moaned Ruth. She stood. She watched the door. She pushed her palms into the sides of her head, but the throbbing would not stop.

She heard a galloping of horses and a yowling of warriors. They were shrieking for the battle and riding for the attack. They rode toward Place of Peace.

Should she go to Salah? What could she do? If she helped the trapped one, she would trap herself. She was not a fool.

Fool. Who counseled her? Wind Maiden? "Are you here, dead one?"

When would the Beloved return? She slid across the floor toward the door. From the shadows, she glanced outside.

The scavengers still looted the cabins of the teachers. They swung their stuffed bags. They hooted like victorious warriors. But the only battle they fought was among themselves over scraps of cloth.

Sister Philipina scooted toward the cabin of John Martin, stepped inside, and reappeared with him. Together, they hurried along the line of cabins, carrying blankets and a sack.

Ruth could follow them, ask them about the teachers.

In the street, she might be seen by ...

She would slither in shadow.

She hurried out before fear could answer.

"Sister ..." she whispered to the back of Philipina as that sister turned between the cabins. She did not hear.

"Sister ..." Ruth croaked louder.

Philipina and John Martin looked back.

"What do you know?" Ruth asked.

"Nothing ... yet," replied John Martin.

"That is why we go," said Sister Philipina. She looked toward the hill. "Join us. My bag is heavy. Carry blankets or carry the bag." She thrust out her full arms for Ruth to choose.

"I ..." began Ruth. She could not help Salah, and she would lose Ruth if she went.

The chant began. "To the practice," the Saviour said.

"Upon the bluff?" she asked.

"Where I lead you, there you dance."

"With the warriors?"

"With the prisoners," he corrected.

"I am not ready."

"You would not practice."

"To the prisoners?" she asked.

"To Salah," he said.

Ruth took the bag from Sister Philipina.

They ran toward the camp. Warriors ran with them. The roar of confusion rose from the camp.

They peered into the dark huts of the Delamatteno.

Ruth crouched and gazed into one hut. "Friend!" She rushed toward Salah.

"Sister," whispered Sarah. Had Ruth been captured, too?

"Blankets and food," said Sister Philipina from beside Ruth.

"Where are the brothers?" asked John Martin from behind.

"Brother Christoph, Brother Senseman, and Brother Edwards are there." Sarah pointed. "Snip calls to another hut." She pointed to her right. "Brothers David and Heckewelder must be there." She looked up at John Martin. "I cannot see them. I only hope ..."

If they were not there, where ...

John Martin hurried toward the hut where Christoph lay.

The small, dark Indian, Sarah's guard, crawled toward them.

Philipina took the bag from Ruth and opened it. She placed bread in Sarah's lap.

"Prisoner," grumbled the guard. "Not guest!"

"Full of child," replied Sister Philipina. She crouched and nudged the blanket against Sarah's leg. "Sit on it," she whispered. "Hide it for nighttime."

"You conspire." The guard pushed Philipina. She backed away, turned, and followed John Martin.

The guard glanced at Ruth. She dropped her eyes and raised them. She tried to make a trading woman smile. He smiled back.

"I may stay?" she asked.

His smile broadened. His gaze said, "Stay all night."

She smiled again.

He crouched near her. She could stay, but how would she get away? She knelt beside Salah.

Dark clouds clustered in the sky. The wind stirred.

"You should not be here," said Sarah.

"I know." Ruth huddled against Salah.

They watched the warriors flock back to the camp from the village. Some strutted past, wearing the hats, coats, shirts, boots of the teachers.

"Awoooooooo; Awoooooooo; Awoooooooo; Awoooooooo; Awoooooooo; Awoooooooo."

Sarah clutched at her apron.

"They count your scalps. They want to frighten you," explained Ruth.

"What will they do?" asked Sarah. She rubbed the small of her back. She uncrossed and recrossed her legs.

"I do not know," answered Ruth. The deepening shadows of the hut carved into the face of Salah the lines of death. What Ruth did know would only lengthen the lines.

She knew that the warrior's howls and yells would make him stagger. His mind would scream. He would thirst for blood. When his parched mouth cracked from thirst, he would kill.

Sister Philipina and Brother John Martin appeared again at the entrance to the hut. Their path was blocked by the dark Indian.

"We pray," John Martin called to Sarah.

The Indian grunted.

"He is not hurt," Sister Philipina said, pointing toward the hut where Christoph lay.

"Come," Sister Philipina called to Ruth.

The Indian looked at Ruth.

She wanted to run past him, sneer in his face, spit. But, after she fled, he would sneer at, spit upon ... he would kick Salah.

"I am made glad by your coming," said Sarah. "Go, now."

Ruth hesitated.

"Pray for us," whispered Sarah. "I cannot pray." She swallowed and held back tears.

Ruth rolled from her knees to her feet. "You cannot hear the rhythm of the dance?" she asked. Salah was in the midst of the dance.

"Too many dances," said Sarah.

"I shall pray. I shall dance for you."

Ruth crept toward the dark Indian. She told her eyes to whisper of desire. She made her body sway and say, "I want to, but how can we?" She hurried past him and ran behind John Martin and Philipina. He could not follow; he must guard.

She ran. Running made her want to run. Not from the little, dark Indian. From Black Wolf.

"Friend!" called a woman's voice.

Ruth hurried after her sister toward Huts of Grace, toward her cabin, toward the darkness and the rock.

"Wait. Are you afraid? Shall I beckon another friend?"

Ruth stopped. A trading woman strutted down the hill. She clinked with buckles on her stroud and bells upon her moccasins.

She swung her body like South-Wind-Blowing.

"Afraid?" asked Ruth. "Of decaying things? Of you?"

"She covers herself with the cap of the White woman but her voice and pride are Lenni Lenape. Friend. I am happy to see you again."

Ruth glanced up to see Sister Philipina and Brother John Martin hurrying down the hill. "Not friend," said Ruth, stepping back. "I do not greet you."

"No greeting?" cried South-Wind-Blowing. "Your tongue is a ragged stroud, snagged on a bush, flapping in the wind." She stepped forward. Her buckles rattled. "No greeting? The dying cannot greet the living?"

Ruth turned away. Let the noisy thing laugh; it mocked itself.

"Ho! You go? But, wait. Shall I tell the mighty fighter that I have seen his rabbit rushing to its hole? You might not be large enough for a warrior to eat, but to chase after and to play with? You are big enough for that."

The clanging thing would awaken the Wolf. Was Ruth called the rabbit? She would be the rabbit. She fled down the hill.

Rain fell. She was not crying. The rain wept down her cheeks.

Inside the hut, Sarah spread her skirt over the blanket and peered through the rainy darkness but could no longer see Christoph.

Her guard crept near her. Other Indians were crouching inside the hut, out of the rain. They watched.

"I need that," growled the guard, pulling at her apron.

Sarah tried to untie it, but he broke the band.

He felt the linen of her skirt.

"I need that," he repeated.

"Coward!" called one of the crouching Indians. "Do you lead the battles? Do you fight? You attack a woman. You fill my mouth with bitter waters. Get away."

The dark Indian tucked Sarah's apron into his breech clout. He crawled toward the other Indian. "My prisoner," he sneered.

"Prisoner of the Delamatteno." The other Indian rose up as if he were about to spring.

The dark Indian grumbled and turned back toward Sarah. He watched her.

Her arms shook. She pulled the blanket out and wrapped it about her, praying that fear and shame would keep the dark Indian from claiming it. The shaking would not stop. It traveled down her chest to her legs.

Warriors lit orange-glowing fires between the huts. The fires sputtered in the rain. Some Indians began to dance around poles, stabbing, taunting, yelling.

From toward Salem, the scalp yell was cried. The sentinels along the trail echoed back the cries until it seemed the sky would shatter.

"Awoooooooo ... Awoooooooo ... Awoooooooo"

Sarah's scalp tingled.

Horses galloped to the edge of the camp.

"Awoooooooo ... Awoooooooo ... Awoooooooo."

The warriors dismounted with Brother Jung. Sarah could see him in the light of the fires.

"Good evening, my brethren," he cried. "Our earthly career appears to be near its end, and we on the borders of eternity. Well, if they put us to death, we die in a good cause."

He bent to look into huts he passed. "Brother Heckewelder? Your wife and child are safe in Salem. The Indian sisters begged the warriors to place them under their care for the night. Tomorrow, they must come to Gnadenhutten."

Tomorrow — would they run the gauntlet?

Brother Jung was a prisoner of the Monsey; the warriors pushed him through the Delamatteno camp to their own.

Sarah lay upon the damp earth. She faced east. She watched for the first light of the rising sun. Her sides ached. Pain shot below her stomach and down her legs.

"God.." she prayed, "... help ..."

Before the light of morning, the scalp yell sounded five more times from the north along the Muskingum toward Schoenbrun. The camp roused and howled back. Sarah pushed herself up from the dirt.

The cries rose higher, reverberating back and forth. Up from the river came Sister Zeisberger, Sister Jungmann, Sister Senseman with her four day old infant, and Brother Jungmann. Two women and two men shoved them toward the camp.

A tall Monsey shook the hair of Brother Jungmann: "I greet you, my brother!"

They shoved the sisters toward Sarah.

Soaked, clad still in their night garments, they stumbled toward her.

Sarah wrapped her blanket around Sister Senseman and her baby. The sisters tucked their gowns about themselves and huddled together.

"They told us they had come to save our lives," Sister Jungmann murmured. "We helped them pack our bags ..."

"How long have you been here?" asked Sister Zeisberger.

"Through the night," Sarah whispered.

Their guard crept around them, poking at their gowns.

The sun hazed grey against the sky. Sarah saw a stirring in the hut where Christoph lay. The captors were leading him and the other brethren toward the women.

Brother David wore a frayed woman's gown; the other brethren were clad in less. They stumbled, barefooted, toward their wives.

Sarah clutched Christoph's cold and wet muslin shirt.

"They agree to release you if you promise not to attempt escape," murmured Christoph.

Sarah glanced up at him. Circles hung beneath his heavy eyes. "I shall stay with you." She might never see him again if she were taken away.

"The baby," scolded Christoph.

She had not thought. "Yes," she said.

"I am sorry ... I ..." His eyes filled with tears. He wiped his hand across his eyes and forehead as if to throw back strands of hair.

"You have no guilt, Christoph."

He stared at her.

The guards pulled the sisters and brethren apart.

The sisters shuffled toward Gnadenhutten.

The village was broken and scattered. Gnadenhutten was no more.

Brother Schebosh offered the sisters his cabin. They clustered there.

Warriors banged open the door. They commanded the sisters to sew stolen linen into shirts.

The Indian sisters brought food and wept over them.

They slept around the fire pit upon the floor; they whispered back and forth. Sarah gazed at Sister Senseman clutching her baby in her arms as she slept. Soon, she, too, would cradle a child. How could a baby survive? She was glad David was not with them.

"They captured Isaac Glikkikan," said the Beloved from the door opening of their cabin on the morning after the second night of the captivity.

Ruth rolled over on her mat.

"The daughter of his sister stole the horse of Captain Pipe and rode toward Fort Pitt," explained the Beloved, crouching before the fire pit. "They shrieked for his scalp. They accused him of sending her to Fort Pitt."

Ruth sat up. She crossed her legs. A chant thumped behind the words of her husband.

The Beloved continued, "Glikkikan said, 'I was a warrior, and no man would have captured me. That was when darkness encircled me and God was a stranger. I am converted. I am innocent, but I will not resist you. I do this for the Saviour."

The Beloved folded his arms around his legs. "They released him. His enemies feared him because he was not afraid."

"Why do you tell me this?" She was shouting at the Saviour, but it was the Beloved who heard.

"I thought you would want to know," her husband replied. "Are you going to Salah today?"

"Yes, yes," she grumbled.

~ ~ ~

"Tassmanane," she said as she laid the food folded inside leaves beside Salah.

Sarah unwrapped one of the leaves and looked at the tassmanane. Her eyes were deep, dark caves. She nodded.

"Waiting," said Sarah, "it is not good."

Ruth knelt beside her.

"We see our husbands each day for only the blinking of the eyes," sighed Sarah. "He does not have moccasins, my husband. Captain Elliot will not return them."

Ruth rocked on her knees. "The warriors will not kill the teachers," she said. "They waited too long and they no longer stalk for the kill."

"No," agreed Sarah. "They wait for us to bow our heads and follow them."

Yes, to follow; but Ruth had decided: she could not go.

"Brother Jonah gave me moccasins for my husband," Sarah said.

Ruth rocked to her toes.

"Please take them to him." Sarah stood and reached for the moccasins upon a ledge.

Ruth bounced onto her feet. Her muscles flexed for running.

Sarah offered her the moccasins. "I tried to give them to my husband this morning; but the warriors guarded like vultures so I could not slide them into his hand.

"I cannot go." Ruth was pleading. South-Wind-Blowing would tell Black Wolf to watch for her. He would be waiting.

"When Sister Philipina takes blankets to the teachers for the night, you can take these."

"Sister Philipina can carry the moccasins ..." Salah did not need her help.

"The sisters say that the warriors will steal the moccasins if I give them now. But you understand." Sarah swung the moccasins to her side. "I lie awake at night. And, when I sleep, I see the red, blue, swollen feet of my husband."

A pounding and a chant began inside Ruth's head. "I shall take them," she said.

At the sun-setting, Ruth wrapped the moccasins inside a blanket and followed Sister Philipina into the camp. She pressed the bulge of the moccasins to her chest.

With unmoving eyes, she walked toward the husband of Salah. She plopped the blanket into his arms and pressed the bulge against his hand.

If the husband of Salah wore the moccasins, the warriors would steal them. If he hid them inside his blanket, would they warm his feet? No. But Salah would dream of warm feet. Ruth was the slayer of nightmares.

He smiled. His cheeks crumpled like leaves. The sleeve of his shirt hung, torn, from his shoulder. A ragged cloth was tied around his waist and fell to his knees.

Ruth crouched. She waited for Sister Philipina. She was too small to be seen. A flea.

The flea leaped up to flee with Sister Philipina. But upon the edge of the camp, darkness overcame them. The Wolf waited.

"You return to me," he said.

Ruth did not answer. She tried to hurry after Philipina.

He was close. She smelled the clotted blood upon his breath.

"Wait!" He grabbed her arm.

She wanted to yelp. She stopped.

"I shall take you with me. Death is here."

She could not speak. If she opened her mouth, Wind Maiden might blow out like a spirit-wind.

"Sister?" called Philipina from ahead.

"I come," murmured Ruth.

"Can you not hear?" The words of the Wolf lifted like a hatchet above her.

The feet of Sister Philipina shuffled back toward Ruth. "She goes with me." She twitched her nose and showed her teeth like a bitch defending her pup.

"Fat pig. You snort and root and do not know what you eat," growled Black Wolf.

Other warriors were raising their heads and rising to see. He glanced around. He drew back his claws from the arm of Ruth. "Stay," he snarled.

But Sister Philipina yanked her other arm.

The squirrel was released from the trap. Ruth scurried away.

"Do not ... repeat ..." Ruth stammered as they ran.

"Another hungry warrior?" asked Philipina. "What is there to tell?" She rolled her head back toward the camp. "He watches."

The words of Philipina cramped the belly.

~ ~ ~

The morning after the third night of the captivity of the teachers, Ruth crouched over her grinding stone in her cabin. She felt the fineness of the maize she ground. She could not see it.

The Beloved returned from pulling a fly-buzzed, putrid pig from in front of their door.

"Pull back the skin and grind in the light," he suggested.

Ruth did not answer.

He wrapped back the skin and turned. "The teachers are released today. They say, 'We follow the Delamatteno.'"

"We will not go," exclaimed Ruth. She dropped her rock.

"Wife! We cannot stay."

"We can build our hut deep in the forest. He ... no one will find us." She stood.

"Why must we hide?" The Beloved tried to take her hand, but she pulled back.

"The ... enemy!" The enemy would kill her. The enemy would kill the Beloved.

"I shall protect you. Walk into fear, and it will flee."

"No!" cried Ruth. She must protect the Beloved and she must protect herself. "We must not go."

"Do we abandon the teachers and the believing lenno?"

"They must not go," she replied.

"The warrior will not let them stay."

"You would go to death?" she asked.

"With my brothers — to death."

"Salah will understand that we must stay," she said.

She wrapped herself in her blanket and cowered in the shadow of the door.

"A warm day," said the Beloved. He pulled the blanket from her shoulders.

Ruth glanced back into the darkness then out into the sun. She wrapped shadow about her and stepped out.

"You must not go," said Ruth when she saw Salah.

"We should not," agreed Sarah, "but they will not let us stay."

"I would have died to save the work of the Saviour in our villages," Christoph had said to Sarah that morning. He had pressed his forehead with his hand. "The warriors refuse to slay us. They eat our villages from the inside until only hollowness remains. The Delamatteno will take the believing lenno to enlarge its nation. The teachers must follow to care for what we can. It is over. We can do no more. We are defeated."

"You have obeyed the Saviour," Sarah had objected. "You cannot fail."

He had gazed at her, his eyes glassy. He was taken away by his captors.

"We can hide," Ruth exclaimed. "You do not know the warrior. I know him. He will let us starve. We shall follow him to death."

"We do not follow the warrior. The Saviour. We follow Him," replied Sarah. Surely, he would not leave them desolate.

Moreover, she was tired enough to follow anyone as long as the end was rest.

Ruth backed from her and turned away because to look into the face of Salah was to cry deep inside.

She hurried through the street.

Hide. Where?

"I can never find you. Now, here you are," screeched the Twitterer, rushing toward Ruth. The Shadow cast itself at the bird's side.

Ruth slid toward a cabin and tried to walk past.

"Sister." The Twitterer stopped in front of Ruth. "I did not know the warrior would take our teachers."

From over the shoulder of the Twitterer, Ruth saw South-Wind-Blowing strolling toward them. Trapped!

"Go!" She shoved the Twitterer sideways and tried to step forward.

"I was wrong," persisted the Twitterer. "I wail with my sisters."

"Get away," hissed Ruth.

"Still, I am glad to go. We follow the warrior."

Ruth kicked her.

Both sisters jumped back. "You're as wild as the warriors. You belong to them," grumbled the Twitterer as she and the Shadow scuttled past.

Ruth watched South-Wind-Blowing saunter toward her.

"He takes many scalps; and he has many pelts; and he is the warrior," said South-Wind-Blowing when she was three steps away.

"Scat, mouse," whispered Ruth.

"Tongue! Do you shoo me?" mocked South-Wind-Blowing. "I shall help you. I bear words. Can you hear, stubborn one?"

Ruth did not move; she did not answer.

South-Wind-Blowing smiled. "Black Wolf sends me. He sniffs the air to catch the scent of the bleeding bitch. He rises for the mating."

Ruth lowered her head. "Why does he send you? He is a warrior. He can take. Does he hide behind you?"

The nostrils of South-Wind-Blowing flared. "Oh, he will come, I warn you; and when he comes, he kills. Now, he calls to talk. A secret place."

"He talked yesterday in the camping place of the warriors where shame released my arm." What would break his grasp if she stood in front of him ... alone?

"Fool. He is not a puppy that you can tempt. He will explode like a rifle fire. First he comes gently."

Squeezed gently or pulled, the rifle would still explode, decided Ruth.

"A secret place," repeated South-Wind-Blowing. "The forest. Until the sun is high, he waits."

Ruth could not go; she could not! He might dig back the dirt that covered the bones of Wind Maiden. Would they move, stand, take life — from Ruth? And if she did not go, he would stalk his prey in Huts of Grace. The Beloved would see and would attack and would die.

Ruth stepped back. She would hide until her whole body pulsed with the dance. She would follow the chant and would know what to do. She wanted to go to Salah, but Salah was lost, too. She turned from South-Wind-Blowing.

"The other way," warned South-Wind-Blowing. "He must not wait. He blazes."

Ruth stopped. The words were sharp and straight even though the mouth that shot them was strung loosely from many heavy lies.

"Go to him," coaxed South-Wind-Blowing. "His wife is fat and dirty. She is no longer Laughing One but has become the Cackling, Nagging One. He will take you instead. These praying lenno are dead. You could live."

Who could live? Wind Maiden? Ruth? Slowly, Ruth circled round. She watched the mouth of South-Wind-Blowing.

"Do not be the fool," purred South-Wind-Blowing. Ruth heard the soft rattle of her throat.

Fool.

Go to him.

Hide.

Do not die.

She might die if she went to Black Wolf, but the Beloved would die if she waited here.

She must go. But not alone.

Ruth widened her eyes to make the gaze of "friend."

"Go, too," she said. She tried not to vomit.

They walked behind the cabins and toward the forest. She wanted to shuffle and stomp until she found the rhythm of victory. But the rhythm she heard was of her heavy breaths knocking against the beating of her heart.

Inside the forest, South-Wind-Blowing stopped. "He does not wait for me." Her mouth twitched. Fear.

"One step, two more," pleaded Ruth.

"No!" South-Wind-Blowing fled.

"Saviour?" Ruth whispered. "Sing," she begged.

Silence answered.

She wandered beside the Elk's Eye.

He did not appear. He had always been there: a tall, black chasm falling through the trees. Too near, she would tumble ... faster ... faster ... deeper. She stopped. Legs apart, she balanced herself and leaned back against the fall.

The chasm widened toward her. She looked up. She was falling, and, still, she had not moved.

He pushed back her cap. She gagged; the ribbon ripped. He threw it aside and rubbed his hand against his bare chest. "The White Man!" he growled. He grabbed at her hair. Her head snapped back, and her hair fell down her back. "Dark and thick. Lenni Lenape. The White Man tries to hide it."

He took up her hair in his fist and rolled it back and forth in his hands. "Come with me," he murmured. "They," he jerked his head toward Huts of Grace, "belong to Pomoacan. They will starve on the land he will give them." He bowed his head; his breath was warm against her forehead. She could not look up. "Come with me."

"I came once," Ruth answered. The words tumbled in a gasp. Who came once? Wind Maiden. Not Ruth. "You took and killed and left."

"I chose the one who chews off ears with whining, who eats like a warrior after the battle but works like an old, crippled woman. She does not pack tassmanane for me when I go to hunt. She scrapes the pelt of the buck of my kill and gives it to her friends but not to me. The village where she lives knows her: the fat, lazy one. They will click their tongues and say I am wise if I take another." He grabbed back the hair that slipped through his fingers. "I take you. You are ..."

"I am married," whimpered Ruth. Her voice fell softly; it was not the cry of protest.

"To the limper. I have watched, and I have heard. No children. You could leave him. Maybe he will leave you."

Ruth turned her head to one side. She struggled to breathe. "Among Lenni Lenape, yes. Not among the believing lenno."

"You are Lenni Lenape!" he bellowed.

She closed her eyes; she suffocated. Kick or bite. Tell him to go. Too near ... she was devoured. Could Wind Maiden take back life from Ruth?

"Our village, upon the Sandusky River ..." His words caressed. "... Your mother and your father, they live there. Old. No one to bring them flesh and pelts, to build their fire. They die with no one to wail over them. Go with me to them."

Mother, soft and warm: "You are my daughter ... You are Lenni Lenape ..." Father, fierce and proud ...

"I am of the believing lenno." She rolled her lips together; she begged.

"They cast a spell on you, these White Men, these teachers!"

"No spell," she mumbled back. The Saviour: "Look. I fall," she wept inside.

"Live. I shall give you buckles and bells and pelts and blankets!" cried Black Wolf.

Buckles, bells, pelts ... they would put skin upon the bones of Wind Maiden and make her live. Move back, move back or die. Black Wolf, he alone covered the sky and air and ground.

"Live." He looked down at her stroud, the stroud of the White woman. His hands rose to her chest.

Wind Maiden ... Wind Maiden ... His hands opened onto her breasts.

"Remember. Can you forget?" he whispered.

She raised her hands and slid them over his. His hands were wide and thick. Heavy. Cruel ... Wind Maiden ...

Her fingers trembled with the memory of the touch of the Beloved. She slid her fingers beneath his and thrust out.

Ruth!

His hands slipped away. His eyes opened onto her face. He would pounce.

Bells rang from deep inside, swelling within. Saviour! She opened her mouth. "I am not Wind Maiden. I do not remember you." The words rose from the bells.

Did he hear the bells? He stopped to listen.

"My husband is Jacob. We are of the praying and believing lenno. I do not remember you."

"You will die." His teeth clenched. The muscles of his neck tightened wide. "You die!"

Would he kill her? "I listen to the call of the Mighty One who saved me from the deepest, darkest, and coldest death. I fear no other death," she said, lifting her head.

He watched her with the eyes of an animal. His hands clenched into tight, skin-whitening fists. Ruth saw — he wanted to pound and crush the thing that pricked his skin and slid its splinters deep beneath his flesh. But he could not find where to turn or strike.

"Step now, step now. The practice," the chanting Saviour said. "The path is clear; the movements of the dance are made, all made. Prepare. The dance."

She bent and retrieved her cap. She turned to him her back. He was not a wolf that she should fear him.

With the Beloved and with Salah. With the Saviour. Up to Sandusky.

She walked away.

"Fool!" he cried against her back.

23
OCTOBER 4, 1781 – FEBRUARY 4, 1782

The cold, so cold, her feet were freezing with the cold. The water crept higher, first to the ankles, then to the knees, then to the hips and waist. Sarah looked around. The lightning flashed, and she saw the brethren and the sisters standing all about, many lifting children higher, higher in their arms lest they drown in the flooding water. She stretched her hands to Sister Anna to take from Anna's aching arms her sister's baby boy… Banging, crashing … trees falling all about, and, then, the pain as one fell upon her and darkness flooded through.

"Oh," she murmured, struggling to push off the tree, "The baby, he will drown."

"No," a voice whispered from far away. Christoph? Where was he? "Rest, Sarah. Do not thrash."

"Christoph? Did the tree strike you?" she whispered back.

"No. The storm passed many days ago. You lie on a mat."

"The pain," she gasped. It exploded in deep waves upon her abdomen wherein her baby lay. "The tree fell across my hips. The baby! He is crushed!"

"No tree fell across you in the storm. You are safe, the baby, too. Your time is near," floated back the reply.

"Oh," she sighed. But, still, the lightning flashed and the wind and the rain battered the brethren.

"Faster, faster," bellowed the Delamatteno captors. Sister Zeisberger fell once, remounted, and fell again, the hooves of her horse catching in the thick ooze of the marsh soil.

"Sister!" called out Sarah as the foot of Susan Zeisberger caught in the stirrup, and she was dragged. "Help her," she wept.

"Help whom?" asked the distant voice of Christoph.

"Who? See, there. Sister Zeisberger. Look where she fell!"

"She fell upon the trip, but she is well."

"The trip? Yes," replied Sarah. "Look. She fell!"

"The journey has ended, Sarah; we rest in Sandusky now."

"Sister Zeisberger ..." began Sarah.

"I am well," said the sister who had fallen. The words came not from the body thrashing in the marsh but from some other place where Sarah could not go.

"Tell them the sisters must be allowed to stop, to rest, to nurse their infants at their breasts. Sister Heckewelder, Sister Senseman, the other sisters, lest their infants die. Tell them, those warriors. We are not cattle. Tell them lest they, lest we die." Oh! The pain! She, her baby, they would die.

"It is over. Sarah. It is over," came the reply.

"Over?" She saw the lightning flash. Another tree fell toward her. Its trunk struck low where her baby lay. It grew heavier, heavier. "My baby. He is crushed," she wept.

"No," whispered Christoph. "You were brought to bed with child this morning."

"Brought to bed? Yes. Tell the warriors we must stop now. Sister Sabina needs to rest. She must lie here. Water for her. Bring it to me. The head of the baby appears!"

"Sister Sabina and her baby girl prosper. She is two weeks old," replied the voice of Sister Zeisberger from deep within the blackness.

"You are giving birth to our baby now." The voice of Christoph rustled beside her ear.

Our baby? "David?" Sarah asked.

"No — the unknown one you carry."

The Delamatteno warriors drove them onward. No food, no water ... "I thirst," she gasped.

An arm lifted her head. She smelled the warmth of the body. "I have come to help."

"Ruth?" asked Sarah. She looked for her but could not find her.

"She burns." The voice slid away as the arm released her head.

"The fever ..." a distant voice replied.

She shook with the cold; it froze the bone. Lightning emblazoned the sky; wind battered; trees creaked and fell. Her horse stumbled in the marsh; she lurched forward; and she fell, she fell, she fell.

"Push, Sister Sarah. Push. Push!"

She pushed against the tree that trapped her stomach and legs. Harder, longer, deeper ...

She pushed free.

"A son, Sister Sarah."

"David," sighed Sarah.

"No. Another."

A blanketed bundle was laid inside her arm. Not David. Another.

~ ~ ~

The cry was high and light. Sarah turned her head toward it. Ruth sat crossed-legged beside the fire pit clutching against her chest a ball of blanket.

"He says he is hungry and he does not know how to wait," said Ruth. "He says the world does not welcome him as it should and that he will return to the warm darkness of his first home." She crawled around the fire pit and knelt above Salah.

Sarah peered up into the black eyes of Ruth. "My baby?" she asked. She gazed toward the bundle.

Ruth nestled the baby against the breast of Salah. "He knows the rhythm of your beatings. Hold him tightly and he will think that he has returned to his home." She hoped Salah understood. She had seen tiny ones grieve for their lost dwellings and die because they would not live without them.

Ruth rubbed her palm across the cheek of her friend. "The burning is extinguished," she murmured.

Sarah rolled onto her side and pulled back the blanket from the small, flailing body. Opening her breast to him, she slid him close against herself.

She stared into his face. No, he was not David. And she loved him.

"He drinks; you must eat," said Ruth, still leaning over Salah. The spring of milk would dry up if its source did not end the long, hot drought. Ruth lifted her blanket around her shoulders and crept out of the hut.

"What is your name, my son?" asked Sarah. "Who are you?" He sucked, rested, then sucked again. He slept.

Ruth slid through the low door opening of the small hut. She cradled a steaming gourd in her hands. Behind her appeared Christoph.

"Eat," commanded Ruth.

"Water, only. I am not hungry," replied Sarah, gazing at Christoph. She felt shy. She rolled the baby out from her breast. "Our son," she whispered. Of course he was. How foolish.

"I did not ask, 'Are you hungry?'" scolded Ruth. "I said, 'Eat.'"

Sarah shook her head. "His name?" She watched the light of the fire flicker against the face of Christoph.

"The Lenni Lenape would call him, 'Running Horse' because he stomped through the forest and the deep, thick, mud-streams and still pushed out with strength," said Ruth.

"Eat," she repeated, "and I will bring water." She almost said, "Drink the stew; it is more water, less stew."

"My father was Johann Friedrich," said Christoph, crouching at Sarah's feet.

He glanced at Ruth who had cocked her head and was watching him from beneath a lowered head. "Water, Sister," he requested.

Ruth plopped the gourd on a flat rock near the fire. "Eat," she mumbled before crawling out.

Christoph gazed toward the fire.

Sarah nudged her finger inside the small, grasping fist of their son. She tried to focus her eyes upon Christoph, bowed by the confinement of the hut. "Shall we honor your father? Do I hold Johann Friedrich Zundel?"

"Honor?" Christoph asked. "I do not know." He rubbed his forehead, pushing his hair back from his eyes. "He disowned me when I adhered to the Unity of the Brethren. Perhaps in death he disowns our son."

"No, Christoph," Sarah whispered. Another thought eluded her; it refused to wait for her to capture it with words.

Ruth appeared in the door opening. "Water," she grumbled. "Now eat."

Sarah forced herself upon her elbow: "My husband, take Johann Friedrich."

Christoph hesitated above her then reached and slid the infant from her arms. He huddled into the shadows.

"He does not sleep, your husband, since first you lay down with fever," murmured Ruth.

Sarah lifted the knobby wooden bowl to her lips and gazed across its jagged rim. Christoph was raising his son in his huge hands. He stared into the tiny face.

~ ~ ~

Sarah rolled up her sleeping mat. Into one arm, she scooped the sixteen day old Johann, swaddled in one of the two ragged blankets she and Christoph still possessed. She tried to grab the mat into her other arm.

Sister Senseman peered in from outside the hut. "Wait, Sister," she protested. "I can help."

"No help," mumbled Sarah. Sister Senseman's own son, Christian David, was but one and one half months old, and she found strength. No one needed another cripple in this wilderness. It was little enough she could do to lift her own son and her own mat. She had contributed nothing else to the construction of the village of their captivity.

She crawled toward Sister Senseman, through the opening, into the light. She tried to stand. Her sister took the mat and lifted her by the arm.

Pressing Johann against her chest and pulling down the grey stroud Sister Christiana had given her, she shuffled toward the new-built village of sorrows. It cowered upon the north bank of the Sandusky River. Woods ... woods? A small cluster of trees shielded it from the flat, extensive plains. The grass was so high that, if she perched upon a horse's back, Sarah could not see over it. Yellow against a yellow-grey sky, the grass swayed in rustling rhythm. What else could prosper here?

Sarah gazed around the village. Crudely-built cabins and huts huddled together beside the river. Few and small. More than three hundred believing Indians squatted here. Three villages had barely contained them in the valley of the Muskingum River. Sisters were stuffing moss into the chinks of the cabins. Children were pulling away cattle that had strayed into the village. Brethren were still laying the roofs.

"Our cabin is there," said Sister Senseman, pointing east along the river.

Sarah continued toward it, pulling back her shoulders to greet the sisters she passed. She paused outside the cabin and peered through the chinks to see the fire burning inside. She glanced at her sister. Christoph, Johann, and she would dwell with Brother and Sister Senseman and their son in a cabin less than half the size of their cabin in Gnadenhutten. She squeezed through the door. The clay soil beneath her feet gave way to her tread. How would they keep out the water when the rains began again?

Sarah crouched beside the fire pit and eased Johann onto her lap. "We must build benches above the wet earth for the little ones," she said.

She wanted to rest. She sat upon her mat which Sister Senseman had unrolled for her. She was a frail, old woman. Curling upon her side, she pulled Johann up against herself. She dreamt she was the bench upon which Johann slept.

~ ~ ~

"You could stay ..." Sarah's voice trailed off. If Brothers Jung and Jungmann could remain behind, then why could not Christoph? Brother Jung had neither wife nor child. He could go, instead. She said none of this but stared up at Christoph.

"Sarah ..." The voice of Christoph held a tinge of exasperation. It should. She had repeated these words at least twice before.

They had only moved to their village five days ago. Many dwellings were not even completed. Not enough wood had been chopped for burning. The Delamatteno descended from their home nearby to scavenge like vultures.

Sarah needed Christoph. She *needed* Christoph.

"The Commandant demanded that all teachers, men and women, with their assistants, appear in Detroit," he said. "Pipe and Wingenund allowed us to leave behind our wives and two brethren. It was a concession, Sarah."

Sarah repeated her second argument that they could all go. "Not through the Black Swamp," Christoph objected. "You almost ..." He hesitated.

"... Died on our trip here," She concluded with a sigh.

The believing congregation huddled together in the small clearing. Brother David and Brother Heckewelder were already harnessing their horses.

Christoph would be imprisoned in Detroit or would die trying to get there. She, their son, and the remaining sisters and brethren would freeze or starve.

Christoph rubbed his forehead. "I commit you to God." He glanced behind Sarah's shoulder to where Ruth held Johann. "I am sorry ..."

Those words haunted Sarah. Almost daily, he mumbled them, sometimes to her, usually in apparent prayer.

"When the brethren return from the Muskingum with maize, we shall have enough," said Sarah. Two days before, the older Brother Schebosh with his wife and several others had gone back to the Muskingum to harvest. She hoped their efforts would help. She had only enough maize for a single day.

"Yes," murmured Christoph. "Can God forsake us forever? I am ..."

"Take my blanket," she said.

"I do not need it." He pulled around him the rag he called a cape.

He adjusted the reins on his horse. He mounted.

Christoph, Brothers Zeisberger, Heckewelder, Senseman, and Edwards with the assistants — Brother William, Isaac, Tobias, and Joshua — rode away.

~ ~ ~

Pecking grain like a winter bird, Sarah lived upon the generosity of the brethren. No relief would come from the Muskingum because Brother Schebosh and his workers had been captured and carried to Fort Pitt as prisoners. The maize still waited in the fields.

The milch cows, without proper feed, stopped giving milk.

They slaughtered some of the small, black cattle that survived the journey and the warriors' attacks, but the cattle were more bone than flesh.

The sounds heard throughout the village of captivity were not songs and prayers but wails of babies and children.

Each morning, Ruth watched the Beloved limp out to hunt for deer or rabbit or bird. She knew he would finally fall upon his knees to dig up roots for them to eat. The hunter, digging through the snow, chopping apart the frozen earth, trudging home with roots slung across his back where a carcass should have hung. He sighed from the weight of failing.

Ruth watched him limp. On the trail from the Elk's Eye, he had stumbled many times in the marshes. He had slept in pools of wetness and awakened to the patter of rain upon his face. His limp had deepened, his gait had slowed. The water had soaked through to bone. The bone softened and was rotting.

Her body cried out with the throbbing of the dance which beckoned her along the path toward the Elk's Eye, to the fields of maize. The swayings, the shufflings awaited her there.

She subdued her body because the Beloved was weak and could not follow the trail with her.

~ ~ ~

Sarah folded the blanket over Johann's head. Large flakes of snow, falling like thick, billowing linen cloth, muffled the weepings of the children today. Although she could not hear, Sarah felt their tears in the dryness of her breast and heart.

Sarah crawled into the cabin of Sister Amelia. She crouched beside the fire and poked up the flames. She glanced at her sister, asleep with her four-day-old daughter encircled by her body. Laying Johann back from the sparks of the fire – He slept; but, soon, the pang of hunger would awaken him, and he would cry – she stirred the broth in the kettle above the heat. The maize had barely thickened it. Sister Amelia needed better food, but what could Sarah do? She had nothing to offer. Her own milk was drying up. She glanced at Johann.

Sarah gasped in tears; her breath rattled out. One month had passed since the teachers had been summoned to Detroit by Major DePeyster. A trader had appeared yesterday, saying that he had spoken with the teachers in Detroit. They were imprisoned, he claimed, and were awaiting removal to Quebec.

Christoph and the brethren with him would escape death. "Praised be the Lord," she tried to say. But here in Upper Sandusky, four children and one sister had already died. It was only November; winter had not yet begun.

Sarah rubbed her arm. Her body, every joint, ached. At night, she fell upon her mat, exhausted. But she did not sleep. Instead, she prayed. She cupped her hands around her shriveling breasts and begged for fullness.

Sisters and brethren scooped small handfuls of maize from their own meager piles and fed her day-by-day. They dug in the earth for roots. They boiled and chewed the bones of their cattle.

Perhaps they would die from the cold. They could stop searching for firewood upon the plain. They could welcome the wind that whistled through the wide cracks of the cabins where moss had fallen out. The snow was already deep; the wind froze the flesh. It would be easy to die from the cold.

She glanced at Johann. "Forgive my unfaithful thoughts," she prayed, more from habit than from conviction.

She slipped off her blanket and wrapped it about Johann. She pulled up her leggings. She pushed a log deeper into the flame for penance.

The log crackled and crunched in half. Sarah recalled the nightmares of her delirium after the birth of Johann wherein the tree was ever crashing, crushing her abdomen, and Johann came forth stillborn.

Finally, she had awakened. More real to her was her delirium than was the reality. What was reality?

She did feel, how could she not heed it, that whether by separation or by deprivation, time for reconciliation with Christoph had fled.

The days were always the same: The infant in the arms of Amelia awakened and cried. Johann roused and wailed. The mothers nudged their little ones against their breasts and pretended that their babies were being fed. She and Amelia ate and pretended that the pottage sustained them and that they had strength to endure. Nothing changed.

Time had starved to death.

The infant stirred; the dream was about to begin. But another part of a different dream, the deepest nightmare, broke in. Wails shrieked upon the wind. Ruth appeared to take Johann, and Sarah stumbled out in feverish delirium to confront death.

"Mary is weak," whimpered Sabina when Sarah crept to where she cowered in the corner of her cabin, cradling her baby in her arms. Mary had been born on the journey and was never strong. "She is tired, too tired to cry. She must not die."

Sarah touched the cheek of the baby. A layer of ice had formed beneath the skin. Cold. Death cold.

She said nothing.

This baby had died before? No, it was another. How often would it die again?

Sarah sat cross-legged beside Sabina. Soft, light tears fell into thick silence.

She and Sabina were dead, dead together. They were buried in one casket, pressed against each other, the stone-cold infant in their center.

Hope without hope.

Sabina wept. Sarah leaned forward and pressed her cheek against the tear-wetted cheek of her sister. Together, they cradled the baby in their arms.

In the nighttime, Sarah roused herself to touch the face of Johann. She felt for ice beneath the flesh. Subduing the urge to crawl around the fire pit and feel the cheek of Christian David asleep with Sister Senseman, she pulled Johann against herself and dozed upon the surface of sleep.

The cry of an infant broke apart dreams. Sister Senseman lifted the whimpering Christian into her arms. Sarah sat up. Thus each day, day upon day, began.

What was today? It was not still yesterday. It was November twenty-second, Thursday. And so it was wherever Christoph lay. They shared the day.

"Lord," she prayed, "Must we arise to endure another day? I do not give. I take from the brethren in order to live."

She could only wait. Endure the moment.

She could not trust, for hunger stared at her through the eyes of her son.

She unwrapped him, yowling, and unbound the wet rag which covered his blistered bottom. She rubbed a greasy black salve made by the sisters onto his oozing wounds and wrapped him in a dry and urine-stiffened rag. Sealing him in the blanket, she rocked him high in her arms, close to her cheek.

The congregation gathered inside the fenced enclosure beneath an open sky for morning worship. Afterward, sisters and brethren dropped their kernels of maize into the gourd of Sarah.

She ground her maize inside her cabin while Johann wailed. She waited for Ruth to join her.

"Your Running Horse neighs again," said Ruth when she appeared. "He is a wild one like the Lenape and not tame like the White Man." She sat beside the fire pit and bounced Johann in her hands.

He sputtered. Sarah knelt over the rocks upon which she ground. She smiled. "Lenape, yes," she agreed. Christoph was Lenape; he and Johann were one blood. What was she? She looked down at her shirt, her stroud, her leggings, her moccasins.

Ruth laid Johann on his back upon her legs. She tapped her fingers upon his chest. His arms and hands waved. "He knows the dance," she said.

"You still practice?" Sarah asked. Ruth believed there was a future, but there was only the present, only the present. Until, through death, eternity.

"Always practice." Ruth looked up. "I must be ready."

"For what?" asked Sarah. She had asked this before.

"I do not know." Ruth thumped her palm and fingers on the infant's chest.

"Sister!" called a voice from the cabin opening.

Ruth did not need to look to recognize the tweet of the Twitterer. "Do you go again to hunt for sticks in the thick forest in this land of the Delamatteno?" asked Ruth. "Go alone, for if you go with another, you will find that you grab the opposite ends of the same stick though you search at far ends of the 'forest'." Ruth smiled. Her words were well sharpened.

"Sister," whined Rebecca.

"No more," warned Sarah, looking at Ruth.

The mouth of Rebecca curled down in a pout. "Runners. Brother Jonah saw them coming from beyond the ... the trees."

They crawled from the cabin to stand shoulder to shoulder with the congregation and to gaze toward the trees where the runners would appear.

"The teachers return," puffed the runners when they were close enough to be heard.

Sarah cupped her hand over her mouth to suppress a sob. She clutched Johann and whispered into his ear, "Your father returns."

They appeared, attired in new garments. From the backs of strange horses, they slid, untying packages and sacks of grain and easing them to the ground.

In one arm, Sarah clasped Johann against her shoulder; the forefinger of her other hand pressed against her mouth. She stood behind Christoph. Had he seen her yet?

He turned. Tears filled her eyes; she bit her finger.

"Sister." His hands clasped her waist for a moment then slid away. "So thin," he almost choked. He pulled back the blanket from the face of their son and swallowed.

"Everyone is thin ... or dead," she said.

"You are too strong to die."

"I am?" she thought.

"You look well," she said. His face was full and ruddy. His mouth was set in a wide smile above his square jaw.

"Sarah, we shall all do better now." He clasped her elbow: "God hears our prayers again."

Sarah stared at him. She had heard that voice before. Was he refilling himself with the vision? Could it find substance in this village of misery?

"The Commandant at Detroit, Major DePeyster, sent sacks of grain, packets of blankets and cloth," Christoph said. "It is a sign from the Lord."

Sarah smiled.

Christoph affirmed that they would live. She wanted to believe him.

Time revived.

That same day, brethren and sisters returned from the Muskingum with sacks of maize slung across their horses' backs. Harvesting with jumping fear, they had glanced over their shoulders while they worked lest soldiers from Fort Pitt might find them and carry them away prisoners as they had carried Brother Schebosh, his wife, and four other brethren the month before. The harvesters had hurried back with what they could carry. Much still stood, dry and frozen, along straight rows in the fertile plantations in the valley of the Muskingum.

The brethren licked their lips in hunger for their forsaken home.

In the nighttime, a high fire blazed. The believing congregation crouched around it to hear the story of the journey to Detroit.

"Major DePeyster had brought us here to the Sandusky because he had heeded foul-smelling words spoken by lenno who despise the Saviour," Brother David was saying. "'Send the White teachers back to other White skins where they cannot spread lies and confusion among lenno,' our enemies had demanded of him."

Sarah sat upon the ground. Johann snuggled against her, pulsing, it seemed, with her own blood. She stared at Brother David who stood above. He gazed about at the congregation which encircled him at the fire's edge.

Christoph, once dead, lived again, not in presence only but through reborn hope nourished by the renewed flow of the vision. He sat beside her. She wanted to be glad, but she could not forget privation and death.

Brother David continued, "Major DePeyster called a conference in Detroit of captains and teachers to hear the accusations. Captain Pipe stood. Had he ever been our friend? No. And did he now condemn? No! On the day of accusations, the Saviour held down the tongues of liars. Captain Pipe said we had once written letters to the Big Knife, but the council of the Lenni Lenape had guided our hand. He said the teachers helped all lenno. We were 'friend.'"

Christoph whispered, "Judgment is past. God will fulfill His call."

Sarah nodded. Why had God needed to judge them at all?

"DePeyster issued passports to the teachers," Christoph continued. "We can roam through all this land."

"He promises food and supplies to compensate for what we have lost," Christoph concluded.

Sarah looked at him. A confident grin replaced his once tense-faced gaze.

"Shall we build a meeting house in gratefulness to the only God?" Brother David asked.

"Yes," the congregation agreed.

Ruth, close beside the Beloved, strained to hear the beatings of the dance. When the believing lenno were starving, and now, when they were saved, the rhythm of the beatings was the same.

~ ~ ~

Days blew cold; nights blew colder. The small fires sputtered as wind whistled through holes in the cabins. The cows could not graze upon the plain. They huddled among the trees. They died.

Major DePeyster lacked supplies to feed all the starving Indians who shivered near Detroit. Because the believing congregation did not fight for the English, their needs were supplied last. And no food remained for the last.

The maize gathered from the Muskingum was consumed.

The congregation chopped flesh from the frozen carcasses of their cattle. They ate the meat and gnawed upon the bones. But the carcasses thawed and refroze and most flesh rotted before it could be consumed.

"Go back to the Elk's Eye to harvest," advised Brother David. "Go while snow covers the ground and while the marsh is still frozen. Wait until the earth thaws, and the mud will be deeper, steps will be slower, stomachs will be emptier. Warriors will be roaming then."

In small groups, they wandered back.

Ruth pounded her hand upon her leg in eagerness to follow. She watched the Beloved. His leg was frozen like the waters and like the earth below the snow. She watched him rub it and pretended that she did not see.

Ruth shuffled her feet while gathering sticks, while searching for roots. She bent herself toward the place of the dance where the Saviour waited to call out the story of the movements. When she bent or scratched the earth, she tapped with her fingers the rhythm of the chant which she could almost, almost hear.

When the sun melted the snow and thawed the earth in an early thaw, the ground inside the cabins became puddles of mud. Cold wetness made joints to stiffen and bones to ache. Sleeping mats and pelts and blankets were hung to dry.

The young, the old, the weak died.

"God has so soon forgotten," Christoph said, his shoulders slumping to their weary mold. "Sarah, I did hope for better ... I am sorry ..."

Again. "You have nothing to regret," she said.

"God judges us still," he lamented, "and I do not know of what to repent."

"He will redeem us yet," she consoled. And if they died, death would be rest.

"You have always been strong," he said. Sarah discerned resentment in his voice. "Whom ... what have you ever needed?"

Those should have been her words, not Christoph's. She wanted to exclaim, "You are wrong! I need you. I love you!" She yearned for release, but weakness, not strength, held her back.

~ ~ ~

In early February, the six who had been captured and carried to Fort Pitt returned. "The Big Knife is our friend," they said. "He fed us. He built our fire. Return to the Elk's Eye. Do not fear. Gather maize. The journey is only seven days."

Lifting their bags and carrying straps, mounting their horses, the believing lenno returned.

The Beloved rubbed his leg. Ruth stiffened against the poundings within.

Upon an afternoon while Salah hung skins and blankets to dry during the thaw, Ruth held Running Horse and scolded Grandmother Earth.

"Go back to sleep. Freeze," she grumbled as to a naughty child. "Why do you awaken now? What mischief do you plan? We do not want to play." She rubbed the toe of her moccasin into the mud and pop-popped the mud beneath her foot.

"Can the earth thaw unless wind warms?" asked Sarah. "Do not spank the Grandmother; she only obeys the wind. And do not scold the wind. Should she grow bitter again?" Sarah slid beside Ruth upon the log where she perched. They stared at each other from the corners of their eyes. Sarah began the game, a game that required no smiling.

"No, no, I understand Grandmother Earth better than you do." Ruth was bowing her head and kicking up the clinging clods of mud. "She could have painted her face with sand, but she chose clay to glob upon herself. Why? So we could sink up to our knees in the oozing ground. I cannot practice the dance when my feet cannot pull free."

"You still practice?" Sarah's question was not part of the game. She had lost, anyway. She would never win against Ruth.

"Yes." Ruth gazed at Salah.

This dance was like Christoph's vision. It would consume a life until nothing remained except the engorged vision, mouth dripping with the blood of the once-living, now dead.

"Live now," said Sarah. "Forget the dance."

"Yes. Live now," agreed Ruth. "The practice is now. I rock the Running Horse. I mingle words with you. These are motions of the dance."

"I do not understand," sighed Sarah. She could more readily endure her increasing lethargy than the sight of Christoph: silent, brooding. Ruth must not succumb to similar obsessions.

"No, you do not understand," agreed Ruth. "I do not understand. Understanding is not part of the dance."

"The Saviour gives us 'now' to live; not 'tomorrow,'" persisted Sarah.

"Yes. Now. But 'now' is nothing without the dance." Ruth wanted to tell Salah that the dance was for her, too. She did not know how to say it so she closed her mouth.

"I do not understand," repeated Sarah. She could almost hear a child's voice inside herself whimper, "Do not make me understand."

Not many of the believing ones were in the village that day. Some were visiting the Shawano to beg for maize; others worked at a camp nearby, dripping the brown, sweet water from the sugar trees; and some harvested along the Muskingum.

"Where are you going today?" Sarah had asked when Christoph had returned to the cabin after the morning worship and had grabbed his rifle.

"Hunting."

When had he last returned with even a rabbit? "When will you be back for ..." She had hesitated; she could not call their kernels of food a meal.

"Do not wait." He had stood near the door opening, hunched over like a tubercular old man. "I must fish ... chop wood ..."

"And eat," she had added.

"Yes. While I hunt."

What would he eat? A piece of bark? A blade of grass? He was starving himself so that she and Johann might eat.

"Do not go today," she had pleaded.

He had paused. "Sarah, let me do what I can."

He had disappeared.

Now, she sat beside Ruth, feet sinking into the mud formed by rains of weeping.

Without Christoph, waiting for the salvation ... or was it the starvation? ... of God.

Years of hidden longings for Christoph clamored for expression. But reticent and frightened habit held them back.

From beyond the woods, a brother's yell warned of visitors. Soon, Pomoacan, other Delamatteno, and some White Men appeared upon horses.

The few in the congregation who were still in the village ran to meet them. More who had been in the woods or along the river followed behind the riders. Christoph was among them.

Sarah stood. Christoph was talking to Isaac Glikkikan, rifle held down in one hand, the other hand grasping air. He glanced around. He looked at her.

The warriors swaggered around the village. They guffawed at the moss-plugged cabins, at the rags which covered the grey flesh of the brethren, and at the black cattle which lay dead upon the ground.

"Proud ones," they scoffed, "now you live as we."

The praying lenno did not answer.

Ruth shook her head against the drumbeat. Running Horse screamed; Salah lifted him from the arms of Ruth.

Christoph nudged his way past the brethren toward Sarah, mouth forming words she could not hear. Brother David caught his arm; he paused to talk then turned away.

Christoph stood before Sarah. She looked up, and she recalled the day when first they strolled together in Bethlehem.

The visiting warriors demanded food, so Isaac Glikkikan searched the village and returned with nothing. "Consume with us the cattle lying dead upon the ground.," he said. "When you were in Huts of Grace, you asked for tea, bread and butter, milk, pork, and beef. We gave you all you desired. Then you said we should not regard our fields of crops but arise and go with you. We would find all and more than we had left behind. You brought us here and gave us nothing."

Pomoacan and all who followed him stared away and closed their mouths.

Johann cried. Sarah rocked him in her arms. She breathed in tight gasps. The hand of Christoph rested on her shoulder. She breathed again.

Ruth watched Salah. She watched the jawbone and the bone-encircled eyes. Dead flesh was already drying against the bone. Salah was becoming the Aged Woman.

"They murder us," snarled Ruth.

"They starve, too," Sarah replied. "What can they do?"

"Leave. Let us die alone." Ruth rubbed her nose and frowned. She could bring flesh-fattening maize to Salah. Soon.

The Beloved stood with the men beside the warriors of Pomoacan. Ruth hurried to him.

"We die," she said. The breast was dry; the little one died. She complained, "Grandmother Earth, she has poison, not milk, in her breast. This land is death." Ruth stomped her feet. She danced.

The Beloved looked at her. "The marsh thaws."

She did not answer.

Finally, he said, "Tomorrow ... toward the valley of the Elk's Eye."

24
MARCH 1, 1782 – MARCH 8, 1782

The sisters crouched together beside the fields of brown-dry maize. Ruth rolled an ear between her palms and slipped back the blanket of husk from its hard and shriveled body. She laid the ear in the pile beside her. Her blanket slid from her shoulder; she yanked it up.

A baby cried. The wail rose from the bundle beside Susanna ... Martha, size of Running Horse. Ruth's arms trembled to lift her. She hugged her blanket. She looked around at the Twitterer, the Shadow, Eyes-of-Mother, and Sister Lovel.

The Beloved carried a full-bellied bag toward the sisters. His leg bowed out from the knee. He limped; he did not complain.

"We have ripped maize from all the stalks in this field." He looked at Ruth as he spoke. Lifting his sack, he poured the maize onto the pile in the center of the circling sisters. "Tomorrow, we shall gather from over the hill."

"Sons!" called Sister Joanna to Gottlieb and Benjamin crouching beside the Elk's Eye. They glanced back at her. "Pack and carry. Now!" They jabbed sticks into the water then ran to help the Beloved.

Maize. More maize than could be eaten — ground, boiled, baked — in one night, ten nights, two moons. They would not starve. Salah would eat, and Running Horse would suck flowing milk.

"Look where the husks have scratched my palms," said the Twitterer, holding her hands out to Ruth.

Ruth squinted and wrinkled her nose. Maize gave the Twitterer strength to complain.

"I am glad for the scratches," chirped the complaining one, dropping a husk. "They are better than the scratches of emptiness in the belly." She looked around at the sisters: "But we have many more days to work. Our hands should rest."

"Words of truth," said Eyes-of-Mother."We have no warmer fire to flee to than the one we build here in Huts of Grace, and we have nothing to flee from when we are here. We can wait until tomorrow."

The sisters pushed aside the maize and raised their bags and carrying straps.

Ruth did not rise. "No," she mumbled into her rubbing hands. Salah's arms were not long enough to gather this maize.

"Go with us," she had said to Salah on that day before Ruth and the Beloved had left. "Your fire burns low here. It will blaze beside the Elk's Eye."

"I cannot go," Salah had replied. "The warriors who raise the hatchet for the Saggenash fear we might carry messages to Fort Pitt. They will not cut the rope that holds us to Upper Sandusky."

"Then I shall come back, and I shall tie myself to the rope that binds you," Ruth had said.

Ruth grabbed another ear of maize. She would finish quickly and hurry back to Salah.

She felt the hand of the Beloved upon her shoulder. His touch was always light, but his fingers spread wide in power. "No?" he asked.

Ruth tilted her head sideways to look at him. "We do not have until tomorrow. They wait in the nameless place for food."

"We will send maize tomorrow," he said. "We will rest here and, still, remember our teachers."

Ruth laid aside the maize. She stood. A thump broke against her chest. The Beloved was wise; they would not hurry; they could rest. The thumping rose into her throat and pounded in her belly. Rest. She followed the Beloved. She stomped one foot and then the other.

In the nighttime, when she lay down beside the Beloved, she asked him, "Do you hear the thump?" He lay so close against her that he must hear.

He pulled his leg around and looked at her. It had swelled upon the journey, and the swelling had not gone down. "No thump," he said. "What do you hear?"

"The pounding of the dance. What does it say?"

He did not answer; he did not know.

They lay together upon a skin in their own cabin in Huts of Grace.

"We are safe here. You must not fear."

"The teachers said we should not build our fires inside the villages," she whispered. "They said danger might prowl near."

"You heard with me. And do you forget?" asked the Beloved One. "Our brothers came back from Fort Pitt where they were carried prisoners before the snows fell, came back and told us that the warriors at Fort Pitt were friends. They said, 'Do not hide but build your fire beneath the open sky.' We do not need to fear."

"I remember," said Ruth. But the pounding did not remember. She rested then and did not dance until stillness settled upon them and dreams stepped out to fill the night.

The next day, four warriors and one prisoner appeared at Huts of Grace. The warriors bragged about attacking White Man lodges. With mouths stuffed with ground maize they mumbled, "We clubbed the clawing White bitch and her screaming pup."

Ruth spat upon the ground to cleanse her mouth from the taste of their words.

Eyes-of-Mother fed the prisoner.

"Speak English?" he asked.

"Yes," she replied.

They talked.

"The prisoner, he says, 'Flee,'" she reported to the brothers and sisters. "He says Big Knife warriors will gulp down the fire water of fury and follow the trail of the murderers. The trail runs here. Flee!"

"Straight words," mumbled the warriors. Then they chewed more maize, lifted their heads, and smiled: "Trade with us before you flee. Look: A stroud for women and cloth for children. Hats and moccasins."

"We have a rule and it says that we do not trade with warriors," said the believing ones.

Ruth blinked and looked at the Twitterer and at the Shadow. They gazed at the strouds and sighed. She blinked again and opened and closed her hands.

She snapped her tongue and pounded her feet. She said, "Throw our bundles upon the horses. Why do we wait? We must go."

Runners carried the warning from Huts of Grace to Place of Peace and Beautiful Spring where other brothers and sisters worked. The assistants built a fire in Place of Peace. They listened for the counsel of the Saviour.

The assistants returned to Huts of Grace upon the day of rest. In the meeting of the morning, Brother John Martin said, "We do not raise the hatchet. The believing lenno are taught that to kill is evil. The Big Knife knows this. He reads from the great Book of secrets that our teachers read from and which he and we obey. We warned him when the warriors attacked. We have been punished because we are his friend. Why should we run from our friend?"

The brothers agreed to harvest three days more. Four nights, and, then, they would return to the village of captivity.

Ruth smiled and laughed at the Beloved. They were going back. She teased the Twitterer and poked the Shadow. She watched the children playing above the Elk's Eye and held the tiny Martha of Susanna.

She danced. Her laughter rose in rhythm to the beating of the drum and high and low her laughter and her voice sang with the ringing of the chant. She thumped her hands upon the maize, pulled back the husks and made them quiver, stroud twirling, in the sun. She stacked them one by one, beating and bouncing with her hands.

On the day before the final night in Huts of Grace, Ruth pulled back the last husk from the last ear of maize in her pile. She laid it in a sack. She stood and looked across the field at the brothers, sisters, children. She clapped her hands. She sighed. Tomorrow ...

She watched Eyes-of-Mother ... mother ... mother. Toward the forest ran Sister Lovel chasing Hannah. Young Brother Schebosh and Sister Schebosh stood together, talking, and then Brother Schebosh walked into the forest. John Martin and his sons, Paulus and Anton, packed sacks of maize onto the backs of three horses. They mounted and rode into the forest to hide maize inside a hollow tree or hidden crevice to await another journey from Upper Sandusky. The belly had roared in hunger during snowfall but now grunted in fullness with the thaw. Ruth shuffled her feet then stepped forward, heel to toe.

The Twitterer stood, back towards Ruth, hands on hips, legs apart. The Shadow crouched behind. Sister Joanna chased her sons and called them back into the work. Little ones, wrapped in blankets, hung like packs from the backs of mothers who crouched and stood, reached and lifted.

Ruth tapped with her fingers the palm of her hand. All the sisters, all the brothers, all the children moved to the rhythm of the dance.

The Beloved stood beside her; he watched the fingers leaping, thumping in her hand. "The dance?" he asked.

She smiled back.

Big Knives!

From over the hill and toward the Elk's Eye first one man and then another and another appeared.

The beating stopped.

"Friends!" called the White Men in Unami of the Lenni Lenape.

Ruth counted them upon her hands and, then, upon her toes as they approached — thirteen.

The brothers and the sisters set down their bundles and their maize.

"Yes. Put down your maize and leave your work," they said in words that Ruth could not understand. But the Beloved and Eyes-of-Mother changed the words so that all the believing lenno could hear.

"We have heard how you starve in the village where you were carried by the wild warriors who punish you because you are 'friend' to the Big Knife. From Fort Pitt we come to save you. Give us your rifles, your knives, and your hatchets. Follow us to a new home."

"Give our rifles?" asked the brothers. "We must hunt with them."

"Friends. We shall give you food. Go without weapons. Are you not the peaceful Indians? In your new home, you will have your rifles again."

The sisters and the brothers hesitated.

"You are the praying and the peaceful Indians?" the Big Knives repeated.

"We are," the brothers insisted. They lifted their rifles, their hatchets and knives, and laid them in the arms of the Big Knives.

"Friends," said the White Men.

"Friends," agreed the believing lenno.

Shoulder against shoulder, they walked toward Huts of Grace.

Ruth wanted to cry, "Stop! Come back. Dance." But they would not understand. She glanced at the fields of maize and beyond toward the village where Salah waited.

She ran to the Beloved. They followed after. She could not remember the rhythm of the chant.

In Huts of Grace, many more Big Knife warriors waited. They swarmed through the street like bees.

"Gather your belongings. We shall help," they said. "We can leave tomorrow. Are there more of you?"

"Yes, in Beautiful Spring and Place of Peace."

"Tomorrow we shall bring them," said the White Men.

The Big Knives smiled; they said, "What did you bury in the forest before the Delamatteno carried you away? Lead us. We shall help you dig it up. Then you can take it with you to your new home. Why leave it buried in a land that is 'home' no more?"

With eagerness, the sisters and the brothers obeyed. Eyes-of-Mother led a tall, young, White Man into the forest. They returned with metal kettles and pans. Brothers Luke and Philip led three more and brought back the cups for the drinking of the blood of the Saviour. Abraham, white-haired and slow in walking, took two to gather plows and hoes.

Ruth and the Beloved watched, for they had buried nothing.

While the sisters and brothers worked and talked with the Big Knives and while the dark-skinned youth ran and played with the white-skinned boys; Anton and Paulus, the sons of John Martin, returned from the forest where they had been hiding maize. "Our father rides to Place of Peace. He will tell them that the Big Knife walks in amity in Huts of Grace," they said.

Before the fading of the day, Brother John Martin, with Adam and Henry from Place of Peace, returned. To Williamson, the captain, they said, "The lenno from Place of Peace ask you to lay your arm of protection around their shoulder. They, too, will follow you to safety."

"Friends," exclaimed the White Men. "We shall go to them in the morning. Today we help our other friends gather their belongings. Tomorrow we shall gather their possessions with them."

When light faded, Sister Schebosh walked to the edge of the village and stared into the black forest.

"My husband," she said to the sisters, "before the Big Knives came, he went to find the horses. He should have returned."

"Horses roam far in search of crisp grass," said Sister Joanna. "He followed them into the night. Soon, he will come back."

The brothers built a tall and smoking fire to sit around. Ruth crouched behind the Beloved and listened to loud and whispered talk. The blazing fire stole light from twilight. Dark darkness hovered near.

"Brothers. The only God has sent the Big Knife to us," said the Beloved in Unami.

He looked across the fire and spoke in the droning sounds of the White Man. The Big Knives bounced their heads up and down. They smiled.

"You are good Indians," replied the tall captain of the Big Knife warriors. "You obey our God. We shall warm you with our blankets and raise our rifles to protect you."

The Beloved leaned backward and whispered to Ruth, "Williamson. I led him and his warriors along the path toward the Mengwe and the Delamatteno."

"He shot you," murmured Ruth.

"No," retorted the Beloved. He dropped his eyes then raised them to hers: "I have wondered ... No! Those who wounded me, they were evil, not like these White Men."

"The White Man ... can his mouth utter truth?" asked Ruth.

"Yes," replied the Beloved. "If he serves the Saviour, he must serve Truth. Our teachers are White Men so some White Men must be good."

"Live forever beside us," spoke out a White Man.

"We can invite more teachers to join us at our new home so that we shall not forget our Saviour." The long, white hair of Abraham glistened with the fire as he talked.

"You are good and peaceful and Christian Indians," the White Men said.

Sister Schebosh paced outside the circle around the fire. Her husband did not return.

In the nighttime, Ruth pulled her bearskin up close to the Beloved. She lay down at his side.

"You are cold?" he asked.

"No," she replied.

He took her hand and pulled her arm against him. "The Saviour delivers us."

"Salah ..." began Ruth.

"We can send a runner to tell them we are saved and that the maize waits for them. We shall not need it now."

"Yes ..." murmured Ruth. To herself, she whispered, "No."

The orange glow of fire vibrated without sound upon the ceiling of the cabin, through the air, and upon the walls. A final click-click of White Man feet clomped out to the edge of the village and then was gone. The wind was lazy and did not blow; the cabins did not creak.

The believing lenno were safe.

She turned her head toward the Beloved. The hand which covered hers lay open on his chest. His mouth was parted as, without sound, he breathed. He slept.

She could not sleep.

Salah — when would she see Salah again? Running Horse — who would play with him?

Thump. She listened to the beat of her heart. It bumped against the silence. She tried to sway to the rhythm of the hollow, banging sound, but she could not follow. She listened for the singing of the chant. Behind the beating heart, behind the silence she looked. She waited for the thumping, thumping of the drum.

"Saviour. I listen. Where are you?"

When the White Man came, the chant ended and silence began.

The praying lenno arose when Grandfather Sun pushed first brown then orange then yellow past the trees to the sky above and spread his bright arms across the fields and street of Huts of Grace. This was the day they would have returned to their home without a name.

Out from the bluff above the Elk's Eye came the White Men. They came from the same camping place where the Delamatteno and Mengwe warriors, many sorrows before, had built their fires and had slept. They flowed into the village. They gobbled the ground maize the sisters boiled for them then lifted their heads and smiled.

The Beloved ate beside Ruth. He placed his empty bowl into her hands. He rose and walked along the street toward the forest. As he stepped toward the path, a Big Knife called out, "Jacob! Where do you go?"

The Beloved glanced around. "I search for Brother Schebosh who went to find the horses yesterday. I shall help him bring them in."

"We shall bring them; you wait here," said the Big Knife, walking nearer.

"I know where they find the most tender grass," explained the Beloved. "You may come, but I shall lead you."

"No."

Ruth put down her bowl and dropped her blanket. She looked about. The sisters and the brothers turned to see and stood to hear. From the side of her eye, she watched the Big Knives slither like a long, black snake and circle round. She stood. One light step upon another, she walked toward the Beloved.

"We cannot pack our blankets, skins, our pans and tools unless we lead in our horses," explained the Beloved.

"You will stay here," commanded the Big Knife.

Three White Men slithered behind the Beloved and blocked the path. A rustle and click; their rifles were lifted. From beside and behind, the snake rustled. It rattled.

Ruth scurried toward the Beloved. A Big Knife grabbed her arm. She pulled away and spun into the arms of her husband.

"Into the street. Everyone!" shouted Williamson.

A fat White Man pushed his rifle against the back of the Beloved. Ruth held him for one thumping longer. He rubbed his face against her cheek; he tried to clutch her waist. They stumbled apart. He grabbed her hand. They were pushed and butted forward.

From further away than deep within, the chant, low, silent, rolled. The drum thump-thumped and hushed the heart. Ruth shuffled her feet. The dance began.

Close together in a circle, the sisters, the brothers, and the children stood. Around them circled and swayed the Big Knife.

"We arrest you, warriors and murderers!" the White Man cried.

"No! No! We are the peaceful lenno. Our Saviour, He is your Saviour, too."

"Murderers," the White Man hissed back.

The sisters rocked and wailed. Some clutched their little ones in their arms. Ruth squeezed the hand of the Beloved.

"We shall make a trial," Williamson cried. "Men to one cabin." He pointed with his hand. "Women and children there."

"Aaaaaaaaaaaaaaaa," screeched the Twitterer, then the Shadow, then another and another. Ruth huffed and huffed. The scream rose up but she pushed it down, far down, beneath the hum of the chant.

"Hear! We are the praying lenno. Hear!" the Beloved cried.

"You will not die without a trial," Williamson said.

"Die? Why do we die?"

Williamson raised his arm again. He pointed at two cabins: "Put the men there, and women and children there."

The brothers and the sisters were torn apart. Ruth and the Beloved clutched hands.

"I can do nothing," he whispered. Their eyes intertwined like their hands. "I believed the lie again."

"Can you love me?" she murmured back.

"Yes. Though the heart stops beating, I shall ever love you. "

"Then you are my Beloved. I am satisfied," she replied.

Stone hands pulled the twining hands apart. "Dance. Dance now. Dance!" a voice cried in her head. The beating exploded inside.

The chanting rose to fill the sky. The rhythm was pounded on the chest of the earth. Ruth reached and clasped back his hand.

"The dance!" she cried.

His eyes opened wide. Tears filled the bowls; he blinked and set free the flow. He looked to the sky where now the chanter sang. "Yes, the dance," he replied.

Then he was gone. Still, in her shufflings deep within, she took his hand and thumped, first toe then heel, beside him in the long, circling line.

They pushed her into the cabin. She stumbled and fell. The door banged behind. In the darkness, the sisters wept.

The cabin — Ruth gazed around — it had been the home of Salah. She pushed her back against the wall and patted the hollow-sounding wood with the tips of her fingers. Salah stood with them, hovering, like the smell of the old smoke made by the fire built during the previous year. Ruth pulled her hand from off the wall and wound her arm through the waiting arm of Salah.

"Watch and listen," she whispered. "I shall lead you in the steps that we must follow."

"The Saviour will deliver us," said Eyes-of-Mother to the sisters.

"Yes ... yes ..." they one by one replied.

Ruth glanced back toward Salah. Looking forward, she envisioned the Beloved. She followed him in the circle.

Some sisters clustered near the high, small windows. Ruth crouched against the wall.

"Big Knives come from the forest with our horses," said Sister Lovel from a window opening on the other side of the room. "And look, over there. They carry our blankets and pelts."

"Our bowls, our kettles, our rifles, our hoes," continued Sister Schebosh.

Ruth closed her eyes. She shivered. She heard the words of the chant.

The Twitterer huddled beside her. "What do you sing?"

"The song the teachers taught us about the blood of the Saviour that flows from his side," Ruth replied.

The Twitterer sang with Ruth. The sisters and the children listened. They sang.

Grandfather sun crawled along his path. The children whined for water. Sister Lovel hugged her Hannah. Joanna held the hands of Gottlieb and of Benjamin. The little ones, clutched in arms, wailed.

"They come from Place of Peace," exclaimed Sister Schebosh. Her voice fell: "The Big Knives push them forward."

The door opened. The sisters and children from Place of Peace stumbled into the darkness.

Ruth squeezed the shoulders of Sister Amelia. Amelia's little one was wrapped in her arms.

"They said, 'We are friends and will feed you and protect you from the cold,'" Amelia sobbed.

Ruth sighed.

"They say they will hold the council now to learn our punishment," said Anna Benigna, wife of Glikkikan.

"What have we done?" whimpered the Twitterer.

No one replied.

They waited.

"Saviour. Defeat the enemy," all prayed.

"They stand, one long line," said Eyes-of-Mother, staring through the window. "The first among them, Williamson, carves a line with a stick into the dirt. He speaks. A few – their counting would not fill the fingers and toes — step over."

She continued, "They go to the cabin where our brothers are kept." She paused. "They are here."

The door banged open. Grey light crept in. Big Knives stood with rifles to their chests.

"We made a trial," a tall, dark one snarled. Eyes-of-Mother opened the meaning of what he said.

"Sixteen stepped forward to vote to carry you prisoners to Fort Pitt. All others stood back for death."

"Why? We follow peace," the sisters exclaimed.

"You are of the warriors."

"We are women and children. Our husbands raise the hatchet against no man."

"You have horses, pots, cups, rifles, strouds taken from murdered White Men."

"No. All our own. Our teachers would tell you. All our own."

"Children and wives of warriors, you die."

"We have a Saviour. He is your Saviour, too."

"The one who saves me would never save you."

The sisters sobbed. They huddled together.

The White Man spoke again: "Your warrior husbands ask for time to pray and prepare for death. The day is old. We cannot begin until the light. Pray and prepare until morning ... if you can." He laughed.

"Big Knife. Tongue swollen with the poison of lies," Martha hissed.

"Salt beasts," agreed Elizabeth.

The White Man slammed the door.

"Sisters. It is too late to boil hate," warned the wife of Glikkikan. "Soon we shall behold the Saviour. Do not go with shame."

"Does weakness make the Saviour hide?" demanded Martha.

"Never," responded Ruth, for she had heard Wind Maiden in those words. She recalled the first and second deaths and the birth of Ruth. "He saves us from the deepest death but not from dying."

"What is the meaning of your words?" asked the Twitterer.

"I know the meaning here ..." Ruth circled her hand, palm forward, in front of her face, "... not here." She tapped her head.

"You are White; you do not need to die," said Martha to Anna Benigna.

"I am a believing one. I must die," she replied.

"Love the enemy," urged Eyes-of-Mother.

Ruth looked up and she saw the chanter banging upon his drum. His hands were open and flat and stiff. He paused and raised one. She saw a red hole through the palm, and light, not blood, streaming through.

They sang.

The Twitterer whispered in her ear, "I am evil. Forgive me. I wanted to be you. When I could not, I tried to make you me."

"I forgive," Ruth murmured back. "I am evil. Forgive me."

Into the darkness behind the Twitterer ... no, behind Rebecca ... Ruth looked to find the Shadow. "I have not loved you. Forgive me."

The Shadow ... Leah ... clasped the hand of Ruth. "I have loved you, but I am always afraid. You are not afraid. Pray for strength for me."

They sat shoulder against shoulder. They swayed. Little ones slept in arms and laps. The sisters breathed with one breath. "Father, forgive. Saviour, receive us," they whispered.

The ceiling opened into the nighttime sky, and the black sky broke away. Light shone long before it was day.

When the grey haze of morning ascended, the Big Knives pounded through the village. They entered the cabin of the brothers and reappeared with two.

White Man screams and howls, cackles and yowls rumbled along the street.

Sisters Martha and Joanna watched at the window. They called out the names of the brothers as the Big Knives led them to another cabin, returned to the first, and soon appeared with two brothers, again.

"There! The sons of John Martin. They flee!" exclaimed Sister Joanna. Rifles popped. Sister Joanna pounded her head with her fists.

Martha looked back at Ruth. "Your husband ... he goes."

Ruth pressed her back against the wall. She would not watch. He was within the touch of her hand.

"Why do we die?" asked Rebecca.

"Hush," whispered Ruth. She was Star-at-Dawning staring at her daughter. She was Salah talking to Ruth. "Do not ask. We die. First, we dance."

"Dance?" Rebecca nudged the leg of Ruth. "When?"

"Now. In a great circle, rising toward the sky."

"You lead me, and I shall follow."

"No," cautioned Ruth. "Look up. Follow the light through His hand."

Ruth leaned past Rebecca. She grabbed the hand of Leah and pulled her forward. "Dance until sweat flows, your legs cramp, and you fall. Then you will have no strength to follow fear."

Ruth ran ahead of thinking, following the Beloved

Joanna called, "They come."

Anna Benigna pushed her way to the door. "Mahicanni, Shawano, Lenni Lenape," she cried. "Make straight your back. Do not scream. Die the warrior for Him, for Him who died and took away the pain of death."

The warrior. "You are Lenni Lenape," Star-at-Dawning said.

Anna Benigna and Sister Schebosh were grabbed, hands tied behind their backs. Thrust through the door, they disappeared.

Soon, the White Men, eyes wide, were back. They seized two sisters more.

The children huddled beside their mothers in the corners. Not even the Big Knife could take them until his belly, throat, and mouth were filled and he was reeling, drunk with blood.

The White Men, hands opening and closing like Black Wolf, appeared again.

Now.

Ruth shuffled forward. They yanked the ropes around her wrists. Clutching like the Twitterer, Rebecca grabbed her arm. They tied Rebecca's hands.

Ruth breathed the sparkling air. She slid her feet against the face of Grandmother Earth. She looked down the street of Huts of Grace, toward the forest, toward the Elk's Eye. And above, she watched puffs of cloud float across the grey-black sky.

Through the cabin door ... into the red, blood-clotted air ... she saw ...

... Sisters ... ragged piles against the wall, heads crushed open, scalp locks chopped off ...

Red-spattered hands thrust Rebecca down. "Saviour," she murmured.

A mallet poised.

Thud.

Rebecca ... smashed upon the floor.

The chanting pulsed wider, higher. The drum boomed through the earth and air. Ruth gasped quick breaths. She grabbed the shoulder of the Beloved, clasped the hand of Salah.

She stepped into the final shuffle of the dance.

25
MARCH 23, 1782

"I cannot!" exclaimed Christoph. He was pacing the small bedroom in the cabin of Mr. Arundle, the English trader who had offered lodging to the teachers when they had arrived in Lower Sandusky four days before.

"You can read from the *Harmony of the Gospels* about the triumphal entry of our Lord," said Brother David. "That is not difficult."

They were speaking in German, not Unami. No believing Indian was near.

"You read tomorrow," fumed Christoph, nudging his head toward Brother David. "Or any of you!" he bellowed, sweeping his hand to include Brothers Heckewelder, Senseman, Jungmann, Jung, and Edwards who sat on benches or along the floor.

"I cannot read on Palm Sunday. I shall not be a hypocrite." He pushed his fingers through his hair.

The entire room was silent. Sarah held her breath, trying to hold down the panic that had been so hard to control ever since they had first learned that the Commandant demanded the appearance of all the White teachers in Detroit.

"What triumph do I proclaim?" Christoph was saying. "The triumph of Girty, Elliot, McKee, and the Delamatteno in convincing Major de Peyster that we should be driven from Indian land back to Bethlehem? The triumph of the sisters ..." He glanced at Sarah, then at Sisters Heckewelder, Senseman, Jungmann, and Zeisberger. "... and of our children in surviving the trip through marshland to arrive — where? — in a half-starving Delamatteno village? Do I proclaim the triumph of evil?"

No one tried to reply although any, especially Christoph, could have said, "Our Lord triumphed for a season then was overcome by evil unto death, yet he reigns victorious in the end."

In the end ... in the end ...

They waited for the end. Waiting seemed less endurable than any end. They waited to hear from the brethren and sisters who had gone to the Muskingum and to whom they had sent a messenger on the third day of March saying, "Return. Bring horses. The Saggenash at Detroit take the teachers ..." and from whom they had not received reply.

They waited for a boat from Detroit to carry them to ... an end.

They waited for death, the final end.

Sarah stared across the still-quiet room at Christoph. He would not meet her gaze.

A door banged in the outer room. "Brother David!" Indian voices called in Unami.

The babies, sleeping in that room, sputtered and wailed.

The teachers hurried from the bedroom.

Brother Joshua and a boy, the son of Rachel, bent over, panting.

"Water," breathed Joshua.

Sarah listened to the gulpings. Ordinary. Ominous. Rachel and her children had been on the Muskingum.

"Sit, brothers." Christoph motioned toward stools beside the fireplace.

Joshua flung apart his hands: "This is not a sitting message."

They began the telling. Sarah pressed the head of still-whimpering Johann to her chest.

He had been confined, the son of Rachel said, with the sisters and other children in one cabin. Which cabin? Yours, Brother Christoph. "... I, with Jonathan, lifted the plank to the cellar. We slipped through and hid. The Big Knife led most to another cabin to ... to ... Was too crowded to kill all there ... The last — mothers, young ones — they clubbed and scalped above our heads." He rubbed his hands together. "Blood flowed through cracks, dripped on us."

"Darkness came. I squeezed through a hole. Jonathan ... The hole was small; he was fat ... he stuck. I pulled. Boots stomped. I ran."

"They burned the cabins where brothers and sisters lay. I watched. I heard the screams of Jonathan. I hear them now.

"I hid in the forest. Found Thomas hiding, too. He had been clubbed and scalped; he came back to life, lying in the heap of dead. Slipped through the door. Escaped.

"We wandered. Together. Slowly. Thomas fell and shook and foamed. Sisters and brothers from Beautiful Spring ran, too. We made one path and fled together."

He gazed at the teachers. He opened his mouth as if to speak but did not.

Brother Joshua continued, "The brothers at Beautiful Spring had received the runner you had sent. They sent a messenger to Huts of Grace to call the believing lenno back to Sandusky. The messenger found the body of Young Schebosh. Shot. White Man bootmarks in the ground. He ran back to Beautiful Spring. The lenno fled toward Sandusky, no food or horses."

"Your two daughters were at Huts of Grace," said Brother David.

"Dead," replied Joshua. He closed his eyes. He pursed his lips.

He began the recitation of names.

Near ninety were numbered.

"No!" Sarah heard herself exclaim. She ground her teeth. She wanted to strike her head against the wall.

Ruth, her black hair sliced from off her head, blood streaming down her smashed face. Rebecca. Leah. Anna Benigna. Isaac Glikkikan. Amelia. Piled like scraps of debris, ignited, burned.

She heard herself whispering, "Hush ... hush ..." above the head of Johann.

"... martyrs, passed to the Saviour's arms and bosom ... forever resting, protected ..." someone was saying.

"Consolation?" a voice erupted. "Only one prayer: God! Look down upon our nakedness, upon our bruises and our wounds! How long will you despise and consume us?"

Sarah gazed up. "Hush ... hush ..." she murmured. Christoph was looming above them. He stomped from the house.

"Christoph?" She murmured.

Ruth was swaying; her hands were clapping. Her husband, Jacob, stepped in front of her. They danced away from Sarah.

"Wait," she pleaded. She was looking through Ruth toward the door which had closed behind Christoph.

Ruth glanced over her shoulder. She reached back her hand.

"I cannot," said Sarah.

Ruth shuffled her feet and moved out until Sarah saw only her eyes and the outstretched palm of her hand. They faded.

"No!" exclaimed Sarah. She slid Johann into someone's arms.

She pursued Ruth out the door.

"Christoph?"

He stood with his hands clasped behind his back and stared out over the bay. His head turned but stopped before his eyes reached her.

"Christoph ..."

He looked, again, toward the water.

Ruth waited. Her hand, fingers wide, reached.

"Come back ..." Sarah moaned. Ruth ... Jacob ... Christoph ...

"Back to what?" A hard laugh flung out over the bay. "It is over for me."

"The vision ..." began Sarah.

"A curse." Christoph swung around and glowered at her. "A lie. Lambs to the slaughter, led by a lie."

"No. A ... Christian Indian state ..." she began. Someone had dreamt of that long ago.

"Populated by ghosts. Who massacred our people? White-skinned Christians. What Indian will join the accursed ones now?" He put his hands to his head. "Not really Christians. Devils. But the Indians will say, 'Believe the words of no White Man. Cast out his Saviour. The Big Knife killed the praying lenno, the harmless lenno, who were his friends and brothers. What, then, will he do to me? I touch nothing the White Man offers. This Saviour ... He is strong? What does He save? Scorched bones?'"

"Our own Indians who yet live, they ..."

"God help them. We cannot," Christoph snapped. He sighed. "Why has the Saviour severed us from them now? How can they survive? The world is overflowed. The dove flies out, but it never returns with the olive branch."

Sarah's teeth chattered. The wind prickled her flesh. The mallet swung onto the skull. With a nauseatingly hollow thud, it shattered the skull which popped open like a melon.

She sobbed. "Christoph, I need you. I ... love you."

She could feel against her palm the pressure of the clasp of Ruth. And she knew that if she dared to look she would see the long, long line of dancers weaving through and beyond the air.

With her other hand, she groped for Christoph until she felt the rough and heavy tips of his fingers.

In both his hands, he cupped hers. He bowed his head into it and wept.

She wrapped her other arm around his heaving shoulder and slid it across his back. He grabbed her in his arms and pulled her against his chest.

They joined the circle, shuffling, swaying. In their midst, the Saviour led the dance.

The End

ABOUT THE AUTHOR

JoAnn Hague is an Ohioan by default and, eventually, by desire. She began her professional life as a high school and college English teacher. Soon, however, the writing compulsion assaulted her. Encouraged by a faithful spouse and a circle of dedicated Yellow Springs, Ohio, writing friends, she plunged into full-time writing.

The massacre of the Moravian Christian Indians became her passion as she strove to tell their story in the way they would have recounted it. How, she wondered, could she make sense of a brutal, senseless act? She concluded that telling the story, thereby passing along its memory, helped to shape meaning out of a shapeless, heartbreaking event.

JoAnn invites you to contact her at www.joannhague.com

Made in the USA
Charleston, SC
21 November 2012